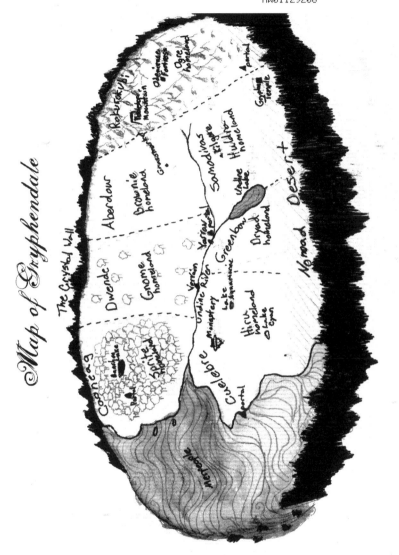

GRYPHENDALE

By Lara Lee

Bite-Sized Exegesis · Texas · USA

Bite-Size Exegesis (2016-09-28).
GRYPHENDALE

ISBN-13: 978-1539181385

ISBN-10: 1539181383

Visit www.laraswanderings.wordpress.com

TABLE OF CONTENTS

Dedicated to my mother
Elizabeth Lee Barnoske

CHAPTER 1: THE BEGINNING

If there is a door, it must have led to something, thought the young woman as she examined the solitary structure in a small opening of the forest. The oak leaves on the forest floor crunched under her tennis shoes as she walked around the ancient stone platform upon which a set of large double doors stood. She searched the ground for a building foundation or path that gave the doors a purpose, but nothing else was there. She proceeded to examine the nine-foot-tall doors. They were held up by a green marble door frame engraved with patterns of blowing leaves, flying creatures, and fairies. The woman couldn't find any indication that the marble door frame had been attached to any other structure.

"How strange!" she muttered to herself. "Perhaps it's a monument."

The doors themselves were a dark wood trimmed in gold. The panels were engraved with a medieval-styled gryphon. The door handles were also gold, and above the golden handles, they were barred with a heavy wooden beam. The woman struggled to remove the beam from the gold holders and tried to pull on the handles. The doors were firmly locked.

The woman walked around to the opposite side of the doors. The back of the doors had no handles. Instead, a colorful mural depicting an epic battle filled the smooth surface of both doors. The warriors in the battle consisted of a variety of mythological creatures and humans. In the foreground, almost life-sized, were depicted two men face to face in combat. One was a human male with dark hair and a sword. The other was a moth-winged man with light hair, pointed ears, and fire coming from his hands. Diagonally at their feet lay a dark-haired woman with pointed ears and a mortal wound to her abdomen. Her face looked peaceful, as though she had been sleeping. Above all this chaos, was painted a flying blue gryphon staring straight at the viewer.

The woman was studying this art piece when the doors began to rattle and creak. Just as she looked around the corner of the door frame to see who might be playing with the handles on the front side, the doors flew open inches from her face, forcing her to jump back. She rushed around the open doors to the front to see who opened them, but she only caught a glimpse of a blue tail and the back foot of a large feline disappearing through the doorway. The woman darted around the structure, back to where she had been before the rattling, and was shocked to find that the doors with the mural on them were still closed.

"Are there two sets of doors?" she asked herself.

She returned to the front with the open doors and looked directly in. She could see through the doorway to the trees on the other side. The woman then walked around again to the back. The smoothly painted doors were still closed with the same mural she had observed before. She continued around. The front of the doors were open so she could see through. After completing this circle a third time, she stopped and stared through the opening. *It must be an optical illusion,* she thought to herself.

She reached out her right hand and walked towards the opening to touch it. Her hand went through as though nothing was there. Suddenly, a force shoved her from behind, and she stumbled through the doorway landing on her knees. The sting of the fall on her hands reverberated through her like the hollow sound of wind through an empty cave, sweeping away her memories. For an instant, she started to look back, but the sight of the blue feline tail disappearing into the brush took hold of her attention.

"Hey, wait!" she shouted.

She decided to go after it and see what it was, forgetting anything about the doors she had just gone through. She took off in a sprint toward the forest edge where the creature had entered the brush. The sun sat low in the sky, causing visibility to diminish rapidly. She ran wildly to keep up with the sound of the creature somewhere close in front of her. The woods were increasingly dense and dark as she followed the sound. After some time of fighting through the brush, she found herself drained of energy and short of breath.

"Stop! I can't keep up. Who are you?" she gasped.

The closing branches around her entangled her reddish hair as she rushed by. Her clothes felt heavier as she tired. She tripped over her own feet and splashed into the muddy ground.

"Dadgummit!" she shouted in anger.

Now she was lost, too. There was no way she would be able to catch up to the noise, now distant in the far brush. She pushed herself up and wiped the mud off her trousers. Her clothes had become much too big, and her shoes had grown three sizes too large. She looked down at her hands. They had transformed into soft, round, child-like hands. The girl felt panic welling up inside of her. How did she get here? She could not remember. Who was she chasing? She did not know. Why was she chasing it? Who was she? Where did she come from? She could not remember anything at all from before running into the forest. Tears welled up in her eyes.

"If anyone is out there, I give up. I'm ready to go home."

No one responded.

She walked over to a nearby oak and plopped down under it. Then she wept, feeling helpless and alone. She could do nothing to fix her situation. Even if she could get out of this forest, she didn't know where to go.

The girl stopped crying as she got an idea. She searched her pockets, finding a set of keys, some gum, a pocket knife, a cell phone with a dead battery, and a little money. She also discovered a picture, and in the darkness, she was still able to see the person in it. The black and white photo was a beautiful light-haired lady with rich, dark eyes. Her thin face was perfectly framed by her long hair, and she was laughing cheerfully.

The girl studied the picture closely in the darkness. No writing was on it, and there was nothing to indicate the identity of the lady in the picture or when it was taken. She carefully folded it back up and placed it in her jean jacket pocket with the rest of her stuff.

Just at that moment, the girl heard the rustling again. The wind then blew through the branches as though following the creature in the brush.

A voice on the wind spoke, "Don't be afraid. I am with you."

The voice faded away as the wind died down. The girl heard the creature begin moving through the forest once again, just out of sight.

"Wait. I'm coming with you," the girl shouted after it.

She jumped up to follow. This time her clothes were so baggy that she had to hold up her jeans so she could hobble forward. After a few yards, she stopped, took off her shoes, and rolled up her jeans before proceeding. The creature seemed to be barely moving forward as though it was waiting for her.

"Thank you. I'm ready to follow now," the girl shouted to it.

She progressed slowly through the dense brush. Even though she was certain that she was following the creature, she was astonished to notice that its passage through the brush left no bent branches or trampled ground. It did not struggle as she did.

She ducked under the last branch and emerged into a clearing. As she looked up, she gasped at the landscape before her. The clear night sky glittered with stars like diamonds on a black velvet gown. A huge moon the size of a giant porcelain plate barely touched the horizon. At the base of the moon, a hilly forest stretched into the distance. A misty lake which began a few yards in front of her mirrored the moon and night sky. Everything was an eerie pale green in the lake's glassy surface.

A high-pitched wail pierced the silent night revere. The girl shivered and turned to her right towards the sound. The wail repeated, this time lower, like a sob, followed quickly by a louder cry. The sounds appeared to be originating behind a group of large rocks on the lake's edge. She cautiously crept around the stones and saw an elegant woman sitting on a simple wooden chair with her back to the girl. Next to her was a basket filled with white garments. The woman's hands appeared greenish against the pale robe she was washing.

The greenish woman, sensing an observer behind her, turned her face towards the girl and the rocks. The girl gasped at her vividly red eyes. The greenish woman's skin around her eyes was also red as if she had been crying for days.

The strange woman rose to her feet, faced the girl, and called out, "Child, are you lost?"

The girl started to slink away from view, but then gathering courage, stepped forward and responded, "Yes, I..."

The girl faltered, unsure what to say. She considered asking for directions or information, but she blurted out, "Why are you crying?"

"I can see that you are not from here. You are a human child. Well, child, I am Mara of the Sorrowful Lake, Queen of the Banshee." She paused, but seeing that the girl did not understand, she continued. "The Banshee are a people given to the task of mourning. We weep over every individual who dies. We also foretell the nearing demise of the noble, preparing their burial clothes in advance for their coming doom. This night my sorrow is exceedingly bitter. The garments I have washed are for a very great hero deserving the attention only a queen could give. The robes puzzle me for it is rare not to know who the clothes might be for. These are perhaps the size of a small Sprite or a tall Brownie, but I know not of one who fits this description."

She sighed and dropped the garment she was holding into her basket next to the wooden chair. Then she looked up.

"Now tell me about yourself. Who are you and how did you come here?"

The girl lowered her eyes from the majestic woman and began to dig in the dirt with her sock-covered toe.

"I don't remember," she mumbled. "I don't know where I am, how I got here, or where I'm from."

"Do not worry, child." The queen reached out her hand with a kind smile. The girl stepped forward and took it. "I sense the good in you. I will help you. What is the last thing you do remember?" The queen sat in her chair to look into the girl's eyes. "It might be imperative."

"Well, I remember running through the woods after something..." As the girl started her story, a violent rustling came from a bush at the forest edge.

A voice cried out, "Off! You horrid arachnids! Die, I say!"

The violent rustling continued.

The queen stood up, and the girl hid behind her.

"Whoever you are, show yourself immediately!" demanded the queen.

A bundle of fur leaped from the forest edge and rolled around, dropping a bright orange top hat and matching umbrella. Finally, it stood up, brushing itself off. He was a small satyr, about the girl's height. He wore a white long-sleeve shirt, a fine patterned orange vest, with a chain coming from the pocket. He had a reddish goatee, sprinkled with streaks of gray hair, and a mop of the same red and gray curly hair on his head. He walked over and picked up his hat and umbrella.

The little satyr then gave a grand bow.

"Your Highness," he addressed formally.

"Puck!" the queen exclaimed, then sighed. "Why are you here? There is a price on your head."

13

"I had a vision about the wind portal and journeyed here to verify its security. I was resting nearby when I was awakened by this girl's running through the woods. I pursued her until those terrible beasts assailed me," he explained. "The girl arrived here on her own, but she will not be able to return. I do not know how, but the portals were unlocked without being opened."

The queen gasped.

"Unlocked?"

Suddenly, a huge crow began to fly straight for the girl. Puck stepped in the way and whacked him with his umbrella. He then waved his free hand, creating a clear bubble around them.

"A spy," said Queen Mara.

Puck nodded.

"The shield will make us invisible for a little while," he said to the girl.

After a moment of silent thinking, the queen said, "The girl is here now, and she must be kept safe from the eyes of Maldamien. I think she is under a curse. We are not safe here. Maldamien will know she has arrived. I cannot bring her to my court. There are spies everywhere, even in the Banshee palace."

"Let me take the girl," Puck volunteered. "I can both protect her and teach her how to survive. I also have to stay away from Maldamien's eyes."

"That would be best. Thank you, Puck."

The queen pushed the girl around in front of her and knelt to her eye level.

"What is your name, child? Do you remember?"

The girl looked into the queen's bright red eyes.

"Yes. My name is Autumn."

Queen Mara frowned and stood up, looking at Puck.

"That is a portentous name."

Puck shook his head and shrugged.

"It is a lovely name," he replied.

The queen's frown softened.

"Yes," the queen agreed, a smile briefly touching the corners of her mouth. "Puck, we must hurry. Autumn is definitely under the curse of the portals. She has the smell of magic on her. She has no memory, and whatever her previous age, she has been transformed into a child. As her guardian, I would like to bind you two together."

Puck and the queen seemed to have a quick exchange of expressions until a silent understanding passed between them in that momentary pause. She looked at Autumn.

"This would magically help you both keep track of each other. If you are separated for any reason, you will always be able to be found by Puck. Also," she turned to Puck, "I can give you papers to help you travel securely as master and slave. It would be less suspicious if she is disguised." The queen smiled at Autumn. "This will only be a disguise for your safety. Trust Puck. He was once a school teacher, and he will take care of you."

"I am afraid that your plan would be best, but I detest slavery, even the image of it," grumbled Puck. "At least the magic bond will be there in a worst-case scenario, but the girl must be willing."

Autumn looked at both adults. She had just met them. She felt like she could trust them, but to be magically leashed to someone seemed drastic. Puck took the girl's hands.

"I know you must be confused and afraid, but I will try to help you get home."

Autumn jerked her head up and looked into Puck's eyes.

"I don't want to go home."

Puck looked at the queen, then back at the girl.

"What?"

"We must hurry, child." The queen looked around. "I feel eyes upon us." The queen waved her hand, reinforcing the dome around them. "This will help for now."

"I don't know why, but I know that I have no home and that I am looking for something. I can't do anything until I get my memories back. I will be bound if you will help me break this curse and help me find what I was searching for," the girl stated more confidently than she felt.

She didn't feel like she had much choice. It was either go with them or wander around alone.

Puck nodded.

"So be it," said the queen as she held out her hand. Puck placed his hand in hers. "Autumn, place your right hand over Puck's."

Autumn obeyed. As she touched Puck's hand, multicolored rays of light shot out of the queen's hand. A ring of writing appeared on Puck's and Autumn's wrists. The girl removed her hand from Puck's, and Puck picked up three pieces of paper from the Queen's hand. Autumn looked at the green symbols encircling her wrists. She felt anxious, hoping she hadn't just made a mistake.

The queen tiredly addressed them.

"I have helped you as much as I can, but now go. My magic will go with you for as long as possible, but it will fade soon. My hopes go with you as well."

The Banshee queen turn towards the lake, which moved out of her way revealing a hidden staircase. She walked down into the depths, the water closed over her, and she was gone.

CHAPTER 2: THE CABIN

Puck took Autumn's hand in his and ran into the woods, pulling her along with him. She had to hold up her trousers to keep from tripping on them. Branches whipped Autumn in the face, and even though she asked for Puck to slow down, he didn't stop until they were deep in the forest.

"I can't keep running like that," said Autumn, panting.

"We shouldn't have to in the darkness of these woods," said Puck. "The magic protecting us can only last minutes these days, and we know that we have been seen. You are in great danger just by being in this world."

A drop of water landed on Puck's nose. He wiped it off and looked up at the sky.

"Puck," Autumn started, "where am I? Where are we going? How are we going to break this curse? Why was it put on me to begin with?"

Puck looked at her blankly.

"Oh! Of course! Let us keep moving as I explain. You are in the world of Gryphendale. It is often referred to as the faerie realm in your folk tales. It is a floating island within the center of the earth. I will draw you a map and explain much more tomorrow. We must not talk much lest we are discovered. You look very tired, but we must hurry."

As Puck had observed, Autumn sensed overwhelming exhaustion coming over her.

"I have so many questions," she whined mostly to herself.

Puck placed her arm in his and patted her hand. He continued walking quickly.

"Lean on me if you need to. I am stronger than I look. If you faint, I will carry you."

"I will not faint," the girl stated resolutely standing taller than she had been a moment before.

Puck regarded her, then chuckled gently.

17

"I have taught many students over hundreds of years, Autumn, and determination is, in my opinion, the single most important factor in a student's success. Don't let it go. I will answer every question you may ask and some you won't know to ask, but it will be tomorrow."

Autumn sighed.

Rain began to pour down at that moment. Puck opened his umbrella, but it did little to stop the fierce windblown torrent from soaking them. There was nothing they could do but continue on. Puck soon grew tired of trying to push his umbrella through branches and closed it back up. They walked quickly arm in arm through the woods for a couple of hours. Autumn let her tears mix with the rain on her face. Could the day get any worse?

Puck continued his fast pace with the girl stumbling next to him in the heavy storm. The girl barely noticed where they were going in her exhaustion. Everywhere looked like the same dark, dense forest as she had been in before, but she kept her word and did not faint.

They arrived at another clearing, much smaller than the one they had been in with the Banshee queen. Within a few yards was a stony hill. They turned to their right to walk around it. It was not long before they approached a log cabin with a nice chimney. The back half of the cabin was built into the hill. It almost seemed as though the hill had landed on the cabin or the cabin had grown out of the side of the hill. They looked as though they always had existed together.

They both sped up toward the house, trying not to slide in the mud. Puck opened the front door and went in first. All was black darkness until Puck lifted his umbrella that had been hanging on his arm and a light shone from the end of it. He quickly found the hearth and started to build a fire. Autumn timidly followed behind. She stood in the middle of the room and looked around. The room was very large, but it was the only room in the house. The hearth was in the wall to the left of the door. Farther down was a wooden partition set up in the corner. A single bed was pushed up against the far wall. A few tables, boxes, and mirror lay against the wall opposite the hearth. Against the wall next to the door was a large table with four chairs around it and miscellaneous objects on top of it. The girl was pleased that nothing looked too strange. Perhaps this world was not so different after all.

Puck soon had the fire blazing, and the heat felt as though it was thawing her fingers and toes out. Her eyes began to close involuntarily.

"We will be safe here in the storm. You can have the bed," Puck told her. "I'll move the partition, so you can take off your wet things."

She nodded, did all that she was told, laid on the bed, and fell soundly asleep.

In the midst of her deep sleep, she dreamed of a myriad of colors swirling in every direction. Bubbles floated around her, each reflecting a separate image. Autumn reached out and gently grabbed a bubble with an image of a man sitting at a desk writing vigorously. He looked up and smiled at Autumn, then the bubble popped. She reached for another bubble. This one had an image of a crowd of people cheering. That bubble popped. Autumn began to get desperate to grab more bubbles, but they were all popping before she could get them. Rays of light began to shine in on her, and her dream faded away.

Autumn opened her eyes. The memories in those bubbles seemed to be so close, but just out of reach. She sighed.

"So, you are finally awake. Would you like breakfast or to bathe first?" Puck called out. The sound of pouring rain came into focus.

The night had passed extremely fast. The girl sat up on the bed still hidden by the partition and saw her dry clothes next to her. She dressed and moved the partition. The room looked transformed. The dim light shining through the cracks of some window shutters by the door was not the only difference to the room. The boxes and furniture had been rearranged so that two chairs sat in front of the fireplace with a small round table sitting next to one. The big table was cleaned off and remained under the only window in the house, which was next to the front door. The boxes and trunks were organized and stacked next to the hearth so that all their contents would be easily accessible. Another partition hid a tub, a small table, wash basin, and mirror. One only had to move the end of the partition to be completely hidden.

"What time is it?" asked Autumn.

"It's late morning," replied Puck.

"Are we still safe here?"

"As long as the storm rages, Ogres will not venture out to find us. We may even have a day or two of security afterward since our trail will be lost."

Autumn noticed the steaming cauldron in the hearth that Puck was stirring. It smelled wonderful.

"I think I would like to eat first if you don't mind."

Thunder rumbled.

Puck smiled. He ladled some water from the cauldron to a tea kettle and placed it on the large table. He picked up a bowl from the table and poured some grain from one of the boxes into it. Autumn walked painfully to the table and sat as Puck placed the bowl before her. Her body ached from the exercise of yesterday. Her feet felt raw, but the flowery smell of the cauldron energized her. Puck poured the water from the kettle into the bowl and then into two teacups also on the table.

"I ate this morning already. This purpleberry tea will help diminish the effect of the curse. I made enough for you to bathe in it because that is the most effective way to use it. Even so, it will take a couple of weeks for the curse to be washed off, and then your body will have to grow into its normal self which can take quite a bit longer, I'm afraid."

Autumn looked into her bowl. It was bright purple.

"It works as a sweet tea for your stewed bread. It is safe for you to ingest." Puck continued as he went to pick up scrolls from another box. "We will have to adjust some to what we both can eat. For instance, I do not ingest meat, and you cannot eat some of my favorite berries. Fortunately, I am well versed in human dietary needs."

Autumn took a small bite with her spoon. The stewed bread had a texture of oatmeal but tasted like buttermilk pancakes with blackberries. After a few bites, she realized Puck was seated across from her and watching her eat casually.

"How do you like it?" he asked as he sipped his tea.

"It's wonderful!"

The food was helping to improve her mood.

"Good. Would you like to ask me any questions while you eat? We won't be able to do much else today with the tumultuous weather, but I think you could use the time to get more familiar with your new situation."

Autumn looked at him. "Yeah. What's with the portals? How did I get here and what happened to the creature I was following? Who is this Maldamien guy? Why is he after us? I feel so overwhelmed and confused. I want my memory back. I want to know who I am, where I am, and what I was searching for."

She sighed. It had poured out without her control.

Puck nodded.

"I am sure you have plenty more to ask too, but what is the most important question to you for now? I will try to help as much as I can."

Autumn thought for a moment.

"Could you explain how I got here or the portals or something like that?"

Perhaps that could reveal some more of what happened to her and how to fix it.

Puck nodded. "I cannot tell you specifically how you arrived here, but I will do my best to explain the portals. This world is called Gryphendale and is a floating island located in the center of the earth. The only way to travel between the two worlds, at least that I had known of, was through the portals. There are four portals scattered throughout Gryphendale and four in the human world. The wind portal connects to the wind portal in the human world, the water to the water, the earth to earth, and the fire to fire. A hundred years ago, our queen, not Mara, but high queen of all Gryphendale, Queen Anemone, locked all the portals and was trapped in the human realm. This created a problem in which the portals could not be opened. I will have to teach magic to you to explain why, and I will do so later, but not right now." Puck sipped some more tea. "Anyway, the portal has remained locked until yesterday."

"So, can the portals be used now that it has been unlocked?" Autumn asked.

"No. You see, only one is unlocked. All four have to be unlocked first, and then a special spell must be performed before they can work again." Puck smiled. "I thought you didn't want to return home."

"I don't," Autumn said with her mouth full. She swallowed, then continued. "I just don't like being trapped."

"Understandable," Puck nodded.

"So how do this curse and the Maldamien guy fit into this?"

"Maldamien is the dictator of our world, and his presence is felt everywhere. He took over the world soon after our queen disappeared a hundred years ago, and he has spies hidden among the most remote corners of Gryphendale He placed a curse on the portals to weaken anyone who might go through them so that he can capture them easier. He is afraid of our queen returning through the portals one day."

Autumn looked at Puck.

"I'm assuming he is a terrible ruler?" Thunder rumbled outside followed a little later by a flash of lightning. Autumn smirked at the dramatic timing.

Puck stood up, pulling out a pipe.

"He is quite evil. He is a very powerful wizard, perhaps the most powerful I have ever known of. He is power hungry and does not care who or what he hurts in his obsession. He is after me for constantly opposing and doing all I can to protect people. You are automatically hunted because you came from the human world. Anyone from the human world may be a connection to our queen."

Puck paced as he spoke, puffing on his pipe.

Autumn thought on Puck's words.

"Did you say he took over a hundred years ago? How old is he?"

"Two hundred thirty-nine, to be exact. Time moves very differently here than in your world. Time moves quicker here, but we are also ageless. We haven't always been, but we do not age beyond our prime, or the age we were when the miracle took place. We do not die of any diseases or poisons, we only die in battle. I do not know if it will affect you or not, so I don't want to take any chances." Puck paused and looked outside. "Let me prepare your bath. I hope you can take a few of these baths before we have to leave, but once a day is probably all your system will be able to handle."

Autumn gasped as he carried the entire cauldron to the tub and poured it in with his bare hands. He was not only stronger than he looked, but also impervious to the heat of the cauldron.

"See if the bath is warm enough for you. I observed that humans like everything tepid," Puck said as he returned the cauldron to the hearth and poured a waiting bucket of water into it. He then opened the door and put the bucket outside to catch rainwater.

Autumn walked over to the tub. It was still steaming. "It will be fine," she replied. She looked around the make-shift bathroom and saw everything she needed laying out neatly.

"I found some clothes that would make a good disguise. With a little magic," Puck said with a smile at the girl as he closed the partition, "I made them cleaner and closer to your size."

Autumn undressed and soaked in the small tub, enjoying the water's floral scent. If Puck continued to use the same tea for everything, she would probably get tired of it eventually, but she couldn't imagine that at this particular moment.

The storm continued outside; the sounds were both comforting and frightening. Autumn was deep in her own thoughts. What was it that drew her here? It was curiosity, but what specifically was that blue creature? Was it a lion or a gryphon, like the painting on the portal? The portal! She remembered the portal!

"Puck!" Autumn screamed. Something sounded like it jumped or fell over.

"What?" he shouted back. Thunder crashed outside.

"I remember something!"

"Good. Good. What is it?" he made his way closer to the partition.

"I remember the portal! I fell through it following a blue gryphon. Well, I don't remember the portal much, just the gryphon."

"Are you sure?" Puck asked with sudden tension in his voice.

"Yes, I'm certain. Why?"

There was quiet for a few moments. Autumn felt restless waiting for his answer. She decided to finish up her bath before continuing the subject.

"Puck."

"Yes."

"I think I will need another bath soon. This water is very dirty." Autumn dried off as she spoke.

"That's the magic that was on you."

She looked at the new clothes set aside for her. Each item was a different shade of brown. She put on the dark brown trouser that tied around the waist loosely, then put on the tan long-sleeved tunic with an embroidered pattern around the neck. Finally, though she was indoors, she put on the plain brown cloak and looked in the mirror to see the effect. She smiled. It looked like something from a Medieval costume party. She looked back at the leather boots that somehow were supposed to strap around her legs. She decided not to mess with them and let Puck show her. She found a strip of patterned cloth under the boots and decided to tie it around the waist of her tunic. Autumn opened the partition and looked for Puck. He was sitting on one of the wooden chairs smoking his English style pipe, staring deep into the fire. She almost touched him when he looked up at her.

"Well!" he exclaimed with a smile. "It is a little baggy, but you already look a little older. I think you will grow into it very quickly."

"Autumn held out the shoes. "I can't figure these out."

Puck laughed. "I will demonstrate for you. Sit down."

He stood up as she sat in the chair opposite to him. He knelt down and expertly showed her how to strap them over the legs of her trousers up to her knees. "There, you look like a true Nomad."

"I thought I was supposed to look like a Dryad."

"Well, this will work for any identity," he said as he took his seat. "We have to work with what we have."

"So," she began, "why were you so surprised when I told you about the gryphon and the portal?"

Puck smiled sadly at her. "I like that you push for answers." He looked back at the fire. "I told Queen Mara that I had a dream that led me to check the portal. Within that dream, I saw the gryphon." He leaned forward and tilted his head to look at her. "You see, the blue gryphon is a character from old legends and mythology. Very few have ever seen him in physical form at all. He is the most powerful being that exists. Some say he is the creator incarnate, most everyone else says he does not exist at all."

"What do you say?" asked Autumn.

"I thought I knew at one time," replied Puck sadly. "Either way, we have a big puzzle to figure out. It cannot be a coincidence that a blue gryphon led both of us to the portal. How did you get here with only one portal being unlocked? Why you are here, and why you do not want to go home? You don't seem like a warrior. Had you been the High Queen Anemone, I would have recognized you. I really am quite puzzled."

"So, what can we do to figure it out?" asked Autumn. She wanted answers as much as he did. Perhaps more.

"Well," Puck rubbed his beard, "we don't have much in the way of resources to do a lot of traveling, but I would like to go to a few friends of mine for advice and help. Thyme would know the most about magic spells and the stories of the blue gryphon. Until we can save up enough money and resources for that trip, we will try to see what you can remember. We can assume the Ogres won't travel in the rain to get to the portal, but we may have two weeks at the most before we will have to move. Until then, we need to make some potions to sell in the village south of here and teach you some basic survival skills to live in this world. You need time for the curse to wear off, and time is hard to come by when one is on the run."

"Does it always rain this much?" Autumn asked as thunder crashed again, shaking the house. "I'm glad that the roof doesn't leak."

"I'm glad, too," Puck responded. "To answer your question, no, it hasn't rained here in months. Since Maldamien took over, the magic of this world has been slowly disappearing. Some time ago, some elders had to do elaborate spells to help the seasons to change and the crops to grow. Now the seasons are frozen, and as the world dies, it looks more like fall. The few crops that exist are grown in magical domes that mimic the seasons. A few months ago, it stopped raining entirely. I suspect a little magic entered this world from your world when you came through the portal and that caused the rain."

"So how did Maldamien effect the seasons?"

"I'm afraid that I haven't been able to prove that he has. Some say it has strictly to do with the portals being closed, but I asked why our magic is disappearing entirely. I think it is being drained somehow, but I don't have any theories on how."

Autumn looked out the window at the storm. Everything he was telling her seemed so strange. Had she not been getting all this information from a mythological creature, she would not have believed it.

They were in their own thoughts for a while. Autumn began to feel bored and started to look through the boxes to see what was in them. Puck just sat by the fire and watched. Autumn was a little disappointed at what she found: everything was mostly grains and food items, with some dishes, tools, and blankets mixed in. Finally, Autumn went and got her old clothes and emptied the pockets on the floor before the fire. She then folded her clothes and put them under her bed. The contents of her pockets seemed to pique Puck's interest. He sat forward and picked up an object from the pile: the photograph.

"That's all the stuff that I have to connect me with my past," Autumn stated. Puck did not respond. He was closely studying the picture of the young woman that had been in Autumn's pocket.

"She's pretty, but I still can't remember who she is," Autumn said picking through her other objects. She put the pocket knife in the pocket of her trousers and began to analyze the keys.

"It's Queen Anemone," Puck almost whispered.

"What?" Autumn jumped up to look. The picture had not changed. It was still the light-haired woman with dark eyes. "She looks human!"

"She was or is... a powerful magician herself, but even without her

25

wings and pointed ears she is exactly the same as when I last saw her."

Autumn's heart beat rapidly. What did this mean? She had somehow still thought she was there by accident or that eventually, Maldamien would find out she wasn't the one he was looking for. But what if she was exactly who he was looking for? She couldn't remember anything, but now her own possessions made her completely involved.

"What do I do?" Autumns asked, panicked.

"Hide this and don't ever let it be seen by anyone at all. Loyal or not." He paused and grabbed the keys from her hand. He picked out one old-fashioned skeleton key. "This is the key to the portal! You must have met or known the queen."

Puck looked around at the boxes, still holding the picture and the keys in his hand, and found a piece of cloth. He mumbled some words and a pocket appeared on it. He placed the picture and keys into the pocket and carried the cloth to Autumn.

"Tie this around your waist under your clothes. Don't lose it."

Autumn went behind the partition and did what Puck told her. She felt nervous. What was she doing with that picture and the key to the portal to begin with? Was the queen still alive?

"Autumn," Puck called out as she was finishing.

"Yeah."

"Why did you not want to go home?"

"What?" she asked as she came out from behind the partition.

"By the lake, you told me you did not want to go home. Why?"

"Oh... well, I felt like I was looking for something or going somewhere. No, maybe... a... it was some kind of emotional thing that came up. I feel like I have nothing to go back to, for some reason."

Puck nodded. "We must figure this out because the queen could be waiting to get through that portal. But why did she send you and not herself? With the spell on the portal not broken, the key should not have worked either. There are so many questions."

Autumn looked out the window. She felt a shiver of fear run down her spine. "Puck, could anyone be listening to us right now?"

Puck looked out the window into the rain. "I placed a magical shield that would alert us if someone was near. We always have to be careful. Shutters and a simple magic spell won't protect us forever."

"Puck, I feel frightened."

Puck led her back to the chair by the fire. "Be cautious, but don't be afraid. Maldamien may know a lot of things, but I am certain he does not know who it is that came through that portal or what you have. The Ogres must travel here from the nearest fort, which is two weeks away. His spies and other agents won't take any action without the Ogres in this type of circumstance. Next week, we will go to the house of my friend Ezekiel, so you can hide and bathe. If we have too, we will continue moving whenever we need to. For now, we must concentrate on breaking the curse and teaching you how to survive in this world. Knowledge will be our strongest weapon, right now."

Autumn nodded. Puck poured her some tea. "There is nothing we can do today. We will concentrate on the practical skills for the rest of the evening to keep your mind clear of worry. Why don't I teach you the contents of these boxes and how to cook lunch?"

Autumn smiled weakly and nodded.

At that moment the front door creaked opened causing Puck to turn suddenly, dropping the pot of tea. He pointed the umbrella that jumped into his hand from the wall where it leaned towards the intruder.

A small black shadow slipped through the crack in the door and made its way towards the fire. The firelight revealed the indifferent form of a black cat. She sat down and began to lick her paw as though no one else was in the room.

"Who are you and what do you want here?" demanded Puck, stepping between Autumn and the cat with his umbrella still pointing at the creature.

"That is a bit rude since I let you sleep in my house," said the cat. "In fact, it is very rude since I came to save your lives."

Puck dropped the point of his umbrella and bowed. "Sorry, my dear. One cannot be too careful."

"Indeed," replied the cat who had stopped cleaning herself and sat staring at them with her slitted yellow eyes. "The news I bring is not of what you would hope. The crow, the gossip that he is, has just told me that a Nomad and two Ogres will be here by this evening to search the area for the magical disturbance. I would suggest you leave now, even in the rain if you hope to survive the night."

Puck and Autumn looked at each other. Within the hour, the two figures departed into the rain with all the supplies the cat allowed them to take.

"Thank you," said the girl to the cat.

"Live child," said the cat, "live through this night, and that will be thanks enough."

CHAPTER 3: ODEMIENCE

The massive sandstone fortress called Odemience stood solemnly in the midst of tall reddish mountains like a squat king enthroned with his councilors encircled behind him. On one of the ledges of a nearby ridge overlooking the west side of the fortress, two observers hid, staring intensely at the structure through the early morning mist.

"I can't see how they are getting out of the force field around the fortress. There are no gaps or ripples!" growled the younger of the two.

His eyes turned from purple to black, and his fox-like tail swished slowly for balance.

"Perhaps they have a trap door somewhere, or perhaps they are being transported magically to the outside of the fortress," suggested the older man who had large, flopped-over, pointed ears and wild white hair. He adjusted a series of lenses mounted to his head by multiple leather straps and wooden tubes.

"How close can you see with that thing?" the younger man asked.

"Well, this bi-ocular-head-mounted-magnifier could show me the stain on one of the Ogres' teeth, but I cannot see around rocks or over the walls of that fort." He sighed.

"Then it just leaves me going down there for a closer look." The younger faerie's eyes changed from black to blue.

The older man removed the device from his eyes in time to see the change. He shook his head. That was not a good sign. "Sage, don't get too close!" he whispered.

Sage smiled.

"Don't worry, Toble. I'm always careful."

He silently slipped away as the old man shook his head again and placed his contraption back over his eyes to watch.

Sage expertly crawled through the maze of rocks. He navigated back away from the fort, then around the ledge and down the steep path toward the fortress, his tail hidden under his dark brown cloak. He traveled carefully, stopping often to listen for footsteps. It was best to do this during the day since Ogres were night creatures who preferred the cool caverns in the mountains to the heat of the mid-day sun.

Sage crouched down to crawl as he reached the base of the cliff nearest the fortress edge. Only a few yards in front of him was the edge of the massive clear dome that magically secured the fortress from intrusion. Sage could clearly see the sandstone outer walls of Odemience lined with eight guard towers. Slightly inside a small courtyard was the keep, also constructed from a ruddy sandstone. The keep itself had four towers, and its flat roof was densely manned with Ogre guards. The back of the fortress was carved into a mountain. Sage and Toble had spent months searching that mountain for tunnels or secret passages. A few times they had gotten lost in different caverns, hoping they would not stumble on a garrison of Ogres. They found nothing that was promising. If there was a way in from the mountain, it was magically hidden.

Sage quickly concealed himself behind the rocks upon hearing voices moving towards him. Two large Ogres stopped to talk not far from where Sage had been just a moment ago. The Ogres were the largest of the races on Gryphendale, from six to eight feet tall, and also the most varied. Their appearance as a race looked like someone had borrowed features from a variety of beasts and meshed them together to create the most intimidating combinations. The visual effect was also not far from their collective personality. They were fierce, cruel, animal-like warriors who, in combat, could not be beaten by strength alone, though their fighting styles varied as much as their looks.

"Yep, it happened a couple of days ago, right before all the rain," a bearish Ogre guard was saying to another taller Ogre who looked slightly more reptilian with spikes down his back.

"Did Cowtongue's unit there check it out yet?" asked the tall one.

"Naw, Rattler, they had been waitin' for a good night to go. Their Nomad has been gone since they took that there Sprite king, so they've been lazy. I think a few of the Shenlong guards are there now."

"That's no good for us," said Rattler. "Grizzle, do ya think we'd be sent up there? What an awful march that'll be!"

"You're telling me! I heard that Lord Maldamien is furious though."

Rattler swallowed hard. "So what's going to happen?"

"Since Cowtongue didn't act right away when the wind portal

opened, he is going to have to come here and answer for that in person."

"That's a death warrant for sure!"

"The next nearest unit has been ordered to check on it," said Grizzle.

"What if they can't find anything now? It's already been a few days."

"You know how it goes. They'll just round up peasants and start killin' until they get someone who'll turn in the local underground leader. Then they'll question him till he talks."

"I've heard reports that the school teacher guy is in that area," said Rattler, licking his lips with his forked tongue and looking around anxiously.

"Yeah, I'm sure they'll look for him. He's sure to be in the middle of things," nodded Grizzle.

"So do ya think the queen has returned?"

They were quiet for a while. Sage let the thought sink in, too. Could she really be back? He and Toble would leave immediately to find out. The months they had spent here had been a waste, anyway.

"I don't think she is," Grizzle answered as he played with one of his large bottom tusks nervously.

"Why's that?"

"Well, I think Lord Maldamien would've known that."

"What makes ya think he doesn't?"

"Ya might be right."

A third Ogre, who had two horns sticking out of his head like a cow, walked up.

"Hey, have ya heard what's been happenin' in Shenlong?" he asked.

"Yeah, we've been talkin' about it," grunted Grizzle.

"Well, I heard some news just now," the scaly cow-like Ogre teased.

"What is it? asked Rattler.

The cow-like one leaned closer, conspiratorially.

"I heard that he's goin' to send a whole battalion and... Turmeric."

Sage's eyes widened.

Rattler swallowed nervously.

"I hope it's not my unit."

"Or mine," agreed each of the others.

"What are you three gossiping about?" shouted a familiar voice.

Sage could just get a glimpse of the Nomad speaker walking up to the guards. He ducked down completely. It was Turmeric himself. The tall Nomad's pale skin and high voice were unmistakable. Sage's eyes turned red. He took some silent breaths to calm his rising instinct to attack.

"We were, uh..." mumbled Grizzler.

Rattler was just frozen in terror.

"Well, it doesn't matter. Which one of you is the captain of the eighth mobile unit?"

"I am," replied the cow-like Ogre.

"Prepare your unit to leave at nightfall. Tell your troops to pack light because we will be traveling far very quickly."

Turmeric turned to go but then stopped and looked up.

Sage felt a chill and looked back in the direction of Turmeric's gaze. It led straight to the ledge Toble was on. A flash of light off of Toble's contraption met Sage's wide, green eyes. Panic filled him. Before Sage could hear Turmeric's next words, Sage was running soundlessly up the path he had come. He could see Ogres coming around to the wider path that came up from the other side of the ledge. Sage's eyes turned red again as he heard Turmeric's voice giving a series of orders.

As Sage came to the ledge, Toble was digging in his large bag. "Toble, come on! They saw the reflection off your glass spectacle thing. We need to leave now!"

"What?" Toble asked.

"Let's go!" Sage yelled.

Toble swung his bag onto his back and thrust a smaller bag into Sage's arms. They both took off down a hidden path away from the fortress, down into the caverns. It was a risk going into the Ogres' strongest environment, but it was the only open way. Sage and Toble ran hard and fast, having explored this cavern thoroughly during the two days of rain. The series of passages and sharp turns would have easily lost anyone who was not familiar with the dark, damp tunnels, but not the Ogres. Toble expertly threw spiky foot traps and round barbs from his bag which went easily unseen among the stalagmites. When they reached the other end of the progression of chambers, they could hear the Ogres howling in pain. Sage and Toble continued running in the woods that began only yards from the cavern's edge. Sage and Toble breathed a little easier but were not ready to relax, yet.

In the woods, they had the advantage. They ran for about ten minutes until they were deep inside the dense foliage. Sage jumped up at a low branch and disappeared into a tree. Toble continued a few yards and looked around for Sage.

"Tree! Turn into a tree!" Sage shouted.

"Right!" replied Toble.

He stopped and quickly lifted his bag over his head. Roots sprang from Toble's feet and branches from his arms and torso. He grew in height as his legs and torso merged into a solid trunk of a great oak. The growing branches from his arms consumed his upper half, arms, and head in moments. When he finished transforming into a large oak, his bag was hidden in his branches.

The troop of Ogres was not far behind. They poured into the woods after Sage and Toble, running past them. A few minutes later they wandered back, smelling the air like a pack of wild dogs.

"Where'd they go?"

"Don't know."

"I stopped smellin' them right here."

"Did they vanish?"

"Turmeric won't be happy that we lost them."

"What else can we do?"

The herd of Ogres grumbled on for a minute more before returning the way they came.

Sage waited a few minutes more after he had stopped hearing them before climbing from branch to branch into Toble's oak tree. "Toble, I think they are gone."

Sage then jumped down, and Toble changed back into his faerie form.

"Let's keep going before we stop for the night," suggested Sage.

"We are not returning to the fortress?" Toble asked.

"I overheard a conversation between some of the Ogres. Then Turmeric came and confirmed the gossip."

"Turmeric? That's serious," mused Toble.

He swung his bag in front of him as they continued their fast pace. He began to dig through the contents.

"What could be so important that it would bring Turmeric out of his hole in the ground?" Toble asked from almost inside of his bag. "Oh dear! I misaligned my goggles."

"It sounds like the Wind Portal has been opened."

Toble stopped and jerked his head up.

"What? Has the queen returned?"

"I don't know. One of the guards mentioned that Puck or 'the teacher guy' was in the area. I think we need to find him and learn what has happened. Turmeric and a unit of troops are also going to Shenlong, and we need to warn the Underground."

"You would think Puck would be more subtle after his stunt last year," mumbled Toble with his head back in his bag as they continued walking.

"You haven't forgotten that we helped," teased Sage.

"No, we did not. I remember that," Toble stated.

"Yes, we did! That was right after Puck gave you some ointment for your ears."

"Oh," Toble replied sheepishly. "I guess that's right. I'm almost out of ointment. I think I will see if Puck could make me some more."

Sage smiled. "You don't happen to have any food in there?"

Toble threw Sage a cloth pouch. Sage opened it and poured out a few black dried up nuggets.

"What are these?"

"Blackberry nuts," replied Toble as he found some sort of contraption that he had been looking for.

Sage tossed a nugget into his mouth, then spit it out making a horrible face. Sage inspected another nut.

"I think blackberries are from the human world and are not nuts. How long have you had these?"

"I do not remember, but they taste like nuts to me," Toble replied, taking one of the black nuggets and eating it absently while analyzing a small wing of his device.

Sage poured the nuggets back into the cloth pouch and put it into Toble's bag.

"Do you think a lot will change if the queen has returned?" asked Sage.

"Of course," answered Toble absently, lifting up the device and letting go, trying to make it float in the air.

Sage sighed.

"My father died trying to save her. She must be a great lady. There are so many legends about her."

Toble looked at Sage. "What?"

"Never mind." Sage sighed again. "What would I say to her? 'Hey, I'm Sage. My father died trying to save you.' I wonder if any time has passed for her. She would have only remembered me as a little boy. Would she expect me to take my father's place in protecting her?"

"If you wanted to," replied Toble as he continued messing with the wings on his device. "A lot of things change in a hundred years, Sage. No one is expecting you to be your father. By the way, I think I've invented a way for someone to fly without wings or magic."

They continued traveling until late that night and made camp on the rocky edge of a mountain, so they would be hidden by the dense woods in front of them. Sage ate some herbs he found, and Toble ate some blackberry nuts because a fire, even for cooking, would be too risky. Toble quickly fell asleep leaning over his bag. His oak tree shape was bent over with his flying contraption in one branch and another branch laying in his bag. Sage lay against his own bag, but couldn't sleep.

It would be weeks before they could get to Shenlong, but he felt like it was not long enough or short enough. He had long ago given up any hope things would really change. He had gone to Maldamien's fortress hoping to free thousands of prisoners that Maldamien held as slaves in his fortress, but he never thought he could really change things. Now that change was inevitable, he felt his past coming back to haunt him. There were so many things he had never dealt with. He'd just buried them and forgot about it. He had been able to ignore the past, using the daily struggle for survival as an excuse, but now he would have to deal with it.

CHAPTER 4: POTIONS

Autumn looked out at the clear morning sky as she stood in the cave in which they were hiding. They had spent the last few days hiding under trees and in caves waiting for the rain to stop. The days were not wasted though. Puck taught her how to cook various plants, taught her about many different types of faerie creatures who inhabited the world, even explained how they were in the northwestern corner of Gryphendale and how to keep a sense of direction in the dark. He explained how the atmosphere around Gryphendale mimicked the atmosphere around the surface of the earth and that the sun, moon, and stars were not real, but reflections of light magnified and transmitted through the earth's oceans. She asked lots of questions trying to see if anything brought back a memory or held a clue to why she was there. It didn't reveal anything about her past, but it had at least been a distraction from the miserable weather and wet clothes.

"Are you ready to gather some herbs in this wonderful sunshine?" asked Puck as he put on his dried cloak and stomped out the low fire next to Autumn.

"Am I ever!" Autumn exclaimed, almost bounding out of the cave when Puck caught her shirt and pulled her back.

"Wait!" shouted Puck. "Let me check first." He walked out into the daylight slowly and looked both ways, then allowed Autumn to proceed before him. "We must be very careful."

Autumn looked around in awe as they walked. This was the first time Autumn was able to see Gryphendale completely in full daylight, and it was beautiful.

Flowers were blooming, and trees were bright fall colors. She looked at the chirping blue jays that were as large as house cats.

She and Puck jumped at a loud pop behind them as they walked. They turned to see an owl flopping on the ground and standing up to fly back into the tree.

"Those clumsy owls are always falling out of trees," stated Puck as they turned to continue walking. Autumn giggled, and Puck laughed with her.

Autumn breathed in the crisp morning air as they entered the denser part of the woods. Mushrooms were bright colors and large enough to sit on. Ferns accented their path as light peeked in speckled patterns through the tree branches. Autumn quickly fell in love with the world around her.

She swung her arms out at each side and began to spin happily, laughing. "This is wonderful!"

Puck looked back at her and smiled sadly. He continued walking on slowly.

"What?" Autumn asked running up to him. "Did I do something wrong?"

"No," said Puck, "you need to be aware of your surroundings even in your joy, but you did nothing wrong."

"Then why are you so sad?"

"The way you see the world right now is but a shadow of what it once was, and even this much won't last very long." Puck glanced at Autumn's saddened face. "Come," he said kindly, "pull your hood up and prepare for a beautiful sight." Puck also pulled his hood closer around his face as they reached the edge of the woods and peered into a huge field of wildflowers. Autumn gasped at the sight.

Puck grabbed her hand suddenly and pulled her to the ground. "Hide!" he whispered. Autumn fell flat into the mud next to Puck. The shadows of the woods hid them well. Autumn looked up to see what Puck had buried her in the mud for. She followed Puck's gaze to a single lady dressed in red with fiery red hair.

"Are we hiding from her?" Autumn asked annoyed.

"Quiet!" Puck whispered.

"But she looks harmless. Is she an ex-girlfriend?" the girl teased.

"No, she is a Red Lady."

"Well, that seems obvious."

"No, I mean she's a man-eater and works for Maldamien. She may be looking for us or checking the portal."

"A man-eater?" the girl looked at Puck to see if he was joking. He was not.

"I think humans call them vampires, but these are all female

Nymphs."

"I thought vampires didn't come out in the day." Autumn thought about an old black and white movie she had seen one time.

"Ever since Maldamien started ruling, they have been more and more comfortable everywhere and at any time of the day." Puck glanced back at the field. "No one has ever been able to kill them because they are very strong magic users. Unlike other culture's magic, theirs uses some kind of hypnosis or will-power possession."

When the Red Lady disappeared into the woods opposite them, Puck sat up in the mud looking disgusted at it. "It couldn't be helped. I hope that you understand that we are still in a lot of danger. Just because we haven't met any trouble doesn't mean it isn't still after us. I will do my best to keep you safe, but please take this to heart." He sighed and wiped mud off his arms.

"Don't worry, Puck, I will listen to you. It just feels safer when it isn't dark and stormy."

Puck smiled at Autumn's words.

The seriousness only lasted a moment as Puck and Autumn tried to help each other up in the mud. Each one fell back into it once before they made it out. They found a large puddle nearby that they used to wash off some of the mud. Then they began to pick flowers and herbs on the edge of the field. Autumn used her pocket knife, and Puck used a hunting knife to cut the plants. A few times Puck had to stop Autumn from cutting a poisonous version of an herb she was told to look for, but by noon she felt like an expert of at least the varieties of herbs in that field.

As they sat under a maple tree eating some nuts and berries for lunch, Autumn began looking around nervously.

"Are you feeling the coolness in the breeze?" asked Puck.

"Yeah, it's strange. What is it?"

"It's messages in the wind. You have a gift in the magical arts," said Puck, smiling.

"What is the wind saying?" asked Autumn.

"Maldamien is angry," Puck leaned back against the tree. "We are being careful, but we are going to have to be very aware of any sign that he might have spies around."

Autumn nodded then tilted her head. "So, what does having a gift in the magical arts mean? After all, I'm human, not faerie."

"Here it makes little difference who you are. Humans have strange beliefs and practices of magic in their world that are against the order of things. Here, magic is necessary for life. It runs through things in different ways, like currents in your oceans or electricity. We use what is there like an artist paints a picture. Everyone can paint, but some people are better at it than others. Unlike the human world, we don't use superstition or some other manipulative force. It is purely physical here. One can create magic through potions like my people do, or with special gems like the Ogres. The Sprites channel it through the wind, Hiru through fire, the water peoples use water, and so on. Here there is magic in everything, but one has to learn how to access it. Now, any of us can use any technique we want, but we tend to use only what we grew up with. Some, like Queen Anemone, and her grandmother Queen Audrey, learned all the main kinds of magic out there. I am not certain if Maldamien has learned as much as they did, but he somehow channels more of it."

"So, do you think I could learn a lot of techniques?" asked Autumn.

"Yes, if you really want to."

They finished their lunches and continued working until late. Then they wrapped the herbs in the blankets they brought and tied them with rope. Puck carried the larger bundle on his back. Autumn struggled along with her smaller load. As she walked with Puck, he took out a small set of pan pipes from an inner pocket. He began to play a soft low wistful tune. Autumn saw a rabbit large enough for someone to ride on peeping at Puck as he played. A small green and purple tiger came out of the depths of the woods and sat in their path. Puck continued playing his song as he walked up to the tiger. The tiger turned and began to walk ahead of them. The sun began to sink down low as they slowly walked in a line after their guide. The tiger walked up to the entrance of a shallow cave in a hill. Puck stopped playing his song, and the tiger disappeared back into the woods.

Then Puck dropped his pack from his back so he could make a low fire. Autumn also dropped her bundle and began to gather some dry twigs that were nearby. Once they got the fire going, Autumn stretched her feet and hands towards the heat.

"So, what are we going to do with all those herbs? We aren't going to eat them all."

"No, we are going to make potions to sell in town when we arrive at

Ezekiel's place. I hope that we might be able to make enough to sell so we can get supplies to take a trip to visit Thyme. We will need a lot of supplies for that trip because he is a very difficult person to locate. Talking to him would help us find quite a few more answers. If we could be ready soon enough, he may be able to break your curse faster than bathing would, especially since you haven't had a chance to bathe since your first day here. At least at Ezekiel's place, we can give you a week to bathe and see what you can remember."

Puck stood up. "We are going to need some water. Stay here, and I'll be back."

He didn't take long and carried the water in a huge hollowed out gourd which he placed on the fire.

"Puck, I was thinking while you were gone. Why was the queen trapped in the human world? Why was she trying to close the portals in the first place?"

"A little over a hundred years ago, Queen Anemone ruled Gryphendale from the palace at Vervain. If you can imagine a map, Gryphendale is sort of an oval bowl shape. I had told you we are in the northwest. Vervain is in the center of our world. That is where generations of rulers have governed, and it is near an even older ruin in which the Ancients once ruled the whole world. Queen Anemone had been ruling there already for a hundred years when these events took place.

"Maldamien was once an adviser of Queen Anemone's grandmother, Queen Audrey, so it followed that he continued in that role for Queen Anemone, but he was greedy for power and control. Queen Anemone discovered that Maldamien was building a fortress called Odemience in the land of Rokurokubi far to the east with slave labor. She was furious, had him arrested, and tried for treason. A great deal of proof was brought against him of not only his tendency towards slave labor but also for his conspiring against her. He was found guilty even though it was becoming more obvious that he had supporters throughout the government. The night after the verdict was given, he escaped. The queen received various secret messages that many thought he was after control of the whole world, even the human realm. A group of trusted advisers and she made the decision to contain him here and protect the human world. The queen performed a complicated spell, then sent four groups out with the keys to lock the portals and complete its sealing. Maldamien magically arrived at each portal moments after they were sealed, killed many in each group, and stole the keys. The last group was led by the queen herself, and they were in the process of closing the wind portal when Maldamien arrived. In trying to protect the queen, the captain of the guard threw himself in front of her, blocking her from being hit by a mighty fireball, and was killed himself. Either the force of the fireball or the captain's last efforts shoved the queen through the portal with the key as the door was shut. Her life was spared, but the portal was sealed with no known way for it to be unlocked. The queen had no husband and no heirs, so Maldamien seized the throne immediately and killed anyone in the palace who might oppose him. It was a horrific massacre. The city was left abandoned after half of it was burned and most of the citizens had been taken away as slaves." Puck sighed and leaned forward, absently playing with his English smoking pipe.

"That's dreadful," said Autumn. She observed his pained face and sympathized with his watering eyes.

After sitting quietly watching the water and waiting for it to boil, Puck finally looked up. "I would say you look as though you could be about eight years old now," said Puck. "Perhaps the rain helped wash a little of the magic off you."

"How old did I look before?" asked Autumn.

"I would say about five or six. I wish I could speed up the process for you, but I'm afraid that might be quite painful."

Autumn nodded. She already ached with various pains just from traveling as it was. "So, what are we doing with the water?"

"We are boiling the potions to bring out their properties. We will do as much as we can every evening now before we get into town."

He unwrapped his bundle of herbs and grabbed a handful of silver grass. He picked up his knife from the bag and placed everything on a flat rock near the fire.

"Cut this as finely as you can, and I will sort through the bundles. When you finish, just ask for more silver grass."

Autumn began cutting.

Puck started making piles of the different herbs. He looked over at Autumn's work. "Very good. We need to cut all the silver grass this same way because it will be the foundation for our potions. I will teach you how to make five different ones today. We will see how well it goes before I introduce some more."

Autumn felt pleased. She expertly handled the knife even though it seemed very large in her child-like hands. She wondered if she had been a good cook in the human world since the motion of cutting seemed so natural.

When she finished, Puck scooped some of the grass and threw it into the gourd holding the boiling water. He waited a moment and frowned. "We may only be able to make three potions today. This grass is very weak. Look, it should have turned the water a dark blue, but it is only a pale blue right now."

Autumn looked at the pale blue water and nodded as though she knew what he was talking about.

"I think we have plenty of silver grass in here somewhere," said Puck as he continued sorting.

Autumn began to cut the purple flowers Puck handed her as he separated stacks of herbs all around the cave.

"So," said Autumn after a while of silence, "what do these potions do?"

"The first one helps mend wounds, the second helps stomach ailments, and the third is a balm for aches in the muscles and joints," said Puck.

"That doesn't sound very magical to me. It's just herbal medicine like we use back in my world. Anyways, I thought you were all immortal."

"These are basic level potions, and they are quite magical. You must think of magic differently here than what your folklore invents. As to immortality, we do not die of natural causes, but injury, poisoning, and pain are just as real to us as to you." Puck trailed off as he began to wrestle with some thorny weeds that were tangled together. "Go ahead and put the purple daisies in the pot."

Autumn did as Puck asked, then began to stir. A puff of smoke popped out of the liquid hitting the girl in the face.

Puck shouted, "Don't stir!" and jumped up, knocking over some of his stacks of herbs. At seeing Autumn's face, he began to chuckle.

Autumn reached up and touched her face then felt something protruding from her forehead. "What is it?" she asked as panic began to fill her.

"It's just a flower growing out of your forehead. Don't worry. We

42

will cure you soon enough. These spells are pretty safe, but I am impressed that you were able to create something so advanced from your mistake. Most students just let the magic escape and make the solution useless." Puck looked into the gourd.

Autumn was not comforted by Puck's casual tone. "Well, what do we do to fix it?" asked Autumn.

"With every spell or curse the cure is connected to how it was cast," said Puck, "so I would like you to construct the cure... but not yet. Let us talk it out first."

Autumn looked around, "Well if it's connected to what caused it, would it use the same ingredients?"

Puck grinned broadly, "Yes, exactly! Now, what is the one thing that must change?"

Autumn looked at the water intensely, "Well, I stirred it to get a reaction, but if I don't do anything, then that won't help. Do I stir it the opposite direction?" Puck nodded, "Very good! Very good indeed! The catalyst, or whatever caused the reaction, is the only step you must do backward. Now, do you remember which way you stirred?"

Autumn closed her eyes and mimed the motion in the air. "Clockwise."

Puck motioned toward the gourd.

Autumn nervously took the wooden spoon that was still in the cauldron and stirred counter-clockwise. Another puff of smoke came out of the pot and hit her in the face. She reached up to feel for where the flower was. It was gone. Autumn sighed in relief.

"I'm glad that wasn't permanent," said Autumn.

"No spell is permanent unless it is one that can't be reversed in any way," said Puck.

"Like what?"

Puck frowned a little. "Like the dark spells that require something or someone to die to cast it."

Autumn shivered and made a sour face.

"You will never learn a dark spell from me, though knowledge of what kinds of magic exist may help you to protect yourself from them," said Puck as he lifted the gourd. "This potion is used up. I'm going to pour it out and get some more water. Would you cut some more silver grass?"

As Puck walked out of the cave, Autumn cut the silver grass Puck had piled next to her. When Puck returned, Autumn had some questions ready for him.

"It seems like magic isn't too hard to do. It's just a matter of learning recipes, but can it be done with just movements too since Queen Mare cast a shield thing with her hands and did other stuff? Also, how do spells get a moral quality? What makes a dark spell dark?"

Puck looked a little surprised, then continued to put the huge gourd on the fire. "A tool, such as a knife, has no moral value," began Puck, "but the one using it can use it for good or evil. Magic in this world is the potential in every object to do certain things. Humans like to call it science or creativity. We call it magic. The religious may even call it created purpose. Whatever you call it, there are many ways of using it for many purposes. Dark magic may just be an evil purpose for a spell, or it may be unethical ways of creating spells even if it seems like it is for a good purpose."

"I think I understand," said Autumn.

Puck picked up the silver grass that Autumn had cut and put it into the gourd as Autumn continued cutting. He then settled by the fire with his English smoking pipe.

"Many students become so excited by magic and spells that they became superstitious and addicted to the power. When they see that they can cure illnesses, give sight to the blind, or many other such things, they start doing anything they can to get more powerful. Something good then leads to something evil and darker by seeing themselves as gods. I don't know if you believe in gods or a god, but when you start to feel that the world revolves around you, that is what you are doing. Dark magic goes against the reason magic exists. Dark magic controls people or things against their purpose or will. It intrudes on one's rights, steals, deceives, and even kills."

"Wouldn't it be better not to practice magic at all?" asked Autumn.

"Again, you see magic as something out there like reading or writing in which one can just choose to never learn. It is more like walking or running. We all do it, but some can train to be very good at it. We were all created with an ability. None of the races have a monopoly on those skills. Some races just tend to be better at one thing then another, but sometimes you will find an Ogre who likes animals, or a Sprite that uses water. The point though is that this is a natural gift for the harmony of life in working together as a community. There is a responsibility with the gift to use it responsibly. When one starts twisting the magic in the world for their own purposes... well, just think about human history... if you can remember it."

"You mean like wars and such?" asked Autumn.

"Sort of. I mean the weapons of warfare, gunpowder, swords, various tortures, and even the creative forces of strategy and manipulation. Those are examples of the life-giving creativity of man being used for negative purposes. The same thing can be done with all the races' gifts. Dark magic can be obvious, but it can be subtle too."

Autumn looked into the fire. She felt a burning within her. "I want to learn, but I can see that it is like you are teaching me how to use a sword. I can use it to help, or I can destroy everything around me with it."

"Even yourself," added Puck.

"It's a big responsibility," said Autumn, "but I want to do it."

"Good," said Puck. He looked out of the cave at the fading sunlight in the distance. "You will need it."

CHAPTER 5: TRAP

Sage checked his grip on the branch before swinging upside down to tie the rope to a rock jutting out the side of a waterfall. He swung back into a sitting position and then jumped gracefully to the branch in front of him like a gymnast swings from bar to bar.

Once he was over the solid ground, he jumped down. Voices started to approach. Sage dived into a nearby bush almost landing in Toble's lap.

"Are you finished?" whispered Toble, regaining his position.

"Yeah. How about you?" asked Sage.

"Yes. Wait perhaps I... No. Yes, I'm done," said Toble.

They waited and watched. This morning they had seen in the distance the Ogres with Turmeric marching towards Yarrow River. Toble and Sage quickly decided it would be best to slow them down and prevent these troops from getting to Shenlong as quickly as them. Whoever they would find in Shenlong would need time to escape. They developed a make-shift plan to pick off the troops. This was their third trap already today.

Six Ogres came plowing through the forest first.

"...after we go there, then we'll go to Vervain," said a greenish colored Ogre.

"Why would we do that?" asked the brown warty one.

"I overheard the captain and Turmeric talking about a ring or something," said the greenish one.

"That place gives me the creeps," said the pig-faced Ogre.

At that moment the Ogres stepped on the rope lying on the forest floor. A giant wooden arm swung right into them, knocking the group unconscious.

"Great!" said Sage.

"Drat!" said Toble. "It was supposed to knock them over the waterfall. I suppose I should have shortened the back rope or..."

"Too late now!" Sage said as they sprinted off into the woods. He smiled. They successfully knocked out fifteen troops with all the traps. Turmeric would have to leave a couple of soldiers with each group so that they could rejoin the unit when they recovered. That made six more troops delayed. Almost half of the fifty-soldier unit were now detained.

"I thought you were behind this!"

Sage's hair on the back of his neck stood on end at the familiar cold voice. He immediately pushed Toble down into some brush and then dove the opposite direction as a silver fireball landed where they had been moments ago. Sage rolled and jumped back onto his feet, drawing his short, curved sword from its sheath on his belt. He quickly looked around to see where Turmeric was.

"Are you afraid to fight me like a real man?" Sage called out. He knew Turmeric was watching him, but none of Sage's skill would be able to see through the magic that Turmeric used to hide. "Are you on one of your master's errands like a whipped dog?" Sage baited.

Another fireball headed towards Sage. He barely jumped out of the way, rolling in the dirt again. He quickly got to his feet and charged the direction the fireball had come from. He could see a slight ripple in the air and swung his sword at it.

Clang!

Sage's sword met Turmeric's long straight sword. The magical illusion disappeared as Turmeric lost concentration on it. Sage swung again.

"You have lost your touch, Turmeric," Sage taunted.

"You prefer brute force, but I have used my time better!" Turmeric blocked Sage and then held out his hand towards Sage to shoot a small fireball.

Sage tried to dodge it, but it seared his leg.

He cried out in pain. He then attacked Turmeric with a series of skillful moves with his sword. Turmeric met each attack with equal force, blocking then attacking in turn. With his free hand, Turmeric shot darts of various spells that Sage blocked with his sword or dodged. The fight lasted only a few minutes before Sage could hear the other twenty-five Ogres heading towards him. His wide eyes turned yellow. He was going to be trapped in a moment if he didn't do something.

Turmeric sneered, and he held his sword pointed at Sage. "Don't worry. I'll make your death quick. I would never risk keeping you as a prisoner."

Sage glanced behind him as he moved back slightly. He was at the edge of the waterfall.

Turmeric's smile faded as Sage sheathed his sword, smirked at Turmeric with a nod, turned around, and jumped off the cliff.

"No!" shouted Turmeric as his troops arrived seconds too late. The Ogres froze in fear of Turmeric's rage.

Sage had jumped off the cliff aiming towards a large oak growing from a lower ledge. He grabbed onto a branch as he fell towards it, then swung himself onto the ledge, and rolled into the wall of the cliff. The landing shook his whole body with pain.

The large oak transformed back into Toble. "That was a close one," he said.

"You should have seen it from where I was standing!" said Sage as he sat up and began to take inventory of his limbs.

Toble knelt down and examined Sage's wounds. "These are pretty bad," said Toble as he spotted the burn on Sage's leg.

"Do the best you can. We need to get on with our journey as soon as possible. I'm not too eager to try to delay Turmeric at this point."

Toble nodded. "I agree. We would do better in traveling faster than them. We can use the river to get into the kingdom of Caoineag in two weeks and then go to Shenlong on foot. The Ogres are afraid of water, so it will take them longer on foot even if they do travel fast. I could add a sailor, perhaps I could rig..."

"Yes, but remember that we won't have time for something complicated," said Sage as he braced himself while Toble helped him to his feet.

"We will still beat them by a few days. I will clean your wounds and then get a quick raft built. We should be off within the hour."

Sage grimaced as they made their way down the side of the cliff to the bottom of the waterfall. It didn't take very long, but the color was gone from Sage's face by the time they reached the bottom.

"Leave me by the water," said Sage. "I'll take care of my wounds. I am not going to be much help in building the raft, at least not until my leg is tightly wrapped."

Toble left Sage with his bag of supplies and walked into the woods a little way. Sage half watched Toble as he was fixing his wounds. Toble grew roots into the ground and then began to wave his arms. The trees around him began to shake their branches so that dead limbs fell into a pile around Toble. With the waterfall masking the sound, it looked like a silent dance as vines came at Toble's summing to help create the raft as quickly as Sage could bind up his leg. It was not long before both men had completed their tasks. Toble even fashioned some quick oars to guide the raft, and they were on their way before dark.

The raft smoothly glided down the river at a steady but quick pace. Sage put down the oar he was using and lay on his back as Toble continued to steer.

"Toble, I heard one of the Ogres talking about a ring at Vervain. Do you know what ring they could be talking about?"

"Well, I imagine they would be talking about the queen's royal seal. It is a special ring with magical properties that can only be activated by the rightful ruler. I always assumed that Queen Anemone was wearing it when she disappeared, but I suppose she could have left it behind in the palace. If Maldamien could sense a magical disturbance in Shenlong, perhaps he sensed the ring getting activated in Vervain."

"What could Maldamien want with it after all these years?" asked Sage. "If he is not the rightful ruler could he even use it anyway?"

Toble shook his head. "Maldamien can twist almost any magic. I am sure he could find a way to use it. It seems like a lot of things are happening all of a sudden after so many years of nothing."

Sage pushed himself up onto his elbow. "I was thinking the same thing. I guess when the queen takes back her throne..."

"Don't start assuming things," cautioned Toble. "We don't know if the queen really has returned or if it is just some magical burp or misunderstanding. Also, we haven't seen anything change yet."

"I'm just really eager for this all to end. It's hard to imagine a life settled down somewhere. I had once thought that when the queen returned I would be able to have a little house, a wife, some kids, but that dream faded so long ago. I would be content with just a little bit of peace in which I didn't have to look over my shoulder at every moment." Sage sat up completely and checked his leg. It felt horrible. The pain seemed to pulsate through his body.

"Are you all right?" asked Toble.

"My leg hurts, unlike any burn I have ever had. When we stop for you to rest, I'll get some willow bark for the pain."

"I can go a long time before resting. Are you sure you don't want to stop now? Your burn will be very slow to heal because of the type of fire spell Turmeric used. It looks like a flesh-eating type of burn."

Sage re-wrapped his leg tighter. "I think you are right, but I still would like to stop as little as possible. When we find Puck, maybe he will have something for it."

"When we start our trek, we will need to find something stronger than willow bark. The trip from the river to Shenlong will be at least four days."

Sage frowned. "Do you hear anything?"

"Yes. Why?" asked Toble.

Sage picked up his oar and dug a deep stroke into the water. Toble understood what Sage was doing and followed suit. They rowed until the raft was hidden under an overhanging willow tree.

"Have you checked the shore?" Turmeric's voice demanded.

"Yeah. We have been checking for miles!" growled an Ogre.

"Fine! If we can't find a body, than he is not dead. Get information. We will be running the whole way there."

The whole group of Ogres began to grumble.

"For being so athletic, you all are incredibly lazy. Next grumble I hear, and the rations will be halved. Do you hear me?"

"Yes sir!" said the chorus of Ogres.

As the pounding of footsteps and the light of torches faded away, Sage sighed in relief. He looked back at Toble who had already begun his transformation in the water. After fifty or so years on the run, Toble had learned to rest whenever they had a moment. As a Dryad, he got his main energy, nutrition, and rest from the earth in his tree form. He could store that energy and travel for days without sleep. Not all Dryads had made the most of this potential, but as a team, Sage and Toble made extensive use of anything they could.

Sage got his sword out and eased into the water. Since they were under a willow tree, he would gather as much willow bark as he could. Providence was looking out for them.

Sage scraped the bark of the willow tree with his sword. His weapon was not a proper sword, but a very useful mix of a cutlass and a curved dagger. He used it for everything, but for a real battle, he would give his hind teeth for a long sword. Right now, much of his life centered on survival so that the old Nomad blade had become his best friend.

Sage stacked the bark on the raft until he got enough to last at least two weeks. Then Sage made his way to shore. The water on his leg felt good, but once it was exposed to air, it began to burn again. Sage stopped to rest a moment, so he could collect himself and deal with the pain. He then gathered as many nuts and herbs as he could. Food was hard to find these days, so anything edible was collected. In the dark, some things not edible might have been collected too, but he would worry about that later. Once Sage returned to the raft with the supplies, he woke Toble up and they were on their way.

"How did they not see us? I know it's dark, but not that dark," said Sage.

"Or hear us?" said Toble. "We were talking louder than we should have. I don't know. Perhaps after you drowned that one Ogre last year, they are afraid to get near you and water."

"That wasn't easy to do. I'm not sure I could do that again," said Sage, settling down for a nap on the raft.

Toble shrugged. "Doesn't matter. It's just the potential that scares them. Anyways, I am not planning on stopping until we get to the kingdom of Caoineag."

Sage started to chew a piece of willow bark. "It will be quite a race to get there, and it will be just as hard to get away."

"Is it any different than it always is?" said Toble.

"True, but this time it's going to be harder with my bad leg. It'd better be worth it!"

CHAPTER 6: SHENLONG

Autumn and Puck had prepared disguises the day before for going into town. Puck had been growing a full beard and dyed all his hair black, which was quite a task considering his goat-like legs had to be dyed too. He also decided to wear rags and pack his nice clothes for later. Autumn's disguise was mostly pale make-up, rubber pointed ears, and black hair with white streaks in the fashion of the Hiru who lived in the Nomad lands. Since the mysterious Hiru were not common in this area, in fact not common anywhere, being disguised as this race would be the more convincing than any other race. She had few options when it came to disguises since she was too tall to be a Gnome or Brownie, didn't have wings like the Sprites, and couldn't mimic the eye color changes of the Huldra. Her only options left were the Dryad, Undine, and Hiru. Puck would be posing as her slave this time since he would be carrying the bigger load and since the Dryads were slaves that just left the Hiru and Undines. With the mysterious nature of the Hiru being less known to the public, Puck decided she could pull it off. Hopefully, no one would want to see their travel papers. The papers that Queen Mara had given them had completely different identities, with Puck as master and her as a Dryad slave.

They left the woods early that morning and followed a dirt road through an open field. Autumn immediately tensed, having been trained by Puck to keep hidden at all times.

Puck pulled out his pan pipes from his bag. "Some music will help you relax and help our disguise. We don't want to look like we are on the run. We are just travelers minding our own business." They had been running and hiding from the various creatures that Puck knew served Maldamien for the past couple of weeks. It was nice to travel slow and comfortably for once.

Puck began to play a song that he had never played for her before. It was simple but very beautiful.

52

"Puck, does that song have words?"

"Yes, but it is hard to play and sing at the same time," he said with a twinkle in his eye and continued to play.

"Would you teach it to me?" Autumn asked.

Puck's face turned serious for a moment.

"I'm sorry," said Autumn. "Did I say something wrong?"

"No. Not at all," said Puck. "I would be very honored to teach you the song. It is... Well, a song that holds some memories. Playing the melody is one thing, singing the words is a bit more personal. Well, let's get on with it," said Puck. In his airy tenor voice, he sang:

"Ancient roads we want to travel,
And our foot upon the gravel,
Paths for us to explore,
The trails beyond the shore.

Touched by the gryphon's wing,
Beyond common censure,
Drawn to the dusty road,
Beware of the adventure,
Touched by a gryphon's wing.

Highways lead us somewhere too far,
Far away from our childhood home,
To chase the distant star,
A happy life just lived to roam.

Touched by the gryphon's wing,
Beyond common censure,
Drawn to the dusty road,
Beware of the adventure,
Touched by a gryphon's wing.

Autumn felt the awe of the beautiful folk melody. Puck repeated the song line by line with Autumn mimicking his pitch. They worked on it for a little while before Autumn could faithfully sing it on her own.

"That is such a pretty song!" said Autumn.

"You won't find anything like that at Ezekiel's. The Sprites have odious taste in music. They also sing traditional songs to non-traditional tunes. It is quite awful! There is no rhythm, no melody, and no musicality. Oh, how I despise it!"

Autumn giggled. "In fairytales, the Sprites sang well."

Puck raised an eyebrow amused. "I see you are regaining some memories. Well, human fairytales mix a lot of stories together. Many cultures in this world have beautiful music, but the Sprites are not one of them. Well... that's not true." Puck scratched his beard.

"I have told you that the Sprites use wind for their magic. That is how they fly. Wind is used for music too. Thousands of years ago they were some of the best musicians in any world. Perhaps the tales come from that era. Since then, they became bored and began to experiment with various sounds, rhythms, pitches, and harmonics to the point of senselessness. So now their songs are so convoluted that it just sounds like noise."

"Well, if it is so bad, why do you go there?"

"Because Ezekiel is one of my closest friends. I have found that friendship is one of the most valuable things a person can have."

Autumn and Puck sang or talked until about noon when they rested for lunch on the edge of some woods with unusually tall trees.

"I'm sore!" said Autumn as she plopped down under a large chestnut tree. Puck always traveled hard, and every day she felt horribly sore. It seemed like her body would never get used to constant walking.

She unpacked the lunch from her bag, and Puck sorted out their rations. Autumn looked around and noticed that something was different.

"Puck, I haven't seen any flowers all day. Everything is so brown. What happened?"

"They all died a couple of days ago. This is the state that this area was in before you came."

"It's so different!"

"Yes, it's all deteriorating," Puck took a bite of purplish root vegetable. "You are now going to be able to see with your own eyes that I wasn't just telling you stories."

They quickly ate and continued their journey. After only a few more hours of walking, Puck walked up to one of the largest trees in the woods. They walked around it and came to an ornately decorated structure shaped like a giant hollow budding flower. Puck swung opened the gilded door, they both walked into it and closed the door. Immediately, the structure lurched upward gliding easily around the tall tree in a spiral.

"Put the hood of your cloak up," said Puck. "That will help your makeup look more believable."

Autumn did as he suggested.

The bulbous structure eased to a stop in what looked like a small floating city of tree houses. Buildings sat on branches as if they grew from them. Giant leaves ornately covered the tops of the houses. The large village was almost empty. Some of the buildings looked abandoned, and others were in need of repair. A couple of men and women Sprites were flying here and there with their moth-like wings, hurried but almost in a secretive manner.

Puck dragged Autumn out of the blossom before it moved back down.

"This is amazing!" said Autumn.

"Indubitably," said Puck.

They walked out on one of the tree limb roads that thankfully had ornate guard rails on either side. It seemed to be the main road of the village with a few roads shooting off from it. Very few people were walking, so the rails were not necessary for the wide walkway, but Autumn still felt safer with them there. The few people who were out seemed to be uneasy about their presence and moved out of their way. One gnarled creature that Autumn took to be an Ogre nodded at them as he passed.

"Why are people staring at us?" whispered Autumn. "I thought we were supposed to not be noticed."

"The Nomads are loyal followers of Maldamien and tend to have high positions in his government. The people will fear you, but that's good because no one will get to close to you either."

The branch roads twisted around each other and connected each of the closely built buildings to each other. From the main street, they turned right onto a smaller narrower branch, and then left to a dark corner of the village. They reached a small shop on the edge of town where Puck stopped and turned to her.

"Remember what we practiced. I will handle the negotiations. You just look important. Pay attention, though, because things don't always go as planned."

Autumn nodded. She was glad she had the hood to hide some of her expressions. She straightened up with the best air of authority she could muster. Puck opened the door for her and followed her in. She stood in the middle of the shop looking around with as little movement and expression as she could. She waited for Puck to speak to the old Sprite behind the counter as her agent. Once the conversation was fully engaged, Autumn slowly strolled around the perimeter of the room. She looked over the floor-to-ceiling shelving that held hundreds of small potion bottles. Each one cured some ailment, grew hair, helped plants grow, dye any part of the body from wings to eyes to toes. Autumn came upon one extremely dusty shelf. The bottles cured colicky babies, pain from growth spurts, and other childhood ailments. The untouched nature of the shelf caused Autumn to pause and wonder at the strangeness of it.

"Mistress, is this an acceptable price?" Puck called out in an earthy accent. Autumn calmed herself from the jump at the surprise. She slowly turned around as composed as possible and looked at the old man with a stringy herb sticking out of his mouth and a smug look of victory. Puck calmly watched her, obviously willing to accept any answer she gave.

"Is it the price I asked for?" Autumn said in the most important voice she could create. She had not heard what the price was.

Puck smirked. "No, but it's only a little lower."

Autumn tried to hide the pleasure she felt at answering correctly with a look of severe displeasure. "Then it is not acceptable."

She turned around sharply because she could not keep her face serious. Then she hesitated only for a moment before walking to the door slowly. She heard some shuffling and shifting of glass jars behind her. The shuffling stopped with the sound of some lowered talking.

"Mistress, I believe our friend is willing to buy all of our potions," Puck stated after a moment.

Autumn turned around and looked at the old Sprite.

"Thank you," she said with a little nod. Puck finished unloading his bag and collected the money as Autumn left the shop. He then hurried out of the shop behind her, passing her to lead the way. Once they were out of view of the shop, Puck whispered, "Well done. Very clever!"

Autumn smiled weakly. Her insides were still shaking. The slight adrenaline caused by the unpredictable situation was exhilarating. They quickly reached another lifting device and Puck stepped into it.

"Are we going farther up?" Autumn asked while looking up at another level of buildings above them.

"No. Ezekiel lives on the ground level," Puck said. "His inn houses many travelers who may or may not like to sleep in trees. Ezekiel himself fell out of a tree when drunk one time and thought he would either have to abstain from drinking or move to the ground. He chose the latter." Puck chuckled to himself as the wooden flower blossom began to move. "You will enjoy our stay. It is well hidden, and only friends of Ezekiel know of it. Of course, the underground movement meets every week too."

"The underground movement?" asked Autumn.

"Oh yes." Puck shifted nervously. "I guess I forgot to mention that they are meeting tonight, but we don't have to be seen."

"I didn't know you were part of an underground. I guess it makes sense," said Autumn as she tried to calm her surprise about it.

"Well... a... Actually, I'm one of the leaders of it."

It was starting to get dark when they got off the lift. Autumn could not read Puck's expression, but she felt used and deceived. Was he going to use her as a pawn for some kind of plot to overthrow the government? She had to process what he was saying.

"A leader?" She paused as her brain recalled various conversations over the past week. "I should have guessed when Queen Mara said you had a price on your head. I mean I have only known you a week, so I don't really know all that much about you."

"Shh," said Puck as they passed a couple of Sprite travelers on the forest floor.

Autumn obeyed, but she still felt betrayed, her mind spinning.

"I think you are imagining an army of people ready to go to battle or a massive network of revolutionaries. This is just a group of poor folks still loyal to Queen Anemone who sit around gossiping and complaining. I wasn't concealing a huge secret from you. Queen Anemone has been absent a long time, and nothing has been accomplished in over seventy years. I would have informed you of it had it come up in our discussions."

Autumn relaxed a little as they weaved through trees on the forest floor. "Perhaps I can learn more about what is going on at the meeting," offered Autumn.

"Perhaps, I doubt that there is much new."

"Everything is new to me!" said Autumn.

Puck smiled. "Of course."

They made their way to a very large boulder. Puck glanced both ways, walked up to the boulder, and knocked a special rhythm. The rock transformed into a thatched roof inn. The door of the inn burst open. There stood a large over-weight Sprite with tiny wings holding his arms wide open.

"Friends! Welcome!" He grabbed both of them in a huge hug and practically carried them inside with him. "Puck! It's been a long time! I thought you were on the run. I haven't seen that disguise for some time, must be uncomfortable! Martha! Brown tonic! Who's this? A Hiru?" he looked closer at Autumn. "Oh! It's make-up! Fabulous! So, you found a student. Good for you! Hey Martha! Where is that tonic?" He continued talking until a large woman, also with undersized wings, came out of a back room with a tray loaded with drinks.

"What are you hollering about? I know we have guests as well as you. You would think that I was deaf!"

She passed out drinks to everyone at the table they had landed at.

"Puck! Good to see you! What are you doing in these parts? My goodness, what an enchanting girl! You have a lot of talking to do." When Martha slid a drink to Autumn, Puck pushed it away.

"Don't drink this. It would burn your human throat," he whispered to Autumn as their host and hostess continued to fuss over everything.

Autumn was overwhelmed at how two people could create so much noise and bustle.

Puck gulped some tonic and laughed. "Ezekiel! You haven't changed a bit!"

At this Ezekiel laughed and slapped Puck on the back, causing Puck to spill some tonic on himself. Puck pulled out a handkerchief from his pocket to wipe up the spill, and Ezekiel took another long drink of his tonic.

Autumn looked around for the source of a strong smell.

"What's wrong?" asked Martha.

"I smell cinnamon somewhere," said Autumn.

Martha and Ezekiel laughed heartily. "Why, that's what brown tonic is...brewed cinnamon!" said Martha.

Puck interrupted the chatter. "Could she have some sweet milk? She is too young for tonic."

Both Ezekiel and Martha looked at Autumn intensely.

"Really?" said Martha.

Autumn dropped her hood, and Martha nodded. "Of course! The disguises! I will get the sweet milk and a rag, so you can wash your face. We don't need disguises here. It's been so long since I have served a child ..." She chattered on as she left the room through some swinging doors.

"Now Puck, we need to hear your story," said Ezekiel. Puck set down his mug and opened his mouth to speak as a knock came from the door in the same rhythm Puck had used. Ezekiel was up to greet his new guests.

"Welcome! Welcome! Zachery, Caraway, Philip, and Daniel! Come in! Nice to see you Tabatha!" and on he greeted as guests continued to pour into the room. The noise also increased exponentially.

Puck stood and picked up his pack lying on the floor next to him. He motioned for Autumn to do the same. They moved from the table nearest the door and in the front of the fireplace to the table in the opposite corner of the large room. There were only eight tables of odd sizes in the room. The one they chose was tiny and could fit only the two of them comfortably. The table was also shaded by a staircase disappearing into the second floor. The only view the stairs blocked was the swinging doors that Martha bustled through carrying a crowded tray of drinks.

Martha expertly navigated the moving mass of people filling the room so she could deliver drinks. "Philip, how is your wife? Tabitha, what a lovely dress! Zachery, how did you get that black eye?"

Autumn placed her hood back over her head as she and Puck settled down at their table. Martha slid a cup of white liquid and another mug of tonic onto their table as she passed without acknowledging their presence and continued her rounds.

Puck leaned over to Autumn. "Ezekiel and Martha have seen me in almost every disguise I have ever used, but most of these people have not. Until we can tell them what we have been up to or we make our presence known, they will act like we don't exist. We are very safe with them. Just sit back and enjoy."

Autumn looked around the crowded room. Most of the guests were light-haired moth-winged Sprites. Many looked like they were in their thirties. A few looked older. Some men were standing along the back wall with a mug in their hands. Everyone was facing the fireplace in expectation, talking loudly as they waited. Puck took a drink of his second mug of tonic, and Autumn tasted her sweet milk. It was thick and sweet like velvet cake.

As the last Sprite entered the room and the door was closed, Ezekiel called for everyone's attention with his arms stretched up. "All right, the meeting is about to start!" boomed Ezekiel even louder than he was when he was greeting people. "First things first! A moment of silence for King Coriander."

Puck sat up with a start. "What!" he whispered.

The room was silent in reverence. Then Ezekiel raised his glass, "A toast to his widow. Long live Queen Shasta!"

The room shouted the salute after him, "Long live Queen Shasta!" Everyone drank long gulps of their tonic.

Autumn leaned over to Puck. "Who are these rulers?"

"They were the King and Queen of the Sprites. Every kingdom has their own rulers, but they all answer to Maldamien. Apparently, the king has been killed somehow. This is the first I have heard of it."

Ezekiel then asked, "Who would like to lead our national anthem?"

Puck growled under his breath. "I wish they would do without this part!"

A gaunt Sprite with a stringy goatee stood up from the front table by the door.

"Go ahead, Philip," said Ezekiel.

Philip started to sing in a very high tenor voice as others followed:

"Our land is the beauty of the flowers.

The anthem we sing pledge our allegiance..."

A light breeze flowed through the room, making an awkward accompaniment to the song. Autumn muffled a laugh. It really was awful. There was no rhythm. The melody just trailed away. Even the words bordered on nonsense. It was a choir of tone-deaf clamor. One thing she had to admit was that every voice was crystal clear and strong, but apparently all singing a different part.

When the song finished, Ezekiel stood up to speak again. "Friends, you all remember how last month King Coriander was 'escorted' away to speak with that tyrant, Maldamien. Some of you may not have heard about how he 'accidentally' died on the way. This is the reason Queen

Shasta took action in court to oust the adviser to the throne, that spy of Maldamien. We had talked last week of Queen Shasta's own arrest, but these details were not made public. Her bravery and courage to oppose Maldamien were in part from her grief, but we all know that King Coriander would have been proud of her. He was able to subtly resist Maldamien for nearly a century, but I am afraid that has ended. I can say today that Queen Shasta is still alive and well, but things don't look good. I expect she will be taken all the way to Maldamien's fortress in Rokurokubi."

People began to grumble and talk among themselves. Autumn noticed Puck looking very grave.

"So that is why we haven't seen much trouble," mumbled Puck.

Ezekiel held up his hands to quiet everyone. "Now I am placing for discussion the question of what we should do about Lord Jacob's coronation tomorrow?"

People started to shout out things. "Kill him!" "Banish him!" "We should capture him!"

Puck rolled his eyes and took another sip of his tonic.

A nicely dressed male Sprite stood up. "Wait a moment! I got back from Cowtail village, and I haven't heard about all of this. What happened to King Coriander? Did anyone do anything when Queen Shasta was taken?"

Ezekiel nodded. "Those are good questions, Paul. A month ago, a convoy of four Ogres and a Nomad arrived at the palace. King Coriander greeted them with hospitality even though it is well known that he was no friend of Maldamien. Supposedly they wanted him to create a new law raising the taxes on food production even higher. He has always been able to walk the line between bowing to Maldamien's wishes and undermining him at the same time. Apparently, it was too much. He knew the tax would leave the people absolutely nothing. It seems like Maldamien really just wanted to get rid of King Coriander or test his loyalty, because they arrested him on the spot for treason and led him to the West Caoineag Outpost near the Dwende border. From there he was going to be taken to Maldamien's fortress, but somehow there was an 'accident' of some kind. I believe the king tried to escape. His body was returned to the queen to bury. I suppose that is more than the Brownie king received, but it was a terrible blow. Queen Shasta was an emotional mess. Who could blame her? It was less than a week later that the same Ogres and Nomad came for her. Lord Jacob and Maldamien's court-appointed 'adviser' have been ruling since."

"Well, Lord Jacob would be the one Maldamien would choose!" exclaimed a woman at a table near Autumn and Puck.

"Did anyone try to protect Queen Shasta?" asked Paul.

"What could we have done?" asked an older man standing against the back wall. "One Ogre could kill twenty of us!"

"And the Nomad's magic could burn down the city!" said another man sitting by his wife or girlfriend.

"Well, the royal guard did try to protect the queen," said Ezekiel. "Turner's dead, and Juniper is missing a leg. The others only received minor wounds before standing down."

"How is it that an entire city of people could not have saved our king and queen from five captors?" said Paul.

"Tell me," said the old man, "would you have led the charge?"

"No," said Paul, "I'm no hero. I am certainly not like Sage."

"Well, Sage wasn't here," said the old man, "and none of us want to turn out like the Hiru or the Brownies. Their nations are in ruins for their rebellion. At least we can live to fight another day."

"Gutless," mumbled Puck. Autumn looked at Puck in surprise.

"But when will that day be?" asked Paul.

"Sage and Toble have been doing the best they can," said Ezekiel, "but no one can do it alone. One day we will have to fight."

"They are wasting their time," said the old man. "They go from skirmish to skirmish, risking their lives for one person here and one person there. They live in a dream world."

"I wish that we all lived in that world!" said Ezekiel. "A little hope wouldn't hurt anyone. Each person they save is one more who will live to fight another day. Are you saying that we should just accept the injustice and violence? Should slavery be our normal way of life? If it takes another hundred years, I would still fight for at least the hope of a better future."

Autumn looked at Puck as he leaned over to whisper to her. "If you don't understand what they are saying..." he began.

"Who are Sage and Toble?" asked Autumn.

Puck looked confused momentarily. "Sage is a Huldra, son of Queen Anemone's captain of the guard. Sage's parents were both killed by Maldamien when he was a child. He was raised by Toble, a Dryad

Ambassador, and close family friend. They had disappeared into the desert for some time, but in the last fifty years, they have been going around helping people and causing problems for Maldamien. It all started when Turmeric decided to go after Sage to get some family revenge or something. He didn't bargain on setting Sage on a vendetta. It was the worst mistake Turmeric has ever made." Puck chuckled to himself. "They have certainly built a reputation for themselves."

"Kind of like Robin Hood," said Autumn. "It sounds like you have a reputation too. How did you get a price on your head?"

"I helped break up Maldamien's birthday party executions last year. There were a lot of people involved, but I was the only one seen." Puck said casually and turned back to the main conversation in the room.

A white-haired Sprite was standing and finishing a long speech. "We have become a scared people! We cower from any trouble. We hide from conflict of any kind. We have become slaves in our land. We work to feed Maldamien, his friends, and his army. Two hundred years ago we lived in a golden age of productivity, art, and culture. We overcame death, and all our fears seemed to disappear. Since then we have grown weak and afraid. We are terrified of death. Our magic is disappearing. Why? Why can't our people have children anymore? Why is it so hard to live, to survive? Where are the happy days? Why hasn't anyone figured out why we have fallen so far?"

Puck sighed. "He gives that same speech every meeting!"

The old Sprite sat down, and people mumbled their agreement. Philip stood up. "That reminds me of a song."

"Of course it does!" replied Puck. "That means the serious part of the meeting is over."

Philip began to sing:

"Maggie was quite an ordinary faerie..."

Martha walked over to their table and discreetly whispered, "If you want to retire, your rooms are the last two on the right." Then she left.

Puck leaned close to Autumn. "Now they will sing, drink, and dance late into the night. It was actually a shorter meeting than I remember, but when anything gets really serious or too hard, they just want to escape and not deal with it. Just meeting together helps them feel like they are doing something for the cause of freedom."

They looked up as the tempo of the music sped up. Autumn wasn't sure if it was supposed to be a jig or a waltz for someone with one leg shorter than the other.

Autumn saw an intoxicated woman get up to dance, swishing her long skirt to the right and left, completely off rhythm. Some other people were stomping and clapping. Autumn still struggled to figure out where the beat was since all the stomping and clapping was staggered. Instruments of various types appeared in the group.

"She decided to ask his name.

A diddly da, a diddly da!"

Puck leaned over. "Maybe my memories of these meetings are more pleasant than reality. Do you want to retire or stay longer?"

Autumn looked at the three mugs in front of Puck and wondered that he wasn't up dancing like the others when they had had less to drink. "We can go. I am sore from all our traveling."

Puck noticed her glance at his mugs before answering. "Yes, I did have too much to drink," he admitted. "Just push me forward if I start falling back." He picked up his pack and started up the stairway. Autumn followed, hoping Puck was teasing.

"She almost couldn't help but dance. She twirled and leaped and spun in the air," the room sang. "You have a dancer in your soul..."

Puck made it up the stairs fine and walked down the hall to the very end. Then he turned to the two doors on the right. "I will take the first one. Sleep well, and I will see you in the morning," Puck said as he walked into his room.

"Good night," Autumn answered. Before she entered her own room, she listened for the end of the song.

"A diddly da, a diddly da!"

CHAPTER 7: IN TOWN

Autumn woke up happily giggling at the memory of last night's music. She dressed quickly, put on her rubber ears, and her cloak. She studied the marks on her wrist that she had received when she and Puck were bound. It looked like a green tattoo of symbols or some script that encircled her wrist like a bracelet. She would have to remember to ask Puck about the significance of it because so far it had done nothing.

She walked out of her room quietly and gently closed the door behind her.

"How are you doing, honey?" Martha said loudly.

Autumn nearly fell over in surprise. "Good!" she gasped trying to regain her breath. She then asked, "Is Puck still asleep?"

"Yeah. A little tonic will do that," said Martha. "You don't have to worry about being quiet. Everyone sleeps well after the meetings. Why don't we go to the kitchen and get you something to eat?" Martha led her downstairs. Autumn was stunned at seeing the main room littered with half a dozen snoring bodies.

"Don't mind them." Martha led Autumn through the mess to the swinging doors. "These poor souls get to escape their misery every once in a while, but they pay for it with a hangover like you can't imagine."

Autumn looked back at the room. She had a dark feeling of dead bodies lying about rather than sleeping Sprites. Autumn shook the feeling away.

"Are you cold?" asked Martha. "Some hot cocoa will cure that."

"You have hot cocoa?" said Autumn.

"Sprites invented it you know," Martha said with a wink.

Soon Autumn was sitting at a large work table in the middle of Martha's kitchen with a warm mug of the best hot cocoa she could ever remember having. The smell reminded her of Christmas mornings.

"We will have some nut loaf in a few minutes," said Martha.

A few minutes later Puck came walking in with dark circles under his eyes.

"Are you feeling all right?" asked Autumn.

Puck sat in a chair across from her. "I should not have drunk three mugs of tonic when I haven't had any in such a long time!" Puck moaned. Autumn suppressed a giggle.

"Dear Puck," said Martha. "Have some hot cocoa."

Puck took the cup Martha offered and then she poured a dash of tonic into it before he could take a sip.

"That will take the edge off the headache," she said in response to his look of disgust. Puck sipped it carefully.

"So how long are you going to stay with us?" asked Martha.

"If you don't tire of us, we will stay for two weeks," said Puck. "We have a lot to talk with you and Ezekiel about, Autumn needs to bathe often to get rid of the curse on her, and we need to hear if there have been any unusual activities happening recently. But for now, I may retire back to bed to wallow in my chastisement." Puck moaned as he got up and walked bent over, as though lifting his head any higher would cause more pain.

"Is there anything you want me to do?" Autumn asked Puck before he left the room.

"Why don't you help Martha with her chores or errands or whatever. I'll fix the brew for your bath tonight. See you later," he mumbled.

"Hope you feel better," Autumn called after him.

Puck waved absently and was gone.

"So, what are you doing today and can I help?" Autumn asked Martha.

"Well..." Martha pulled the nut loaf out of a stone oven and set it on a rag on the counter. "I need to visit a few homes before we open the brewery today. We used to be just a tavern, but with our going into hiding with such a select clientele, the brewery is our main source of income. We make the best tonic anywhere."

"Can I come on your errands?" asked Autumn.

"Sure, sure. I will need to pack some things. Now that I think about it, maybe I can get Ezekiel to open the brewery without me. I would like to take my time today. I'll be back. Just help yourself to the bread." Martha bustled out of the kitchen, and Autumn made her way to the bread.

Autumn.

Autumn looked around for Puck. It sounded like his voice was in her head.

Autumn, put your two fingers on your wrist with the markings and communicate with me through your thoughts.

Autumn looked at the marks around her wrist on her right hand. It had turned inky black.

She put her fingers on it and thought, *Can you hear my thoughts? Why did you not tell me about this before?*

I can only hear your thought when you touch the marks. It didn't come up before. It just occurred to me that if you and Martha go out today, you will need to know how to communicate like this if you get into any trouble. When either of us is searching for each other, the marks will turn red. You will only need to touch them to see what I see. Also, don't touch the marks when you are very angry. There is a reason these were used on slaves. I hope that covers everything. Take care.

Autumn watched the marks turn green again before cutting the bread for herself and sitting back down.

There was a lot of things Puck hadn't gotten around to telling her, she mused.

Autumn only had a few minutes with her thoughts before Martha came back into the kitchen with a large bag and whisked Autumn out the back door of the house with her. Autumn put the hood over her head again.

They walked a little way into the woods silently. Then Martha turned to Autumn. "Before we go too far," said Martha," I want to let you know that we have known Puck for many years and even have helped him invent some of his disguises. I know you are a human child. I could tell this in the morning light, but don't worry. I won't press you to explain anything. You are safe with us. Puck will tell us when the time is right. I told you this though because I want to ask a favor. We are going to visit some very hurt people. Being human, you should have a leaning toward some healing spells. Could you help them some?"

Autumn's eyes widened. "I haven't learned any healing spells."

"Just follow your instinct. I think it might help," said Martha.

Autumn shifted her weight from one foot to the other uncomfortably.

"I'll do what I can."

67

"That's all I ask." Martha turned to continue walking.

Autumn followed behind. Everyone seemed to know more about her abilities than she did. She was in a sour mood by the time they reached a rough lean-to next to a large tree.

"This is our lift." said Martha, "We don't use the main ones because I don't like the busy-bodies on Main street knowing what I am up to. Very few people know of this one, and I like it that way."

They walked into it, and Martha pulled a rope hanging out of the window to start it. It jerked to a start as the sound of gears groaning began. The lack of a door and the violent way the lift shook convinced Autumn that she needed to hold onto the irregular wood on the walls to keep from accidentally falling out. The whole thing began to move in a slow jolted motion straight up. After what seemed like an eternity, the contraption stopped. Autumn followed Martha out onto a bare branch with no railings. Autumn tried to look at only where her feet were going and not down below. They walked a few yards and turned left, then a few yards more and turned right. Autumn could see the town in the distance. It looked much smaller than she had remembered it the day before.

They continued on to a tiny house on the edge of town. Martha knocked on the shaky wooden door.

"Come in," said a very old woman.

Martha and Autumn came into the dark one-room house.

"How are you this morning, Abigail?" asked Martha.

"Oh, I feel terrible!" said the old woman.

Autumn's eyes adjusted to the darkness, and she saw that the voice came from the direction of a bed in the farthest corner of the dusty house.

"What ails ya this morning?" Martha asked as she dug through her belongings.

"My bones ache, and I think I have a cold. Nothing to worry you about," said the old Sprite woman.

Martha shook her head and smiled kindly. She poured out some warm soup from a container in her basket and took a piece of bread from a larger loaf on the other side of the same basket. She took them over to the woman while leaving her things by the door.

"Abigail, this is a friend of mine. Her name is Autumn, and she is helping me with my errands," said Martha.

"How nice it is to see a young one again even if she is a Nomad, or is she a Hiru? I can't tell," said Abigail.

"She is a mix from the Nomad lands," lied Martha. She quickly changed the subject. "So has your grandson been by to see you?"

That subject immediately got Abigail going on a discourse about how no one comes to see her anymore. Autumn soon tuned out. She was distracted by how cold and dirty the house was.

"Do you mind if I light your fire?" asked Autumn.

"Do whatever you want, dear," said Abigail.

Autumn walked over to the fireplace to get the fire going. She had to sort through stacks of stuff to get things away from the hearth, so they didn't get burned. She also had to dig through a stack on the table to find a type of match that Puck had taught her to use to light the fireplace. As the light began to fill the room, she realized it was much dustier than she had originally thought. Autumn rolled up her sleeves, found a bowl and rag, and filled it at a sink in the tiny kitchenette. She moved clutter and scrubbed every surface in the house while refilling the bowl with clean water over and over again. She moved papers and books into neat stacks and filled empty containers with smaller items. She opened the window to let in more light, so she could see what she was doing.

"Oh! Don't do that!" said Abigail, but Martha quickly distracted her with more questions.

"So, when did the Ogre last collect taxes from you? That was very brave of your brother to stand up to him. You must be so proud," said Martha.

Abigail was happily talking again.

Autumn was amazed that she was getting things clean as fast as she was and that she even felt brave enough to interfere with another's belongings, but she had told Martha she would help and that was what she was doing... she hoped.

It was another hour before Martha got up and packed up the empty soup bowl.

"Well, we need to go and make some other visits. It was nice talking to you," said Martha.

The house was transformed into a cleaner, warmer, and more comfortable place, and Abigail looked around in amazement.

"My, my, my!" said Abigail. "My house looks brand new! Why I think that dust must have been what was causing my cold. Well, thank you, my little Nomad!" Abigail stretched out her hand to Autumn. "Here! Take this for your hard work."

She placed a small wooden charm of a flower on a gold chain into Autumn's hand. "This would look lovely on you."

Autumn took the gift and put it on without lowering her hood.

"My, that looks nice," said Abigail "Good luck with the others. Bye."

"Bye and thank you!" said Autumn as they left the house.

They turned towards town. As they walked, Martha was humming to herself. Autumn looked around at the handful of people on the street. Everyone looked as nervous as she felt. An Ogre began to walk towards them as people moved out of his way. Autumn looked at Martha who also moved calmly out of the way. Autumn followed her lead. The Ogre stopped and looked at them.

"You, Nomad, I haven't seen you before. Are you here on business or for Maldamien?" he asked.

Autumn remembered the role Puck had told her to play when they were in town yesterday and put on an air of authority.

"Who are you to question me about my business? I am here to visit my uncle. Would you want me to tell him about how I was treated like common trash?"

A look of surprise came over the Ogre's face. As Autumn hoped he was so flustered that he didn't even ask who her uncle was.

"A... a... no. I'm sorry. I'm just doing my job."

"That's fine. Continue on. I won't mention it," Autumn said with a wave as she turned to go in the opposite direction than that of the Ogre, even if it was the wrong way.

"Right... a... thanks," said the Ogre as he hurried off.

Martha walked up beside Autumn and whispered, "That may have been the only thing you could have done there, but we are going to have to hide you. Once he tells his authorities or one of his friends and realizes that you never mentioned who your uncle was, he will try to find you again. The next time won't be so easy."

Martha led them to a large house right in the middle of town. Autumn felt jittery from her encounter with the Ogre and jumped when Martha knocked on the door. A young Sprite woman opened the door.

"I am so glad you were able to come," said the Sprite.

Her bright eyes seemed out of place in her worried face and poor clothes. She let them in, and Autumn could see that the house was much bigger than the previous home and very clean, in fact, bare. As they walked through the entry and into the sitting room, Autumn saw no furniture.

"Daniel would be so glad for the company. He is still in so much pain," said the young Sprite.

"When Ezekiel told me about him, I had to come," Martha said. "Jackie, this is Autumn. She is just helping me with my errands. Can we go to see Daniel now?"

"Oh yes," said Jackie.

The Sprite floated across the room barely touching the ground. A light sound of wind chimes seemed to follow her. Each room they passed to get to the stairway was also empty. They went up the stairs to the first room on the right.

As they entered, Jackie sang, "Daniel, you have some visitors."

The bedroom was also very bare. The bed Daniel was in was finely crafted, but the only other furniture were two simple chairs and a little round table.

Daniel was a Sprite in his thirties, lying uncomfortably in the bed with his left leg out on top of the covers. His leg looked grotesque, and he had other more minor injuries on his head and arm. Some of his sores looked infected even though he seemed as clean as the house.

"Oh my!" exclaimed Martha. "Why did they do that to you?"

Daniel's face turned from a deathly pale to a vibrant red.

"Those Ogres weren't satisfied with our last piece of copper. That is all we have left, and yet they thought they needed to show me a lesson in not paying my taxes!"

He was shaking with rage. Jackie rushed to his side to try to calm him, which seemed to annoy him more.

"Look around! What else could we have sold? No one wants to buy this house. No one can afford this house! We pretty much just live in this room and only light that fire. We work as much as we can at the orchards, but the harvest is bad, and we weren't cut out to be field hands."

Daniel grabbed his wife's hands and showed Martha and Autumn her palms.

"Look at this! Look at this! An artist! A musician! And yet her

71

hands are regularly shredded by the rough work, yet that isn't enough!" Jackie took her hand back as Daniel had to rest from his tirade.

"We all suffer," said Jackie. "I just wish it would end. I keep thinking that it can't get worse and then it does. Is Maldamien not going to be happy until he kills us all?"

Martha walked over to Jackie and put her arm around her shoulders.

"Someday it will end, and a good ruler will be back on the throne. Until then, I brought some potions that Autumn can use on Daniel. If you don't mind, my bag is so heavy. I would just like to leave all of this food here."

Jackie gasped, and Daniel swallowed. He answered as Jackie left the room for the moment.

"I really appreciate that. You know I would repay."

"No, no, no. I don't want to hear about repayment. Now Autumn, here are the potions I brought."

Martha dug into her bag and pulled out a few bottles and a couple of rags. She handed them to Autumn as Jackie returned with slightly redder eyes.

"Jackie, could you show me the kitchen, so I can unload this, and we can fix some lunch?"

Jackie just nodded and led Martha out. Autumn could hear Jackie muffle a sob in the hall.

Autumn set the bottles on the table, opened the one she needed, and soaked the rag with its contents.

"Are you fine with me applying this to your wounds?"

Daniel nodded. Autumn dabbed the wounds on his face first. Jackie came in with a bowl of water and set it on the table.

"Just in case you need it," she said.

Autumn smiled at her. "Thanks."

Autumn rinsed the rag and reapplied ointment and began to dab his arm. The solution seemed to bring out a clean, healthy color in the wound. She would have expected more though if she had been some kind of healer, but she had to remind herself that magic here wasn't always obvious spells and such, just talents or whatever.

Daniel watched her work for a few minutes and then said, "You're a Nomad."

Autumn didn't say anything.

"I know that Ezekiel and Martha have friends from all over, so most people aren't surprised by anyone that they have with them, but your people have allied themselves with Maldamien. How did you end up here and cleaning my wounds?"

Autumn's heart raced. It was a harder question to answer than the Ogre's, even though they were similar. She tried to keep her voice calm.

"No matter what we were born to, we each have a choice. We can become what people tell us to be, or we can rise above that and be different. A lot of people let the things around them affect them and change them into something awful. When you choose a different way, it just carries you along. I guess you can say I was carried here."

Autumn wasn't sure if he would believe her obscure answer. She rinsed out her rag again, applied more ointment, and began to dab his leg.

"It's a tough thing to do, being different," said Daniel. "I hear a lot of guys at the orchard who are bitter and full of anger, and others who are so beaten down that they can't even look up. I see myself turning into one of them. They aren't even people anymore. They are shells of their former selves. What if what Martha says is true and the queen returns, what happens to them? How do they live in a restored world? I think you are right. One does need to rise above and try to be something better. I may never look at this time with any pleasant memories, but I don't want to have regret over who I was added on to it too."

Autumn nodded as Daniel talked, but she was amazed at how quickly his mood had changed. Autumn rinsed out the rag, emptied the bottle on the rag, and re-dabbed his leg. It was a deep wound that would have needed stitches in the human realm. Daniel didn't express any pain, so the ointment must have numbed the wound.

Martha and Jackie came in chattering and carrying lunch. Autumn asked Martha for some more of the rags that were in her bag. With those, Autumn wrapped up Daniel's leg tightly. Jackie took the bowl and showed Autumn where she could wash up. Once Autumn was done washing her hands, Martha was saying good-byes and handed Autumn a peanut-butter style sandwich while pushing her out the door, too.

"Bye!" said Autumn as they left.

"Bye and thank you!" they called out to them.

Martha had already pushed her nearly down the stairs, and they were soon out of the house. Martha was humming happily as they walked down the street.

"What was that about?" asked Autumn.

"I don't know what you did to Daniel," said Martha, "but he was nearly in tears apologizing to Jackie for being so angry all the time and hard to live with. It seemed like it was a good time to leave."

Autumn was stunned. She didn't know what happened either but took a bite of her sandwich as they walked along. Martha quickly turned to some smaller branches and out of the way paths.

"You are a natural healer," said Martha. "I would like to take you to a lot more homes this week, but I think we need to have a talk with Puck first. That Ogre has seen you, and your abilities will not stay secret too long in this town if we don't limit it to the underground. It's such a shame too when so many people could benefit from you, but we can trust so few."

"I didn't do much," said Autumn. "He just talked."

"You didn't heal outside wounds, but the people we left felt hope and more full of life than they have in years. There is more to healing than you seem to think, and you have a natural talent for it. Mark my words, one of these days you will see a healing that defies your expectations, and then you will understand how magical it actually is."

CHAPTER 8: THE TOUCH

Autumn rushed into the washroom of the inn, stripped off her clothing, threw them out the door, and plunged into the bathtub.

This week had been hectic. At dinner that first full day they had been there, Puck told Ezekiel and Martha Autumn's whole story. Martha told Puck what had happened in town, and Ezekiel set to work on getting information from his contacts that night. The rest of the week was a constant flow of people and news. Victims of the Ogres' cruelty were brought to the inn instead of Martha going to visit them just so that Autumn could be around. Bits of information about Queen Shasta, various military outposts, and other underground groups were coming in from a collection of odd-looking visitors. Tucked into every free moment, Puck taught Autumn from a map of the various countries, cities of importance, and major roads. He wanted her to always know where she was.

He taught her a little more about magic, but there never seemed to be enough time for him to get very far into it. Autumn felt like he was skirting around a major key. The main thing she knew was how to make the potion to wash off the magic from her curse. It was slow, and her body could only handle two baths a day without having horrible growing pains. They were all impatient to cure her curse and find out what her memories held, but it took time. Time was not on their side. They couldn't stay there much longer without getting discovered, and they still did not have enough money for the long trip to visit Thyme. Puck was considering visiting other friends as they tried to save up. Today, Puck and Autumn had to go out to get supplies for their next journey. They took back roads to various strange shops and had just come back. In a few minutes would be another underground meeting. Puck needed to alter her clothes since they were getting small, so she was taking her second bath today early.

A knock came from the door. "Your clothes are finished. I'm

throwing them in," said Puck. "People are already arriving, so you will want to be quick."

Autumn submerged in the purple water to her chin. "Okay, you can throw them in," she said.

The door opened briefly, the clothes came flying in, and then closed again. Autumn dried herself off and dressed. The clothes were slightly too big again, but with all the growing she was doing it would last only another week. It was the second time this week Puck had magically let them out. Autumn also put on her new larger fake ears. Her hair had to be re-dyed as well. She covered her damp hair with the hood of the cloak and checked herself in the mirror. She looked eleven years old. She sighed. Would this curse ever go away? After her quick assessment, she left the washroom to head downstairs.

The main room was already crowded with people.

"Hi Autumn!" said Daniel. Jackie was smiling next to him. "Look, my leg is getting better. I have crutches, but I'm getting around!"

"That's fantastic!" said Autumn.

"Autumn!" called an old male Sprite who had come to visit yesterday with a black eye. "I just wanted to let you know that I am courting Abigail now. You were right. No one is too old for a little bit of happiness. I should have courted her years ago, but I was always afraid. Anyways, she would have been here, but she decided to go shopping with her sister. She said she hasn't bought a new dress in over a decade and had a little money saved up."

"Tell her hi for me when you see her," said Autumn.

Autumn greeted a few others before making it to the table Puck was sitting at. He had shaved his beard back to a goatee a few days ago and had resumed wearing his top hat and vest the day after they arrived. Many in the room recognized Puck and had greeted him. He had chosen to sit closer to the front and center of the room.

Soon after Autumn took her seat, Ezekiel stood up to call the meeting to order. Philip volunteered to lead the room in the Sprite national anthem. Martha came out and delivered more drinks. Autumn was amused to see that Puck chose to enjoy sweet milk along with her. In fact, he hadn't had another mug of tonic since their first night there.

Ezekiel stood after the song finished.

"Friends, we may all now know that Lord Jacob is officially king of Caoineag and has made the Nomad Angus his top adviser."

The room booed.

Ezekiel continued.

"Queen Shasta has been moved from the East Caoineag outpost. I can't say for certain, but we believe that she is on her way to Rokurokubi."

"May the Gryphon be with her!" shouted a Sprite woman near Autumn.

"She will need more than a myth to save her!" said a Sprite man standing against the back wall.

Paul stood up.

"I have just come from the capital yesterday, and a bill has been signed to raise the taxes. If we can't pay, we will be shipped to the Ogre mines as slaves."

"Is it true that Maldamien eats his slaves?" asked Philip.

"I have heard that Maldamien doesn't know where the magic in the land is going, so he is raising taxes to feed his troops," said Paul. "I don't know what he does with the slaves, but it wouldn't surprise me."

"Well, I heard differently," said the Sprite man in the back. "I heard that he is storing the magic and trying to kill us all off, so he can have a world full of only his supporters."

"That rumor has been around for decades!" said Daniel. "What does it matter if it is true?"

Autumn could feel the unreasonable panic filling the room. "Friends, this is not good for us! These rumors are just causing fear and panic. We need to encourage ourselves and think about things we can affect and change. We need to have some hope. What can we do to fix this or help ourselves?" she said.

Philip stood up after her.

"Well, I have always said that we should make someone else our king in place of Maldamien, but no one listens to me!"

"That's because you worship Sage and want to make him king," said a woman Sprite by the door.

"So, what is wrong with that?" said Philip. "At least it's an idea. What idea have you come up with?"

"Let's say we made a king," said Daniel. "Then what happens? What army would he have? What would happen to Maldamien? We can't even stay in control of our own country let alone worry about the world's politics. I think what Autumn was saying is how can we do something right here and right now."

"I still think that would help with the right here and now," said Philip. "The whole problem is Maldamien."

"Yes," said Ezekiel. "You are right. Maldamien is the problem, but until someone can figure out where he gets all his power and learns how to lead an army against him, any action would be a repeat of the massacre at Samarium Pass. Until we can find a realistic way of taking larger action, we must be content with smaller things to help and preserve each other."

"I agree with Ezekiel," said an old Sprite woman by the staircase. "Do you not remember the uprising forty years ago at Threnody county or the one eighty years ago in the Nomad Desert? Do we not remember the near extinction of the Hiru people or the destruction of the Brownie government? Listen, it might make good talk to discuss grand plans, my husband died for grand plans, but we need to survive. What are we going to eat tomorrow? How are we going to have a roof over our heads? That is the kind of plans I want to hear. Some folks can fight Maldamien if they like, but I just want to live!"

Some in the room clapped in agreement. Puck nodded.

"That woman is at least honest with herself," he whispered. "By the way, can you understand what she was saying?"

"Of course," said Autumn, "Why do you ask?"

"She was speaking the Sprite language. You seemed to understand everything last week, too. That has been puzzling me."

Puck took a drink of his sweet milk.

Autumn looked at the old male Sprite who was answering the woman's comment and noticed that the things she thought she understood did not match the sounds or movement of his mouth. A chill crawled up Autumn's spine.

"So how often does that happen? Why don't they always speak their native tongue? Why do I understand them?" asked Autumn.

"As far as I know you have only been exposed to the language at these meetings. It's illegal to speak anything other than English. Maldamien's father was an Englishman, and he thinks that forcing everyone to speak English creates a more human-friendly world or some such rubbish. Most educated people knew English anyway because one of the portals opens in England, but such arbitrary laws are a common thing with Maldamien. Meetings with more than five attendees are also illegal to keep down uprisings or rebellion or whatever. There are many laws that I just ignore." Puck finished speaking and looked at the old Sprite who was giving his weekly monologue.

"We have become a scared people! We cower from any trouble. We hide from conflict of any kind. We have become slaves in our land. We work to feed Maldamien, his friends, and his army. Two hundred years ago we lived in a golden age of productivity, art, and culture. We overcame death, and all our fears seemed to disappear. Since then we have grown weak and afraid. We are terrified of death. Our magic is disappearing. Why? Why can't our people have children anymore? Why is it so hard to live, to survive? Where are the happy days? Why hasn't anyone figured out why we have fallen so far?"

Autumn turned to Puck. "I think that was word-for-word the same thing as last week."

"Yep," said Puck.

Daniel leaned over to their table. "He gives it every week, then Philip stands up and says it reminds him of a song and the party begins."

Autumn laughed. These people were stuck in a rut.

As Philip stood up as if on cue, a sudden banging came from the door in a familiar rough rhythm. It was loud and rushed. People in the room mumbled to each other, and some started to sound panicked.

"For the Gryphon's sake! Let me in!" came a masculine voice from the other side of the door.

"Relax people. Calm down," said Ezekiel as he looked through the peephole of the door.

"It's Sage," he announced as he proceeded to open the door.

"Of course it's me! Who else would bang on your door in the middle of the night?" Sage said.

A crowd of people immediately stood up and gathered around the doorway so that Autumn couldn't see. The room had erupted in talking and shouts of welcome.

"By the Gryphon! What happened?" shouted Martha.

Autumn decided to stand on a chair to see what was going on.

"Autumn!" called Martha.

"I'm back here!" she answered.

"Go get some ointments and rags quickly!" said Martha.

Autumn jumped from the chair and nearly hit Puck who had just risen to his feet. She dashed into the kitchen. Having not seen what the damage was she grabbed three different potions, a bowl of water, and as many rags as she could find. She shoved the ointments and rags into all her pockets and carried the sloshing bowl of water through the crowd of people until she got where the new arrivals sat.

The old Dryad was dirty from head to toe. His long distinctive ears flopped over a bit on either side of the wild white hair on his head. Even in the dirty Nomadic clothes, he looked tall, thin, and scholarly and not like the Robin Hood-style outlaw Autumn had imagined. He seemed nonathletic, but he was practically holding the younger more dashing Nomad up in the chair. The younger man's eyes sparkled with a type of fire and charisma that is hard to explain to someone who has never encountered it. His messy black hair, scruffy face, and worn out clothes couldn't hide his confident presence and magnetic demeanor. Martha was busy taking their bags and cloaks from them and pouring them drinks. The Dryad finished telling everyone a summary of their adventure when Martha spotted Autumn.

"Autumn, take care of Sage's leg there." Martha pointed to the younger man's leg where a bandage was nearly falling off. "You two are filthy and must be tired! I'm going to fix you something to eat!" Martha then bustled off to the kitchen.

Sage seemed feverish and sweaty but looked at Autumn with clear blue eyes. It made Autumn feel jumpy and nervous inside. As Autumn knelt down to place the bowl at his feet, she was taken back by his tail.

"I guess you have never met a Huldra before," he said softly.

"No sir," she said. She tried to hide her embarrassment by immediately undoing the bandage and unloading the supplies from her pockets.

"Has anyone seen Puck lately?" asked Sage, looking around.

"I'm here, Sage," said Puck. The crowd parted some so Puck could get through.

Sage nearly jumped up, and the old Dryad pushed him back down.

"Oh! I wish you weren't here! You are in great danger!" said Sage.

"Why?" said Puck. "How do you know this?"

"Puck, I have no idea what you have been up to, but the Ogres who were chasing us were sent here to look for you!"

Puck and Autumn looked at each other. Sage noticed the exchange curiously.

"Are you certain?" asked Puck looking slightly pale.

"Yes, I overheard their conversation. That is the reason I came here." Sage looked at Autumn and then back at Puck. "No matter what you are working on, you need to leave here tonight!"

"Who else is in danger?" asked Ezekiel.

"I would say that you and your wife should take a short vacation. The rest of you should go home and pretend you never saw us," said Sage.

"All right everyone!" said Ezekiel. "Time to go home! We will let you know when we will meet again!"

As Ezekiel ushered everyone out, Autumn was finding Sage's wound perplexing. She had already cleaned it twice, applied a potion for burns, and it was still just as ugly as before. She sighed.

"It's a magical burn caused by a fireball," Sage said. "You have done quite a bit of work on it..."

Autumn nodded. That explained it. She was still determined to do something more though. She suddenly put her bare hand on the wound. As she did, an image of a blue Gryphon flashed before her eyes. She looked up at Sage and saw his eyes roll back.

"He is going to faint," said Autumn.

Three men grabbed the chair before it fell backward. Sage revived immediately with the jolt of his chair.

"What happened?" asked Sage.

"What did you do?" asked Martha who came up in time to see the whole thing.

Puck rushed to her side, looking at the wound she had been treating. The leg now had a bright pink, newly-healed look to the skin replacing the open burn. A large grin spread on Puck's face as he patted Autumn on the back.

"She did what she needed to," Puck said.

Sage and Toble both looked down at Sage's leg and touched the smooth skin as though it were a strange substance.

Autumn calmed the jittery excitement inside her by calmly getting up and saying casually, "Do you have any other wounds that need treatment?"

Sage looked up at her with a dumbfounded expression.

"No, that's good. Thanks."

It took Ezekiel a while to drag out the remaining Sprites who were all exclaiming over the miracle and trying to find out if Autumn could visit a relative or friend of theirs who could use some sort of healing.

Sage, Toble, Puck, Autumn, and Martha were seated at the table when Ezekiel finally closed the door.

"Wish it hadn't taken so long to get everyone to go home, we really need to talk fast," said Toble.

"Puck," said Sage, "what has been going on here? I have heard things about a magical disturbance in this area, and Maldamien is so upset about it he has sent Turmeric out to investigate. He specifically mentioned finding you. It seems very serious."

Puck rubbed his chin. "I was expecting something like this to happen for two weeks now. What has taken so long?"

"I expect the situation with Queen Shasta and King Coriander tied up the troops around here. A good portion of them are traveling to Rokurokubi right now," said Ezekiel.

"What happened to the king and queen?" said Sage. "I was gone for a few months, and the world has turned upside down!"

"Well, King Coriander is dead, and Queen Shasta is being taken to Rokurokubi. Lord Jacob has been declared king," said Ezekiel.

"What? Why? How does that have to do with the magical disturbance?" asked Toble.

"It's a complicated series of events, but it doesn't have anything to do with the disturbance," said Puck. "Autumn, why don't you tell Sage your story."

Autumn blinked dumbly for a moment then lowered her hood and peeled off her pointed ears.

"You're human," said Sage.

"More than that," said Autumn. "I am from the human world. The last thing I remember is following a blue gryphon through the wind portal. After that, I met Queen Mara and Puck. Apparently, I've been cursed to be a child again and can't remember anything about myself."

"So the portal is open?" asked Sage.

"Only one," said Puck, "but I don't know how she came through because the rest are not open, and it is still unusable."

"So the queen has not returned," said Sage, disappointed.

Puck looked at Autumn. "What made you think the queen had returned?" asked Puck.

"What else is one to think when you hear the portal might be open?" said Sage. "I had hoped it was true, but... well…"

"We still don't know if the queen was involved," said Puck. "We don't know where Autumn is from or why she is here. Maldamien cursed the portals to wipe her memory and make her as helpless as a child. The queen may have sent her, for all we know."

Martha couldn't sit still.

"Isn't it obvious! The Gryphon brought her, and the Creator opened the portal!"

Sage's face went blank, and his eyes went from green to black quickly and then back again.

"Well," said Sage, "we can't just sit here. We also heard that Turmeric and the Ogres are going to look for a ring at Vervain. Toble and I will be leaving right away to go there before them. How about the rest of you? You can join us if you want, but then again it might be safer if we all split up."

Ezekiel said, "No, I think we will stay with Martha's mother up north. That way I can continue getting information from my sources."

Sage nodded. Puck spoke next.

"We will go to Pech in Dwende and see a friend of mine named Tanner. I think we might need his help. You might remember him. After that, we might join up with you at Vervain if you are still there."

Sage's eyes turned yellow.

"Be careful. I have heard that the Gnomes have shifted in their allegiance."

"I could never believe that of King Fitzwilliam. He is as loyal as King Coriander was," replied Puck.

"A lot can change over the years," said Sage. "Look at how much has changed these last few months. Mentally, I have heard he isn't all there anymore. Just be careful."

Puck shook his head. "Nonsense."

Sage shrugged. "Well, good luck," he shook hands with Puck warmly. "We will be off then."

"Oh! Don't leave yet!" said Martha. "You need food and clothes and some supplies," she said as she rushed into the kitchen.

Sage grinned. It was the first big smile Autumn had seen on him since he arrived.

"Yeah," he said. "I think I'll wait around for something other than

Toble's blackberry nuts." He elbowed Toble.

"They are very nutritious," said Toble.

"Are they the same blackberries as in the human world? I thought they were fruits, not nuts," said Autumn.

"Ha!" said Sage. "I was right!"

Toble shrugged.

Martha appeared with their things, and their bags were stuffed full. "You both could stay here with us and leave tomorrow," said Martha.

"You look exhausted," said Ezekiel.

Sage shook his head as he stood up and put his cloak on.

"Toble can't sleep inside, and I will be fine. Autumn saw to that."

Sage messed with Autumn's hair like a big brother does to a little sister as he passed by on his way to the door. They said bye and were off.

The inn seemed remarkably quiet for a few moments before everyone got up to prepare for their own journeys. Puck and Autumn went upstairs and began to pack.

Autumn had very few possessions of her own, just her things from the human world. Her sack was quickly ready, and she carried it into Puck's room to see if she needed to carry any supplies.

She had just walked through Puck's door when she heard banging and lots of noise downstairs. The sound of slamming doors and hurried voices made both Autumn and Puck pause and looked at each other.

"Puck! Autumn! Hurry!" shouted Martha.

Autumn moved into the hallway as Puck rushed by her with his half-packed bag. They both rushed to the edge of the stairs to see what had happened.

"Hurry!" panted Sage from downstairs. "They're here!"

CHAPTER 9: THE SECRET PASSAGE

The turmoil in the house reminded Autumn of an angry ant bed. Puck had rushed back into his room and shoved everything on his bed into his bag in a disorderly fashion. Autumn and Puck were downstairs following Ezekiel and Martha who each had sacks and were just shoving everything they could from the kitchen shelves into them. Sage and Toble had already rushed past them and into the brewery. They moved a heavy table and rug out of the way and were working on opening a trap door.

Banging came from the front door.

"Hurry up!" said Sage.

Everyone descended into the hole in the floor. Ezekiel went first to lead the way, followed by Martha, Autumn, Puck, Toble, and then Sage. Sage bolted the trap door from the inside.

The banging on the front door was loud and intense as though they were trying to break the door down.

Ezekiel passed around torches down in the underground cavern and then returned to the trap door. He waved his arms in slow movements.

Autumn could hear the slap of the rug and the grinding of the table moving above them. When Ezekiel was satisfied with his work, he walked through the group and led them down the tunnel deep into the darkness beyond.

Autumn could hear faint sounds of crashing and angry voices back above them in the direction they had come. The sounds were getting fainter as they continued forward into the tunnel at a running pace.

The tunnel looked like a mine shaft with beams supporting the walls and roof. The structures were strong and secure, but Autumn trembled with the idea of being trapped underground.

"We will be safe in the vault," said Ezekiel. "Whoever betrayed us could not know about this place because everyone who helped with this project is here. Only Toble and I know how to work the vault itself."

"I do?" asked Toble.

"Well," said Ezekiel, "just myself then."

"I smell smoke," said Puck. "I think they are burning your house down, so let's hurry."

Autumn sniffed the air. She could smell nothing but the torches that they held. The group came to an open, round stone door. The group rushed through as Ezekiel stood by waiting for them to pass. Sage, Toble, and Ezekiel all pulled the door to close it. Then gears began to move to lock it.

"What a great idea!" said Toble as he inspected the edges of the door. "It even has a soft lining to make it airtight. Who invented this?"

"You did," said Ezekiel as he dumped his bag in one corner of the large stone room.

"Did I?" said Toble.

He leaned in to examine the door even closer as if trying to remember it.

"I think we should stay here tonight," said Ezekiel. "There are vents in this room to bring in the fresh air, and there is another door over there, but we can leave that open for now. I think it might be hard to escape this region since the whole forest around the inn is probably crawling with Ogres and Nomads."

"I agree," said Sage. "I didn't think they were that close behind us. We had intended to get at least a day's distance between us."

"I don't think that was your Ogres," said Puck. "Turmeric would have magically opened the door. No, that is the local brute squad. I think someone betrayed us."

"Why?" asked Autumn. "What would have been so significant about tonight?"

Toble sat down with his bag and said, "Because of your little miracle, my dear. You didn't do anything wrong, but anyone who knows anything about magic and the Hiru would have known you were not what you appeared to be. If Maldamien was sending a unit to find Puck in so specific a place as the portal and there is the talk of the queen returning, I think an order would have also gone out to look for a girl cursed by the portals. I think a little girl with very magical abilities would be very suspicious in such circumstances."

"Do you mean Maldamien might think that I am the queen?" said Autumn.

"Not Maldamien per se, but his minions may not know what he is implying by his orders," said Toble.

Autumn sighed and sat down next to her bag and Puck's. The room was larger than the tunnel, but six people were not going to be sleeping with lots of space between them. Autumn felt oppressed by the room and the things Toble was saying.

"Don't worry," said Sage as he walked around the room and put everyone's torches on the brackets on the wall. "We all are on the run for some silly thing or another. The point is just to not get caught, whatever the reason. Even if you weren't mistaken for the queen, he would still make you a slave just for being human. It's unfair any way you look at it."

"Thanks," Autumn muttered as he took her torch.

"So, are we still going to the same places we talked about earlier?" asked Martha, trying to change the subject. Her hands were shaking.

"Yep," said Sage. "Why not?"

Autumn moved over to the other side of the room to sit by Martha. "Are you all right?" she asked.

"My house is burning down," she said. "I can't help but think about the antique dresser my grandmother left me that we have been able to keep this whole time and the pearl necklace my father had given me at my wedding. I am losing paintings my children had made when they were little and the hope chest that Ezekiel carved for me. It's all gone."

Autumn couldn't think of any way to comfort her except to take her hand and squeeze it. Ezekiel slid over closer to Martha on the opposite side, put his arm around her and squeezed.

"It's all right, darling," he said. "I will make you new things. At least everyone is safe. If Sage and Toble hadn't warned us …"

"If you weren't prepared with this tunnel …" said Sage.

Toble sat next to Sage and was beginning to sprout leaves all over. Autumn had never seen such a thing.

"Toble, can you rest in here with all the stonework?" Puck asked.

"No," said Toble tiredly.

"There is dirt just a little way beyond the door," said Ezekiel.

Sage picked up his bag to follow Toble, but Toble stopped him. "Stay here with everyone; I'll just be on the other side."

Sage dropped his bag by the door.

"Sure," said Sage.

87

Before he could even sit down a branch of an oak tree grew just in view.

"Did he just turn into a tree?" asked Autumn.

"Yep," said Sage. "He's sleeping. He hasn't slept in days. It will be good for him to rest even if it is cramped."

Autumn moved back next to Puck as everyone started to shift their belongings to get comfortable to sleep. Everyone pointed their feet towards the center of the room. Puck and Autumn faced one wall, Martha and Ezekiel the other, and Sage was next to the open door.

"I don't think I am going to be able to sleep at all," said Autumn.

"I don't think I will be able to either," said Martha.

"Puck, why don't you tell one of your world-famous stories," said Sage. "It's hard to sleep when one's mind is worried and stressed."

"How do you fall asleep, Sage? You have been on the run all your life. You must have some method," asked Martha.

"When you are always on the run, you sleep when you are exhausted. If I am trying to get rest when I am not completely exhausted, then I relax my mind and imagine a perfect place or dream of what I wish my life was like. It usually works."

"I guess a story can create that perfect place feeling then," said Martha.

"Hmm," said Puck, "I am assuming that requires a happy story with a happy ending. It has been a while since I have told a story like that."

"You told one last year at least!" said Ezekiel. "Get on with it."

Puck patted his pockets, pulled out his English pipe, and stuck it in his mouth. He didn't light it, but it seemed to help him think better.

"I think I have a good story.

"Before time began, there was a Creator. He made all that was made. He formed his realm of light and all the marvelous creatures that abide there. He formed the universe and painted it with colors beyond imagination. He created galaxies, stars, planets, and heavenly bodies. In this vastness, he created a tiny planet with deep sapphire oceans and a lush green island. Upon this bountiful island, he created a menagerie of life. He formed things that fly and things that walk and things that swim. He also formed four rivers in this garden to maintain all that he created. These rivers were not of water, but of the substance we call magic. The source of these rivers was him, and they flowed all over the world. Only then was the world prepared and filled with various plants and animals. The Creator stepped down from the heavenlies in the form of a majestic blue gryphon. He stood where the four rivers met, and from its flow, he formed the six races of faerie: the Sprite, the Undine, the Gnomes, the Brownie, the Hiru, and the Dryads. All other kinds of faerie derive their lineage from one of these six, and even these six may not have looked the same as we see them today, but this was not enough. The Gryphon looked around the world and the greatness that he had made, but it was missing something. This brought a tear to his eye. From this tear that fell into the dirt, the Gryphon made humans. After he had finished creating, he gave each race a gift and responsibility. To the Sprites he gave power over the wind, to the Gnomes he gave charge over the animals, to the Brownies he gave care of the earth and ground, to the Hiru he gave the strength of fire, to the Dryads the wisdom of the trees, and to the humans he gave the touch of life. The Gryphon placed the races in a garden and hid the four rivers.

"The Gryphon told the races, 'Your gifts are your charge. Use them well, travel to the ends of the earth and enjoy what I have created for you, but do not seek the four rivers or stand in the midst of them or you will destroy yourselves because only I am the source of the four rivers and none other can take my place.'

"For a hundred years the races lived in peace. Each one was learning about their gifts and caring for the garden that they lived in. The Gryphon even appeared to many at that time and walked and talked with them. The unicorns and phoenix seeing the beauty and peace of the earth asked the Creator if they may leave the heavenlies and dwell among the mortal ones. The ruins of Yarrow are the only remains of those most ancient of days."

Puck leaned back with the end of his story.

"That's not right!" said Autumn. "What happened next? We don't live in a garden anymore, so what ruined it?"

"I was trying to keep it happy and end it in a happy place," said Puck.

"You're teasing her," said Sage. "If you had wanted to tell a happy story you could have told a love story or a comedy or something else. What made you pick this story?"

Puck nodded. "Yes, I could have told a different story, but your talk about what life should be like, and a perfect place, reminded me of this."

"So, is it a true story?" asked Autumn. "I am assuming that it is true."

"It is true to those who believe that the Gryphon is real," said Puck. "I used to believe it very strongly, but... well…"

"If the Gryphon is real, than why has he let all of this happen?" said Sage. "Why doesn't he just step down 'from the heavenlies' and fix it instead of letting so many innocent people suffer?"

"Sage, you don't mean that do you?" asked Martha. "And Puck, I thought you really believed!"

Puck chewed on his pipe silently, and Sage flopped lower down, covering himself with his cloak like he was going to sleep.

"Whether or not anyone believes, I would like to hear the rest of the story," said Ezekiel.

"Me too!" said Autumn.

Puck took the pipe out of his mouth.

"Yes, well the rest of the story isn't as happy as the beginning," said Puck. "As the races grew and had children, the world became a more violent and greedy place. The races separated themselves into nations and wars were commonplace. Each nation tried to conquer the other. Races were enslaved, fortresses were built, and the memory of the Gryphon was purged from the memories of the people. The Human king named Adam used his gift of life in a twisted way to kill and conquer. His only rival was the Sprite king named Gregory who was just as evil. Their kingdoms were constantly at war, and their battles are still told in legends. King Adam, though, wiped out much of the faerie populations. He then heard a distorted version of the creation tale I just told, and dreamed of standing in the midst of the four rivers because he believed he would become a god. King Gregory soon heard of King Adam's plan from his spies. He decided that he would beat King Adam there so that he could become a god first and destroy the human race forever. The two evil kings raced to Yarrow, believing that was where the four rivers were hidden. The fortress was very old even at this time, and was only guarded by a sorceress who was half human and half faerie named Kara, and her servants. She was able to hold off the kings for forty days with the power of the Gryphon, but at the end, the fortress was destroyed, and the Sorceress Kara was killed. The kings did find where the four rivers met inside of the fortress. Within the fortress, the kings turned against each other and fought to get to the rivers first. King

Adam mortally injured King Gregory and stepped into the midst of the four rivers. The world suddenly shook, and the waters from the deep came forth. Instead of becoming a god, King Adam was destroyed. The great island on the planet broke apart. The inhabitants of the earth fell to their knees and called on the Gryphon to save them. The Gryphon heard their cry and came to Yarrow. He made a covenant with the people of all the races that if they obeyed him, he would always protect them, but if they turned on him, he would let destruction overtake them. They all swore to the covenant. The Gryphon saw the pride in their hearts though and knew that they would continue fighting each other. He split the world into two. The greater for the humans and the lesser for the remaining fairies. He then split the rivers into the four portals. He did this to save the world from destruction, and it has remained that way to this day."

Ezekiel and Martha were both asleep, but Sage was propped up on his elbow watching Puck with a strange expression. Autumn was feeling sleepy and curled up under her cloak.

"That ended happily," said Autumn. "I don't know what you were worried about."

"It was bittersweet," said Sage. "Kara still died."

Autumn frowned.

"That's true, but the world was saved."

"No debates over the story," said Puck. "We need to rest."

Autumn felt disturbed by Sage's comment. She ended up staying awake for some time thinking about what it would have been like to have been Kara. Where had the Gryphon been for her?

CHAPTER 10: GNOMES

The trip to the Gnome homeland of Dwende seemed endless. The group escaped from the passage early in the morning four days ago and went their separate ways. Puck put his rags back on, let his beard grow, and redyed it. They also changed Autumn's disguise by washing out her hair dye to let her naturally red hair show and gave her large floppy ears like Toble's. Puck also dyed her clothes to a disgusting green color.

During the entire trip through the Caoineag forests, they carefully avoided any public roads or passing under villages. They had no tent, so they camped whenever they were tired. Puck also talked on and on about various aspects of the world as though he was giving one lesson after another. At first, his lessons were interesting tips about camping or survival, but after a couple of days Autumn just zoned out and wallowed in self-pity.

"All I want when we get there is a bath!" said Autumn interrupting Puck's lesson on the Gnome succession of kings. "I am hot, dirty, sweaty, and tired!" She was walking slowly and dragging her feet. This was the first full day of walking in tree-less fields, and she hated it.

"Yes, one usually needs to work up to a trip like this," said Puck. "We can rest if you like. Your body is having to cope with a great deal of growing so fast and exertions you have not trained to do. It is understandable." Puck shifted his pack so he could reach into his pocket. "This is willow bark. Chew on it, but don't swallow. It will help with the pain."

Autumn took the leathery strip from Puck's hand and chewed on it while making a disgusted face.

"Well, how about I teach you some Gnomish words?" asked Puck.

"Please don't. My head is too fuzzy for any more lessons today," said Autumn. She was on the brink of tears. She wanted to go back to the inn and curl up in bed.

Puck pointed to the horizon. "Look, those are the great trees of

Dwende. That will be the capital of Pech."

The grouping of trees had sprouted out in the middle of nowhere. Puck had told her that unlike the Sprites, the Gnomes lived on the ground and carved their homes in the trunks of these enormous trees, building up into them five stories or more.

Unfortunately, the trees created an optical illusion because they were so big and their distance was hard to judge. They didn't arrive in the city until late that night. Right before they entered the city, Puck shaved his beard by firelight and replaced his rags with his normal clothes. "We will be going to the palace," he said. "I need to be presentable."

Autumn was practically sleepwalking as Puck finally navigated through the massive trees. Whatever kind of city Autumn was expecting, this wasn't it. They didn't see a single person, no lights to show paths or roads, nothing that indicated anyone lived here at all. Autumn was able to barely see the gravel road they were walking on by the light of thousands of lightning bugs flying overhead. As Puck reached the center of the city, Autumn still could not make out any visible doors or windows.

Puck navigated through the massive cluster of trees to the largest of them and firmly knocked on the trunk. Autumn checked the hood of her cloak to make sure it was shading her face. When nothing happened, Puck knocked again louder. The bark of the tree where he had knocked faded into a large elaborately carved door that slowly opened. A little round man in long deep red robes stood at the door and grimaced at the two intruders.

Puck took off his orange top hat and gave a deep bow. Autumn followed his lead with a curtsy.

"We have come to pay our respects to his Highness William Fitzwilliam the Great. Please inform him that Puck and his young student, Holly, are here."

He then presented the paperwork that verified their identities.

The little man, no taller than Puck and much shorter than Autumn, looked at the paperwork dismissively.

"The king has gone to bed, and it is past curfew. Come back tomorrow."

"We are not from around here. We are sorry we have broken curfew. If you could wake Tanner, I am sure he will allow us to stay with him tonight. Then we will be off the street and off your hands."

The Gnome grumbled under his breath and closed the door. Autumn wondered if he had just left them outside and went to bed. A few minutes later the door flew open, and a Gnome in all brown with a tall pointed hat hurried to greet them.

"Puck! How good to see you!"

The Gnome pushed them inside, closed the door, and practically dragged them through the grand parlor and up a massive, wooden, ornately carved staircase. They then hurried down some dimly lit hallways until they reached an ordinary door on the very end. The Gnome opened the door and whispered, "Aurora." Then he closed and locked the door behind them.

The room lit up to reveal a little sitting room with a couple of doors around it and a small fireplace.

"Puck, it's been years!"

The Gnome hugged Puck and then took his bag and hat.

"Who is this?" he asked as he also took Autumn's bag. "The doorman said Holly, but I know you, Puck, better than to trust that."

He placed their things in a nearby closet.

"Tanner, this is Autumn."

Puck proceeded to tell Tanner their story as they made themselves comfortable in the over-stuffed chairs around the fireplace. Autumn heard very little of their conversation and nearly fell out of the chair as she dozed off.

"Oh! I am so sorry," said Tanner. "Come in here and sleep on the bed. Puck and I will be talking for a while yet."

Tanner opened a door into a bedroom.

Autumn managed to take off her complicated shoes before crashing onto the bed fully clothed and fell asleep.

Autumn slept hard all night and didn't wake until close to noon the next day. When she did wake, she ached all over and debated whether any movement was necessary. Finally, the feeling of grime covering her convinced her that bathing was more important than not moving.

She slowly climbed off the bed and made her way out the door.

The two old men were smoking pipes by the fireplace where they were sitting last night and laughing at a joke.

"Did you guys even sleep?" asked Autumn.

The two men looked up. "Oh, yes. We just camped out here," said

Tanner. "If you are looking for the washroom, it's the door next to you."

"By the way," said Puck, "you may want to take extra care with your makeup because we have been asked to present ourselves to the king this evening."

Autumn looked down at her dirt crusted clothes. Last night she had vaguely thought they had escaped that embarrassment. Tanner and Puck looked at each other.

"I could see if there is a Gnome dress in the palace that you can use, but I'm afraid you are about two feet taller than any Gnome," said Tanner.

Autumn went to the closet that had her things and picked out her bag.

"No, I'll make do," she mumbled as she stumbled to the washroom.

It was a couple of hours later before she emerged in her over-sized human clothes and bright pink skin. She had worked hard to scrub all the dirt off herself and her Nomad clothes. The Nomad clothes were lying around the washroom drying. She would see if Puck or Tanner could whip up some magic to dry them in time for meeting the king.

She joined the others in eating her first meal of the day. A tray sitting on one of the side tables held various slices of bread and cheeses on it. When Autumn sat down with her little plate full of food, she noticed two bags packed by the door.

"So, are we leaving tonight? Are you coming with us?" she asked Tanner.

"Puck invited me to join you, and I would be honored to come," said Tanner. "This mystery is very interesting, and I hope I can be of assistance. We need to leave soon because this palace is not as safe as it once was. It would be safer to be traveling. I am sorry that you won't have a chance to wash in a potion to help cure your curse before we go."

"I updated him last night," explained Puck, "and it turns out that Sage's warning about the king is correct. We must keep our identity secret from him. Why are you not dressed in your tunic?"

"Just cleaned everything," said Autumn between bites of cheese. "I was hoping one of you can help me dry them."

Puck got up and left his plate.

"So how do you know Puck?" Autumn asked Tanner.

"We knew each other when we worked at Vervain," said Tanner.

"You both worked at Vervain?" Autumn wondered when she would stop learning new things about Puck.

"It was nothing big," said Tanner.

He put down his plate and leaned back.

"He was the royal tutor, and I was the gamekeeper, like I am here."

"Oh," said Autumn.

She looked at Tanner anew. He didn't seem like he belonged in a palace. He was clean-shaven, but rugged at the same time. He wore nice clothes, but they were practical for hard work. His hands were large and leathery. Yes, he may be a good person to have in a survival situation.

"Puck and I were some of the very few who survived Maldamien's attack on Vervain. Almost everyone was killed. I tried to keep that fact hidden while working here, but with things becoming more and more dangerous, I needed an excuse to leave," said Tanner.

"Your clothes are ready," said Puck as he entered the room. "I enlarged them for you as well."

Autumn shoved the last bit of bread into her mouth as she disappeared into the washroom. It wasn't long before she was ready, packed, and waiting to be summoned by a servant for their time to be presented to the king.

Puck and Tanner both smoked their pipes and talked about various people they both knew.

"Do you remember Kory's baby girl?" asked Tanner.

"She would be at least eighty by now," said Puck.

"Well, she has joined Maldamien's army."

"What?" said Puck, "Her parents must have been upset."

"They died ten years ago with an Ogre raid on their village," said Tanner.

"What a shame," said Puck. "What would have made that girl join with her parent's killers?"

"I don't know," said Tanner. "I have concluded that it is either fear of being killed herself or the desire to have all the benefits and comforts that come with serving Maldamien. Soldiers don't suffer from hunger."

Puck shook his head. "Yes, but there is more to life than one's stomach."

A knock came from the door. Tanner stood up and opened it.

"The king is ready to see you," said another Gnome in deep red robes.

"Well," said Puck as he got up and emptied his pipe in the fireplace, "wish us luck."

Tanner patted Puck on the back as he passed and shook hands with Autumn.

"I'll be waiting for your return. May the Gryphon be with you."

Puck and Autumn followed the servant down the hallway back to the large parlor they had entered last night. Today it was well lit by a large chandelier.

"Wait here," said the servant as he disappeared behind two large doors at the end of the parlor.

There were beautiful wood carvings everywhere. As they waited to be announced, Autumn noticed that the room was old and worn out. Many engravings were damaged and dust laid on most things. The rugs were faded, and even the chandelier was filled with dark areas.

"Walk this way, please," said the servant when he reappeared.

Puck and Autumn followed him into a great throne room lined with people on either side. A large throne sat on a platform in the center. All the well-dressed aristocrats were small and round like the servant and Tanner. The servant stepped aside as Puck continued his approach to the throne. Autumn walked next to him trying to match his pace. As they reached the throne, Puck took off his orange top hat and bowed low. Autumn curtsied slowly to keep the hood of her cloak in place on her head. The result was a graceful dignity that got the room buzzing with whispers.

Autumn looked up slowly and straightened when Puck did. She then took a better look at the king. He was a tiny round man with a white beard that looked even whiter against his dark blue robes. Everything around him, including the throne, made him look remarkably smaller than anyone else in the room. Autumn suppressed a smirk at the fact that he was called "the great." Autumn also noticed the Nomad standing slightly behind the throne. She was glad she had her hood shading her face well. The hair on the back of Autumn's neck stood on end.

"Puck, it is so good to see you. Will you amuse us with some of your stories? It is strange to see you with a pupil. You have traveled alone for such a long time. She is very pretty. Come, man, speak! Tell us about your adventures!"

The king was shaking with excitement over the presence of Puck.

The girl couldn't help but wonder if he had been extremely bored lately or if Puck's stories were really that legendary.

Puck placed his top hat back on his head. "This young lady is the cleverest youth that I have met in a hundred years. I immediately thought to myself, 'Self, you are getting old and have not passed on your knowledge to anyone completely. This wise youth is willing. Wisdom without knowledge is wasted, and you haven't taught in such a long time.' So, we have been traveling together since." Puck pulled out his pan pipes from his waistcoat pocket. "We will now entertain you with a song."

Autumn looked at Puck to see what he was doing. He smiled at her and began to play the familiar tune to the song she had learned from him. She took a breath and closed her eyes.

> "Ancient roads we want to travel,
> And our foot upon the gravel,
> Paths for us to explore,
> The trails beyond the shore.
>
> Touched by the gryphon's wing,
> Beyond common censure,
> Drawn to the dusty road,
> Beware of the adventure,
> Touched by a gryphon's wing.
>
> Highways lead us somewhere too far,
> Far away from our childhood home,
> To chase the distant star,
> A happy life just lived to roam.
>
> Touched by the Gryphon's wing,
> Beyond common censure,
> Drawn to the dusty road,
> Beware of the adventure,
> Touched by a gryphon's wing."

"Very good! Very good!" said the king as the music Puck played faded.

Autumn kept her eyes closed to calm her nerves from singing before the king. When she opened her eyes, she was taken back by the king hopping down off his throne and coming towards her.

"Come, my dear," the king said as he grabbed her hand and led her to a window on her right. The courtesans parted as they approached. "I was so impressed with your performance that I want you to stay here for a couple of weeks and perform for me."

Autumn looked at the king in surprise, but he continued. "Look at this magnificent city. You should go and see all of it. Buy some souvenirs, enjoy our theater, and experience our finest restaurants!"

Autumn looked out the window where he pointed. The city was transformed from what they had seen last night. Shops and produce were open and out to see, windows were open and lit up, people were crowded on the streets fighting for room with carts and merchants. It looked like a human metropolis. Autumn then noticed Ogres within the mass. Many Gnomes were being ordered around loading carts, not for merchants, but for Nomads. The shops were not selling products but collecting produce from the population. The entire city was enslaved.

Autumn looked back at the king and could see his eyes were glazed over. He didn't see what she saw at all. Autumn calmed a rising sense of panic and responded as though she could see what he saw.

"We would be glad to accept your offer. Your fine city would be a treat to explore," said Autumn as sincerely as she could muster.

"Good! Good!" he patted her back. "I will send a servant to give you a tour tomorrow. Tonight, we will have a feast that you must attend."

"Yes," said Autumn. "I will head straight to my room and prepare for it. Will we be entertaining you this evening?"

"Of course! You and Puck must perform again," he said as he turned around to look at Puck.

Puck bowed. "We will be delighted," said Puck.

"Good! Good!" The king waved for them to go as he returned to his throne.

Puck and Autumn walked out of the throne room silently. A servant opened the double doors, and another followed them. When the doors were firmly closed, and Puck and Autumn were almost to the center of the parlor, they heard a muffled noise. Both of them turned around instantly to see Tanner with a cloth over the unconscious servant's mouth and nose. Puck lifted the servant's feet, and they laid him across the front of the doors.

"The king is mad, and the whole city is enslaved," whispered Autumn.

Tanner nodded.

"Not now. Follow me," he whispered back.

They went into what looked like a closet door and down a narrow staircase to a kitchen busy with servants. Tanner led them through the kitchen into a large pantry. Tanner shoved a stone into the wall next to one of the shelves and the shelf and wall swung open. They hurried in, and Tanner closed the door and whispered, "Aurora." Torches on the wall lit up, and each of them grabbed one.

"That's a useful spell," said Puck.

"Learned it from the Hiru," said Tanner.

"Where are we going?" asked Autumn.

"I found out that you both were not going to make it back to the room after your meeting with the king. Ogres were waiting to take you prisoner in the parlor. The meeting with the king was a sham just for the Nomad to get to see you both and make sure you were the ones they are looking for. I have your bags down here. There are lots of secret tunnels that only the servants know about. They would never volunteer the information, even if they were loyal to Maldamien. It's just not done." said Tanner.

"What happened to the Ogres?" asked Puck.

"They got a report that you had escaped already," said Tanner. "They are hunting for you by the stables. No one knew I was helping you, but I definitely won't be able to go back."

"This tunnel doesn't happen to lead out of the city, does it?" asked Puck.

"No, it only leads to the outside of the palace, but I have new disguises," said Tanner.

They reached their bags and piles of rags were next to them.

"What do you have in mind?" asked Puck.

"We are going to ride out with the trash."

****

As the sun set, the kitchen boy dumped the last of his trash into his cart, hopped onto the driver's seat, and flicked the reins for his fox to start running. The hidden passengers held their breath hoping no Ogre or Nomad decided to stop the cart. Luckily, the boy who drove this cart drove it every night and just nodded at the Ogre who was blocking the way out of town. The cart stopped at the garbage dump, backed up to it, and tilted the cart back with a lever, pouring the contents into the ditch, then he quickly drove away. Tanner, Puck, and Autumn climbed out of the pit and made their escape south away from the city and toward Vervain.

CHAPTER 11: RED LADIES

"Autumn, Autumn, Autumn," Sage said into the campfire and then sighed.

He couldn't help it. He was disappointed. He expected to see the radiant queen who his father died to save, but he found a preadolescent human girl instead. She wasn't a normal girl. She had healed his leg which was saying something, but she wasn't a hero or warrior, just a child. Then again, she was under a curse. Who knows what could be in that brain of hers or what she would be like when she was back to normal again, however long that takes? Still, he was disappointed.

Sage stared at the great oak tree opposite him and the campfire. Toble had traveled the longest he had ever gone without sleep to get to Ezekiel's house in time. They traveled for only half a day into the remote part of Shenlong for him to rest. They could have tried to beat Turmeric to Vervain, but Toble would have fallen asleep on the way anyway. Knowing Turmeric, Sage predicted that they would still beat him to Vervain since Turmeric would be combing the area searching for Puck's trail first. Even so, Sage was not terribly motivated to go to Vervain. He hadn't been there since the night they had fled a hundred years ago. He had hoped that he would be going with a powerful queen to regain her rightful throne instead of sneaking into a deserted city haunted by the most painful memories of his past.

Sage sighed and threw another piece of wood on the fire. This was the first campfire they had had in weeks, and he was going to enjoy it. He leaned back against his bag with his feet stretched out towards the flames. This was about as nice as it got for them. It was such a difference from the way it was when he was a child. His father was a folk hero and legendary warrior. Sage's mother was one of the queen's ladies in waiting. Sage lived in the palace and was raised like a prince. When Toble saved his life, they had to flee. They did what everyone who wants to disappear did: they went into the desert. Toble had some friends there, and Sage spent his teenage years living and training as a Nomad. He would have just stayed there had Turmeric just left him alone. In many ways, Sage's conflict with Maldamien and Turmeric came down to wanting to make them pay for ruining his life twice.

Sage watched the flames dance. This is what always happened when he had time to sit and think about things. He always ended up depressed and angry. He had to learn to control his anger to survive. Blind rage would get you killed. Even so, he was angry. When he was younger, he just wanted his parents back, but now he was glad they didn't have to see what the world had become. After so long fighting, he just wished he had a normal life and family. He was now older than either of his parents were when they died, but he had never gotten to experience the joys of a home as they did. He was tired of being on the run, fighting battles, and worrying about friends. He wanted a little bit of happiness, but that was just too much ask for in a world where he was just lucky to be alive.

He had long ago given up hope for those things and saw his destiny as being one who helped others try to live the life he couldn't. He wanted to bring a father doomed to Maldamien's gallows back home to his family. Sage wanted to help a young mother to have enough food to feed her family. He wanted to hurt those who were out to hurt the innocent. In all of this were his purpose and one day he would not be lucky enough to live through it. That was fine with him.

Still, hope would creep through his self-inflicted suicidal mission, birthed from a fatalism that was not natural to him. In times of quiet, Sage still hoped. He knew it was only his stubbornness and unwillingness to give up without a fight that kept any hope there. There was nothing to hope for. Yet in rare moments like these, he would look into the fire and see a small house in the woods with a wife and four or five children. He would see peace and happiness. He would see all those things that hurt and ached in the depth of his gut, but he just could not kill it and stay sane or rational.

Toble began to transform back into his faerie form.

"Welcome back," said Sage, relieved to have his thoughts interrupted.

Toble yawned.

"How long was I asleep?"

"Two days."

"Why didn't you wake me?" asked Toble.

Sage shrugged. "You needed it."

"Hmm," said Toble as he picked up his bag and stomped out the fire. "Well, we had better be off."

Sage slowly grabbed his bag and followed. When Toble was annoyed there wasn't much arguing could do to stop him. Not that Toble needed to be stopped. It was time to move on.

They worked their way southeast through the dense forest. It wasn't an easy walk because they were far from any trails. At some points, Sage had to pull out his short, stocky sword to cut down brush that wouldn't listen to Toble's magic or let them pass.

They traveled for a week, eating as they went, and stopping only to sleep. Their agreed goal was to continue until they came to a market road in the southeast corner of Caoineag that followed the river and would take them on to Vervain. There wouldn't be any reason to avoid the road at that point since the forest ended there. After a week of travel and trailblazing, they hoped to reach that road today.

"So Toble, do you really think that ring is very important?" asked Sage still feeling like he wanted to turn around and head back to Shenlong. Going to Vervain was his idea, but he regretted it every step they took.

"Yes," said Toble. "I just hope we can find it."

Sage's memory of the palace was from when he was twelve, and he didn't remember the palace being a very complicated place.

"If the Ogres have been there, they will leave a mess. If not, we just search the jewelry boxes. How hard can it be?"

"I used to work there," said Toble.

Sage's confidence vanished. Toble meant he invented something to hide it but couldn't remember what it was.

"What kind of things did you invent for the palace? If you could list them off, maybe we would have a clue what we were looking for."

"You know, traps doors, secret passages, hidden compartments, complicated locks, the usual security things."

Sage sighed. There was nothing usual about Toble's inventions. Sage had yet to meet anyone who created devices as complicated as Toble's.

Toble continued.

"Queen Anemone was the first one to implement such measures.

104

The palace was surprisingly insecure before her reign."

"That's ironic," said Sage. "Then again, she may have tried to secure the palace because of Maldamien's rising in power."

"Yes, that's exactly right. She couldn't find out what was specifically happening around her kingdom, so she started to make a general plan. She sensed that things were not right years before she was able to point at Maldamien."

"The queen was an amazing woman. She ruled all those years alone. How did she know what to do? How did she not become power hungry like Maldamien? Or become overwhelmed with people's problems and internalize their struggle?"

Sage started to hack another stubborn bush. Toble followed behind.

"She was just like you and me. She was confused, overwhelmed, felt alone, and was even vain at moments, but she listened to advisers and did the best she could. People sometimes become legendary for just being lucky or in the right place at the right time. She wasn't perfect, or Maldamien would not have been able to get as powerful as he did, but she did make a lot of good and even lucky decisions to hold him back for a while."

"Pretty amazing," said Sage. "No wonder my dad admired her. He said she was a natural leader. Mom always had good things to say, too."

"Your parents were a good judge of character. Your father also said that you were a natural leader as well. I think he would be proud of you."

Sage frowned. It wasn't that he didn't appreciate Toble's compliment, but he didn't feel like was doing anything to show natural leadership, or even to make his dad proud. He existed. That was about it.

They continued on for a few yards when Sage heard rustling in the distance to his left. Sage stopped suddenly, and Toble slightly bumped into him. The movement continued towards them more aggressively. Toble lifted his bag and began to transform. Sage grabbed a low branch, swung up into a tree next to them, and scrambled for a higher, more hidden position.

"Please, miss, let me go!" said the whimpering male's voice.

Sage watched as two Red Ladies led a bound Undine man through the forest right under him. The Undine man was well dressed, had bare webbed feet, pale, rubbery skin, and was shaking in fear. The gills on his neck quivered as he looked nervously around and swallowed sobs. The tall older woman who was leading the group and holding the rope turned to her prisoner, hissing and showing her huge snake-like fangs. The Undine man fell to his knees and hid his face in his rope-bound arms.

The younger prettier woman who was behind him sighed. "Do you think we can eat him now? I'm hungry, and he is so loud."

She shifted her hips in the ragged red dress. Her pouty lips emphasized the crossing of her arms in irritation.

"You have no right to complain. You didn't do any of the work," said the older woman.

She straightened up her gaunt frame to try and tower over the young woman.

"That wasn't much work," countered the younger woman, putting her hands on her hips and bringing her chin forward. "We are far enough from the road. No one will hear us."

"And no one will hear him as he is. You know the rules," said the older woman waving the woman away and turning back to their path. "We have to share him with everyone."

"Maldamien doesn't do that," said the younger woman still planted in the same place. "Why should we?"

"Since his reign, we have been able to eat anytime we wanted," said the older woman, talking to the woman behind her and pulling the rope to get the Undine moving. "We used to be lucky if we could get one person a year before."

"Don't just defend him because he is your son," said the younger woman catching up to the taller woman. "He could share his slaves as easily as we share our prisoners. If he can have as much as he wanted to himself, I don't see why we should have to split this one among the twelve of us."

"Hush you tiresome bore! I don't have the patience for you today. I may decide to eat you and be done with it!" she said.

"You wouldn't eat me!" said the younger woman. "You're soft and a hypocrite. You talk about rules, but you are supposed to eat your sons and only let your daughters live. You broke the biggest rule of them all."

The older woman sighed.

"You always bring that up when you don't get your way. Fine. We will eat him now and catch another one for the others. They can't complain about that."

"Please, ladies, I beg of you!" wailed the unfortunate Undine as the two ladies turned on him and showed their fangs.

Sage drew his short, curved sword. He couldn't just watch. He never could. He jumped down behind the older woman, wrapped his arm around her neck and stabbed her in the back. She twisted around and looked at him. She laughed as Sage pulled his sword out of her. He backed up into a tree, surprised at the reaction. Before he could think, the younger woman was quickly next to him. He vaguely remembered stabbing her in the gut as she grabbed his face and brought it close to hers, nose to nose. Sage's eyes were drawn towards her red piercing gaze. He let go of his sword. A haze came over his mind. He felt lost and alone as he drank in the intoxicating images that were shot into his brain. Reality and nightmares were melding. He looked at his life like it was a storybook that he had read one time. The hellish nightmare of fire and shadowy demons was his new reality. His strength was disappearing.

Then, suddenly, it stopped, and Sage fell to the ground sweating and pale. Had he given into their hypnosis? Was he in their power like the Undine man? As he began to come back to himself, he took inventory of his limbs and mental functions.

"Sage!" shouted Toble into his face. He was shaking him. "Sage!"

"Did you get her?" said Sage in more of a groan than normal speech.

He suddenly felt pain all over. He opened his eyes. Toble was pale and breaking into a sweat. His wrinkled face showed relief.

"That was the dumbest thing you have ever done!" said Toble as he helped Sage to stand up slowly.

"Dumber than jumping off a cliff?" he asked.

"Yes! This tops them all," said Toble. "You know that Red Ladies aren't like other faeries or humans! You can't just swing your sword around and kill them! What in the world were you thinking? You know as well as I do that they are some of the strongest magic users in the world!"

Sage had never seen Toble so angry, but even so, he knew it was because Toble was afraid of losing him.

"Are you all right?" asked Sage.

107

"Am I all right!" said Toble. "No one has EVER killed a Red Lady before and lived!"

Sage looked around still feeling stunned and hazy. The Undine man was loose, and the two Red Ladies were laying at his feet with their faces mutilated.

"What happened?" asked Sage. "I killed the first one, and I thought I stabbed the second as she grabbed my head, but what happened to their faces?"

Toble shook his head.

"You didn't kill either of them. You just distracted them. I guess there are still some things we both don't know. As they were dying from the wounds, they were trying to heal themselves and get their strength back by killing you somehow. They were so focused on you that they didn't see me free the Undine."

The Undine man joined them.

"They heal themselves magically. They steal the life energy from you. They usually do it by eating people physically, but they can do it magically too when they need to. They were both fighting over you when Toble cut me loose. If you hadn't stabbed both of them, we all would have been in trouble. I knew that they were using their eyes to hypnotize you since they were feeding off of you magically instead of physically. I have experienced a little of that myself. We slashed through their eyes, and that stopped it and finished them off."

"So now they are really dead?" asked Sage feeling light headed.

"Yes," said the Undine man. "We need to leave though because there could be more around. We were just fortunate that you surprised them. I doubt we could do this again."

Toble grabbed his bag from the brush, but Sage stumbled to a nearby tree, leaned against it, and puked in the bush. He still wasn't all there yet from the magical encounter, but that helped a lot.

The Undine man offered to carry Sage's bag. Even without the weight of the bag, Sage still had to lean heavily on the Undine and Toble as they worked their way towards the river. They had to stop two more times for Sage to puke in the nearby brush. Once Sage was able to walk on his own, the Undine man began to make conversation.

"By the way, my name is James," said the Undine man, holding out his webbed hand towards Sage as they walked.

"Thanks for helping me out," said Sage, shaking the hand. "I think

I'll manage tomorrow."

"Hey, it's the least I can do for saving my life," said James.

"No, we are even. You saved my life, too," said Sage.

"Are you Sage and Toble, the legendary heroes of the Fenodryee Rebellion?" asked James.

Sage sighed. What about that was heroic? They lost, and hundreds were killed or captured.

"Sure, I guess that's us."

"Wow! And you lead the underground army too, right?"

Sage's eyes narrowed. There was no underground army, just a bunch of gatherings and gossip clubs.

"Who are you?"

James turned a little paler and brushed some of his dark hair out of his face with his webbed hand.

"Sorry. I'm not trying to pry. I am the Undine king's steward. I was asking because we are about to enter a war with the Merpeople, and we could use more warriors."

"What? Why?" asked Toble.

"The Merpeople are trying to take over our river. We are just struggling to keep our economy afloat, and they say that we are stealing from them," said James. "If they want a fight, then we will give them one."

Sage had a hard time imagining James in any sort of battle.

"It's a bunch of foolishness," said Toble.

"Don't you think that is drastic measures considering the fact that we should be fighting against Maldamien?" said Sage.

"Well, we aren't going to start it," said James. "We are just going to defend ourselves."

The situation seemed strange to Sage. Two more governments were now taking their eyes off of Maldamien's activities. The rumors about the Gnomes and the events with the Sprites left no loyal governments intact. It seemed to Sage that Maldamien was somehow behind this war. After a hundred years of allowing these governments to exist in submission, why overturn them now? Also, why do this so subtly? Why not march an army in and just take over things like with the Brownies and Hiru?

"Well, I hate to disappoint you, but we can't make any detours," said Toble.

"Oh, a secret mission!" said James. "How exciting! Well, you both would be welcome at the Undine palace at any time. Just ask for me if you need anything."

They reached the edge of the forest and could see both the market road and the river.

"I'll be leaving you here," said James. "I would feel safer swimming home, if you know what I mean." James handed Sage back his bag.

"Sure," said Sage. "No Red Ladies. Totally understand."

They shook hands at the bank and James jumped in and bobbed back up. "Remember, you have an open invitation if you change your mind!" He waved and then disappeared under the water.

Sage and Toble continued to travel a little farther on the market road. When they finally decided it was safe to stop for the night, they didn't make a fire, but just got comfortable on the edge of the river and off the road. Sage decided to sleep up in Toble's branches that night like he used to do as a teenager. He was still unnerved by the day's events. He totally understood James' preference for swimming miles upstream to the chance of encountering another Red Lady. It was an experience he would never forget.

CHAPTER 12: YARROW

Autumn stood on the hill staring off into the distance. Puck and Tanner had told her that on a clear day you could see Vervain from here even though it was still two days' travel away. It wasn't a clear day, but a cloudy night. Autumn still stared off into the darkness. Tanner and Puck were eating dinner lower down on the hill and talking about old times around the half-buried fire. Autumn had climbed the hill for time to think alone.

What was she doing here? She was getting more of her memories about childhood and instead of making sense of what was going on, it just confused her more. The curse was wearing off slowly. Puck and Tanner asked her daily if she could remember anything more. They were all eager to get to the bottom of this mystery. She could not even remember her family. Who were they? What were they like? She struggled to remember the end of her schooling and anything after that. Even if she did remember everything, would it change anything? She didn't want to go back home for some reason, but she didn't want to always be running for her life. What if it was all a mistake, and she had just found those items from Queen Anemone lying around on the ground? Would she even have a choice about going home if the portals were never opened? Would she have to hide for the rest of her life? Would she join the underground and try to survive? Maybe she could go back to the little cottage in Shenlong, fix it up, add some running water, start a garden, and live there. Why did she not want to go home? What was she looking for?

Autumn tried to see if she could make out the form of Vervain in the darkness. The idea of the abandoned palace reminded her of the story of Sleeping Beauty and her castle covered in impenetrable vines. Life didn't seem real here. She felt like one of these days she would wake up like Sleeping Beauty and find that it was all a dream.

The visit to Vervain was a minor detour though. Tanner and Puck had intended to try and convince Sage to go with them to the south to search for Thyme. Puck believed he was the only one who could instantaneously cure her curse and help them get some answers. They planned on being in Vervain as little as possible.

Autumn turned around to look at the direction they came from. The open land all around covered in brown grassy hills made their escape difficult. They only stopped when they could find a place to hide, and so Autumn ended up chewing a lot of willow bark to help her muscles cope with the pace of travel. This was the first night she hadn't fallen right to sleep as soon as they stopped.

In the distance was a glowing light. Autumn stared hard at it thinking it was a lone star, but it was getting closer quickly. Soon she was able to tell that the light itself was a figure running in their direction.

"Puck! Tanner! Something is coming!" said Autumn.

The two men were in action in a moment. Tanner dumped dirt on the fire and Puck ran to her side.

"Where?" Before she could answer, he shouted back to Tanner, "It's Apollo."

"Who is Apollo?" asked Autumn.

"He is a very old creature, as old as the earth or older. He is a unicorn, and he is the only one left to intervene in the affairs of faerie and man," said Tanner as he walked up.

"We are very lucky to see him," said Puck. "It is said that to spot him will bring good fortune to the observer."

The three of them watched as the pure white unicorn galloped through the tall grassy field. His course did not alter as he headed directly towards them. The large stallion slowed to a walk as he got closer. He approached Autumn so that they were looking eye to eye. Autumn stared into his crystal blue eyes. It seemed to her that she could see all of history and the wisdom of the ages in them.

Then the unicorn bowed. "You are highly favored," said Apollo.

Puck and Tanner looked at each other in awe.

Something drew Autumn to Apollo's ivory white unicorn horn. It was longer than she had imagined a unicorn's horn would be. She reached out her hand, and with the point of her finger, she touched the tip of it.

Pain shot throughout her body and her finger began to bleed. Apollo

112

straightened up abruptly, backing up a little, shaking his head.

"Only one other has touched my horn. This will cause you much woe."

"Look at your wrists," said Puck to Autumn.

Autumn lifted her hands. The runes on her right wrist were copied on her left as well. Both sets of runes had turned silver.

"Those marks will be both a blessing and a curse, but that must be for later," said Apollo. "You are all in great danger here. Turmeric and his Ogres are nearby. They have tracked you here. Climb onto my back, and I will take you to Vervain tonight. First, though, I must also show you something that will affect the destiny of us all."

Apollo knelt down. Puck and Tanner looked at each other and hesitated to move towards Apollo's back. Finally, Autumn climbed onto his back first, then Puck, and then Tanner. Once they were settled and holding on, Apollo leaped up and sprinted towards Vervain. They entered woods, then fields, then woods again. They moved miles in mere minutes. Apollo turned slightly east of Vervain until he reached an open valley surrounded by woods and filled with ruins. He turned directly east into the valley. Apollo slowed to a walk as he reached the edge of a stone foundation. The ruins were not very high. The highest wall standing was only one story and a half high. Most of what remained were piles of rubble and stone pavement that echoed the clicking noise of Apollo's hooves as he walked.

"This is Yarrow," said Puck.

Autumn's eyes were wide. She tried to imagine the fortress from Puck's story about the warring kings and Sorceress Kara. She imagined that Apollo had just passed through what would have been the main gate since there seemed to be a thick low wall on either side of where he walked, perhaps even a drawbridge had existed, and the moat was just filled in with time and weather. He then entered a courtyard that had ruins in the center that may have been a fountain or statue. He headed to the left in which there was a walled-in area. It may have been barracks or the palace part. Apollo turned right into an open room that had the highest walls in the entire complex on the north, sidelined with worn down statues of humanoid figures. Very little obscured the view of the south and west of the valley from where he stood, but in the east of the hall stood a portal very similar to the one Autumn had entered to get to Gryphendale. This one was made of blue marble instead of green, and was carved with images of water creatures instead of leaves and flying things. The structure was identical in every other way. It wasn't connected to any of the fortress structures at all as though it just landed there. In front, the portal was a strange table-like structure covered in gaudy gems. It was so completely out of place that it almost hurt to look at it.

"What is that?" asked Tanner.

"The altar was erected by Maldamien after the portals had been sealed. He completed its construction only this week. It is guarded by a spell and must be of great importance to him. This portal will be the last to open because it was the first one sealed. If it is not opened in three months' time, during the Day of Remembrance, this world will be uninhabitable," said Apollo, "but if it is opened, this altar is witness to the fact that Maldamien is planning some evil enchantment. I suspect it to be also destructive to our world in some way."

"So, we just need to open the portals before he can do his spell," said Autumn.

"It is not so simple," said Apollo. "One must know what Maldamien has already done. I can only see and know things like that of mortals. I do not know what Maldamien intends to do, but I sense that all of you will be key in stopping him. I tell you this to help you on your journey. I will do what I can to help, but I believe that you will find the answers."

"What do we need to do?" asked Autumn.

"Search," said Apollo. "Search until you find more answers. Now we must go."

Apollo turned to leave, but Autumn looked back as long as she could. Apollo could have walked over the walls that divided that room from the direction they needed to go, but Apollo weaved around, exiting through doorways the same way as they entered as though the structure was fully built. Once they entered the open valley, Apollo took off into a full gallop to the west and entered the forest in moments. He weaved through trees expertly. Moments later, when they exited the forest, Autumn could see the dark outline of a city on the horizon and the slightly shimmery line of a river just touching the south of it. Apollo slowed down as they approached the broken-down gate hanging by a hinge attached to the remains of a crumbling wall. He stopped just inside.

"Your friends are at the palace, but it is safer to journey there in the light of day," said Apollo as he knelt for them to dismount. "Be safe and work quickly. The Gryphon is with you."

As soon as they were safely off, Apollo turned and left.

Puck shined a light from the end of his umbrella and led them into the nearest inhabitable building. Most of the structures looked like they used to be businesses with their large open windows to the road. Dirt and dead grass covered much, and nearly all the building had been substantially damaged somehow. Autumn could still see this easily being rebuilt into a thriving city with just a little bit of work.

"Why did you say that this city was abandoned again?" asked Autumn as Tanner began to work on a fire in the old fireplace even though there was no roof on that side of the building.

"Well, it was abandoned a hundred years ago because when the city was sacked the inhabitants were all carried away as slaves," said Puck. "Most folks were scared to move back because Maldamien decreed that this city should be left empty and those who disobeyed would be killed, but I am sure a few people may hide out here as we are doing."

They cleared some of the rubble around the room for an area to lay down. Tanner had a warm fire going, and they settled around it.

"Wow," said Autumn as she laid down to go to sleep, "Three months to save the world. Doesn't sound real."

"I didn't realize things were that serious," said Puck as he leaned back against his bag.

"Does it change our plans?" asked Tanner.

"The main thing I keep thinking is that we really need to go see Thyme," said Puck. "I am certain he would know something. I think curing Autumn's curse is the key. You must know something. If it isn't about the queen, than you would know something about the Gryphon or how you got here without all the portals open, or even why you came here at all. How did you end up here now? The timing is remarkable. The Day of Remembrance is the day 200 years ago that Queen Audrey died and Queen Anemone took the throne. The puzzle pieces are starting to be revealed for the first time in a century and yet there is so much we still don't know. It is more urgent now. I am sure Sage and Toble would want to go with us. I think that we must go see Thyme. All other plans will have to be made after that."

Autumn wanted to stay awake for the rest of the conversation, but her tired body rebelled. She didn't even move until she woke the next morning to Puck shaking her.

"It's daylight," said Puck. "We have got to get going."

Autumn's body was adjusting to travel, but she still had to push past stiff limbs and sore muscles every morning. Tanner handed her the daily ration of nuts and berries and the skin of water. She really would have preferred a good steak instead.

When they left the building, the view of the city was obscured by a faint fog that had settled during the night. It made the city look monochromatic. Puck and Tanner had no trouble finding their way through the city streets. Autumn could read the heavy looks of despair on their faces as they observed every destroyed house and relived the past in their minds. Brown weeds had grown up and covered most of the roads and rubble, but they could still make out remains of broken furniture thrown in the streets, signs of fire on homes and litter of past lives strewn here and there all in various forms of decay and rot.

They walked silently for most of the morning as they weaved from street to street observing the numerous levels of destruction on their way to the center of the city.

After a turn to their right onto a wide avenue, Autumn could see most of the sprawling palace ahead. It was huge, and the fog still hid part of it. They walked up to the massive iron gates decorated with delicate designs of roses and vines trimmed with tarnished peeling gold. The gates squealed loudly as they pushed on them as hard as they could. They still could barely get them open enough to let the group squeeze in. Tanner ripped his cloak while trying to squeeze by.

They walked through an overgrown courtyard spotted with marble statues worn away by weather and time. The gardens were extensive and appeared as though they were once very elaborate. Autumn strained to see the bordering wall around the edge of the property because of the size of it and the frustrating mist. She wondered how hard it would be to bring it back to its former glory if someone wanted to. Even on the path they walked could be seen glimmers of pink marble under all the dirt and grime.

They walked up pink marble steps to the splintered and broken doors. As they stepped past them, Autumn could see that they had been carved with designs of flowers and decorated tastefully with jewels, but most of the jewels were missing. They stepped into a large dusty entry

116

with staircases on either side and with a balcony around the top trimmed with tarnished gold. Autumn could faintly see a remnant of a painting on the ceiling. The group continued under the balcony to two large white doors covered in cobwebs.

Autumn and Tanner each began to pull on the golden handles. As the doors slowly ground open, dirt and grime fell from the ceiling. They entered a great throne room faintly lit by the large windows directly in front of them. Surrounding the walls were draperies with colorful illustrations of scenes from Gryphendale's history. There were eight massive draperies in all.

They split up to explore different parts of the room. Autumn followed the draperies around. Each one detailed a different story of heroes and battles. A couple of them had the blue Gryphon incorporated. Each panel created questions in Autumn's mind of what happened or how long ago it may have happened. It seemed like the stories must have spanned thousands of years because styles of clothing, weaponry, and even the drapery techniques were different for each one.

When she got to the last one, Autumn turned around to see where Puck and Tanner were. Puck was standing in the center of the room studying the floor. Autumn moved next to him.

"I remember the day they made this floor," said Puck. "It was a couple of weeks after Queen Anemone was crowned. This mosaic told the story of the immortality that Queen Audrey died to create. The floor was destroyed because Maldamien didn't want anyone to think about the past monarchs. He wanted to create something new and different. This city is a reminder of all that was. I am surprised he even left it standing at all."

"You haven't told me that story yet," said Autumn. "I mean the story of the spell of immortality."

"Let's find Tanner first, and I will tell you," said Puck.

They found Tanner standing behind the throne looking at a marble wall covered in writing set up in front of the shattered floor-to-ceiling stained glass window across the back wall. Puck and Autumn joined him.

"What is that?" asked Autumn.

"This is the laws of our land since the time Gryphendale was combined into a unified kingdom," said Tanner. "I was just noting how

117

many of them Maldamien has violated."

"Not much of a surprise," said Puck. "I need to tell Autumn the story of the miracle, but I wanted your help with some of the details."

"I don't know why," said Tanner. "You were there. I wasn't even born yet."

"Still..." said Puck as he dropped his bag and sat on the floor in front of the mother of pearl thrones. He indicated for Autumn to do the same.

"This may be information Apollo desires us to explore for answers, so I will try to be as clear and specific as I can.

"Before we were immortal, we lived similar length lives to the humans. This 'miracle', as everyone calls it, occurred at the end of Queen Audrey's reign. She and her husband, King Tarragon, were great and wise rulers who were leading Gryphendale into a time of peace and prosperity. They had seven children and lived long happy lives to a ripe old age. Their seven children loved to study books so much that they isolated themselves from the world into a monastery. Some did marry, but all of them and their followers were called the Asiri. Thyme, the one who I would like to visit, is the only Asiri left. They were hunted and killed by Maldamien when he came to power even though the Asiri had always sworn never to take the throne."

Tanner tapped Puck on the shoulder. "Oh yes," said Puck. "Back to the story. When the king died, the queen sank into a deep depression. Her only grandchild, Anemone, lived with her, but that wasn't enough. She leaned very heavily on the advice of a young human student of mine, Maldamien."

"Maldamien was your student?" said Autumn wide-eyed.

"Yes. As a child, he was found to be very talented and was sent to the palace to study with students from all over the kingdom. It was a new program to cultivate the next generation of rulers, advisers, and government authorities. It turned out to be a bad idea because of the way the palace fostered a superior attitude in those chosen. I taught him, but I cannot say he learned much from me. Many of those students are followers of Maldamien today. It was my greatest failure."

"Puck," said Tanner.

"Right, I am getting easily distracted," said Puck.

"Maldamien convinced the queen that immortality would help the world be a better place where people wouldn't have to lose loved ones like the king. Great skills and achievement could improve without losing scholars and artists. He helped the queen develop a very powerful and difficult spell in which the world of Gryphendale would be frozen in age. Everyone would reach their prime age and stay that age forever, but the old stayed whatever age they were. The seasons did not change. Nothing, including animals, deteriorated from old age. I do not know what this spell entailed or how it worked. It was done very secretly, and no one knew of it until the queen was found dead in a field of rosemary with a letter in her fist, written by her hand and signed with her seal. It was soon after that when rosemary became very poisonous to us. The letter explained that she wanted to create this spell for the well-being of all Gryphendale. It was quite long, describing her dream for the world, but I found it very strange that it didn't talk about her death or say any good-byes like a suicide letter usually does. The world declared her to be a hero and buried her with honor. The Asiri refused the throne, so Anemone was voted in unanimously by each country and crowned as a lone ruler, which was rare.

"Anemone ruled a hundred years alone and ushered in a golden age of progress. Inventors and artists never died, but just got better and better. Fake seasons were simulated with magic. Education increased. Underneath all of this, Maldamien grew more powerful. Political alliances were being formed, and Maldamien built his fortress with slave labor. He circulated information about his involvement in the miracle and gained popularity. Maldamien's work was hidden from the queen, but she continually caught wind of things going on around her. She became suspicious of various people in the palace and tried to fix the problems she saw. Finally, she was able to point everything back to Maldamien, having him arrested for treason and plotting to take over the throne. He not only escaped but formed an army. Queen Anemone received a piece of communication one night as she was in the war council preparing for Maldamien's attack. No one knows what the message said, but she immediately formed four teams of people she trusted.

"Each team was sent to the portals to bar them and lock them with a key. Tanner and I were part of the team sent to the water portal. Queen Anemone went with the captain of the guard to the wind portal. The portals were closed in a specific order with the wind portal being last. The two Hiru warriors who flew to the earth portal near Maldamien's fortress were the first to be discovered and killed even though we had closed our portal first and the fire one was after ours. Maldamien magically transported to the other portals and killed all he saw, stole the keys, then went to the next one. Many did escape. He came upon Queen Anemone as she performed the complicated spell to seal them all when the last one was locked. He attacked her with a fireball, but the captain of the guard blocked it and fell back against the queen, pushing her into the human world as the locked door was closed. Maldamien immediately led his army in a mad rage, burning down the city of Vervain, executing all who were in the palace, and taking the citizens of the city to be slaves. He then hunted down the Asiri, the strongest political allies of the queen, and anyone who was a threat magically, to kill them all."

Tanner added, "Puck and I escaped because we didn't return to the palace right away. When Maldamien had attacked our group, we were able to get away and hide. There was no chance for a fight. We stayed hidden for a while as we argued over what we should do next. That argument saved our lives. When we headed back to Vervain, we saw the city in flames long before we arrived. I am guessing he transported his whole army?" asked Tanner.

"I always assumed so," said Puck. "I have never heard of someone having that much power, but Maldamien has done things similar to that since."

Puck took out his handkerchief and blew his nose.

"Well, we need to find Sage and Toble," said Puck after a bit. "We played tourist probably longer than we should have."

"They were looking for the queen's seal, so I suggest we head to the queen's apartments," suggested Tanner. Puck grabbed his bag, then Autumn and he followed Tanner out of the throne room. Autumn turned around and gave the room one more look. She felt like she almost remembered something important, but then it was gone.

CHAPTER 13: VERVAIN

Puck, Tanner, and Autumn walked down the dark palace halls and up some beautiful staircases to a broken-down door into the Victorian-styled sitting room. The faerie queen's large sitting room had been reduced to remnants of shattered furniture and shredded decor. The group continued through the sitting room to the queen's dressing room. Autumn wandered to the ornate armoire with all its drawers pulled out and emptied onto the floor. The mirror was opaque and cracked. The empty jewelry boxes were evidence of someone's previous search, probably looters. Autumn walked on to the wardrobe while Puck and Tanner searched dressers and trunks. Autumn gently touched a dusty, faded silk gown slightly stiff with age. She wondered why no one stole those. It would probably not look normal to be dressed like a queen, but the luxurious material could be re-used for many other things.

"You have grown quite a bit since the last time I saw you. Is your hair naturally red or black?"

Autumn turned around and gave Sage a great big smile.

"I'm a red-head," she answered.

"It surprised me," said Sage.

Autumn noticed that his sword was drawn, but his arm was hanging at his side casually as he leaned on the doorway. He was a little cleaner and had shaven since the last time she saw him.

"Sage!" said Puck. "Good to see you again. Have you found the ring?"

"No."

"Is this the boy who would chase my cow dogs?"

"Tanner! It's been awhile," said Sage putting away his sword and giving Tanner a hug. He had to kneel down to do so. "I hope you have forgiven me by now."

"What's this I hear?" came a voice from the other room.

"Hoble who half evening by dawn? What?"

Toble came walking in with huge magnifying lenses over his eyes and tufts of white hair poking up between the leather straps holding it to his head.

"Toble, your earplugs!" shouted Sage, and he pulled a wired cork from Toble's ear.

Toble almost blushed as he removed his contraptions.

"Excuse me. I was searching for trap doors in one of the closets, and I have a terrible fear of getting bugs in my ears."

"Same old Toble!" said Tanner. "It's good to see you, Ambassador." They shook hands warmly.

"No titles, Tanner. We don't live in that world anymore," said Toble.

Autumn spoke up. "So, do you have any idea where it could be?"

"The ring?" said Toble. "I had made some secret compartments for the queen that we are still searching for."

"We have narrowed down that the improvements were made only in the queen's apartments," said Sage.

"That would make sense," said Tanner. "I guess we had better start looking."

The group split up and went into each of the queen's rooms. Autumn soon discovered why Toble was afraid of bugs because there were plenty of them in every dark corner. Autumn went into the queen's bedroom. It was a mess with bedding everywhere, and tables knocked over. On the farthest wall from the doorway stood a stunning portrait of the queen with her moth-like wings, light blond hair, and a full navy blue gown with the extra material on the bottom draped around her feet. Autumn checked that she was alone, and then got the photograph from her secret belt under her tunic.

She studied the laughing woman in the photo. They were most definitely the same person except without the pointed ears and wings. Autumn sighed. She was very pretty, but what was she doing with this picture?

"Where did you get that picture?"

Autumn jumped and spun around, meeting Sage's fierce gaze.

"I told her to hide it, Sage," said Puck who walked into the room at that moment.

"How did she get it?"

Autumn was finding him difficult to read. Usually, his eyes were like a mood ring that showed his emotions, but they were changing colors quickly now.

Autumn stood to her full height to face his challenge.

"I brought it with me from the human world."

She watched as both his eyes and his expression changed a couple of times.

Tanner and Toble walked in, and both stopped, sensing the tension in the room.

"You knew the queen?" he asked.

"I don't know," said Autumn. "I am still getting my memories back from Maldamien's curse. I keep trying to remember things, and they disappear."

Sage sighed. "It was probably right for you to keep that hidden, even from us."

Sage sat on the bed. Autumn could see disappointment and tiredness on his face. For the first time, she saw that he was much older than he looked.

"Wait!" said Autumn as she turned to the portrait and tried to pick it up off the wall.

Sage and Toble rushed over to help her.

"What are you doing?" asked Tanner.

"It's like in an old movie," said Autumn.

"A what?" asked Tanner.

"I think she may have found my hidden compartment," said Toble.

The portrait was removed, and a faint square line was marked on the wall. Toble pushed on the panel, and it popped open, revealing a metal panel with the image of a gryphon engraved on it.

"Drat, I don't remember the spell," said Toble.

Sage turned to Autumn.

"How did you know it was there? There are lots of other pictures in this apartment and even just in this room."

Autumn looked around. Yes, there were multiple pictures of various sizes on all the walls.

"I don't know. This one was just compelling," said Autumn.

Sage looked at her as though he was trying to see something more behind what she was saying.

Puck went to the panel and said various phrases, but nothing happened.

"Well, let us camp here for the night," said Puck. "We need to discover how to open that door before we depart tomorrow. I am sure Turmeric or his brutes will be able to force it open if we don't."

"Turmeric?" said Sage. "Did you see him on your way here?"

"Apollo warned us that he was close by and brought us here. He would have been two days away from here yesterday," said Tanner. "We should be just ahead of them if we leave tomorrow."

"Hmm," said Sage.

Autumn sensed that Sage wasn't very confident about Tanner's assessment, but he didn't argue.

Tanner tried to light a fire in the bedroom fireplace, but when it started to smoke up the room, he put it out. Puck and Toble found a bathtub that they dragged in and placed under an open window. Tanner then made a small fire in it. Autumn and Puck invented a stew from a little bit of everyone's provisions. Periodically, Toble or Puck would get an idea, return to the panel, and try a different spell, but nothing happened.

As they ate, Tanner told Toble and Sage of their adventure. Puck added the information about their encounter with King Fitzwilliam. Toble narrated his and Sage's adventure with the Red Ladies. Sage turned pale during Toble's description of the battle itself.

"That does explain a lot about Maldamien," said Puck. "If Maldamien is half vampire, than his use of dark magic is consistent with his past. It still brings up so many questions, such as how was he able to hide it all these years? Why hide it?"

"I also don't like the idea of the water peoples being at war with each other," said Tanner. "Why would Maldamien want to destroy the governments of all these kingdoms now?"

"I think when we leave here, we should go to see the Asiri, Thyme," said Puck.

Sage shrugged.

"That sounds good to me. I hadn't planned that far yet."

"Doesn't Thyme live on a floating island in the Hiru lands?" asked Toble.

"Yes," said Puck. "I hoped the Hiru would help us."

"Not much chance of that," said Tanner. "They may remember you, but I have heard of a few people who went into their land for various reasons, and their dead bodies were sent back home."

"We could avoid going to the Hiru if I could build something that we could fly in," said Toble.

"Yes," said Sage, standing up and stretching, "but we still don't know where this island is."

"True," said Toble. He rubbed his chin as he pondered the issue.

"Why is it so hard to approach the Hiru? Are they allies of Maldamien? I mean why do they kill people who go into their land?" asked Autumn.

Tanner took a small stick from the fire and lit his rough, wooden pipe, then handed the light to Puck.

"They are no friends of Maldamien," said Tanner. "When Maldamien attacked Vervain, the armies of Gryphendale were gathered together there, preparing for war. Without the queen or the captain of the guard there, the generals from various countries lost their nerve when they saw the power Maldamien had. He could kill twenty soldiers with a single fireball. All the allied armies broke rank and fled except the Hiru. The Hiru stood fighting for hours. Maldamien killed a dozen men with a fireball and a dozen more Hiru would fill the rank. They never fled. Maldamien and his army had to kill every single one of them to get into the palace. Even with their efforts, very few of those inside of the palace were able to escape since Maldamien's army surrounded the grounds. The Hiru back in their homeland never forgave the other countries for abandoning their people."

Sage was leaning forward. His face was unreadable, and his eyes were black.

"Toble and I were the only ones who escaped the palace that day. Toble had been with the queen and my father when my father died. I am sure you have heard that story." Autumn nodded. "Well, after my father died, Toble traveled all the way back to the palace with the help of a Hiru. They arrived during the battle. I was twelve and with my mother. She believed that the women and children would be spared, so she had gathered them all into her apartments. She was frightened for me because she was afraid that a boy of almost fighting age might still be in danger. Toble was able to sneak into the palace using a tunnel he had built for the queen. He found all of us. My mother pushed me to go first even though I wanted to stay and protect her, but she kept telling me that they were all going to come. Once I had gotten into the tunnel with Toble leading the way, a fireball caused the entrance to collapse. I had thought that was when she died, but I found out later that Turmeric had executed them all himself. Had I known..."

Toble patted Sage on the shoulder, but he got up and left the room. Toble continued where Sage ended.

"We had to hide and even fight our way out of the city. It was by the skin of our teeth that we made it. We would have been caught if it had been a whole group of us in that same circumstance. I have reminded myself of that because I do wish we had been able to save them. Sage and I went to the Ifrit Desert to hide. We didn't know where else might be safe. We heard news of the things that happened. Sage wanted to search for his mother, but we soon learned that no one was left alive and how dangerous it was to come back here."

"I think that for Sage's mother, knowing that her son was safe would have given her hope and courage," said Autumn.

"Perhaps, but there is no way of knowing whether she thought he was killed when the tunnel collapsed," said Toble.

"No one should go through that," said Tanner.

"I have to say that is one of the few times I have ever heard Sage talk about that day. Perhaps he has finally made peace with it," said Toble.

The group stared at the tub in which the fire had already died. Puck stood up and went to the panel on the wall just to look at it for a while as though that would somehow help him come up with an idea. Autumn, Tanner, and Toble began to settle down for the night. None of them asked about the bed or blankets because the idea of what could be living in that bed after all this time was disturbing.

Sage returned about an hour later carrying a variety of items. He dumped the items on the bed. Some of the items and trinkets looked like they belonged to a child, some belonged to a man, and a few to a woman. Sage put all of these into his bag except the pile of clothes. He picked them up and went to Autumn.

"Here are some traveling clothes. It was the only ones in decent shape. They may fit you if you would like them."

Autumn looked at his intense green eyes. She suspected that they were his mother's clothes because of the emotion hidden in his voice.

"Thank you."

She took them and went to the washroom that was now missing a tub. She closed the door and tried on the clothes that Sage gave her. She was slightly embarrassed when she realized how tight her old clothes

126

had gotten. The clothes Sage gave her were an earthy rose-colored leather. Through all the years of storage, the material had remained soft. When she started to put on the trousers, she discovered a hole in the seat of them. She then remembered Sage's tail. She would have to fix that later. The long-sleeved tunic draped down to her knees. The outfit even had a matching cloak. The beautiful embroidery and comfortable fit made her feel like a woman instead of a child. She looked in the dirty mirror. This coming of age realization was almost humorous in its delay. When she was growing up the first time, she felt like an adult at a much older age. It was so disorienting to keep track of herself. She wondered if she could really be an old woman who came through the portal. Would she continue to age to that point or would she stop at her prime like the others in this world?

Autumn shook her head to stop thinking about it. She left her old clothes there, since she didn't need them anymore, and returned to the bedroom.

The men were all laying around reclined and ready to go to sleep for the night. They looked up at Autumn when she came in.

Puck, Tanner, and Toble smiled like fathers or uncles looking at a little girl who was growing up. Sage just looked surprised.

"My dear, you are becoming quite a lovely young woman," said Puck.

"Thank you." Autumn smiled and sat down next to her bag. "So, what are we going to do about the ring?"

"If we can't open the panel tomorrow morning, then we will have no choice but try to conceal it the way it was before and hope that Turmeric won't discover it," said Puck.

Autumn got up and walked over to the square on the wall.

"Don't worry about it tonight," said Tanner. "We need to get rest so we can rise early."

Autumn ignored him. Something was drawing her again. She looked at the image of the Gryphon. He was with her somehow. She could feel him like she did when she had touched Sage's wound. She reached out and touched the image. As she did the image glowed and so did the marks on her wrists. The metal door opened and revealed a small chamber. In it lay some treasures: a crown, some papers, and a ring. Everyone jumped up and crowded around Autumn looking over her shoulder. Autumn took out the papers. All of the papers were legal

127

documents, including a will. Autumn skimmed over them, but none of them said anything about Queen Anemone's last days. Autumn handed them to Puck and took the large ring out. It had an engraved seal on it with an image of the Gryphon in the center of it.

"Do we want to take anything else out?" asked Autumn.

"No," said Puck. "I think we should leave these papers too. I think everything will be safer here than on us."

"Who wants to carry the seal?" Autumn asked next.

"I think you should," said Sage. "You are the one who found it and was able to open the vault."

"Put it with your other things from the queen?" said Puck.

"So how did you know the spell?" asked Tanner.

"I didn't," said Autumn. "It was kind of like when Sage's leg was healed. I had an image of the Gryphon in my mind."

Puck nodded knowingly. "The Gryphon, yes. I need to teach you more about that when we have the time. I have really neglected your education."

"This Gryphon thing is kind of weird," said Sage as he put the papers into the vault for Puck and closed it.

"Why?" asked Tanner.

"Well, why is he using a girl who doesn't even know him? Why now? If he can break spells, then why doesn't he just save Gryphendale by himself?"

Puck looked at Sage intensely. "He is using you, too. Do you think any of us could have survived without him?"

"Then why did he make it so hard!" said Sage. "Why save one or two and let thousands of others die?"

Toble sighed and walked back to where he had been lying down earlier.

"We could debate that tonight or get some sleep. It's up to you. I'll be keeping watch tonight."

CHAPTER 14: CAPTURED

Autumn dreamed of a beautiful ballroom lit with golden chandeliers. Couriers and aristocrats were walking and dancing about in French silk ball gowns and Louis the XIV style suits. They wore plain white masks over their faces as they glided across the marble floor to soft chamber music. The scene was disturbed by a rumbling in the distance. There were angry voices just beyond the gilded white doors. The sounds of struggle and confusion were getting louder and closing in on the ball fast.

Autumn woke with a jump, hearing shouts in the next room.

"Puck, get the girl and run!" said Tanner.

Sage swung his short, curved sword as he skillfully fought back Ogres at the door. Autumn could only see their clubs and maces swinging at him from the half-shut door Sage was pushing against.

Puck had climbed up a chest of drawers that had been moved to try and keep the door closed and was hitting the Ogres over the head with his umbrella, which was giving them various magical deformities.

"Go back to the dark hole whence thou camest!"

Tanner was shooting arrows past both Sage and Puck with amazing accuracy.

"Puck, get the girl!" he shouted again.

Autumn looked around for a weapon that she could use and grabbed the leg of a broken table. She also noticed that there was no other way out.

"We're trapped!"

"Toble! Where are you?" Sage searched quickly with his eyes as he kicked a large Ogre back through the door. "We are going to have to fight our way through them!"

Sage grabbed a nearby chair and held it up like a shield with the legs facing in front of him. He then pushed forward into the Ogres while still fighting.

"Tally ho!" shouted Puck as he jumped down behind Sage.

Tanner and Autumn followed the slow progression into the next room.

"I'm coming!" came the muffled sound of Toble's voice.

Autumn paused to look around, but Tanner grabbed her arm and dragged her on. The group had taken off into a run while swinging and stabbing blindly. They made their way into the hall, pushing back the three Ogres who were left standing.

"Toble, where are you?" said Sage as they pushed their way to the stairs.

More Ogres were waiting for them near the stairs, and Sage's chair was almost completely broken apart. They were getting overwhelmed by Ogres

"I'm coming!" said the slightly nearer muffled voice of Toble.

From a nearby room, Autumn saw a mass of bed sheets and knotted curtains quickly moving her way.

"Move!" she shouted.

Sage, Puck, and Tanner immediately flattened themselves against the wall on either side of the hall. The moving mass plowed into the dumbfounded Ogres, knocking them all head over heels down the stairs.

Toble's shouts of unintelligible words could be heard from the sheets as they fell.

"Toble!" Sage dropped the chair as his eyes turned yellow. He rushed down the stairs with Tanner, Puck, and Autumn close behind.

Toble had managed to knock out the whole group of Ogres. There was probably eight of them. Sage began to dig through the pile of massive bodies piled at the bottom of the badly damaged staircase.

"He's over here!" said Tanner pointing to the other side of the heap.

Toble sat there, clear of the group and sheets, while grumbling over his broken glasses.

"Toble, you never cease to amaze me," said Sage as he helped the old man up. "Are you all right?"

"Did you hear my alarm?" Toble asked. "I was walking down the hall when I saw them coming and ducked out of the way to not be seen, but got tangled up in all that stuff. I tried to warn you though."

"I heard you," said Sage. "Everyone isn't used to your whistles, but we woke up in time. No more time for talking, we need to go!"

Sage led the way around halls, through the servant's area, and into the kitchen.

"I am hoping they won't be in this end of the palace," he said. "It's the closest part of the palace to the river. As soon as you get to the river, jump in. It's our only hope of getting away. Can you all swim?"

"I don't know if I can," said Autumn. "As far as I can remember, I can't."

"Drat," said Tanner.

"Maybe we can hide her in the bulrushes," said Toble.

The group ran out of the kitchen door into the gardens as they talked. Ogres appeared everywhere. Sage began fighting an Ogre who was head and shoulders taller than him and had a broadsword. Tanner immediately shot arrows into the oncoming mass. Toble did his best to punch the Ogre coming in front of him, but hit the one trying to grab him from behind. Puck continued to hit Ogres with his broken umbrella and to change their arms into rubber or stone.

Tanner had finished his last arrow when Autumn shouted, "Duck!"

As he obeyed, Autumn threw a rock up and hit it with her wooden table leg. It hit the Ogre in front of them.

"Home run!" said Autumn.

"What?" said Tanner as he picked up a dead Ogre's spear and began to use it.

"Grab the girl and run!" Sage told Puck. "We will stay and distract them."

Puck grabbed Autumn's arm and took off running through an opening in the fight. They ran down the hill and around the side of the palace.

"Tanner, you go too!"

Autumn heard Sage's words when she felt a blow to her head.

"Maldamien will be pleased," said a cold voice as Autumn blacked out.

Autumn woke up tied, gagged, and slung over the shoulder of a large smelly Ogre. She barely got a glimpse of Puck over the shoulder of a different Ogre.

"The ring is not here," said a deep voice.

"Then you didn't look hard enough!" said the icy voice.

"Could one of the others have taken it?"

"I feel it still here," said the icy voice.

"We have searched the whole palace."

"Search it again!"

"A...well, could you point out an area in which you feel it?"

"Stupid fool! No. Now search the palace again!"

Another voice began to talk.

"We were only able to take two of them. Do you want us to pursue the others?"

"Do you know where the others are?" said the icy voice.

"They jumped into the river."

"Take three soldiers and go after them! Doesn't anybody around here think?"

Autumn saw the Nomad with the icy voice walk by and talk to the Ogre carrying her.

"You two come with me. Captain, you stay with this unit until they find the ring. I don't care if you have to rip this building to shreds, just find it! You can join the rest of us at Rokurokubi when you're done. All right, let's go."

Autumn couldn't see what was going on. All she saw was the back of the palace where they had come from. The group of Ogres marched off, and the movement up and down made Autumn nauseated, to add to her splitting headache.

Autumn.

Autumn could hear Puck's thoughts in her mind. She realized he must have been able to twist his bound hands to touch his wrist. Autumn tried to do the same thing.

Yeah, I think I got it, she communicated to Puck.

Good. Are you all right? I haven't been able to see you since I regained consciousness.

Autumn touched her wrist again.

I'm fine. Just a headache. How about you?

Autumn looked around for Puck and then received a picture of his point of view which looked similar to her view: huge grotesque Ogres everywhere.

The group of Ogres carrying her joined up with more Ogres. Every time she would try to count them the lumpy Ogre holding her would move. Once they started traveling, she saw the same five Ogres the whole time but could hear the rest marching in front.

The lines of soldiers jogged in unison the rest of the day along a dusty road and camped late that night, straddling the main road north of the river. Autumn's Ogre dumped her like a sack of potatoes next to Puck. A series of campfires were made to accommodate everyone and tents were erected all around them in an orderly circle.

The Nomad Autumn had seen earlier walked by them with three Ogres following him. They then stopped where Puck and Autumn sat. The Nomad stared at them with dark black eyes.

"Have you fed them?" He asked the three Ogres with him.

"No, Lord Turmeric," said the tall reptile one with spikes down his back. "Why?"

"We need to keep them alive," said Turmeric. "Milkweed, you are in charge of feeding them once a day when we make camp. Oh, and give them water, too."

The smallest of the three began to growl under his breath and left to do as he was told. The other two started to chuckle.

Turmeric's eyes turned red.

"Mudroot, Cowtail, do you want to help?"

His tone of voice jolted them instantly to seriousness.

Autumn's eyes were wide as she noticed Turmeric's gray fox-like tail peeking from under his black cloak. He was a Huldra! Autumn was not able to contemplate that for long before Milkweed returned.

The short Ogre was still as tall as Turmeric. He was also wide and warty over his grayish skin. His long lower canine teeth stuck up out of his mouth like tusks. He came with a bowl of some sort of gruel and a leather canteen. He set the bowl and canteen down as he propped Puck and Autumn up back to back. Then took out their gags. He poured water down their mouths, face, and whatever the water landed on. He then shoved a spoon full of food down each of their throats alternatively until the bowl was empty. Finally, he doused them with water again.

As he closed the canteen, Autumn said, "Thank you."

She didn't know why she said it, but Milkweed was startled as much as if she had punched him. Without saying anything, he left.

You did well, communicated Puck into Autumn's mind. *I have been very negligent in teaching you the way of the Gryphon, but you have good instincts.*

Are you going to teach me lessons now?

Then again, what else were they going to do?

I don't know what is going to happen to us and you are not equipped for it. I taught you how to survive physically in this world, but

133

now you need to learn how to survive internally too, replied Puck.

An Ogre walked by with a cauldron of water and glared at them as he passed. Puck shifted to get in a more comfortable position for touching his wrist.

What about escaping? asked Autumn.

Turmeric has a magical shield around us so that I can't use my magic. We would need to not only break these bonds, but also the spell around us. Then the odds of us making it very far in a camp full of soldiers is very low. I will keep thinking of ideas, but right now, I am afraid we can't do much about our situation.

Puck lowered his head like he was falling asleep.

The Way of the Gryphon may provide a way of escape, but more importantly, it will help you to protect your mind. The Order of the Gryphon was once a large, public organization of followers of the Way, but it became less important and less popular as the world became more prosperous and as the people felt confident that they could do anything. The stories and teachings were lost and what few books I knew existed were burned by Maldamien. Most who do believe now believe it like a superstition or as folktales, but even those are few. I know of a handful of people who know the truth. I will teach you everything I can, said Puck.

Turmeric walked out of his tent and came up to them. He crouched down in front of Autumn, staring at her with purpose. Her heart raced. Could he hear their thoughts? He held Autumn's face by her chin and studied it with cold blue eyes that gave her creeping goosebumps.

"A human woman, obviously not from the Nomad tribes, wearing Huldra clothing. You must be the one who came through the portal. You're obviously not the queen, so why are you here?"

Autumn's face grew as cold as his, but her heart jumped into her throat.

"So, you don't want to talk to me. That's fine. Maldamien will enjoy talking to you. Perhaps he will let me keep you as a pet when he is done. You would do well in my collection."

Turmeric studied her face for a response or a reaction, but she gave him none. When he let go of her face, he smiled and walked away.

Autumn sighed, lowered her head, and closed her eyes. She was a prisoner and vulnerable to any evil desire this man had. It hadn't hit her before how much danger and pain would be possible. Would torture, starvation, violence, or death be in her future? She felt the weight of it fall over her. She felt exposed and weak. That was what Turmeric was doing. He was trying to make her afraid. The problem was that it was working, and she didn't know how to stop it. As far as she remembered, she had never been in so much danger. The fear of the unknown future ran hot and cold up and down her spine.

She could feel Puck taking a series of slow deep breaths, then finally she heard him in her mind again.

I had to calm my anger before communicating with you again. These marks were used by slave holders to telepathically punish slaves, keep track of them, and order them around. If I touch the marks still angry, I could hurt you very badly, said Puck. *The purpose of what I will try to teach you will prepare you for fear tactics like this and worse. If we are going to be traveling to Rokurokubi to see Maldamien, we will have two weeks at least.*

Puck shifted to try and make his hands more comfortable, but the chains wouldn't give. Autumn watched as a fight broke out between two Ogres, both of whom were over seven feet tall. It only lasted through a couple of punches, but a full-grown tree was knocked over and crushed by the weight and force of one of them.

The Way of the Gryphon is about functioning the way the world was intended to function from the very beginning, said Puck ignoring the skirmish. *In the story I told you about the beginning, the Creator wanted everyone to be in a harmonious relationship with him and each other. This means knowing the purpose, primary function, and source of everything you encounter. No one knows this about everything, but the more you know, the better.*

Puck shifted again, and Autumn could tell that his wrists were hurting him. She looked around to see who was watching them. The massive Ogres were beginning to leave the fires to retire to their tents for the night. A brownish pig-faced Ogre was leaning against a tree watching them intensely. Autumn speculated that he was the one assigned to guard them.

They don't seem too worried about guarding us, communicated Autumn.

Why should they be? With chains and spells, I am not very hopeful of escaping, said Puck.

So, is there a purpose or function in this? asked Autumn.

Yes. This is a great example and one of the hardest ones to master, thought Puck into her mind. *Let me start with something simpler, and then I will build to our current situation. A leaf is a very simple organic object whose purpose is multiple. First, it must grow. Secondly, it must help the plant grow. Then it may be used for shade, shelter, nests, food, dyes, or medication. When it finally dies, it fertilizes the ground. No part of the leaf's existence is wasted. Every part of its life can be used for good and show off the work of its Creator. This is its primary function. The enhancement of this function is part of the Brownie's magic. They tap into the source of the leaf's function and can encourage it to do more than it would do on its own. The source of this leaf is the plant. The plant's source is the seed. The seed grows because of the Creator. All that is good can derive its source from the Creator. If you are connected to the Creator, then nothing is withheld from you. Even so, you cannot, through the Creator, do anything against the function and purpose of that which he has created. Only dark magic twists and forces things to submit to its will with no regard to its purpose or the will of the Creator. This is enticing to some because they think they can do anything they want, but it destroys things, minimizes the magic potential of the object, and eventually destroys themselves.*

So how does that have anything to do with what we are going through now? asked Autumn.

The tents surrounding them and the monsters who laid inside of them felt impossible to overcome. Sage had been able to fight these creatures, but he didn't use magic. He was just fast and skillful with a sword. Autumn was certain that very few could survive long in a fight with just one of these beasts.

Our present circumstance has many facets, thought Puck. *Each person here was created and given a purpose, but none are working according to that purpose. So inwardly they are weakened from their intended potential. We are hopefully working in our purpose. The more we do so, the stronger we become. This means that no matter what happens to us, it must bring an ultimate good. Once we step out of our purpose, we can't be certain of that.*

How can we be certain that we are working according to our purpose? What does it matter if they are weaker on the inside when they have the weapons and spells over us? Does 'ultimate good' mean we will eventually escape or that we won't get hurt? This is not making

136

a lot of sense to me right now, said Autumn.

She couldn't imagine herself doing much good in opposing Turmeric or the Ogres no matter how much potential she had.

There are two ways to know if you are doing your purpose. The first is to learn as much about the Creator, his creation, and act in accordance to that. The second and even better way is to communicate with him yourself and ask him.

"What?"

Autumn's face went pale when she realized she vocalized that. Puck jumped a little as well. Luckily, the Ogre guarding them was laughing at the joke a passing Ogre just told him. She sighed in relief.

How does one do that? she communicated.

He created you. Mentally, whether or not you know it, you are connected to him. Even without marks, you can communicate with him just as you do with me. When you are in trouble and don't know what to do, bring up an image of him or call to him for help.

Okay, what about my other questions?

I can't tell you specifically what will happen next, but internal strength will keep you from crumbling when everything seems too hard to bear. It will help you to be true to yourself, your convictions, and your loyalties. It may not help you in hand to hand combat, but some things are more dangerous than a flesh wound.

That's a lot to think about, communicated Autumn. *I need to think about that some.*

All right, I will continue tomorrow. We will need to make good use of our time. "Are you comfortable?" asked Puck.

"What?" said Autumn.

We have to talk some, or it will get suspicious that we don't talk at all. "I was just asking if you were comfortable enough to sleep?" asked Puck as he shifted so they might be able to sleep better if they did sleep.

Autumn spent much of the night wondering if they would escape, if Sage would try to rescue them, and pondering Puck's words about the Way of the Gryphon and internal strength.

She looked around at the tents and wondered what her purpose was. She thought about how things might have been before Maldamien came to power. What were these Ogres like then? Autumn imagined Milkweed as a carpenter or blacksmith. It wasn't all that hard. His eyes were not cold and heartless. The terrible monsters around her transformed in her mind into enslaved individuals trying to survive. She looked around at the few Ogres still wandering around, and saw various degrees of coldness. When she spotted Turmeric's tent, she wondered about him. He wasn't trying to survive. He was just evil and twisted. He was the slave master who enjoyed pain and suffering. She had seen it in his eyes.

Creator, she thought, *I don't know what I believe about all of this, but if you are there, don't leave me helpless.*

Autumn looked up at the full moon peeking through the clouds. She saw the shadow of a gryphon pass before it. She gasped. Did he hear her? She watched intensely to see if he would pass by again, but she fell asleep.

CHAPTER 15: LESSONS

The next few days fell into a routine of traveling with periodic breaks for meals, then camp at the same time every day. Milkweed continued to feed them at the same time each evening and Autumn would thank him. For some reason, his negative response to her words made her determined to continue.

Puck continued his mental conversation and lessons throughout the day. He explained the divine purpose of many objects and various situations, then taught Autumn how to meditate on this until she could feel it inside of her. Autumn began to understand the patterns in the world and a sense of a cosmic plan and order.

This is good, communicated Puck as the Ogres marched past another abandoned village. *If we were not always under a magic shield, you would be able to use the potential of these things with your own gifts to create magic. For now, though, it is more important to learn to protect yourself. You must now learn to meditate on your own divine purpose.*

Being carried like a sack of wheat does not lend itself to feeling like I have a purpose. Autumn did not mean to touch her wrist when she thought that, but it had become a habit.

That's true, said Puck. *In fact, this activity is practically impossible until you do a few things. The first is you must now determine and acknowledge the Creator is real and that the Gryphon is he. Do you believe this?*

Autumn did not respond right away. She had seen the Gryphon numerous times, but this did not necessarily mean he was some kind of god or creator. He could be just some animal that had been mythologized.

The Ogre carrying Autumn jolted to a stop. Autumn smirked to herself. She had never thought Ogres were real either, but she couldn't deny she was being painfully carried by one. She also couldn't deny the various times strange things had happened when the Gryphon was around, or an image of him appeared in her mind.

Yeah, I think so, communicated Autumn.

Will you commit yourself to serve him?

The Ogre jostled Autumn on his shoulder as he continued walking. She grimaced. That hurt.

What do you mean serve him? she asked.

One can access the potential in other things and twist it for evil purposes without submitting themselves to the Gryphon's will and purpose, but no one can access their own potential without first submitting to that purpose themselves. In other words, a hammer cannot discover that it was created to drive in nails until it submits to the process of driving in nails.

Autumn was quiet for awhile. To her, it sounded like losing her freedoms, her choices, and being bound like she was in the chains.

So, what happens when someone submits to the Gryphon? asked Autumn. *Would I then have no say in what I do or where I go? Would I become a robot?*

Puck was slow to respond. *I don't recall what a robot is, but no one ever loses free will when that is what they were created to have. I think it would be more like a soldier submitting to a general. One always has a choice to leave but instead chooses to follow orders.*

I can do that, replied Autumn.

I have to warn you, once you start this process, it is all-encompassing. Everything was created by him, and he has a plan for everything. Nothing can be withheld without destroying yourself. I did not instruct you earlier in this because this choice will become a way of life. Are you sure you are ready?

Autumn looked at the feet of the Ogre soldiers. The place she was being taken could be her last, but there was no way to know the future or the 'cosmic plan.' If the Gryphon created everything, he could get her out of this mess. If not, then what did she lose? She had made her choice.

I will serve the Gryphon.

At that moment Autumn felt warmth through her body. She felt an awakening of her senses and a feeling that the Gryphon was near.

The Ogres stopped and tossed Autumn and Puck down so they could make camp. Autumn could see Puck's face for the first time in days.

"You look awful," said Autumn.

He looked thin and gaunt.

"You look older." Puck smiled weakly. "I am proud of you. I can see a change in your eyes. You have been really learning magic well."

Milkweed came over and set them up back to back like usual.

"No grub tonight. Turmeric's orders 'cause rations are low."

He then gave them both water. Autumn thanked him.

"You won't be thankin' me tomorrow," he said and left.

"What did he mean by that?" asked Autumn.

"When Ogres need rations, they raid a village. We will probably have front row seats," said Puck.

Autumn frowned. Just when she was hoping the Gryphon would free her, she would have to watch others suffer.

Now, Autumn, Puck spoke into her mind, *you need to start concentrating on all you know of the Gryphon. It is going to be more difficult as you begin to encounter all the evil in the world.*

Autumn frowned. She thought she was getting a pretty good glimpse of the evil in the world, but it sounded like Puck was preparing her for much worse. A raid would just be a bunch of bullies stealing food, right? She shivered at what might happen.

Puck continued, *You must be certain beyond any doubt that the Creator is good and just. This is a foundation. You must focus on the fact that he has a plan. Just because people suffer does not mean he isn't here or that he doesn't care. Just like I am certain that Sage, Toble, and Tanner have been tracking us, but it has not been the right time to act, so it is with the Gryphon. If you start to feel afraid, lost, or alone, focus on this. It will be fine to doubt or ask why he lets evil things happen but always ask him. If you can't do anything else at all, say, "by the power of the Gryphon." Do you understand?*

Yes.

She felt even more anxious and swallowed a lump in her throat.

We should both spend as much time meditating on these things as possible, Puck communicated.

All right.

They shifted as though they were going to go to sleep and closed their eyes. Autumn focused on the images she had seen of the Gryphon and the things she knew about him. As she did, she felt like she was reaching out to him with her spirit. New things about him seemed to grow inside of her. She seemed to be able to see kindness in his eyes. Just like when she focused on different objects' potential, she searched his potential and found that it was constantly expanding. She gasped at the well of magic and power within him. The revelation hit her so hard that it jolted her. She opened her eyes and began to gasp for air.

You did well, communicated Puck. *Take it slower next time and don't try to use him as a tool. Try instead to open yourself up to be used by him.*

Can a person be used by another person?

Yes, but that often turns to evil. When you want to access the gift of another person, it is better to open yourself up and pour yourself into them. This is more difficult than using them because you have the potential to get hurt or injured, but the benefits are a hundredfold. Using someone will burn them out or destroy them, so it only has limited potential. While pouring into someone has less control and more vulnerability, it also has unlimited potential and exponential power. You can only excel in this by doing this same process often with the Gryphon. This way you are strengthened to channel this power, or it can also destroy you.

There is a lot of risks in this, isn't there? Autumn sighed.

She was already tired. At the same time, a part of her wanted to meditate on the Gryphon again. *It's kind of addicting too.*

It can be. You continue your meditations if you like, but I must rest. Even though there is a magic shield around us, we both are strengthening our abilities, and I haven't done this for much too long. I am very tired.

Autumn stayed awake as late as she could work on the things that Puck had taught her. She felt parts of her that she never knew existed waking up inside her. She was meditating on the Gryphon so much that she could almost hear his thoughts and voice. Instead of feeling like she was intruding, he seemed to help her in. She felt strength and power being poured into her. She did not realize that she had switched from meditation to sleep until she was jostled awake the next morning.

Puck and Autumn did not communicate much because the day was hectic. The Ogres woke earlier than normal while it was still dark and practically sprinted for about an hour. The tumultuous trip caused Autumn's whole body to ache. Then she and Puck were dumped by a tree near the edge of a Brownie village while Turmeric sat by and watched the Ogres proceed into the village itself.

The Brownie people were the smallest of the peoples on Gryphendale, and the tallest of them would have come only to Autumn's knee. The village was very spread out for a people so small, but vegetable gardens and barns surrounded each of the houses. Autumn had never seen one of the hairy Brownies before, but they had floppy ears like Toble and were covered in fur of various colors. They were a simple people dressed in simple trousers and tunics. They were all evacuated to the northeast woods by the time the Ogres had gotten to their village. They didn't even try to fight. The Ogres, instead of just taking what they needed, broke anything they saw and burned what they didn't take. They grabbed a few slower Brownies and threw them to each other like a game until the Brownies died. It reminded Autumn of the way a cat plays with its food. After less than an hour, the Ogres filled a dozen sacks full of food and the village was completely destroyed.

Autumn was nauseated by the few who had died but felt relief that she wasn't a witness to a massacre. She was only half right though. They stopped at two more villages, and those two were horrific. Men, women, and children were crushed, killed, or burned just for being there. The houses were crushed and burned. Everything was crushed and burned. Few escaped. They had somehow not seen the Ogres coming from the first village. The Ogres seemed to transform into savage beasts as they laughed and played with their prey. Autumn was sobbing by the time they resumed their journey to Rokurokubi. The only thing she could think about the rest of the day was the destroyed lives, just for a few meals. Why did the Brownies rebuild when this has been going on for a century? Why did anyone create a home in this world where it could be ripped away at any moment? Why did the Gryphon let this happen? Why didn't anyone try to fight or stop it? The thoughts repeated itself over and over again in her mind.

When the Ogres stopped for the night, Puck began communicating with her.

Autumn, we may be separated in the future. Whenever you get free, and I believe you will someday, find Thyme in the land of the Hiru. Stay there until any of us can join up with you. We only have less than a few months before all that Apollo says happens, but that is the safest place for you right now. You can also learn more with Thyme than I could ever teach you. He is an expert in the way of the Gryphon.

Autumn felt frightened. She always assumed Puck would be with her.

What are you saying? she asked. *You're not giving up, are you?*

No, Puck assured her. *The raids on the villages made me aware of how unpredictable our futures are. I'm not afraid, nor should you worry. I won't leave you unless it's absolutely necessary for your preservation. I have lived nearly three hundred years, and I look forward to the day I can finally rest with my ancestors, but I will not purposely bring my demise. As long as I have breath, I will fight to live every day well.*

Autumn felt his resolve. *I hope I can say the same thing one day, but I feel afraid of death and the future.*

That's natural because you are young, said Puck, *but one day you will choose within yourself whether to let life happen to you or whether to fight for the impossible even if it costs your life.*

Autumn thought about his words. *Puck, you have a lot of faith in me. You seem to think I will always make the right choices even though we both don't know who I was or what I may have done. You have even trusted me with information about the underground and many other things that can hurt a lot of people.*

Autumn, you know I can do a great deal of magic. Have you not felt me pour into you and access your potential? I have not done anything spectacular, but I have seen your gift and your motives. Whatever you were in the past does not matter, but who you are today and right now. I am very proud of you for the choices you have made already, and I know you will do great things in the future.

Autumn looked around the grotesque Ogre camp. It was hard to see the future with the shadows of the raid still haunting her mind. She closed her eyes. She would meditate on the Gryphon and not let Puck down. There was still so much she didn't understand.

CHAPTER 16: TORTURE

The red sandstone fortress, Odemience, in the mountainous land of Rokurokubi, was large and imposing in the mid-day sun as Puck and Autumn were made to march towards it.

Autumn looked around. They had made no attempts to escape. There hadn't been an opportunity, and no attempt had been made by her friends. With every step towards the huge fortress, all hope of escape was fading away. Just fear and dread filled her mind at what would happen to them.

They were brought around the side of the fortress' outer wall to a small door. The Ogre leading them had to crouch down to enter. They then were led around and down many damp, dark passages deep underground. They tried to remember how they came in, but directions soon had no meaning to them after the many turns in the labyrinth of tunnels. They were led into an over-crowded prison the size of a small city. As far as they could see down the halls that branched out from the central area they were standing in were filled with cells. Every barred cell was packed with prisoners.

Autumn was able to observe her surroundings as the tall Ogre who was in charge of her and Puck was discussing his orders with the group of Ogres sitting around a large wooden table eating some sort of gruel and drinking mugs of tonic. The whole prison was carved out of solid rock and iron doors secured every cell. Some cells looked as though there was only standing room in them. It was loud, as prisoners were either shouting at the Ogres or weeping at their own sad fate. The whole place received little light from the low burning torches on the center pillars of the halls just out of reach of any of the prisoners. On the walls of the central area she was standing in hung chains and grotesque tools made of iron. The prison had no windows and seemed inescapable.

After a short time, an Ogre at the table got up and led them to a nearby cell. The Ogre guard unlocked the door to the crowded chamber and held it open, indicating for them to go in. Puck and Autumn began to walk in, but the tall Ogre stopped Autumn.

"Not you. You'll get to go see Lord Maldamien."

Puck's eyes grew wide as he turned around.

"NO!"

Autumn tried to pull away from the Ogre, but it made little difference. Puck was shoved into the cell and Autumn was dragged away.

"NO!" she screamed.

Sobs enveloped her. She felt like all the wind was knocked out of her. Her resolve and training melted away as she felt fear take over. She had never thought she would face Maldamien himself, not alone, not this quickly.

Autumn was half dragged up the halls and corridors to a higher place in the citadel. The lack of outside light still made her feel like she was underground, but she had long ago lost any sense of direction.

They reached a hall filled with massive wooden doors. The Ogre stopped at one on his right. The tall Ogre took a few deep breaths before knocking on the door lightly. At hearing a muffled response, he slowly opened the door, still holding onto Autumn in the hall with his right hand.

"Lord Maldamien, the girl's here," the Ogre said humbly.

"Let her in and go away," said a firm masculine voice. It was not icy like Turmeric's, but deeper and reptilian.

The Ogre pushed Autumn in and shut the door as fast as he could. When she regained her balance, she looked around at the room. It was a small library and laboratory. A large table filled the center of the room, with glass vials, tubing, a small fire, beakers, chemicals, and various disturbing substances covering its surface. The walls lining the room were filled from floor to ceiling with old worn out books. In various places were books that were laying open. The room smelled like an awful medicine Autumn had to take once as a child.

A man in the far corner holding a book turned to the table to mix two of the chemicals. Autumn assumed that he must be Maldamien since no other person was in the room, but she was very surprised by his appearance.

She expected to find a gross old monster or hideous villain in a throne room. Instead, he was a tall young man who stood confident and regal in his luxurious Nomadic-styled robes. His jet-black shoulder-length hair was well cared for and tied in a stylish ponytail. His well-trimmed goatee accented his angular masculine face and very light skin handsomely. He would have been the most handsome man the girl had ever seen except that his deep dark eyes were profoundly disturbing. The most unnerving thing about his appearance was that he appeared completely human.

Autumn stood nervously by the door as he worked, waiting for him to look at her or say something. After a while, she began to relax and wonder why she was there. She took a step forward to get into a more comfortable position. Suddenly, something cold swept over her, and she couldn't do more than blink and breathe.

"I didn't say you could move," said Maldamien casually as he continued to work at grinding up a blue powder in his black mortar and pestle.

Autumn tried to reply, but she couldn't speak either. Maldamien continued working for another twenty minutes. Autumn's body began to ache from standing still for so long. She started wondering if he was going to make her a permanent statue.

Maldamien combined all the various ingredients that he was working with into one vial, which turned into a silver liquid. With tweezers, he dropped a small sprig of rosemary into the silver liquid. Autumn remembered Puck telling her how rosemary was extremely poisonous and wondered what purpose this liquid would serve. As the sprig began to dissolve, the concoction bubbled up and exploded. The flying liquid burned Maldamien's face and hand.

He shouted curses as the wounds began to heal themselves.

"Clean it up!" he commanded Autumn.

Autumn was released from her frozen state, and the chains fell off her wrists. She fell down to her knees. Her arms ached horribly as blood rushed into them. Autumn gasped at the painful return of feeling in her limbs.

Maldamien pointed at her and pierced her with an electric charge as he walked around the table towards her.

"Pick it up with your hands, now!"

Autumn clumsily got to her feet and went to where the spill was, then picked up the broken pieces of glass, placing them in the edge of her tunic. Each piece burned her hands. She let the tears from the pain

GRYPHENDALE

freely fall. When she had all the glass she could find, she sat still and looked at Maldamien.

He was busy creating another vial of silver liquid and absently pointed to a bucket in the corner. Autumn emptied the glass into the bucket, turned, and waited for what would happen next. If he wanted a slave that was fine for now, but she hated him deeply already.

Maldamien handed her the vial with the silver liquid.

"Drink it."

She looked at the glass wondering what it would do to her, but soon felt her body involuntarily move to drink it. The magic he used was so strong that she felt sweat dampen her forehead. She gulped the whole amount of liquid down, then coughed and gagged at the putrid taste. She felt the liquid flow through her veins as Maldamien calmly picked up a dagger she had not seen from the table. He grabbed Autumn's right arm, took the empty vial from her hand, and put it on the table. He then cut open the sleeve of her tunic. She tried to pull away, but again she was frozen.

"I see that you are already a slave," Maldamien said. "Let us see who your master is."

Maldamien put the fingers of his left hand on the marks around her wrist and with his right hand sliced her arm with the dagger.

Autumn screamed out in pain, then the sound of Puck shouting out in pain reverberated through her. Maldamien bent down and licked her blood. The memory of Sage saying that he was a vampire sent chills down her spine.

"Ah!" He smirked. "Puck has a slave girl. How nice."

Maldamien licked his lips as if he was tasting something more, then spat.

"Unicorn has contaminated your blood. A potion no doubt to hide who you are. Even so, I can see you are from the human world and came through the portal. I can taste my curse still in your blood."

He let go of her, and she fell to the floor holding her arm.

"What do you want from me?"

"We are getting to that."

Maldamien calmly walked away from her while playing with his goatee in a pensive way.

He then turned to the table and grabbed a vial of red liquid. He magically brought Autumn up to her feet and to him. He grabbed her

148

hair, pulled her head back, and poured the red liquid down her throat. It burned on the way down. She tried to jerk her head away or scream, but again she couldn't move.

Maldamien then closed his eyes, and she could feel him mentally probing her mind, forcing himself into her memories, invading her deepest emotions and fears. The more he probed, the more it hurt. She wept as he exposed her most personal memories, looking for anything he could use. She began to remember more of her past. She tried to fight the memories. She didn't want them now that Maldamien was searching for them. Maldamien expertly moved through images of her childhood. She could see people. She saw pictures of her father, a college professor, sitting in his cramped office. She saw an image of her grandmother telling her of how her mother died when she was born. She saw her school, teachers, and friends. She remembered her grandmother's funeral during spring break in high school. She remembered old boyfriends, college, her first job.

Maldamien continued to manipulate Autumn's mind, trying to squeeze information from it. She finally remembered her father's car accident and death. The memory of that made Autumn scream in agony.

Stop! Please Stop! she begged mentally.

Her mind surged past some time and almost accidentally came upon images of Queen Mara, Ezekiel, Sage, Toble, and the underground. Maldamien seemed both triumphant, yet already familiar with the information.

"No!" she wailed.

She suddenly felt a force of strength well up inside her. The image of the blue Gryphon flashed into her mind.

Maldamien cried out and dropped Autumn to the floor with a thud.

"How dare you!"

He then grabbed her arm and dragged her to the door.

"Guards!"

Turmeric appeared with two Ogres in the doorway. Maldamien flung the girl at them, catching Turmeric by surprise. He caught Autumn awkwardly and handed her back to the Ogres.

"Teach her proper respect!"

Maldamien's face was red with fury.

Turmeric bowed, and the group quickly left Maldamien's presence. Autumn let herself stay limp. She had betrayed everyone. After all that training and meditating, she had let them all down.

The group traveled down and around a different way than the way they had come, but Autumn didn't care anymore. She had failed.

They brought her down into the tunnels of the prison but stopped in an empty passage in front of an iron door with a tiny opening. Turmeric opened the door, and the Ogres threw Autumn into the tiny cell. They then filed in after her. Without a pause, the Ogres began to beat her and claw at her. She screeched with both fear and pain. They seemed to transform into animals before her eyes, and she put her arms up to block their punches and kicks. She curled up into the smallest fetal position she could as one of the Ogres began to bite her leg.

"Enough!" said Turmeric through the noise and Autumn's screaming. "She needs to be alive for tomorrow's questioning."

The Ogres reluctantly stopped and filed back out the door with blood still on their mouth and clothes.

"Good night," said Turmeric as he slammed the door closed.

Autumn lay in the darkness and wept. She was in too much pain to even think. She just cried until she fell asleep.

She had no idea how long she slept, but in the midst of what she thought was the night, she heard Puck calling in her mind. She mentally jerked to push him away but then, as she realized who it was, she slowly and painfully moved to touch her own wrist. It was odd without the chains she had gotten used to, but now just pure pain replaced it.

I'm here, she conveyed.

Are you all right? What did they do to you? I feel that you are in a lot of pain. His thoughts sounded urgent.

I failed you, she answered. *Maldamien pried my mind, and I remembered the Gryphon too late.*

Are you injured? Is that all? You seem weak.

The Ogres beat me, but it doesn't matter anymore.

Nonsense! communicated Puck. *No one was expecting you to be perfect and no one even dreamed you would have to go through what you did. Anyway, the people in the underground are already scattered, and the inn does not exist anymore. This is not the end. We must not give up. The underground has survived a hundred years of betrayal and failures, but do not give in. Turn to the Gryphon for strength. He doesn't impose himself; you do have to ask for his help. Were you able to remember anything about the queen? Did he restore your memories?*

Autumn tried to push past the pain and tiredness she felt to think about the liquids that he gave her. The red liquid did open up her mind, and she remembered many things, even her father. She began to tear up.

I still cannot remember the queen, but I can finally remember people in my past, including my father.

Her insides ached at the memory of her father's death.

Is this the first time you have remembered your father? Puck asked.

Yes, he was a university professor my whole life. My mother died when I was born, and he raised me. He wasn't very talkative, but he was always there to listen and help when I needed it. He died six months before I came to Gryphendale. I can remember everything up to his funeral and then it goes blank.

Autumn felt the heartache of losing him all over again, but it was a comfort to remember him. It was a healing feeling.

The loss of my father must be why I did not want to go home. I have no other family, and I wasn't very good at keeping close friends.

Sometimes, we need a chance to start over and try again, said Puck. *Through all of this, try to hold onto the good memories and use them to guard against all this life throws at you. I'm going to let you rest now. I had told you to control your emotions before contacting me once, but ignore that now. I will be here for you no matter what.*

Thank you.

Autumn actually felt physically a little better. She wondered if Puck was healing her or if it was herself or even the Gryphon. Something in her said it was all three. She checked over herself and felt a cracked rib, perhaps a dislocated shoulder, and plenty of cuts and bruises. She also could feel the raw areas the Ogres bit. She laid back and focused on the events with Maldamien. It was the image of the Gryphon that stopped him and made him angry. She decided to focus on the Gryphon from now on as much as possible. As she did, she felt peace and comfort pour through her as she sank back to sleep.

It seemed like moments later her cell was being opened, and Ogres were dragging her out again. The pain all over her body was still there, but she felt an inner strength this time. The events followed the same pattern as yesterday with an eerie sameness. The Ogre pushed her into Maldamien's laboratory, and he made the same potion, but this time dropped it on purpose. She was ordered to pick it up even though it burned her, then she was made to drink the silvery liquid, and

Maldamien tasted her blood. This time he made no comments about it. Finally, he made her drink the burning red liquid.

Tell me where the queen is, he spoke into her mind.

Again, her mind felt open. She thought about the power of the Gryphon. Maldamien clenched his teeth.

What do you remember? he commanded into her mind.

"Nothing!"

She cried out as he began to squeeze her arm that he had recently cut and still held the scabbing cut from yesterday. She again thought of the Gryphon

"I know you have been with Puck and the underground. Puck will die tomorrow morning, but you don't have to."

Maldamien's piercing eyes were looking intensely at her, and she was trapped in them as soon as she looked at him. She felt his mind probing hers, and the knowledge of his massive power exploded inside of her. She then realized that it could not compare to the power of the Gryphon.

"You're human. You should not have alliances with mere fairies; they are beneath you. You didn't even know they existed until you came here. I am trying to open the portals, that's a good thing. I am trying to unite the world like in the beginning, that's also a good thing. These mere fairies have lied to you about me."

Autumn was momentarily taken back by his words. What was he trying to accomplish? Why was he so desperate to find out about the queen?

Yes, he whispered in her mind. *We humans should stick together. You will have free access to your home.*

"I don't want to go home!" she shouted and tried to push him away physically, but he froze her again.

His mental probing increased to the point of hurting, and she cried out. He pushed even harder, trying to break down the barriers she had created. She almost sank into unconsciousness as he hammered at her mind.

"No!" she shouted and jerked her face away.

"Yes!" He grabbed her head by her hair and turned it towards him. She lost the sense of the room and felt numb all over. She could start seeing his desire for power, his burning anger, and hatred, even his bitterness towards his past. Finally, she saw his ultimate goal: to be a god!

"By the power of the Gryphon!" Autumn shouted.

Maldamien cried out and slammed her into the ground. This time he had broken a sweat trying to pierce her mind, but failed as the image of the Gryphon remained firm in place at the front of her thoughts.

"Guards!" Maldamien shouted as he stood up.

Turmeric and the Ogres returned.

"Beat her to one inch of her life and bring her back here," commanded Maldamien with his back towards them and looking down at a book on the work table.

Autumn quickly touched her wrist, *Puck, it's getting worse.*

As the Ogres grabbed her to drag her out, Puck answered. *Keep fighting, and I will try to help.*

Autumn felt some healing warmth throughout her body and knew what she must do.

CHAPTER 17: RESCUE

Sage looked at the fortress from his perch in the mountains. He was here again and no closer to finding a way in than he was months ago. He turned around and sat with his head in his hands. He felt like shouting or punching something because of the frustration inside.

Toble and Tanner were sitting around a small campfire watching him. They were being careful around him. Sage had grown short-tempered and moody, and he knew it. He had a picture of the wide-eyed little girl who healed his leg burned into his memory. Autumn didn't belong there. She was pure-hearted as anyone he had ever met. Puck too was a hero and close friend, but at least he was well aware of the cost.

Sage thought back to almost three weeks ago when they were all trying to escape from Vervain. Sage had assumed that Puck, Autumn, and Tanner had escaped and were safe before he and Toble darted to the river and dove in. They had let the current carry them a short distance away and hid in the rushes until everything was clear. Sage would have never known what happened to Puck and Autumn had Tanner not tracked them down. Tanner was the best tracker Sage had ever met, and he was able to find Sage and Toble within hours of Puck and Autumn's capture when the Ogres couldn't. Together, Sage, Toble, and Tanner followed the Ogre unit that had Puck and Autumn. Unfortunately, they had to circle around the palace and the Ogres there before trying to keep up with the pace of the Ogres unit on foot. It took them days to catch up. The Ogres traveled through three kingdoms and there was never the slightest opportunity for a rescue. If they had acted at the wrong time, Turmeric would have killed them rather than lose them. Sage had seen it done before and was certain that was what happened to King Coriander. They had no choice but to watch Puck and Autumn be led into the fortress two days ago.

"Sage, come and eat," said Toble.

"I can't eat," said Sage. "I have to think. There must be a way.

There must be!"

"You will think better on a full stomach," said Tanner. "You haven't eaten in days."

"I said I wasn't hungry!" snapped Sage.

Tanner stood up. "That's enough!"

Sage was startled at Tanner's outburst, but Tanner continued.

"Sage, the world does not revolve around you. Don't act like we don't care either. You have been acting ridiculous for days. Toble and I did not come to watch you save the day, so stop isolating yourself and let us do some real planning."

Sage felt anger building up toward Tanner. It wasn't like anyone had suggested anything useful. He was the only one concerned when they seemed laid back and passive. Sage pushed down the anger to go, sit by the fire, and brood. Tanner was right about one thing. He was isolating himself and trying to do things alone. It was unusual since he always consulted Toble on his plans. This time it was different; he had no ideas to consult about.

"All right," he said, "what ideas do you have?"

Tanner sat down, picking his plate up, and playing with his food. "I wasn't able to come up with one that would work. I was hoping we could talk about our options and come up with something together."

Sage turned to Toble. "How about you? Any ideas or inventions?"

"I was thinking about creating a machine that could throw someone over the wall, but I am afraid that they may be so injured when they landed that they couldn't do anything useful."

"Plus, we would have to get past the invisible shield," said Sage.

"Is the shield mechanical or magical in origin?" asked Tanner.

"It's magical," said Sage. "Toble and I have scouted this area for months trying to get in, but every way is blocked."

"That makes sense since he built this fortress for the purpose of going to war against Queen Anemone. I have even heard that he placed the fortress over a natural spring so the water could not be contaminated," said Tanner.

"It is an ideal structure," said Toble. "I could not have designed one better. It is surrounded by mountains on two-thirds of its circumference. The rest is surrounded by thick high walls, well guarded by Ogres, and structured to protect the Ogres as they guard it. It has well-placed turrets and layers of defenses. Just in case that isn't enough, it is

155

fortified by the Ogre magic through their stonework and other spells from Maldamien. The source of so much magic must be incredible."

"The fortress sits on some old mines," said Sage. "So the structures underground are as elaborate as it is above ground. The Ogre who I overheard talking about that said that he hadn't even seen the bottom of it and that it was like a city full of cells."

"Could anyone get in such a place?" said Tanner.

"I bet my father could have," said Sage. "I wonder what he would have done in our circumstance."

"I don't think General Goliad had a lot of missions with as small of a group as we have," said Tanner. He noticed Sage's frown. "Don't get me wrong. He was a great man and a great general, but no one is good at everything. I remember tracking for him on a hunting trip, and he told me how he hated small missions with just him and a few soldiers. It made him feel exposed and open to attack. He preferred the tactics of an army. He could see how they moved, where they should go, and how they worked as one unit. He was a genius, but not as good at making the most of the people in a small group as you. I wish he could have had the opportunity to attack this place back then with his army. It would have been spectacular, and we wouldn't be dealing with it right now. Since we are looking at this with a small group, I much prefer your style of combat."

"Yeah, barge in and try not to get killed," said Sage.

"No," replied Toble taking over where Tanner left off. "Planning with an army is like structuring chaos, but planning with a small group is an exercise in trust and teamwork. Your father commanded the respect and obedience of his troops. He could play a chess game on the field and win every time, but the rules of the game have changed. We don't have well-trained soldiers for someone to command. We don't have time for large strategies and orthodox tactics. You have to use what you have and make a decision on the run. You're good at that. You don't think in military categories, instead you look at the people you have, search for their skills, and make the most of it at a moment's notice."

Sage thought over Tanner and Toble's words. He was very different than his father. He always knew that, but he saw it as a huge flaw in his personality. He saw his father as an experienced hero who accomplished so much more than him. Sage was older than his father's forty-five years when he died. Could Sage's differences actually be a strength?

"Well, that still leaves us without a plan," said Sage.

The three men sat staring into the small fire, each trying to come up with something or anything. Tanner got up and began to clean up the dinner silently. They each went to do the last bit of chores before the sunset. They sat back around the fire as though they might settle down for the night, but none of them lay down to sleep.

"I guess it is impossible," said Sage, looking into the fire. "And she was our only connection to the queen."

"I was thinking," began Tanner cautiously, "perhaps it is a silly idea."

"It would be better than nothing," said Toble. "My ideas usually start somewhat strange and get better with tweaking."

"Well, when I was a small lad, my grandfather used to talk about the old magic. I believe Puck still believes in it."

Sage and Toble sat forward as he spoke. Fighting magic with magic was a good idea.

"So, what do we do?" asked Sage.

Tanner scratched his head under his pointed hat.

"I don't really remember very much about it, but it has to do with asking for the Creator's help. I think... well, I can mimic what he used to do if you like and we can see what happens."

Sage and Toble looked at each other. Sage had never been religious or magical. He didn't really believe in the Gryphon and had too many questions to follow him even if he was real. Then again, if he was real and had some hidden reason for everything, it would be stupid not to make some sort of peace with him. If there was a possibility that he could help, then what could it hurt to ask him? Sage had always worked in the here and now, but this was different. There were no other options.

"Let's try it," said Sage after musing it over.

The worse thing that could happen is that they look or feel stupid. Not much of a price considering life and death was at stake.

Tanner rose and turned to the east, then knelt, and raised both his arms up. Sage and Toble mimicked his movements. Tanner then sighed.

"I'm afraid I don't remember what he would say. It has been such a long time since I have seen anyone do this that I can't help wonder if this is what went wrong so that Maldamien could take over."

"Let me try," said Sage softly.

He wasn't sure what he would do, but he looked up into the sky and lifted his arms worshipfully. He thought about all the evil that had happened in the world in the last hundred years and felt angry and disappointment at this all-powerful being. At the same time, he felt desperate for something to change and would do anything to see it happen.

"Creator of the heavens and the two lands of earth and all that is in it, we come before you and humble ourselves. Majestic being who controls the destiny of men and faerie, hear our words... a... for salvation for your loyal followers who are in great danger. At least, I know Puck follows you. I may not have ever given you much of a chance at proving yourself. If you are real and everything Puck says about you is true, please forgive my disloyalty, pride, and rebellion. I have long ago realized I can't fix everything; I'm not a god. I can't save them in there. I am not certain that I am even capable of saving myself. I just seem to be lucky. Maybe that's you. I don't know. I don't really know much about this whole deal we are supposed to have with you, but I am asking you, on behalf of all those who can't, please do something. Please intervene. If you can, could you even bring peace to our land again?"

Sage bowed his head to the ground, and the others followed suit.

"So be it," said Toble and Tanner.

They stayed in that position waiting to see if something happened. Sage wondered if anyone was listening. He wished with all his heart that something magical would erupt. He had felt those words pour out of him as his heart raced. He had not intended to say those things.

Sage listened but heard nothing. He finally got up.

"I guess it didn't work." He went over to his bag and lay down. "I'm going to sleep."

Tanner took the first watch, and Toble rested in his tree form.

Sage fell asleep quickly. He dreamed of an open field. In the field, he saw a large tree, wilted and dying. He ran to a nearby stream, cupped some of the water with his hands, and took it to the tree to water it. He repeated this process six times before he realized he was scooping hardly any water. He found some people and convinced them to help him, but they also saw this was doing nothing to help the tree. Out of the distance, a blue gryphon flew down. He walked up to the tree and wounded it with his claw. Out of the wound sprung a root so large that

158

it ran to the river and brought all the water to the tree that it needed.

Sage woke, startled by the vividness of the dream. In the darkness above him, he saw the Gryphon sitting and waiting.

"Come," he said to Sage.

Sage got up quietly and woke Tanner and Toble. One of them had fallen asleep on watch, but Sage had no idea whose turn it was or what time it was. They all followed the Gryphon into the night. He expertly weaved through the boulders and down a path none of the friends had ever seen before. They continued to follow the Gryphon in the dim moonlight for an hour until they walked into a clearing directly behind the fortress on the other side of the wall and the magical shield.

"How is this possible?" Sage whispered in awe.

They had not even entered a cave or cavern and somehow had gotten past every security measure of the castle.

Tanner stated what they all observed. "There are no guards in this part of the fortress! They must not know of this path, either."

The Gryphon led them to a small doorway and opened it with his massive claw. He led them down a long straight passage to where the first floor of prisoners were located. For some reason, the Ogres were lying around drunk and asleep with tonic smell permeating the air.

At seeing the group, the prisoners began to shout and plead for their release. Tanner found the keys on one of the guards and went to the cell with Puck. Sage and Toble tried to hush and comfort them by telling them that they would also be released. The Gryphon just sat in the middle and watched. Tanner had to try a dozen keys before he found the right one to open the door. After opening it, he moved to the next cell.

"Tanner, Toble, Sage!" shouted Puck.

A female voice also called, "Sage!"

Sage looked in the direction of the voices, "Puck, Queen Shasta?"

The fair Sprite queen ran into Sage's arms, cutting off Puck's advancing extended hand. Sage pushed Shasta away and then bowed formally.

"I am so glad we found you. Your kingdom misses you, and we will help you return home if Your Majesty pleases."

The young woman looked elegant and angelic even with a good layer of dirt.

"I am glad you seem well and unharmed," said Sage, "but we need to free the others now."

159

"Oh, Sage!" Queen Shasta stomped her foot like a child and turned her back on him to cry. "I know."

Sage sighed. He knew Shasta well. She was emotional right now, but he knew she would eventually push past it to be a big help with the people. They would deal with their personal issues later.

"Where is Autumn?" Sage asked Puck, but Puck wasn't there.

Sage spotted him kneeling before the Gryphon and in deep conversation. It seemed like no one else could see the Gryphon at all as they walked past. Shasta turned back around with her eyes following Sage's stare.

"What is he doing?" she asked.

Sage shrugged. Puck then bowed and got up.

"Sage, this is taking too long!" shouted Toble, pointing to Tanner with the keys. He was only on his sixth door.

Sage walked up to the Gryphon and bowed.

"Sir... Your Majesty... a... Creator, is there anything that can be done about these prison doors?"

The Gryphon nodded, and every door in the entire prison flew open. People were crying and shouting for joy. The noise was overwhelming.

"Thanks!" Sage shouted over the noise and bowed.

He then jumped up onto the Ogre's table and held up his arms to quiet the people.

When it was finally somewhat quiet, Sage shouted, "Everyone needs to remain silent as we make our way out. Toble, with the Gryphon, will lead the first group, Tanner will lead the next as they filter up here, Queen Shasta will lead the one after, and Puck and I will follow with those who remain. We will make one giant line into the mountain; then everyone needs to scatter throughout the mountains and take different paths home. This will make it less likely for recapture. Hide often and stay in small groups for safety. No one push or panic as we get out of here. I don't want anyone stampeding or causing your neighbor to get hurt."

"We want to fight with you!" shouted a Brownie farmer. Others cheered.

"Those who want to fight will need to meet me in the Sprite capital in two months. Contact the underground in your areas. Will that be all right with you?" Sage asked Queen Shasta remembering how much trouble this was going to cause her.

Queen Shasta's eyes were large and round.

"Yes," she said breathlessly.

"Now, Toble, take this group to freedom!"

Sage jumped down from the table as people began to push forward around him. Toble made his way to the Gryphon, and the Gryphon led him through the way they had come. As people passed Sage, they shook his hands and thanked him, weeping in gratitude. Sage was a bit overwhelmed and tried to find Puck again.

Puck found him.

"Autumn was taken away and tortured." Puck touched the marks on his wrist. "Come with me. You will probably need to carry her."

As they passed Tanner, Sage told him, "I am going to go get Autumn. Organize some fit men to search the cells for those who may not be able to walk to safety. I don't want anyone left behind."

Puck and Sage had to push through the thick crowds of people trying to leave. They finally were able to make their way to some empty areas and continued down a passage that wound down to the lowest level. All the cells on this bottom floor were empty, but Puck went to the door on the farthest end.

"They put her here to die," said Puck as they approached an isolated room with the door standing open.

Puck rushed in. "Oh! My dear girl!"

Sage followed into the damp, dark cell. He gasped at the heap of flesh Puck was kneeling over. A faint silver light was coming from Puck's hands as he stroked the woman's matted hair. Sage had thought he was prepared to see Autumn like this, but the sight of her made him angry to the point of shaking.

Puck moved out of the way for Sage to lift her up.

Autumn groaned when Sage started to move her some.

"Sorry, my dear," said Puck, "but we must get you out of here."

"If you can hear me," said Sage, "this will probably hurt, so hold on."

He lifted her up and shifted her body securely in his arms gently, but firmly. He had heard her gasp in pain and then go limp. Sage gritted his teeth. How could she go through this? Her body was covered in wounds, matted blood, and grime. Had she not been breathing, he could not have imagined her being alive.

"Hurry Sage!" said Puck.

They both rushed out of the cell and back down the hall the way they had come. Sage and Puck joined a group of prisoners who were helping the injured out of their cells. Some, like Sage, were carrying people. Puck checked the cells they passed as the group slowly made their way forward. Every cell was empty. Sage was proud of how, even though these people were desperate to be free, they did care for their fellow prisoners. At least not everything in the world was rotten.

Once they made it to the top floor's central area, Shasta met them. She had taken charge of the situation as Sage had hoped she would.

"Tanner has taken the next group. I sent ten more of the stronger men back to double check each cell for those not able to leave on their own. I think we have everyone out except them and those standing around here waiting for Tanner's group to finish leaving."

"Good!" said Sage. "Take this group, and we will wait for the ten men and bring up the back. Puck, could you see how long the men will be who are checking the cells?"

Puck and Shasta left in opposite directions. It wasn't long before the first of the men arrived to give Sage their report. Only half of them found anyone left. Puck quickly returned with the last couple of men who had a prisoner each. Those who were found may have easily been left for dead, but they had wanted to try and save them if there was any hope.

"It looks as if we are ready to go," said Puck. "We have evacuated a city without a single Ogre appearing."

"I am not one to cheer until there is at least a league between me and this fortress," said Sage. "Let's go."

He led the small group after the last of Shasta's group had filtered out. Puck took the very end of the line. Sage entered the passage the Gryphon had brought them through until they burst into the morning light. After his eyes adjusted, Sage could clearly see the exodus all the way through the magical shield. He led the group to the translucent dome of the magical shield. He then stood next to the hole in the shield to direct people through it while still holding Autumn's limp body.

Suddenly, Sage heard shouts, and a bell began to sound.

"The jail is empty! Jailbreak! Jailbreak!"

He was relieved to see Puck appear at his side. "That's the last of them! The new shift must have found the passed-out Ogres and empty cells."

162

Ogres began to pour out of the fortress like ants on an angry mound. Maldamien even appeared on a balcony of one of the top floors.

"Get them! Kill them all! Don't let them escape, you fools!" Maldamien pointed to the shield, and it began to flicker as he started to remove it for his troops.

The last of the prisoners ran through the shield.

"Go! I'll hold them off," shouted Puck over the loud roar of Ogres.

"But the shield is disappearing! What are you talking about?" shouted Sage back.

Puck pushed Sage through the shield and held both his hands up and still as the shield solidified around them.

"Puck no!" shouted Sage.

"The Creator is with me. Now go, and keep my girl safe," shouted Puck.

Sage turned to go as Ogres bounced off the shield, trapping them inside.

Maldamien shouted and threw a fire-ball at Puck.

Sage turned around in time to see Puck get hit by the fireball. At the moment it flashed at hitting its target, Sage thought he saw the Gryphon appear in the way of the blast, protecting Puck, but when the dust cleared, only ashes remained. Even without Puck there, the Ogres could not get out of the shield.

Sage hesitated, looking for a sign of Puck, but he turned towards the path into the mountain, numb by what he saw. He looked down into his arms. Autumn's body shook as tears fell down her cheeks. She had seen it all too.

CHAPTER 18: WATER WAR

Autumn laid in Sage's arms as he climbed the mountain path to where Toble, Tanner, and Shasta stopped to watch the fortress.

"We saw what happened," said Shasta. "Whatever Puck did to the shield before... The shield will hold until the spell wears off. In other words, he saved us all."

Sage nodded. "And the prisoners?"

"They are all on their way home," said Tanner. "There were many who wanted to continue traveling with us. Some who saw what happened to Puck wanted to turn back and fight, but we persuaded them to go home and join us in two months as you said."

Sage shifted Autumn slightly in his arms. She wasn't very heavy, but his arms were already starting to ache a little.

"Let's go until we are a decent ways away from here. I don't ever want to look at that place again!"

Sage pushed past them, and they followed his lead. They traveled for hours in quiet, each one lost in their own despair at losing Puck. Puck was a great hero. He had lived a long life. He had told Autumn that he wasn't afraid of death, but none of these things lessened the pain.

Waves of despair welled up inside Autumn at losing him. Autumn could still feel the healing spell he had used when Sage and he first found her. She was able to endure the jolting of Sage's steps without losing consciousness because of it, though unconsciousness would have been easier on her just now.

Tanner began to whistle the song that Puck had taught her, and it made her cry.

Shasta started to talk after Tanner had gone through the melody only once.

"I can't believe he is really gone."

"He had a long good life," said Tanner. His voice was rough with emotion. "He will always be honored by those who knew him."

He wiped a tear away with the back of his hand.

"Why did the Gryphon let him die?" said Sage angrily. "Why did he leave us at the last minute? He did so many things to bring us in, why did he just stop in the middle of our escape?"

No one could think of a good reply so they continued in silence. Autumn felt Sage's words echo what she had felt when her father died, and it reverberated in her emotions about Puck. Why did they have to die? The two most important men in her life were so similar in many ways, but most of all the pain in losing them blended together into indistinguishable despair that sapped energy from her.

By that evening, Sage's upper body ached from carrying such a weight all day. His broken spirit weighed twice as much as the woman in his arms. Tanner and Toble had to make him stop for the night, though, because his anger and frustration made him want to push on. They found a cool shallow cave in a grassy hill in the woods beyond the mountains and made camp. This way was the same path that Sage and Toble had traveled a month ago to warn Puck about the Ogres.

"Toble," said Sage as he laid Autumn down in the cave, "do you have your bag?"

"Always," said Toble. "What do you need?"

"We need to clean and mend her wounds."

Toble lowered his pack and dug out some cloth and the very little ointment he had left and handed them to Sage.

Shasta took it before Sage could.

"Let me do it. A woman can care for wounds a man shouldn't see. Now someone needs to fetch water for me."

"I can do that," said Tanner as he placed his large rough hand against the wall of the cave.

He closed his eyes for a moment as silvery light glowed from under his hand.

He looked up and said, "There is a creek just a little way into the woods. I'll be back as soon as I can." He turned and left.

"I'll get the fire going," said Toble as he left with Tanner.

Sage turned to Shasta. "Do you need anything else?"

Shasta smiled in her enchanting feminine way.

"No, but thank you."

"Then I'll find some dinner for everyone," he said and left too.

Queen Shasta tried to make Autumn a little more comfortable by using her own silk cloak as a cushion under the injured woman's head. She looked over Autumn carefully. Autumn saw Shasta's first look of surprise.

"Yes, I'm human," whispered Autumn painfully.

Shasta looked a little unnerved.

"It's not just that," said Shasta. "Though, I do admit that I had thought you were a Huldra or an Undine. I just never thought Maldamien would mistreat one of his own kind so horribly. These wounds are terrible."

Autumn closed her eyes weakly.

"I think I have a cracked collarbone, a cracked rib, a broken wrist, and a broken leg. The worst wounds are the cuts on my right arm and the raw area on my right leg, same leg that's broken."

"Why would he do this to his own kind?"

Autumn's eye flew open, and she nearly sat up in anger.

"I am not one of his kind! I am from the human world. I am a real human, not a monster like him."

Shasta turned pale.

"Please calm down! I am so sorry for my mistake. I didn't mean to offend you. Please don't hurt yourself."

Autumn relaxed. Her nerves felt exposed and on edge. She had to remember that this was a queen who knew nothing about her.

"I don't know what you're talking about unless you are much older than me. The portals are closed. How can you be from the human world?"

Tanner arrived with water in a very large empty gourd. He paused at hearing Shasta's question, but then continued in.

"I can get more water whenever you need it."

He set it next to the queen.

"Yes, we may need it in a little bit, but I will fetch you at that time. Thank you."

Tanner bowed a little.

"Autumn, feel free to tell Queen Shasta your story if you like. We will need her help in all of this before it is over."

Shasta gave a smile as Tanner bowed again and left.

"Only talk if you like," Shasta said. "It sounds like this might be a long story. If you don't mind, I can ask Tanner later if you feel unwell."

Autumn nodded. Shasta washed Autumn's wounds. The open sores and gaping flesh made Shasta even more pale and queasy. Autumn could only lay half-conscious since the conversation had exhausted her. Even so, when Shasta started to remove Autumn's cloth belt that hid the things from Queen Anemone, she grabbed Shasta's hand forcefully.

"Leave that."

"Are you sure? I guess I can work around it."

Shasta tried to apply ointment and wrap as many wounds as she could. She ended up tearing some material from the bottom of her petticoat to finish. Autumn was completely asleep when the queen left with the gourd and some dirty rags.

Toble and Tanner looked up as she approached the fire.

"Where was that creek you had mentioned? I would like to wash some and get more water," asked Queen Shasta.

As Tanner stood up, Sage approached with a small dead goat over his shoulder and some herbs.

"Where did you get the goat?" asked Toble.

"I was picking some herbs, and he tried to ram me."

Sage showed a cut on his arm from his battle.

"No more injuries," commanded Shasta. "We are out of ointment, and I would like to preserve the rest of my petticoat."

Sage dropped the goat where he stood a ways away from the fire and gave Queen Shasta a slight bow.

"How is Autumn?" he asked.

"The woman is resting, but in terrible shape. She will need professional attention very soon. She was able to tell me where all her broken bones were herself, but I am afraid that some of her gaping wounds may get infected if we don't get more ointment."

"Can she be moved?" asked Toble.

"Is there any possibility of her not being moved?" asked the queen. "She can't stay here. It gets cooler every day now and who knows when the Ogres will be free from the shield."

"None of us can stay," said Sage as he took out a small dagger from his boot and began to skin the goat. "The likelihood of being caught is too great, but how much can we move her without killing her in the process?"

"I'm afraid I don't know," said Shasta. "Had she been a Sprite, she would probably be dead already."

"Then we will have to go to the nearest place we can for help," said

Sage. "We will have to go to the Undines in Berehynia. We have to find James, the Undine King's steward at the court and ask for asylum."

"That's still a week's travel from here," said Tanner. "Can she last that long?"

"It is only a couple of days to the river. From there we can build a raft to get there faster," said Sage.

"I don't like that plan," said Tanner. "What if the raft tips over?"

"And I can't swim," said Shasta.

"Then I could go myself and bring some help back with me," said Sage. "That way she could be kept hidden and safe for a couple of days."

No one liked that plan either, but Tanner and Shasta left for the creek and Sage prepared the goat. He finished skinning it, then cut all the meat off the bones and gave a generous portion of it to Toble to roast on the fire. Sage dug a ditch to bury the bones and whatever they weren't going to use, covered it up, then built a frame and tent over it. He placed the thinly sliced meat and skins on the frame and built a smoky fire underneath. The entire process would hopefully have the meat dried and ready to be packed in the skin for travel tomorrow. With meat being so rare, he wasn't going to waste anything he could.

Tanner and Shasta were back by the time Sage took over roasting the meat on the fire. He even made a little stew for Autumn in a bowl Toble had in his bag.

Tanner continued his tale to Queen Shasta about Autumn and the adventures they all had been on. They ate their fill of the meat with the herbs Sage had collected. All of them, including the queen, could not recall the last time they had eaten meat.

When he had finished eating, Sage took the stew into the shallow cave where Autumn was sleeping and knelt beside her. He took off his cloak and put it over her, tucking it in around her. She looked and felt cold. He stared at her peaceful, grown-up face.

"How old are you really?" he whispered.

He gently brushed the hair from her face. She was still the girl who had healed his leg and the one who found the ring. She was pretty, but not exotic like the Hiru or angelic like the Sprites. She had a delicate earthy beauty like a thorny rose. She was tough like a rose too.

Autumn opened her eyes and smiled.

"Hi," she said faintly.

"Hello. Do you want soup? It has real meat in it."

She nodded and tried to sit up.

"Slowly! Let me help." Sage carefully moved her body so she could lean against the wall. "You look better than what Queen Shasta led us to believe."

"I have been doing what Puck taught me. I think I am healing some, but I can't say. I feel terrible," said Autumn in a breathy manner.

"Here." Sage gave her a spoonful of broth. Autumn began to cough and then cried out in pain. Sage helped her back down into a laying position. He looked around for an idea.

"Do you think if I propped your head on my lap, you could drink the broth from the bowl?"

"We can try it, but if it doesn't work, then I would rather skip dinner and just sleep."

Sage sat against the wall, propped Autumn up a little and scooted towards her then tucked Queen Shasta's cloak under her so that she was on a gentle incline. He then helped her drink some of the broth. She was quickly tired, and Sage let her fall back to sleep as he stroked her matted hair.

Tanner came into the cave.

"How is she?" he asked.

"She drank a little broth, but she feels cold."

Tanner sat next to Autumn facing Sage.

"Poor girl. Does she know what happened to Puck?"

"Yes," said Sage. "I think I am going to stay right here tonight."

He wanted to make sure she was well and safe the whole night. He was tired of losing people. She wouldn't be able to wake any of them if she needed something. At least, those were the reasons that he told himself.

Tanner nodded. Shasta and Toble joined Tanner and Sage around Autumn in the small cave.

"We should all sleep in here. I'll keep the first watch," said Tanner.

"As much as I think your plan is good," said Toble, "I think I should take the first watch. I can't sleep in here even if I wanted."

"Right," said Sage, "and keep an eye on the smoking meat. That stuff is as good as gold."

Toble nodded as walked back to the entrance of the cave with his bag in tow.

169

Sage looked down at Autumn as she shivered. That wasn't good. He tucked his cloak better around her, and she seemed more comfortable.

Tanner and Shasta slept close to Autumn and Sage so that the body heat of everyone should have been able to keep it comfortable. Sage fell asleep leaning against the wall with Autumn still laying in his lap, but he woke up in the early morning with Autumn in a sweat and shivering with a fever.

"Drat!" said Sage. "We need to go. Everybody up!"

"What? What happened?" asked Shasta sitting straight up.

"Autumn has a fever," said Sage. "We need to go now and travel hard."

It only took minutes for everyone to pack up and go. They were soon traveling as fast as Sage could carry Autumn. Under his breath, Sage called to the Creator.

"I don't know why you left us or why Puck had to die. I don't know a lot of things, but I do know that when I have asked you before, you have answered. So please don't let her die."

Sage pushed the group all day, not even stopping to eat. Toble put some willow bark under Autumn's tongue to try and reduce the fever. Shasta was struggling to keep up the pace. By that evening, Toble and Tanner were even tired. Sage knew from experience that his adrenaline would not last much longer.

"Poor Coriander!" Shasta whined. "Poor me! Oh, if only he was here to help me! Oh, my dear Coriander. How I miss him."

Shasta was stumbling behind.

Sage sighed.

"We will stop here."

They had been traveling in the woods most of the day, and this place was the same as any other. Sage laid Autumn down as they built a fire. She was deathly pale and still shivering.

"Sage, we had talked of you going off to find help, but let me go instead. I am a better tracker, and I can't carry Autumn if she needs to be moved," said Tanner at seeing Autumn's condition.

"That's a good idea, Sage," said Toble as he began to make a fire.

Sage sat down and leaned back against a tree near Autumn. "I don't think we have a choice. We will keep traveling in the morning even if you are not back yet."

Tanner nodded and tiredly took off into the woods. Toble took off his cloak and laid it on Shasta who was already asleep by the fire.

"It seems like we live from one crisis to another," said Toble, "yet somehow we have gotten this far."

"Puck would say it was because of the Gryphon," said Sage. "Whether or not it is, it must be more than luck. I can't say I don't believe in the Gryphon anymore since I have met him and have seen him, but I still don't know if I can trust him or even believe he is good all the time. I mean look at her," Sage pointed at Autumn. "What secrets does she have locked up in her? Why put someone who has to be a quarter my age through that? Why make her have the potential to change everything and yet not help her or protect her?"

Toble sat down next to Sage.

"I used to serve the Gryphon once a long time ago. Most magic users do learn something about the Gryphon. I never learned much though. I tend to work with tools and gadgets more because they make more sense to me, but in an emergency, I have used magic. In those times, all seems right in the world, and somehow there is an order for a moment. I am certain there must be a grand plan. Would he let the world destroy itself?"

"I don't know," said Sage. "I don't want to think about it, and I haven't had to until now."

Sage laid back. He hadn't said the whole truth. He was a 112-year-old in a 30-year-old body, and he had thought about these things a lot over the years. He had chosen to push it to the side with so many other things so that he wouldn't have to deal with the implications of really choosing.

"I'll take the watch," said Toble. "Get some rest, and I'll wake you in the morning."

Sage agreed and settled down as though he was going to sleep, but his mind continued his train of thought about the Gryphon. Why sacrifice innocent people for this plan? Why let evil rule the world and destroy all he had made? Why not just come down and make everything right? Why not just let the good people live and kill all the evil people instead?

As Sage fell asleep, his last thought was: Because death is not the worst thing one can go through.

It seemed like moments later that Toble woke him up.

"Tanner is back."

It was still dark.

Sage sat up to see a large red and black salamander with an Undine soldier dressed in green leather armor mounted on it. The muscular Undine solder was equipped with at least a spear and shield. Tanner was waking Shasta up. Two more salamanders walked up next to the first.

"That was quick, Tanner," said Sage as he got up.

"They were patrolling the area. It turns out that they are going to war with the Merpeople within a few hours, and they are trying to find their supply lines. They offered to help us since they need to go back and report anyway." Tanner leaned close to Sage and whispered, "Some of the Undines have already made it home, and we are heroes."

Sage stood up, got his stuff all packed for Toble to carry, and picked up Autumn.

"Well, I hope that we can get some fast attention for Autumn then," Sage said to the first Undine soldier who looked like the one in charge.

The Undine captain jumped down from his saddle and walked over to Sage. "I would be honored if you would ride with me. My mount is the fastest."

"Thanks," said Sage. "We would like to find James, the king's steward if you don't mind."

"We were going to take you to the king himself," said the captain. "His personal bodyguard was found a couple of hours ago on his way back from Odemience. I am certain that the king will want to thank you all for what you have done."

"Or get angry that we stirred up trouble so close to his kingdom," mumbled Sage.

Sage had lost faith in the countries who had been loyal to the queen. The governments were getting turned over too easily lately.

The captain shrugged.

"Either way, the king isn't far from here. The Merpeople have made it all the way up river and are pushing hard. At least you would get access to the medical tent if the battle hasn't started."

"Perhaps I can help," said Sage as he handed Autumn to the captain.

"Anything would be welcomed," said the captain.

Sage mounted the salamander, and the captain handed Autumn back to Sage. He then jumped up in front of Sage and Autumn. Tanner and Queen Shasta were with a soldier on the salamander to Sage's left, and

Toble was on the one on his right. The salamanders took off at full speed into the woods. As the captain had said, his salamander was quickly speeding ahead of the others. By mid-morning, they were at a tributary. The salamander continued its pace right into the water and sped along, swimming with its riders above the surface of the water. Autumn was still shivering in Sage's arms. She opened her eyes and looked up at him.

"Hold on. We are going to the Undine king. We will get some help there," said Sage.

"Must talk to... King... Mermaids... spell... Maldamien," said Autumn urgently in a raspy voice.

Sage was confused, but Autumn was asleep again. He wondered if she was hallucinating or if she knew something important about the war.

It wasn't until evening that they arrived at what looked like a floating military camp in the middle of the large river. Tents sat on giant lily pads in rows on either side of a large royal tent in the middle. The Captain called out in his native tongue to the two guards hidden in the trees on either side of the river. He then continued through the sea of tents to the royal tent in the center and finally stopped. He spoke to the guard in front of the tent, and one of them ducked inside.

"He is going to announce us to the king," explained the captain.

The guard returned moments later and opened the tent door wide enough to allow the salamander in with its passengers. The salamander smoothly glided in.

Inside the large tent, on a floating platform, sat the king behind a table looking at some papers. The king was a slightly built, average looking Undine, with brown hair, brown beard, brown eyes, dressed in brown with brown armor. Captains and generals stood around him in their leather armor. James stood behind the king and smiled widely at seeing Sage. The captain bowed to the king from his mount. Sage did a smaller bow with Autumn still in his arms.

"Your Highness," said the captain in English. "This is Sage Goliad, the hero at Odemience. He has come requesting assistance."

The captain dismounted into the water so Sage could be seen. Sage bowed again.

"Sire, this woman is Autumn, the student of Puck. She is in need of medical assistance after being tortured by Maldamien," said Sage.

The captains and generals began to whisper to each other in response to this, but Sage continued. "My friends, Toble, the Dryad Ambassador to Vervain; Tanner, the Gnome royal groundskeeper; and Queen Shasta of the Sprite people are all coming here needing assistance since our escape from Maldamien's prison."

"What happened to Puck? I was told he was also with you at Odemience," asked the king, rubbing his brown beard thoughtfully.

"Puck was killed saving our lives. He enforced the magic shield around Odemience after everyone escaped to trap Maldamien and his forces inside, but he gave his life to do so."

"That is a great loss!" said the king. "We will give you everything you may want or need. My servant will assist you to the palace. As you see, we are at war, and I will not be able to honor you as I like, but we..."

"No!" shouted Autumn hoarsely.

Sage and the king jumped in surprise.

"It's a false war!"

Autumn struggled feverishly to sit up. Sage, bewildered, helped her carefully to see the king.

"What is she trying to say?" asked the king.

"The war..." Autumn swallowed. Her mouth was terribly dry. "The war was started by Maldamien. When I was being tortured, he tried to read my thoughts. He pushed so much that I was able to see some of his. He put a spell on the Mermaid queen to cause this war. I must see her. I must break the spell now. I will not go to your palace until I see her. I must..."

Autumn passed out.

Sage laid her back into his arms as a general whispered to the king.

The king sighed and then spoke to Sage.

"The woman is right. Our spies and contacts have suspected as much, but we have had no idea what to do about it. Years ago, before our fathers died, Princess Oceania was the love of my life. We had planned to wed and unite our kingdoms. We had so many dreams even in this dark time. Her father was killed in a dreadful accident, and my father was murdered by an ally of Maldamien a few months later. We did not talk much as we tried to put our kingdoms back in order. I had to weed out assassins and secure my palace, which is now well hidden. I have been fortunate that Maldamien has not sent an invasion force against me for throwing out all his people, but I also have been very careful not to take aggressive action against him either. We have taken the lesson from the Hiru and just stayed as hidden as possible. Queen Oceania, though, has changed dramatically. Those I had thrown out went to her kingdom. She has been aggressively trying to take over our trade routes and stealing from my people. She has become cruel, the opposite of everything I ever knew about her. She is not just trying to conquer us; she is trying to exterminate us. If this woman can do anything, even in the condition that she is in, then she will need to act now. By tomorrow, most of my soldiers will be killed. As you know, the Merpeople have always been better at war with their steel armor and the strength of the ocean behind their chariots. We are only a nation of fishermen and traders. We can't win this."

Sage looked down at Autumn's pale, moist skin. She was sweating and shivering again. She opened her eyes.

"I must... the spell..." she said to no one feverishly.

Sage sighed.

Then he whispered a little prayer to the Gryphon, "If you save her and preserve her, I swear I will serve you from now on, unquestionably." He then looked up at the king, "We will do what we can."

The king nodded and turned to one of his generals. "See if you can arrange a parley somewhere neutral as soon as possible."

The general bowed, then jumped into the water and was gone.

The king then turned to James, "Go fetch our physician. Afterward, return to the palace and make preparations for our guests."

James bowed and also dove into the water.

"We will get her something to help before our meeting with Queen Oceania," the king told Sage. "Bring them up here with me." The king ordered the captain who held the reins of the salamander. "There is no reason to keep you both so uncomfortable."

The captain led the salamander next to the king's platform, and one of the generals took Autumn from Sage. Then Sage dismounted onto the platform. A wide chair covered in cushions was brought for both of them. Moments later, the Undine physician swam in and climbed some underwater stairs up the platform to look at Autumn.

"Oh, my!" the physician exclaimed upon seeing her. "She needs more attention than I am equipped for away from the infirmary."

175

"Just treat what you can right now," said the king. "She must meet with Queen Oceania in a little while."

As he spoke, the general he had sent to the Mermaid queen arrived, climbed up the platform, and bowed.

"Her Majesty will meet at the grotto in half an hour. She will bring one escort, and you are to do the same. The guests will not count since she is curious about them herself. It appears that some of her people have returned as well."

"That will do perfectly," said the king. "Now, how is your patient?" he asked the physician.

"I have given her a strong pain-reliever and fever reducer. She still may fall asleep or pass out in the meeting. I would prefer to see her wounds and treat her more fully. She is in very bad shape."

"You will get your chance," said the king. "Get everything ready at the infirmary to treat her immediately upon our return."

The captain and his salamander left with the physician. A wide oval chariot pulled by two giant goldfish came in. The Undine driver brought it next to the platform. The general and Sage carried Autumn in her chair onto the chariot. The king, Sage, and the general also got into the wooden chariot. Once they were all comfortable, the driver took off slowly and smoothly out of the tent and towards the grotto.

Autumn could feel the medication beginning to take effect. She felt her shivering settle down and the pain seeping away. She kept her eyes closed and began to meditate on the Gryphon and his desire for peace. Autumn had to push down grief at missing Puck at that moment. She would follow his example and honor his memory in that. She knew what she had to do with a clarity that surprised her.

Sage watched Autumn's facial expression change from a painful feverish look to a calm determined meditation. Somehow at that moment, he saw what Puck had believed in. This woman could actually change the world.

Before Sage could think about this further, they arrived at the appointed place. The Mermaid queen was sitting in a large clamshell with her fishtail folded to her side, and the fins gracefully dipped in the water. The shell chariot was being pulled by a dolphin and a Merman general swimming to the side of her with his spear in his hands ready for action. Both were wearing black armor trimmed in gold. The queen's jet-black hair fell down to her waist. Sage was struck at how powerful and fierce she looked compared to the Undine king's leather armor, brown hair, brown skin, and worried expression.

"All right, Fredrick," said the queen sharply, "what is this about?"

The king turned and nodded at Sage to speak. Sage took a deep breath and looked at Autumn, who still had her eyes closed.

"I am Sage Goliad, and this is Autumn, a student of Puck's. We have just recently escaped from Odemience. While Autumn was there, she was tortured by Maldamien and believes she saw a plot Maldamien has against you and your kingdom."

"So, you went to the Undines?" said the queen angrily.

Autumn opened her eyes and held out her right hand towards the queen.

"As the Gryphon is so shall you see the truth!"

A bright golden light flared from Autumn's hand so that everyone had to turn away. As the light faded, Sage looked back at the queen. She sat pale and stone still, staring at Autumn. After a moment, she began to blink and look around. The general had moved between Autumn and the queen, and had tried unsuccessfully to block the spell with his spear.

The queen slumped forward, putting her head in her hands.

"Oceania?" asked King Fredrick.

The Merman general asked, "Your Majesty?" with his back to her ready to attack his enemies upon her command.

"Oh Fredrick!" said Oceania. "Could you ever forgive me!" She looked up with tears in her eyes. "I have made such a mess of things... Oh! The girl!"

They looked at Autumn. She was limp and deathly pale. Sage knelt down quickly to check if she was breathing.

"She's alive, but barely!"

CHAPTER 19: UNDINE PALACE

Autumn opened her eyes. She was looking up at the roof of a tent. She felt disoriented and confused. She wasn't even sure if she was dreaming. She tried to sit up, but pain shot through her. Nope, she was awake, and everything that had happened to her, the torture, Puck's death, the Merpeople and Undine conflict were all real.

She looked around from where she lay. She was in a bed by the door of a large tent filled with beds. A curtain separated her from her neighbor, but it was still noisy and busy. Next to her in a chair sat Sage with his head back, mouth open, and sound asleep. A white-haired Undine physician walked up to her bed from the opposite direction.

"I see you have woken up. That is very good. Your fever seems to have broken," he said as he felt her head. "I am thrilled. Your friend here would not leave your side. He was very worried about you. I will fetch your other friends if you feel up to it. I will also talk to the king about having you moved to the palace now. I think you are out of danger and would feel more comfortable there."

"Thank you," said Autumn in a hoarse whisper. Her throat still felt dry.

The physician smiled and left. He patted Sage on the shoulder as he walked by on his way out of the tent.

Sage jumped in surprise and smiled at seeing Autumn awake. Autumn couldn't help but smile back. He looked dashing and like a little boy in the same moment.

"You're awake!" Sage pulled his chair closer to her. "You know you're a hero now. You saved two nations from a horrible war."

"You would have done the same thing," she said hoarsely.

"How do you feel?" he asked.

"Better than before. How long have I been sleeping?"

"Two days," said Sage. "All of us have stayed at the camp until you could be moved."

Tanner, Toble, and Shasta walked in and came around her bed. Autumn noticed how Queen Shasta moved around so she could stand next to Sage.

"You gave us a mighty scare," said Tanner.

"Yes. How are you feeling?" asked Queen Shasta. Her giant moth-like wings flittered.

"It is good to see you awake and well," said Toble.

They all looked cleaner and well rested.

"What has been happening while I was asleep?" asked Autumn.

"They are getting married!" said Queen Shasta. "We have all been invited to attend."

"Married? Who?" Autumn tried to sit up again and pain shot through her.

"Don't try to sit up." Tanner quickly sat on the edge of the bed and gently pushed her back down, but Autumn didn't need the reminder.

Shasta's face was glowing with excitement.

"King Fredrick and Queen Oceania! They had intended to marry long ago before Queen Oceania was put under that spell. They decided it was better to do it quickly before anything else happens."

"After the spell was broken, the king and queen have been spending all their time together," said Sage. "First it was just meetings to negotiate a treaty and clarify all the mistaken knowledge between them. Queen Oceania has had to exile some of the people in her court, including the adviser that Maldamien appointed for her. After all of that, they started to catch up on their personal lives. The engagement wasn't announced until this morning."

"Yes, and they decided that the date for the wedding would be one week from today!" said Shasta. "I have asked if I could help. These royal functions can't be thrown together that quickly without a lot of help."

She was floating a few inches in the air as her wings vibrated in excitement.

"I am glad to see you are better," interrupted King Fredrick as he and Queen Oceania walked into the tent hand in hand. "I was glad to hear you were finally awake. We wanted to come and thank you."

Autumn felt honored but was distracted by Queen Oceania's appearance.

"Thank you," said Autumn. "Could I ask an ignorant question?"

"Go ahead," said King Fredrick.

"How is the queen walking? I thought she had fins earlier or did I dream that?"

Queen Oceania looked a little surprised and then smiled. She looked petite and feminine next to King Fredrick compared to the impressive warrior Autumn saw earlier.

"I had forgotten that you are not from here. Your friends have told us your story. You can feel free to ask what you like. I did have fins earlier, but we have magical belts to give us legs when we need them. They are rare, and they become invisible when they are on us. You may not be aware that some of those rescued from Odemience were officials from my court who were wearing them."

"Speaking of that," said King Fredrick, "we would like to hold a dinner in your honor, and your friends of course, as soon as you are well enough to attend. Some of those that were rescued will be invited as well so that they can thank all of you in person."

Each of the friends expressed their gratitude.

"Also," added the king, "I am told you are well enough to be moved so you will be taken to my palace, Tangie. It is the hidden court of the land of Berehynia, and you will be safe there. Maldamien will have a number of things to be angry about today, but he will have to search well to find it. He will never be able to attack it with Ogres either. Ogres sink like a rock."

A group of Undine servants came into the tent and bowed to King Fredrick.

"We will see all of you at the palace. Take care," said the king as he and Queen Oceania turned to go.

The servants surrounded Autumn's bed and carried it out of the tent. The group followed. At the entrance of the tent was a large open shell being pulled by a school of fish. The servants placed the bed into the middle of the shell behind the driver. Then a servant helped the group get in on either side to sit on the edges of the bed.

The carriage pulled away from the floating hospital east down the river. The city of tents slipped out of view, and the river stayed calm and open. Sage looked sadly at the southern shore.

"What is wrong?" asked Queen Shasta.

"A few miles that way," Sage pointed southeast, "is Samodivas and that is the area of the country I was born in. I wonder if my ancestral home still stands there."

Queen Shasta took Sage's hand and squeezed it. Autumn could see them clearly from where she lay.

"But that was never your home, Vervain was. Do you remember as children how much we used to play together at the palace?" said Shasta.

Sage looked at her clear blue eyes. He squeezed her hand in return and then took his hand back.

"Thanks, but that was long ago."

The group watched the brown shore go by quietly for the next hour. The landscape should have been beautiful, but it was all dead and brown. The driver turned right and curved around towards a waterfall. The aquatic curtain magically parted as they entered a cave lit by patterns of glowing rocks on the walls. The carriage floated down a long series of lochs until they were deep underground. They then continued on the smooth waterway until they reached a marble pier. Some Undine servants, finely dressed, met them as the carriage slowed to a stop. They helped Queen Shasta, Toble, and Tanner out before getting onto the carriage.

"There are many stairways in the palace. It would be better if we carried the woman without the bed," the servant explained to Sage who was standing next to Autumn.

"Let me carry her," said Sage.

"I will hand her to you."

Sage got out, and the servant very carefully lifted Autumn and handed her up to Sage. Autumn held onto Sage's neck as her body ached from the movement.

"It's a lot easier carrying you when you are awake," said Sage with a smile.

Autumn just grimaced in an attempt to smile. It just hurt.

An elegant Undine woman greeted them when they walked to the end of the pier.

"Hi, my name is Katrina. I am personally responsible for taking care of your needs and comforts while you are with us. Please don't hesitate to ask for anything. If you will please follow me, I will show you to each of your rooms first, and then I can give you a tour of the palace or guide you to where ever you wish afterward."

She turned and led the group into a hall whose walls were decorated with mosaics in precious stones. A mosaic of white limestone paved the floor in shell patterns. Gold trimmed everything in organic wave-like patterns. They were brought to enormous pearl doors with ancient writing on them. Two Undine footmen opened them to reveal an enormous entrance hall surrounded by doors. The center of the hall contained an open pool in which Merpeople swam to the edge to talk to the Undines. The pool was raised so that one could sit on the edge and talk eye to eye with the Merpeople. Two staircases curved in opposite directions. People were coming and going in hurried activity.

"This palace is one of the oldest in Gryphendale. Our people have made it a priority to maintain its splendor. The other royal residences have been destroyed to offset the expense, but this is the pride and joy of our people," said Katrina.

She then turned to the left staircase and led them up. She turned left down a long hallway and then right to a shorter one with five widely spaced doors: two on each side and one on the end.

"We gave you apartments next to each other and customized the furnishing to suit your tastes." She turned to Toble, "For your unique needs, I will also show you to the atrium if your room is not sufficient."

She opened the first door to her right. Inside the large open room, the bed had been removed and replaced with a large three-foot high planter filled with rich soil. The high ceiling had a sun light installed.

"Oh my!" said Toble. "I believe that will do."

Katrina smiled broadly. It was obvious that was her most difficult room to plan.

"Good. Now for Miss Autumn."

She walked to the next room down the hall. She opened the door and led them into a sitting area.

"Many of your rooms will be similar, except yours, Your Majesty. Yours will be on the end and has apartments that suit your rank. In the rest of the rooms we adjusted the bed size, height and hardness to suit your racial needs. If anything is lacking, please don't hesitate to ask. Now let us go to the bedroom so that Miss Autumn can be made comfortable before showing the other rooms."

Katrina walked into the adjoining room, pulling back the covers on the bed as Sage laid Autumn down. Autumn could feel herself sink into the large soft mattress.

"I will be back with the doctor to get you settled," said Katrina to Autumn. Katrina then turned to Queen Shasta. "I will now show Your

Majesty your apartments."

As she left the room, Sage leaned over and whispered, "I'll check on you later."

It only took moments after they left for Autumn to fall asleep. She was awakened when Katrina and the physician were re-wrapping the bandage on her right leg. The physician re-dressed a few of her bandages and gave her more pain medication. She quickly fell asleep again. She vaguely remembered Sage and Tanner checking in on her sometime that evening.

When Autumn finally woke up sometime in the middle of the next day, she felt the emotions of all that happened rush on her. She allowed herself to lay there and just cry. She cried over Puck and cried over the horrible torture and cried over her father and cried over the world she never wanted to return to. Then she repeated the process. As she was going through her second bout of crying, she fell asleep.

She woke again that evening and saw Tanner sitting next to her in the chair from the writing table and playing with his rough pipe. He had shaved and wore clean brown Gnome attire. Even his brown pointed hat was clean.

"Good evening," he greeted.

"How long did I sleep?" Autumn asked.

"Since yesterday. Would you like some water?"

"Yes, please."

Tanner helped her sit up just a little and drink some. It tasted better than anything she had ever had. Her stomach growled.

"How about some food?" asked Autumn.

Tanner smiled, "I'll tell Katrina."

He left for a moment and then returned. He sat back down. Autumn watched him get his pipe back out and play with it again.

"Sorry, I'm not good with small talk." He put the pipe away in his shirt pocket, but then got it out again. "Well, I want to let you know that you are Puck's girl. I mean, Puck didn't have any children. I think Puck saw you as a daughter or granddaughter or whatever. I just want to let you know that I can't be Puck, but if you need anything... well."

"Thank you," said Autumn. "That means a lot."

"Well, I should be better at saying stuff like this because I have six kids, but the thing is that you're Puck's girl, and he cared for you a lot in this short time. You got to know each other. Puck was a picky guy. He was often frustrated at most people because of their foolishness. He coped with that by laughing or being silly in his younger days and teaching in his older days. There are a handful of people who Puck truly respected and loved. You know most of them, but you are also one of them. I want to help you in whatever you do. That is what Puck had asked me to do at the beginning, and I am more firmly resolved to do just that."

"Thank you," said Autumn.

It was probably the longest thing she remembered Tanner ever saying to her. She was stunned.

Tanner took a deep breath and sighed.

"They will be coming with your dinner soon, and I think Sage is eager to see you. Puck's last words were for him to take care of you. I think he has taken that to heart." Then he smiled. "I think you intrigue him too."

"What do you mean?" asked Autumn.

Tanner shrugged, stood up, and put his pipe away again.

"You're tough and yet still sweet and innocent. It's not every day someone sees that."

Tanner walked out, leaving Autumn wondering what he was implying. Katrina was soon at the door with a tray of food and followed by the physician.

"I am glad you are awake, and you look like you are regaining a little color in your face," said the physician. "I instructed Katrina to serve you soup and work you slowly back to solids. From talking to your friends, you may not have had real food in nearly a month. Now, I also must make some recommendations."

He sat down in the chair Tanner had been occupying and brought it closer to the bed.

"Sage has told me you are a healer. Your wounds are progressing well, but I suggest focusing your healing ability on yourself to help the healing progress and to prevent serious scarring. I also understand that you went through a great deal of questioning and torture."

Autumn looked away. Somehow the reminder of it hurt.

"I understand, but consider talking to one of your friends about it. May I specifically suggest Toble."

Autumn looked at the doctor in surprise. "Toble?"

"Yes. Do you know about the history of the Huldra and the

Dryads?" asked the physician.

"Oh, yeah," said Autumn. "Puck had told me how the Huldra people enslaved the Dryads, but is that still going on... of course it is, but Toble? He was a slave?"

"I will let him tell you his story, but in his younger years, he was very much a slave. Toble was freed and assisted by Sage's father. The Dryad slaves go through many horrible things at the hand of the Huldra. He would be the most understanding, but confide in any of your friends. Don't hold it in. Those wounds must heal too. Now, eat, and I will see you tomorrow morning. I think if you do as I recommend, you could attend dinner with the king and queen tomorrow night. Shall I tell them?"

Autumn was uncertain but nodded in agreement.

The physician smiled. "Don't worry, we won't make you walk or give long speeches."

He left as Katrina helped Autumn sit up. It was much easier. Autumn was amazed at how much better she felt as Katrina placed the tray on her lap. It had a hot fish broth, cold sweet milk, and a little paper flower for decoration.

"Do you think you can feed yourself?" asked Katrina.

Autumn lifted her arms.

"Yeah."

"Then I will return to collect your dishes in an hour."

Sage and Toble appeared at her door before Katrina could leave and had to move out of her way. Sage looked clean, well shaven, and dashing in his hunter green tunic and black slacks. Toble looked every bit like an ambassador in his navy blue robes.

"How do you feel?" asked Sage.

"I feel pretty good. You both look very nice."

"A good bath always helps," said Sage.

"And a good rest," said Toble. "That was the best soil I have seen in years. It probably came from the bottom of this river."

"So, have you both been just bathing and sleeping since we got here?" asked Autumn with a smirk.

"What's wrong with that?" said Sage. "You aren't the only one who had catching up to do."

"Don't you want to look around the palace?" asked Autumn. "I've never been to a palace long enough to explore."

"Why don't we all go then?" said Sage.

"But she doesn't need to be running around until she is healed," said Toble.

"I'll carry her. She'll be fine," said Sage.

Queen Shasta walked in dressed in a golden gown a couple of shades darker than her long straight blond hair. Autumn was struck by her beauty. Every feature was perfect and every hair in place. Now that she was clean and in royal dress, she looked every bit like the queen she was.

Sage, Toble, and Autumn all gave a little bow even though they had not done that regularly before.

"I am glad to see you are doing well," said Queen Shasta as her moth-like wings vibrated enough to keep her barely off of the floor. "I would like to visit with you about the wedding clothes whenever you are well. Queen Oceania wants the colors of the honored wedding guests to be unique from her ladies-in-waiting. I was thinking silver would do well for you. What do you think?"

Autumn felt dirty compared to Queen Shasta at that moment and wanted nothing less than to talk about evening gowns.

"That sounds great. Whatever you think will be fine with me."

Shasta smiled and put her hand on Sage's shoulder.

"I will need your help with the men's robes. King Fredrick refuses to give an opinion on the matter. Queen Oceania asked me to see if you would assist us."

Sage gave a little bow.

"I would be honored," he said formally.

"If you will excuse me for stealing your guest," said Queen Shasta, "I will be eternally grateful."

Autumn nodded dumbly.

"Thank you. I hope you feel better," Queen Shasta said as Sage dutifully escorted her out.

His eyes were an unusual grayish black.

Toble turned to follow.

"Toble, wait," said Autumn. "I would like to talk with you."

Toble stopped and turned. "What about?"

"Well..." Autumn began to fidget with the edge of her bowl of cooling soup. "The physician had recommended I talk to you about what happened when I was tortured."

Toble's expression became a little more serious and surprisingly aware. He closed the door to the room and sat in the chair facing her.

"Are you ready to talk about it yet?" he asked gently.

Autumn realized the doctor was right. Toble did already understand. She pushed the tray of half-eaten soup away. Tears began to fall from her eyes, and Toble pulled a handkerchief from his sleeve and handed it to her.

"I don't know," said Autumn. "Puck was there for me the whole time." She showed Toble her slave marks. "We talked about it some, but I don't feel like I got to tell him everything. I was asleep or unconscious a lot when it was over."

"Don't force yourself to open up," said Toble. "I too went through much as a young man. It will take time for you to heal from it. Now, why don't you start from the beginning and when you can't talk about it anymore, we will stop until tomorrow or whenever you are ready."

Autumn nodded. She told Toble about the first session and her memories. She also told him about the secrets that she let out. Then she stopped and began to feel around the waist of her nightgown.

"What happened?" asked Toble confused.

"My belt, my secret belt." Autumn was in tears again.

Toble walked over to a stack of clothes on the dresser. "Most of your clothes were rags. They wanted to clean you at the infirmary and put you in a nice nightgown. We didn't want to tell them about the belt, so we asked if we could keep the clothes for you. We made sure the belt was with it. Ah, here it is."

Toble held up a strip of cloth discolored by blood and sweat. He handed it to her. Autumn took the cloth and checked the pocket. The ring, the photo, and the keys were still in there. She hugged it close.

"Thank you."

Autumn sighed in relief. Toble smiled kindly.

"Why don't you rest? You have told me a great deal, and any more would be too draining on you. Would you like me to come tomorrow morning?"

Autumn tried to read her own emotions.

"If I don't feel up to it I will let you know."

"Just to let you know, you did very well under Maldamien's hands." Toble's eyes had tears in them. "I did not do so well when my former master questioned me, but we learn and grow and move on."

"I'm going to meditate on the Gryphon as Puck taught me to so I can heal," said Autumn. "Maybe you should try it too."

"Perhaps you are right," said Toble. "I will see you tomorrow."

Katrina was at the door and about to knock when Toble opened it. "Oh, I hope I am not interrupting," she said in surprise.

"No, we were finished talking," said Toble.

Toble left as Katrina started to fuss over Autumn.

"Oh, you look tired. Have you been crying? Your eyes are red. Oh, you didn't finish your soup. Was it all right? Would you like something else?"

"Could I take a bath?" asked Autumn.

"Hmm, well... I will get the doctor's permission. Let me take your tray if you are done with it, and I'll be back in a little bit."

Autumn let her body relax against the pillow behind her. She was getting tired, but she felt more settled in her mind. Talking to Toble was both tiring and healing. Even so, everything in her could not go back to the way she used to be. The mental and emotional wounds left by Maldamien would affect her for the rest of her life, but she was determined to make it fuel her resolve to fight him. The passion of these thoughts brought tears back to her eyes.

Katrina was soon back, unwrapped Autumn's bandages, and helped her into a medicated bath. The effort was incredibly painful. By the time she had finished and was back in her clean bed, she didn't want to move an inch. Autumn realized it was going to take her a lot longer to heal than she was ready to wait around for. She was eager to move past being an invalid and get back to the task of stopping Maldamien, but she was useless in the condition she was in. She had to wait.

CHAPTER 20: WEDDING PLANS

Toble came the next morning as he had promised and presented Autumn with a new sash.

"This has a secret pocket like the old one," said Toble. "That was a tremendous spell to try to do. The library here is excellent."

Autumn pushed away her empty breakfast tray and took her old belt out from under her pillow. "Thank you so much," said Autumn. She was kind of attached to the old belt since Puck had made it for her, so she stuffed the whole thing into the new one. The sash was as smooth as if it was empty.

Autumn and Toble talked about the other torture sessions she experienced. Most of them were the same series of events, but they had come one after another, trying to break her. Toble listened well and shared some of his own experiences. Her anger at Maldamien and her fear of ever going through that again became the theme of the conversation.

"Don't let those feelings consume you," said Toble. "Many people focus on those feelings and become just like the ones they hate. I constantly have to tell Sage the same thing. Negative emotions will turn you into a person you never thought you would be. Forgiveness of all who hurt you, courage over fear, and a positive hope for the future will fortify you and give you strength."

"Have you forgiven your past master?" asked Autumn.

Toble sighed.

"It takes a long time in some cases. I had to start seeing him as the pathetic, scared, hurting person he was. I also had to forgive him over and over again when I thought about it so that I wouldn't dwell on him all the time. It was poisoning me. Hatred consumes you and won't let you go. He was consumed with hatred, and I was becoming just like him. A person can hate so much that there is nothing left of them that is not hatred. I now just pity him and take my experience as something

189

that has made me stronger."

"How in the world did you do that? I mean how do you pity someone who is just pure evil?"

"It's kind of like a wrestling match. The more you fight, the more those feelings put down roots, but when you stop and let go of the pain and hurt, the fight ends. Oh, it doesn't happen quickly. It has to run its course and work its way out of your system, but eventually, you will have to decide what to do with it."

Autumn wasn't sure about the putting down roots part, but the letting go made sense even though it seemed very difficult. "In other words, you can't let go and still hate them."

Toble sat back in his chair next to her and sighed again.

"Sage struggles with the same thing. The balance between fighting for freedom and fighting for revenge is very narrow."

Autumn thought about his words for a while.

"Thank you Toble. I..."

A knock came on the door.

"It must be Katrina coming for the plates," said Autumn.

Toble opened the door, and there were Sage and Tanner.

"I am stealing you away for our tour of the palace," Sage announced.

Autumn smiled broadly.

"Did Shasta let you go? I am sure she probably has other wedding things for you to do."

"Nope. I ran away," he teased.

Sage walked over to the opposite side of the bed from where Toble was sitting and picked Autumn up, bedsheets and all. She giggled like a little girl.

"Hope you are done, old man," Sage said to Toble.

"Yes. I mean no. I think we were done talking," Toble said as he stood up.

Tanner brought in a chair that had wheels attached to it, and Sage placed her in it.

"Toble and Tanner worked on this last night. It was for the dinner tonight, but we ought to give it a test run, don't you think?" said Sage.

"This is great!" said Autumn.

The group was soon off exploring the various halls of the palace at a running pace. Toble and Tanner helped carry the chair up and down the stairs. They found the library, the throne room, the music room, a ballroom, a couple of dining rooms, a couple of studies and sitting rooms, and an atrium all at a high-speed sprint. Autumn was giggling until it hurt, but it felt really good to laugh. They were all laughing like little kids until they ran into Katrina and Queen Shasta. Everyone stopped and froze.

Queen Shasta recovered first.

"Oh Sage, darling. King Fredrick was asking for you. He sent some servants, but obviously, they didn't find you. Katrina was looking for Autumn as well, so it is very good that we came across each other."

Sage bowed a little, and Autumn frowned deeply.

"I will escort Autumn to her room and report to King Fredrick immediately," Sage said.

"No need. Katrina will be more than happy to assist Miss Autumn. I know how noble you are to take care of her so."

Queen Shasta, poised and in command of the situation, left no room for argument.

Sage bowed again and allowed Katrina to take charge of the chair.

"This is a clever contraption," murmured Katrina.

Sage whispered to Autumn, "I'll be back to escort you to dinner." Then he left with Queen Shasta. Shasta slipped her arm in Sage's arm and began to chatter about wedding things as they left.

Tanner mumbled something about desperate women causing trouble or something similar that Autumn could just barely make out. She smirked in agreement.

Toble and Tanner helped Katrina get the chair back to Autumn's room and left her there in Katrina's care. When Katrina closed the door, she served Autumn some lunch.

"Here, start eating."

Katrina set the tray on Autumn's lap while she was still in her rolling chair. Katrina pulled up the chair that was next to the bed.

"Now for a little gossip: Queen Shasta has been handed the responsibility of planning the whole wedding while King Fredrick and Queen Oceania are dealing with the politics of combining their kingdoms and moving the Merpeople court to this palace. Queen Shasta is obviously pleased about that. What I have heard is that after Queen Shasta's husband was killed, and even though she was devastated by the loss, she is convinced Sage is the best one to fill his place. I have seen that happen before. Some people are afraid of being alone. The servants assigned to her have said that she is obsessed with trying to get Sage involved in all of the wedding planning so that she can win him over. After all, what is more romantic than a wedding? I think they would be a good match. A national hero and a popular queen, but I can't believe how openly she is going about it! Some people in the palace say that they used to be an item when they were younger, and before she married King Coriander. I hope she doesn't ruin this by being so forceful, but it would be lovely to have two weddings in a row! There hasn't been this much excitement in the palace in decades. Everyone is talking about it! You must be super excited for your friends. I bet you will be the maid of honor for them. They are such a cute couple!"

"I've noticed Queen Shasta's attention to Sage, but don't you think this is all a little juvenile? I mean do you really think Sage is interested in her at all?"

Autumn inwardly felt horrified by the news Katrina was telling her. They seemed like a horrible match.

Katrina laughed.

"Oh, you are new to palace politics! There is more implied in these things than you realize. Sage and Queen Shasta had a long history together, even if it isn't all romantic. These political marriages should have love and interest in them, but power and security can be just as strong a factor. If Queen Shasta was able to secure Sage as her husband, she would be sending a clear message to Maldamien. At the same time, her kingdom would be the rallying point of all those who oppose Maldamien. If Maldamien could be defeated, they would become the obvious new rulers of all of Gryphendale. She is already a huge enemy to Maldamien. She could do no better than making it public by such a suitable marriage."

Autumn wasn't so sure it was such a big deal as she was making it. It was simple matchmaking and gossip. She saw it all the time as a teen in school. Yet, at the same time, there was a logic behind it, and Queen Shasta was not subtle in her attention to Sage. Could Katrina be right? Would Sage agree to such a marriage? Autumn hadn't known Sage for long, but that seemed unlikely, she hoped.

"I can see on your face you don't believe me," said Katrina. "Well, it doesn't matter. You will see how it affects everything else in the palace."

Katrina continued talking about Sage and Queen Shasta as she helped Autumn return to bed for some rest. By the time Sage came to get Autumn later that evening, Katrina had fitted her in an elegant silver gown with long sleeves that hid her injuries, fixed her hair up with little gem-studded pins, applied lotion and makeup that hid her scars and added some color, and had even thought to add some delicate jewels and perfume. The knock on the door came as Katrina was helping Autumn shakily to her feet. Sage was allowed in.

"Is Autumn ready for dinner?" he asked Katrina.

Katrina moved so that Sage could see Autumn leaning slightly against a chair in the sitting room trying to stay standing on her own. Sage gasped.

"I am if you will help me," said Autumn, pleased with Sage's response.

Sage offered his arm.

"You look beautiful."

Katrina beamed as much as Autumn did. Sage led Autumn very slowly and carefully. He stared at her as though he had never seen her before. Katrina held the door open for them.

"I guess I clean up well," said Autumn nervously.

His gaze was making her self-conscious.

"I think you must be glowing," he said. "Not too long ago, I was afraid you would die, but now..."

"I am amazed at how quickly I have been healing. The Undines don't seem too surprised. They are all very kind to me, especially Katrina."

"The physician is surprised at how fast you have been healing," said Sage. "When he had looked at you yesterday, your bones had all mended. He wanted to keep them wrapped to be on the safe side, but he was practically giddy when he told the king you would be ready to attend a dinner. I don't think he was planning on you walking there though."

"Hmm," Autumn looked around them. "I'm amazed at the beauty and luxury they have been able to preserve here, and so close to Maldamien's fortress."

"It's because they remain so well hidden and difficult to locate. As each of the countries have had less and less magic and resources, they all have had to make changes in priority. The Sprites want to maintain their lifestyles; the Gnomes have tried to maintain their industries, the Brownies focus on subsistence living and their few children, the Huldra mooch off of Maldamien and their slaves. Here, everything is focused on this little bubble of luxury. Many of the villages have been abandoned as people have moved here. The atrium is just a glorified vegetable garden, beautiful, but functional. The cleaning and chores that were done by magic have been taken over by man power. All magic is used to hide and protect this place, so the people can't have children. It is a choice the nation has made. About a thousand servants live here. The villages that remain, work in fishing or trading and pay taxes of fifty percent. The economy has simplified to just that to maintain this."

When they reached the stairs, Sage picked Autumn up and carried her down.

"The king and courtiers have reduced their spending as much as possible to keep up appearances and pay the staff. The staff, in gratitude for the safety of their positions here, do much more than they are asked. It is something that would only work for this culture, but it is truly amazing... and irritating."

Sage put Autumn back down, and she leaned on his arm as they walked to the dining room.

"It makes it feel like the fortress was a lifetime ago or a different dimension," said Autumn.

"Yes, but it is a very fragile illusion," said Sage. "An attack on this palace could wipe out the whole nation."

They entered a doorway facing the end of a very long dining room. Everyone stood up and clapped until Autumn and Sage were seated next to Toble and Tanner on the left side of the long rectangular table. The table was a solid piece of pine with rounded edges and slightly organic curves to the sides. A series of centerpieces made of shells, coral, and various underwater items lined the center of the table. The place settings were simple and elegant with white linen placemats and folded napkins, mother of pearl dishes, ornate silverware, and frosted wine glasses decorated with aquatic motifs. Even though there were nearly fifty guests seated around the table, everyone could clearly see each other in the softly lit dining room. King Fredrick and Queen Oceania came in moments later, and everyone again stood and clapped as they were seated next to each other at the head of the table. Queen Shasta was sitting next to Queen Oceania on the right side of the table across from Autumn, who was next to the king.

"Well, I would like first to give a toast to our honored guests," announced the king. "We have all heard of the heroic rescue at Odemience, the sacrifice Puck made, and the torture Miss Autumn endured, yet risked all to save us from a dreadful war. These heroes are welcome to stay here forever if they like. Thank you!"

Everyone lifted their now-filled glasses by the scuring servants and toasted the heroes.

"To the heroes!"

Sage spoke up.

"I would be amiss to accept the toast without proposing another toast to the Gryphon."

Murmuring filled the table.

"Listen to me first before judging my words. We would not have been able to enter Odemience itself had not the Gryphon appeared in person and led us. He opened the magic shield, he unlocked the prison doors, and I believe he strengthened Puck for his final stand."

"But the Gryphon is a myth," said Queen Shasta, "a children's story. Are you sure you saw him? I never saw him while I was there."

"Oh, he is quite real," said Autumn. "I have seen him too."

Queen Oceania's general, who was sitting next to Queen Shasta and across from Sage, smirked.

"And was Santa Clause riding on his back? Everyone knows that the Gryphon was a made up religious relic to keep people in the dark ages."

Autumn and Sage scowled. King Fredrick and Queen Oceania looked concerned.

"To the Gryphon then!" said the king.

Everyone toasted, but not as enthusiastically as before. The general just chuckled and drank from his glass.

"Then how would you explain the rescue?" said Sage. "I would love to take the credit, but I can't! We spent days searching for a way past the magic shield and could not do anything. That is when Tanner suggested we go back to the old ways and seek the Creator."

"And everything worked out perfectly?" sneered the general as he took a sip of the fish broth that the servants had laid before him.

"Let him finish," said a lady-in-waiting seated next to the general.

"That night I had a dream. When I awoke from the dream, the

Gryphon was there," said Sage.

Another Merman laughed. "And are you sure you weren't dreaming?"

"He woke us up too," added Tanner, "and we saw the Gryphon ourselves."

"So, what happened?" asked Autumn eagerly.

"He led us down a mountain path, through the magic shield, then into the prison itself. He even opened the prison doors on all the cells," said Sage.

"I remember my cell door just opening on its own," said an Undine man down the table.

"But I didn't see him, and Tanner opened my door," said Shasta.

"I don't know why you didn't see him," said Sage, "but he was there."

"Yes, and I followed him with the first group of prisoners back out into the mountain," said Toble.

"What happened then?" asked Queen Oceania as her bowl was taken away by a servant.

"Well, he just vanished," said Toble.

"Vanished?" echoed the general. "Perhaps like a hallucination?"

"I hope you all are enjoying your stay here?" said the king a little louder than necessary to Autumn.

A couple of the conversations farther down the table pause momentarily before resuming.

"Yes, very much. I am overwhelmed by the care of your wonderful people," said Autumn.

"You do look very nice and seem to be recovering quite quickly," said Queen Oceania.

"Thank you."

"This next dish is a white fish to agree with your recovering constitution. I hope you enjoy it. We also have a special dessert that I think everyone will really fancy," said King Fredrick.

"They would have done more courses, but these are difficult times," said Queen Shasta.

King Fredrick and Queen Oceania seemed slightly disturbed by Shasta's comment, but their expressions changed when the food was served.

Autumn looked to her left in time to see Sage, Toble, and Tanner lift their plates up towards their bowed heads in some kind of homage.

"What are you doing?" Autumn asked Sage.

"I thought Puck taught you about the way of the Gryphon? It is about the only tradition I even know about," said Sage.

"He did teach me, but that was after we were tied up and being carried on the backs of some Ogres," said Autumn.

"How did he do that and not get caught?" asked Sage.

"You have to explain the bowls first," said Autumn.

"I think it's just a thanksgiving gesture. I used to see it done a bit in the palace when I was little. I think they thanked the Creator for the food they ate, at least that is why we have been doing it. I am trying to learn some of these traditions and probably going about it awkwardly. Anyways, now it's our turn. How did Puck teach you?"

Autumn showed Sage the slave marks on her wrist. She was surprised he hadn't noticed them before. "They were Queen Mara's idea. She was the first person I met, and she thought it would help Puck and I if we were bound. I wonder if she knew how right she was."

"You never know with Banshees," said Sage. "They excel at prophecy and have an uncanny sense of the future. It's their main magic, but many times they only know partial things like something bad will happen on Tuesday, but they don't know what."

Sage was then distracted by the conversation between Tanner and the general.

"Leaving the old traditions is what is wrong with the world," said Tanner.

"I think that if people would believe in themselves and their own strength, everything would right itself," replied the general.

"Well, I think that these old stories do give us a lot of hope that we have forgotten. We have all forgotten what the world is supposed to be like, and that is preserved in these stories, whether or not one believes in the Gryphon," said Queen Shasta.

"But you must admit that no one is going to fix things but ourselves," said the general.

"I must agree with Queen Shasta," said Queen Oceania. "Living in the wild sea as we do, we all experience things we have no control over. To think that the world is not run by chance is comforting. Otherwise, we all are just blown around by the winds of time and have no certainty that anything will ever turn out right. Such an existence is beyond hope or even our control. Without the idea of some sort of greater order, fate, or a divine being there is no reason to try and force life under one's will. It would be like trying to capture the power behind a storm at sea."

"If what you say is true, than opposing Maldamien could be worse than working within his system," said the general. "If there is a divine order, than how do we know that Maldamien was not placed in power by this Creator being?"

"You assume that the Creator interferes continually with the free will of people," said Sage. "What if he just allows everyone to do as they will and only interferes when asked to?"

"So, you just ask the Gryphon to fix everything and, poof, it's fixed?" asked the general.

"No, the Creator is not a dictator. He won't control people or force people into his will, but he will work events and actions for the benefit of those who follow him," said Autumn.

"So, what about those who won't follow him?" said an Undine woman down the table. "What happens to them?"

"I think they are left with the consequences of their own actions," said Autumn. "I think that those who oppose evil do those people a favor in helping to curve the course of their own destruction."

"I do admire those that oppose Maldamien," said King Fredrick. "Unlike our heroes here, I could not enter a conflict like this because I believe it would worsen the lives of our people to do so."

"The lives of your people will be worse if nothing is done soon," said Autumn. "Maldamien has plans to do even more. Already, two portals have been unlocked."

"What?" cried the king, and gasps filled the table. Conversations all over the table paused to hear what was going on.

"When was the second portal unlocked?" asked Sage.

"Well, technically I don't know if it has yet, but Maldamien was going to do it right after he killed both Puck and me. I feel in my meditations that it has been done, but the only way to find out is to know what the weather is like outside," said Autumn.

"It has been raining since early this morning," said King Fredrick. "In fact, we have gotten an amazingly sudden harvest of fruit as we have never had in years."

"Then the earth portal in the land of Rokurokubi has been unlocked," said Autumn.

"What is Maldamien going to do?" asked Queen Shasta.

"I'm afraid that I don't know exactly," said Autumn, "but I do know he wants to open all the portals."

"It doesn't matter. We must fight him," said Sage. "Every plan he has had has caused pain, destruction, and death. This will be no different."

"I admire your drive," said Queen Oceania, looking at King Fredrick and then back to Sage. "If I could, I would give you the help of my troops, but we are only a navy and don't have enough belts to create a standing force."

"Your Majesty," said the general, "be careful whose side you take. Remember what happened to King Coriander."

"My husband," Queen Shasta interjected passionately, "would have never changed what he did. He stood up for his people and his home. He died trying to escape from Turmeric's forces, and he never gave up!"

Autumn looked at Queen Shasta with a renewed respect. She could be vain and silly sometimes, but she was grieving and still trying to do the right thing. Autumn felt like Katrina had her all wrong.

"Then what are you going to do next?" the king asked Autumn.

It was quiet as Toble, Sage, Tanner, and Autumn looked at each other.

"We are going to find Thyme," said Autumn as she finished the last of her fish.

"Excuse me?" said King Fredrick.

"Thyme, the last Asiri, and his floating monastery," said Tanner.

"Why?" asked the lady-in-waiting.

"We need to understand more about what Maldamien is doing before we can do anything about it," said Autumn. "Puck had told me to find Thyme because he can help us do that."

"Thyme would certainly be the one to do that," agreed Queen Oceania. "I will do whatever I can to help equip you for your journey."

"It won't be easy," said the general. "The floating monastery moves continually throughout the Cuelebre Kingdom, and the Hiru guards it. If you do find it, you will have to convince the Hiru that you come peacefully. As you must know, they don't trust anyone."

The plates were cleared, and King Fredrick stood up. "Well, we still have dessert ahead of us and even a little entertainment, but food and entertainment are not sufficient to honor national heroes." Four servants came into the room with pillows covered in a felt cloth. "First, for our Gnome friend, Tanner of Dwende, we have a finely crafted crossbow of fitting size. This is made from the finest wood in our land, and it's balanced, light, and sturdy. We also have a well-worked leather sling for carrying it and a quiver of arrows." Tanner's mouth hung open. He handled the ornately carved, maple colored crossbow that seemed fitted to him. The leather was also embossed with a matching knot-work design.

"Thank you," said Tanner.

"The servant will deliver the gift to your room whenever you are through looking at it so that you might finish your meal comfortably," said the king. Tanner gave a little bow.

"The next gift is for Ambassador Toble. We selected a fine hatchet and fighting staff. The metalwork of both is of the finest Ogre quality, but the woodwork is by the skill of the Merpeople. The wood in the staff is light, but the hardest petrified wood that can be found in the world."

Toble looked at his gifts. The embellishments were tasteful, and the hatchet could have easily been called a small ax. Toble bowed. "Thank you."

"Now for Lord Sage Goliad. We chose something that is my personal favorite."

The servant uncovered a sheathed sword. Sage stood up and pulled it out.

"This sword is fashioned after the human shamshir. It is made of the finest Ogre steel and forged by the Merpeople with the fortification of magical gems in the bronze hilt. The curved handle is made from a giant conch shell, helping to balance the blade. The sheath is made of thick Hiru leather and embossed by the finest Undine craftsmen."

Sage stood to receive the gift. He admired the long, curved blade and felt the weight and balance of the sword in his hands. "Thank you!"

King Fredrick smiled at how well Sage appreciated the sword. "Good. Well, now for Miss Autumn. We didn't know if you have trained with any weapons, so we decided to be very conservative in our gift. This dagger and sheath are specifically of ancient Undine design, and it was selected from the royal treasury as one of our most valuable weapons. The dagger was made in the golden age of Gryphendale and emanates magic. It is also made of Ogre steal, but this was worked by the Ogres when they used to make the finest weapons and tools in the world. The angular engravings are for the purpose of channeling the magic of the gems into whatever task you use it for. The sheath is a very rare basilisk skin and also magically fortified. Queen Oceania did not think that it suited to give you such a fine dagger without giving you a traveling outfit that matched it and embroidered with the same floral design. This outfit is made of the same leather and should protect you from minor injuries."

Autumn gingerly picked up the dagger and inspected the blade and felt the soft leather of the garment.

"Thank you so much. I am sure these gifts will be invaluable in the course of our journey. Thank you."

"Wonderful! Now, for our dessert."

The servants with the gifts left, and servant with trays of fruit came walking in past them. Everyone began to clap. "For our dessert, we have fruits that have not grown in the lands for a long time: apples, pears, oranges, cherries. These special fruit salads are the product of the strange rain we have had and the creative talent of our chef. As we enjoy this, we also have some entertainment."

King Fredrick sat down, and a small group of elegantly dressed Brownies walked into the dining room with various instruments, and a pair of Undine dancers followed. As the Brownies began to play in the corner of the room, the dancers slowly moved around the table to the music. The movements were smooth and fluid. After a few moments, ribbons of water danced around them, changing into wider sheets and separating into pieces as the dancers moved.

The dinner did not last long after the entertainment had finished. King Fredrick said another little thank you speech, and the guests began to filter out. Some of them came up to Autumn, Sage, Tanner, and Toble to thank them for their own personal rescue from Odemience. Each one had a story to tell, and many were very emotional. Queen Shasta got frustrated at having to wait to talk to Sage and decided just to leave.

When the room was finally most of the way empty, Sage helped Autumn up from the table.

"I am not quite tired," said Sage. "Would you be up to a walk in the minor atrium?"

"Yes, that sounds nice," said Autumn even though she was beginning to feel tired.

They slowly walked out of the dining room and to a nearby door that led to a small indoor garden, about half the size of the dining room they had just left. A waterfall was on their left pouring into a small fish pond. A large tree and circular planter filled the center of the room.

"This is a smaller version of the bigger atrium for this very purpose. I'm surprised no one else is in here," said Sage.

Autumn was amazed at how it made it feel like she was outside at night. It also made her feel even more tired.

"How many gardens do they have?" asked Autumn.

"I think they have six, but the largest one seems to be the one everyone goes to."

"This is beautiful, and so far away from Odemience. It feels like nothing bad could ever happen here."

Sage helped Autumn sit on the raised ledge of the fish pond and sat next to her.

"I know what you mean. I wish it were true, but there is nowhere in this world that is safe. They found me in the middle of a desert, they will find us here too," said Sage.

Autumn looked at the waterfall.

"Sage, when I was being tortured, I couldn't imagine life beyond that or life getting better. I was certain after a while that I would die there. This place has been heaven for me. I have never experienced such luxuries in my life, but this won't last. No matter how much I fear ever experiencing that horror again and no matter how much I want to stay here, the world will end in two and a half months."

Sage sighed and stood up.

"I have been on the run my whole life. It has been a longer life than I was ever supposed to have, but I am still tired of running and fighting."

Autumn couldn't respond. She couldn't imagine how long Sage had lived having known palace life, but being doomed to scrape by.

"Well," said Sage as he walked to a small tree next to the waterfall to inspect its leaves. "I didn't mean to keep you from your comfortable bed to talk about things that could never happen. I just needed to relax some before retiring for the night."

"That's fine," said Autumn. "I was feeling a little anxious myself."

"What about?" asked Sage.

She looked at the purple and gold fishes in the pond.

"The future." She took a deep breath. "What will happen if we are successful and bring Queen Anemone back? When Maldamien is defeated, and everything is recovering, will we all go our separate ways and never see each other again? Where do I belong? I can't stand the thought of going back to the human world. I hated my job, missed my dad, had jerks for friends, and just felt awkward all the time. I really care about the friends I have made here, but when this is all over, if we don't all die at the end, how do I start over?"

Sage turned and looked at her.

"I had not thought about that. In fact, I had not really thought about us succeeding."

He came and sat by her.

"I am sure every kingdom in the world would be open to you. You could come back here. They would treat you like royalty or a national hero."

"Perhaps."

Autumn thought about Puck and the little house, but she wasn't sure she would ever go back there either.

"I suspect that Toble and I will do what we always do and wander," said Sage.

"Is that what you like doing? I thought you said you were tired of being on the move."

Sage smiled.

"True, that isn't what I dream about." He stood up and offered her his hand. "Let's go. You look exhausted. I have kept you out much too long."

Autumn took his hand, and he helped her up.

"What do you dream about?" asked Autumn as they slowly left the garden.

"Of having a family, a home, an ordinary way of life."

They walked quietly for a while. Autumn felt Sage's strong arms supporting her and blushed a little. It seemed like they suddenly appeared at her door.

"Good night, have sweet dreams," said Sage as he opened the door and saw Katrina waiting for her.

"Good night and thank you for helping me," said Autumn.

Sage smiled and kissed her forehead. He turned and went to his door across the hallway.

Katrina hummed happily as she helped Autumn get ready for bed. She didn't ask too many questions, but Autumn guessed she already knew a lot that happened and that palace gossip travels fast.

Autumn's last thoughts before falling asleep were with Sage. What if Katrina was right and Shasta did want to marry Sage? Somehow that really bothered her. She and Sage were friends, and she knew that he needed something different than that. She liked Sage looking out for her, but she also felt like she wanted him to stay in her life. She was trying to sort out her jumbled emotions when she went to sleep.

CHAPTER 21: DINNER

Autumn and Toble visited only briefly the next morning. When Katrina came to collect Autumn's dishes from breakfast, the physician came with her. The physician gave Autumn some potions and checked on her bandages.

"Very good!" he said. "I think you have taken my advice. You may be back to normal, more or less, by the end of the week."

"I can't believe it!" said Autumn. "In the human world, it would have taken months!"

The physician nodded.

"It would have been the same here, but you were given the finest potions in the kingdom, and your healing ability is nothing to take for granted. I have seen healers work, and you are a pretty good one. Sage was not just boasting when he told me of your skill."

Autumn felt embarrassed. She hadn't done as much meditating as she should have, but the Gryphon was still healing her anyway.

"So, what are your recommendations now?" she asked.

"Just keep doing the same things," said the physician as he packed his things back into his bag. "You will be just fine."

He patted her hand and left.

Katrina helped Autumn dress in the soft leather traveling outfit King Fredrick and Queen Oceania had given her. The mauve tunic and slacks looked very feminine with its fancy embroidery. Autumn sat at the armoire that was against the wall at the foot of the bed so that Katrina could fix her hair. Autumn watched her work in the mirror.

Autumn's mind began to wander. She had observed that she wasn't aging anymore. It was also nice to see a familiar face when she looked at herself in the mirror. Autumn had been twenty-five when she entered the portal. It felt good to know herself again. Autumn had all her memories except the few months between her father's death and her arrival in this new world. That may be the only good thing that had happened to Autumn at Maldamien's fortress, but even that good thing had a bittersweet aftertaste. She wasn't what Puck thought she was. She was an ordinary human who knew nothing about fighting, queens, or the affairs of this world. Unless something important happened in the few months that were missing from her memories, there was very little she could do to help, except work as a healer. She had no special upbringing, no miraculous signs, no special destiny, no important family or connections. It could be anyone sitting here, and the same things would have happened to them. She wasn't even adventurous. Her apartment was only a few blocks away from the house she grew up in. She had never traveled the world or done anything exciting until now.

"What are you thinking about?" asked Katrina as she was putting the final touches on the elaborate braid in Autumn's hair. "You look so serious."

"I was thinking about how much I've changed," said Autumn. "I look the same as I did a year ago, but everything is different now."

"Life is strange that way," said Katrina. "Sometimes I wish I was young again, so I could see everything the way you do."

Autumn looked at Katrina. She didn't look old, but she was probably as old as the immortality spell or a little older. It seemed to Autumn that people around here behaved the way they felt, not the age they actually were.

A knock came on the door and Katrina went through the sitting room to open it.

"We came to ask if Autumn would like to have lunch with us in the atrium," said Sage as he walked in with Tanner and Toble.

"I would love to," Autumn answered from her chair in the bedroom.

Sage came in and helped her up.

"You look charming today."

Autumn walked out of the apartment with her arm in his for support.

"Katrina is a whiz at getting me ready. Is Queen Shasta going to join us?" she asked.

Sage's eyes turned a variety of colors.

"Queen Shasta will be busy with the wedding preparations. I have been helping her all morning, so I am hoping that the rest of the day will be free."

Autumn couldn't tell whether he was being hopeful or just factual.

She still couldn't tell how Sage felt about Queen Shasta either. Was he annoyed with her, and if so, why? Did he want to spend time with her but hate wedding stuff, or did he just not want to spend time with her?

It was not far to the main atrium. It was in the center of the palace, like a courtyard that was about three acres in size with paths weaving throughout. The gardens even held birds, insects, and small game. Many of the flower beds had been converted into vegetable and herb gardens while still maintaining their beauty, as Sage had said. The group sat at one of the garden's tables at the edge of an open gravel area. If the sky of the garden was not a large translucent dome revealing the water above, Autumn could have forgotten that she was still indoors.

Some servants came and served them a light meal of angular fruits and some fish.

"So," began Sage, "what are we going to do?"

"Today, or farther in the future?" asked Tanner.

"I was thinking overall," said Sage. "Autumn had mentioned our original plan of going to see Thyme. Should we make plans now, or wait until you have recovered?"

"The physician said I should be recovered by the end of this week," said Autumn. "I don't think we should stay much longer than that."

"That's quick," said Tanner as he took a bite of his food.

"The doctor says it's a combination of the potions and my healing ability," explained Autumn.

"Well, we will still need to figure out how we are going to get to Thyme's monastery," said Sage. "It would be a long trip on foot, plus the monastery floats in the sky."

"I was pondering the idea I have been working on for a flying machine," said Toble.

"The one with a large bubble on top, or the one with the bird-like wings?" asked Sage.

"I decided to combine them. It would be a good solution since none of us can fly," said Toble.

He pushed away his plate to dig in the bag he always carried and pulled out some scrolls.

"I will have to work on the plans a little, but I should be able to build it with some help."

"Let me see those," said Tanner.

"I guess that will keep you busy for a while. How long will it take to build? Can you build a ship in a week?" asked Sage as he finished his fish and started to eat some of Toble's.

Toble pulled his plate back and scowled at Sage. "I don't know. I have to see what we can use."

"You wouldn't have to use as big of a bubble if you use lighter wood," said Tanner from behind a scroll. "Most Undine ships are half the weight you have written here. You based your design on a mermaid ship."

"Huh?" asked Toble as he looked to see what Tanner was pointing at.

"Wood could also replace a lot of this metal work if you choose the right kind," said Tanner. "I thought you Dryads were supposed to know all about wood!"

"Living wood, growing wood, but I never was much of a carpenter," said Toble. "If it was supposed to be natural, it didn't affect me. I grew up working on machines."

"Well, if you let me worry about the wood and finding the lightest and most durable kind, you might be able to make this smaller," said Tanner handing the scroll back to Toble. "And we might be able to use an already made Undine boat to start out with."

"If so, then we might be able to get this done in a week," said Toble looking back at his design.

"Anything I can do?" asked Sage as he stole a second piece of fruit from Toble's plate.

"We will need supplies for the trip and supplies for making the ship," said Toble.

"Just give me a list of what you need for the ship. I can figure out the rest of the stuff," said Sage.

He attempted to steal a third piece of fruit when Tanner slapped his hand with a spoon.

"Stop acting like a barbarian!" said Tanner.

Autumn giggled.

"What about me?" she asked.

"We are depending on you to lead the conversation with Thyme," said Sage. "You know more about what we are dealing with and what is going on than any of us. You also know more about what Puck was thinking and planning."

"I still don't know much," said Autumn. "I had been in the situation of knowing so little for such a long time. I am not sure I know as much as you think."

"Your experience with Maldamien has revealed a lot to you," said Tanner, "and Puck never told any of us why he wanted to see Thyme or what he was going to ask him. You also know more about the events that brought you here than any of us. There are a lot of pieces that seem like they should go together, but you are the only one who is connected to them all."

"The only things I would even think to ask Thyme about would have to do with Maldamien. A lot of the things I thought I knew about Maldamien have turned out to be myths and gossip," said Sage. "All I do know is that he is unnaturally magical. We don't even know what his ultimate goal is. Why does he want to open all the portals anyway? Is he trying to conquer the human world too? Is that why Queen Anemone closed the portals? If the world is going to self- destruct in a little more than two months, is he now trying to save it? Will even stopping Maldamien matter? If we are to stop him, how do we go about doing it?"

"What if Maldamien does keep the world from getting destroyed and does conquer the human world, is that a better option?" asked Tanner.

"I don't think world conquest is his goal," said Autumn. "He has his eyes on something bigger."

"What is bigger than ruling the world?" asked Sage.

"I think he wants to be a god, even if that means destroying the world," said Autumn.

"A god?" said Toble, looking up from the scroll in his hands. "Is that possible?"

"I don't know, but he wants to be greater than anything that is on this planet and perhaps even greater than the Creator himself," said Autumn.

Everyone just looked at each other as they processed the concept. There were still so many questions, but no point in asking them.

Finally, Tanner broke the silence as he got up from his seat.

"I'm going to go and talk to someone about wood."

Toble looked up.

"Ask about a boat too. Any old boat will do as long as it's light."

"And floats," said Tanner as he left.

209

Toble pushed his now empty plate out of the way and spread out his scroll to write on it.

Sage stood up and stretched.

"Well Toble, if you don't need us, I'll go talk to Queen Oceania about the assistance she had mentioned at the dinner."

Toble was already busy drawing and writing in his papers. He just mumbled and waved.

"Where are you going to be later?" asked Sage.

"Huh?" said Toble without looking up.

"Where are you going today?" Sage repeated.

"Here, here. I'm going to work on the ship as soon as Tanner brings me something."

Sage turned to Autumn.

"He will be obsessed with his ship until it's finished. Why don't you join me?"

"Sounds good," Autumn said as Sage helped her up.

They walked through the length of the atrium, talking about various plants and garden features. Autumn wondered some at Sage's attention to her. Was he just bored or did he really enjoy her company?

An Undine woman in simple servant clothes walked up to them sheepishly.

"Are you the human girl, Autumn, and the resistance leader, Sage?"

"Yes," said Autumn.

"They say that you escaped from Maldamien's fortress. Do you know if my husband was there, too? Did he escape?" she asked.

Autumn and Sage looked at each other.

"We checked all the cells closely," said Sage. "If he was there, he escaped. It may have taken him more time to get here because everyone took different routes home to avoid recapture, and he may also have been one who was helping the injured, as well."

"I am really sorry that we can't tell you if we saw him, but I was kept in isolation, so I didn't see anyone," said Autumn.

The Undine woman said, "Thank you so much. When I saw so many people returning yesterday, I was afraid he might have been left behind or didn't make it. I know you did your best. Thank you!" she bowed to them and scurried off.

Autumn wished so much for that woman to have her husband that it ached inside.

"Let's go another way before someone else comes up to us," whispered Sage. "I don't want to promise them anything that I don't know to be true."

"Like what?" asked Autumn.

"What if her husband had been killed? Not all prisoners were kept alive in that fortress. What if he was made a slave somewhere else or sent to the mines?"

Autumn had not thought of that and ached for the woman who had left them.

Sage and Autumn walked arm in arm out of the atrium into a hall. They continued down the hall until they saw an open door on the left.

"Oh, that's the music room!" exclaimed Autumn. "I'm having a hard time remembering where all the rooms were since our full-speed tour. I thought this was upstairs."

"Why don't we go in?" said Sage.

The room was filled with many finely decorated instruments and comfortable chairs. There were stringed instruments in the far corner, cymbals, and drums by the door. Horns and flutes were placed throughout the room. Sage and Autumn sat in the two chairs nearest an angular guitar-like instrument.

"You probably have never seen these kinds of instruments before. There are instruments in here from a variety of cultures. Of course, most are Undine, but this is a Huldranian model, it's called a bolerita."

Sage picked it up and tried to tune it some, and then picked out a rough tune.

"I was beginning to learn this instrument when my schooling ended. It is traditional for the Huldra to learn it, but I have rarely touched one since."

"That's a shame," said Autumn. "Did you really want to learn it?"

"No, not really." Sage shrugged as he put the instrument back down. "There were a lot of other things I missed more. I had just started my year under Puck, and I never learned basic magic, but almost everything else I learned from experience or books."

Autumn's heart twinged at the memory of Puck, but she pushed the emotion down. "Were there a lot of books in the Ifrit desert?" asked Autumn as she picked up the bolerita Sage put down and began to tune it to her own ear.

"Yes, probably more than most places since Maldamien burned

whatever he didn't steal. The desert is a good place to hide things. The people there don't want to be bothered and tend to leave others alone. The Nomads who follow Maldamien are some of the more aggressive tribes. Many of them felt like outcasts because of being a mixture of various races or having trouble with someone back home, but if you earn their trust, you can learn anything."

"Except magic?" asked Autumn.

She looked down at the bolerita trying to figure out what to do with the moving fret on the neck of the instrument.

"Yes, except magic," said Sage. "Magic takes a connection with nature and each other that most people there avoid. Toble tried to teach me one time, but I got frustrated and didn't understand what he was trying to explain. I haven't needed it much anyways. I ended up learning swordcraft and survival skills that were more valuable to me at the time."

"Aha!" exclaimed Autumn.

She had figured out how to push the fret all the way up, so she could play the instrument like a guitar. She began to play Fur Elise roughly. Sage sat forward in his chair impressed. After one time through with lots of mistakes, Autumn returned the fret to its original position and put the instrument down.

"I have never heard the bolerita played that way. It sounded good. Not the way my father used to play, but still very nice. Where did you learn to play?"

"I had a guitar at home that I played. It is similar, but not as pretty."

"The Huldra are a people of many passions. They love art and music about as much as they love war and the hunt. Their enslavement of the Dryads was seen as bringing their advanced culture to a primitive people. The Huldra are such a backward people and one of the few nations to completely support Maldamien as a whole."

"You don't see yourself as part of them. Is it because of growing up at Vervain?" asked Autumn.

"I do, and I don't," answered Sage. "When someone like Turmeric comes to mind to most people, then I can't count myself as one of them. My father, on the other hand, was a great man and proud of being Huldra, but there aren't many like him around anymore."

"I think I understand," said Autumn. "I would have never felt ashamed of being human if people didn't immediately think of

Maldamien and Nomads."

"No one still knows that Maldamien is not completely human," said Sage. "His being half vampire explains a lot."

Autumn shuddered.

"Come on," said Sage. His eyes turned from blue to vivid green. "We have talked too long. You're pale."

He offered her his hand. Autumn took it, but the image of Maldamien licking her blood lingered in her mind. Sage didn't say anything but walked slower for her as they left the music room. After a short while, the effects of the image wore off, and Sage began to talk about the palace itself.

"I believe this part of the palace is newer than the area with the throne room and royal chambers. Of course, I still mean somewhere in the third era versus the beginning of the second. I heard that the oldest part was built 6,700 years ago. Not quite as old as Vervain, but older than pretty much everywhere else."

They walked down to a wing of the palace she had never visited. Sage walked up to a footman in front of a pair of elaborate doors.

"I would like to have an audience with Queen Oceania whenever she is available," said Sage.

"The queen is not here right now. She is being fitted for her dress. I will tell Her Majesty when she returns," answered the footman.

"Thank you, that will be just fine," said Sage. The footman gave a little bow, and they walked back the way they came.

"You are a strange guy," said Autumn teasingly. "How many people can be as comfortable in a palace as they are in the forest or desert?"

"How many people can say that they have lived extensively in both places?" he answered.

"Which would you choose if you could?" asked Autumn.

"Neither," said Sage.

"Where then?"

"I would want a normal house, with a normal family, in a place where I belonged," said Sage.

"Being normal isn't as great as it might seem. I know. When you walk through life invisible to the world, then the world just tries to squash you."

"Then you would choose the palace?" asked Sage.

Autumn thought about it.

"I don't know. I would want to be around those who I care about, and somewhere I felt like I belonged, but I am not sure where that is."

"I don't think our wants are all that different. My adventurous life and your normal life are not satisfying because we are not happy there. I have thought a lot about what makes a person happy. It is not the unwanted drudge of a normal life or an adventure in which nothing is permanent, but a self-built, tailored life of consistent and stable pleasures. A party comes and goes. Good, satisfying relationships and all that goes into building and maintaining those are what lasts. Parties, wealth, adventures, or whatever doesn't matter unless you have people you love to share it with."

They walked into the royal gallery. Portraits of finely dressed deceased royalty hung on the wall, one right next to another. Each one had water-themed backgrounds and various poses of importance.

"Shouldn't we be doing something productive?" said Autumn.

"We can't begin until we find out what Queen Oceania meant in helping us. I need to know what she would like to give us and what we need to purchase."

"True," admitted Autumn.

She wondered if they had any money to purchase stuff with, but decided not to ask. She would just let Sage worry about it.

"Are you getting bored?" asked Sage.

"No, but I am getting tired."

Before they could go farther, a servant walked up and bowed. "Queen Oceania has agreed to see you in an hour."

Sage looked at Autumn.

"Are you up to seeing her?"

Autumn didn't want to part with Sage, but she felt exhausted.

"No, I would like to return to my room."

"Let the queen know that it will be just me," Sage told the servant. The servant bowed and left.

Sage helped Autumn back to her room. She opened her door and turned around.

"I had a very nice afternoon," she told Sage.

Sage took her hand and kissed it dramatically.

"Then we shall repeat it tomorrow."

They said goodnight and Autumn closed the door slowly. She went to the small desk in the bedroom and pulled out a sheet of paper and a silver pen. She began to make a list of things to ask Thyme when they saw him. In her tiredness, she could only think of the questions Sage had asked earlier. Her mind then wandered to thinking about him and how it felt to be walking arm in arm with him.

Was she falling in love with him? This silly crush she was developing was dangerous when he was so different than her and so much older. She knew how easy it was for a lonely woman to fall in love. She already had two disasters in her history. Then again, they saw the world similarly and enjoyed being around each other. This was the first time she felt like she could be herself since being in Gryphendale.

"No," she told herself. "I won't be so easily swayed by my emotions."

Autumn continued her list by putting down: *Ask about ring, picture, and keys.* She folded up the paper. She struggled to undress for bed and put the paper in her sash. She fell asleep with her mind still churning through all her various emotions and questions.

CHAPTER 22: BUILDING

Autumn woke up early in a sweat. She didn't remember what she dreamed but didn't want to risk going to sleep again. Instead, she sat at the desk in her room and continued to work on her list of questions. Katrina arrived a half hour later with the physician.

The physician examined her wounds. He re-wrapped the bandage on her leg and removed all her other bandages. He applied potions to her skin to help with the scarring.

"You are free to do as you like, but don't push yourself too hard. You don't need to be skipping dinner because of exhaustion again," he told her.

When the physician left, Katrina served breakfast to Autumn.

"Toble and Sage said they would not be able to visit this morning. Toble forgot to rest last night, and Sage has to do errands for Queen Shasta. After all, the wedding is in four days!" Katrina informed her.

"That's all right," said Autumn, a little disappointed. "I was thinking about going to the library anyway. Do you think I could have lunch with them?"

"They requested to have their lunches and dinners in the atrium," said Katrina. "I think they were hoping you would join them."

"Then that is what I will do," said Autumn.

After Katrina finished making Autumn's wild hair presentable, Autumn left for the library in the direction that Katrina had described.

The library was a large two-story room with a wall of windows overlooking the atrium below. There were no shelves in the center of the room, just overstuffed chairs, coffee tables, and a couple of small writing desks. To reach the second floor, she had to walk up a small spiral staircase to a narrow balcony that hugged the three walls of books. For being such a huge palace, the library was a little disappointing. Autumn reminded herself that they were probably lucky to even have that many books if Maldamien was stealing them or burning them.

Autumn walked along the shelves, and after covering the whole library once, she picked up a book that looked like an illuminated history or a storybook. She found it frustrating that there seemed to be no books in English in the library either. She had hoped to do some research on the things on her questions list so she didn't feel completely ignorant. A book on magic, the portals, Vervain, or anything related might have helped. Instead, she would have to just scan over picture books and try to gather something subconsciously. Though, she doubted that would help.

She settled into a comfortable chair by the massive windows and curled her legs under her. She looked down out of the window into the atrium. She could see Toble and Tanner working on a boat with supplies all around them. The Viking-styled boat looked like it could seat ten people and some baggage. They'd already erected a wood frame and had ropes all over it.

Her thoughts turned toward Sage. Autumn pushed down the disappointment and tinge of jealousy at his time with Queen Shasta. Autumn could still hear Queen Shasta when she had mentioned Sage and she played together as kids. Sage and Queen Shasta were the same age, she was beautiful, and she was on the right side of the issues. They had every right to be in love.

But it felt wrong.

Autumn sighed. If Sage did end up falling in love with Queen Shasta, Autumn needed to feel happy for them and not keep feeding this school-girl crush, even though it would break her heart.

She shifted in the chair and looked down at her book, trying to distract herself. The pictures were very colorful and expressive in an old medieval illustrated manuscript sort of way. She casually flipped the pages. She noticed a symbol on a child's toy in one of the pictures. It seemed familiar, then she looked at the caption below the image and was able to identify the sounds of some of the symbols.

She flipped to another picture and recognized the word for *queen*. She looked through the text and saw the words for *war* and *killed*.

Autumn flipped to another page and was struck by a picture of a young Undine woman talking to a very colorful fish. Autumn was able to read the caption, "Auriel and the Magical Singing Fish."

Autumn held her breath as she realized she could read everything on the page fluently. She looked around the room. Could she read the Undine language? What did that mean? She remembered how she understood the meeting in the Sprite language at Ezekiel's house. Was she some language prodigy or was this a part of some spell? She decided to ask Thyme about it and wrote it on her list. Until then she was going to make the most of this hidden talent.

Autumn walked to the shelves and read the titles: *History of the War of Tales*, *Why Merpeople are People Too*, *Common Translation Problems of the Ancient Tongues*, and on it went. She found a small children's book that was a history of the world in a hundred pages or so. Puck had taught her the races and some geography with dabs of history that just floated around in her head, untied to any sort of order. She read the book with intensity, filling in the gaps of what she roughly knew about the world. She was only a couple of chapters into the book when Katrina entered the library.

"Did you still want to eat lunch in the atrium? They will be serving in just a couple of minutes. Your friends don't want to get started without you."

"Oh!" cried Autumn.

She left the book in the chair and followed Katrina into the atrium. She would be eager to return to the library later.

During lunch, Toble and Tanner talked about their progress in building the flying ship. Autumn was disappointed at Sage's absence. After lunch, Toble and Tanner showed her how things on the ship worked and what they planned to do next. She tried to show interest. Her thoughts flew back and forth from her discovery in the library and curiosity about Sage's absence. Even so, she ended up helping Toble and Tanner with tasks for the ship. She spent the whole afternoon cutting large sheets of paper for air fins or something like that.

Dinner was eaten in the atrium without any sign of Sage, to everyone's disappointment. Only after dinner was Autumn able to make her way back to the library.

She borrowed five random books of different looking languages and took her children's history book back to her room. She tried to stay up reading but fell asleep sometime after everything became blurry.

Katrina woke Autumn up in the morning. Autumn used her sleeve to wipe up a little pool of drool off of the book she was laying on.

"Well, what the physician doesn't know won't hurt him," said

Katrina as she turned on all the lights. "He won't be coming by this morning because the cook burned her hand pretty badly cooking breakfast. Here are the potions he sent you."

Autumn applied them and then started eating breakfast.

"Katrina, I borrowed some books from the library, and I was curious what languages they are written in. Could you help me?"

"I only read the Undine language. All the rest of those books look like gibberish to me. I could send someone who could help you if you like."

"No thanks," said Autumn.

She didn't want any more attention brought to this issue than necessary. She needed someone she trusted.

"Is Toble in his room?"

"No, Tanner and he got up earlier this morning to work in the atrium. I have never seen two men as excited as they are."

"What about Sage?" asked Autumn. "Is he still in his room?"

"Yes, I believe Sally was just serving him breakfast a moment ago. If you are planning on talking to him, you might want to do it soon. I believe Queen Shasta has another full day planned for him. I certainly hope they get engaged before the wedding. They must be in love the way they are spending so much time together! Oh, and talking about weddings…" Katrina then pulled out a multicolored string. "When you are finished eating, we need to measure you for your dress. I will try to be quick so that you can get going."

Autumn pushed away her breakfast tray and got out of bed. The string began to float around Autumn and measure her by itself. Katrina quickly wrote things down and looked up to say, "Measure the waist," or "around the upper arm."

After a half hour of the string measuring every part of Autumn, Katrina said, "That's it." The string flew into Katrina's pocket. "The day after tomorrow you will need to try on the dress and the wedding will be the next day at dusk."

"Thanks," said Autumn.

As soon as Katrina left with the breakfast dishes, Autumn was dressed and ready to go. She grabbed the library books, walked over to Sage's room across the hall, and knocked on his door.

She heard Sage begin to speak, then trip and fall over something. A couple more tumbling noises later, Sage opened the door. His hair was standing up in odd places, but he was wearing his normal day clothes, though a bit wrinkled. His face relaxed at seeing her.

"Hi," he said opening the door farther to let her into his sitting room.

He picked up the chair he'd tripped over.

"Sorry, Autumn. Shasta had me carry and make stuff for the wedding until late last night. I'm not fully awake yet. I don't know why she didn't ask one of the Undines to help. I'm not in my best form."

He tried to smooth down his hair in a decorative mirror.

"It doesn't matter," Autumn said. "I need to talk."

Sage sat down in front of his breakfast tray on the coffee table and indicated for Autumn to sit in the overstuffed chair across from him.

"Have you eaten?" he asked.

"Yeah."

"Do you mind if I finish while you talk?"

"Go ahead."

Autumn set down her stack of books next to Sage's breakfast tray. Sage arched an eyebrow as his eyes changed from brown to green.

"You have an odd collection of books here," said Sage as he chewed on a roll.

He picked up the top one.

"Do you know what languages these books are in?" asked Autumn. She was shaking inside with nervousness and excitement.

"Sure, this is in the Undine language, next is a Sprite book, then Brownie, then Gnome, and the last one is Mermaidish."

"Can you read all of those languages?" asked Autumn.

"No, I just read English, Huldra, and Sprite." Sage took another bite of his roll. "Why?"

Autumn picked up the Undine children's book and opened it. She looked at the book for a moment and then translated, "The story of the singing fish is one of the most popular tales on common lore, but the truth is not far from the myth."

Sage gasped and stood up, "You can read that?"

Autumn swallowed the dryness in her throat.

"Yes, and I think I may be able to read the others too, but I am almost afraid to try."

"But how? I mean you have never been here before. Did Puck teach you, or are you under a spell or something?"

220

"I don't know," replied Autumn.

"Well, try to read the rest of the books and see what happens," said Sage handing her the Brownie book as he sat back down.

Autumn opened it. Sage watched as Autumn looked over the script. The writing was small and basic. They wrote from left to right just like the Undine and English languages. She was able to pick out words for farm and crops. Then it became clearer.

"The best time to plant a crop is when the magic peaks in the spring. Remember to plant within a clear tent if you are planting at any other time. This will confuse the plant to think it is the correct time." Autumn translated aloud.

Sage handed her the Gnome book. She opened it, and the block letters were even easier to read.

"Don't carve against the grain of the wood or you will be fighting the very nature of the material."

Sage handed her the Sprite book.

"The wind currents move in regular patterns. Keep your head up to direct your flight into the current," she translated immediately.

Sage then handed her the last book which was in the Mermaid language. Autumn stared at the fancy cursive writing with no understanding.

"I can't read this one."

Autumn closed the book and placed it on the stack. "So what do you think?"

Sage leaned back. "Impressive."

He scratched his head and stood up to pace.

"And you don't ever remember being in our world before?" he asked.

"No. In fact, I thought this place existed only in fairytales. Though my father always acted as though it was real. He taught mythology and folklore in the humanities department at the university." Autumn began to wonder about how her father used to talk about Brownies, Sprites, and Gnomes. He was very close to describing them accurately from the folklore that he studied. Did he know the languages? No. Autumn knew very well the stories and sources of his information. His books and studies were not otherworldly. He was very normal. But then again...

"Did you see a Sprite die? Like in the fortress or since you came here," asked Sage.

"What?" asked Autumn, confused.

"Sprites can pass on selected memories when they are about to die. It is a unique trait. They can pass on a skill or a group of memories they want to preserve. It only travels one generation, but it is amazing what children or grandchildren of musicians or artisans can do with such a gift," explained Sage.

"No." Autumn then thought about Puck. "Can Satyrs do it too?"

"I don't think so," said Sage as he sat back down. "Then it must be a spell of some kind."

"But who would cast it?"

"The only wizards strong enough are Maldamien and Turmeric, but Turmeric doesn't really count since he depends on Maldamien to strengthen his magic."

"I could understand the Sprite language before I met Maldamien. I just didn't know I could read it, too. Plus, how would that help him?"

Sage and Autumn sat thinking. It was kind of an awkward silence. Autumn shrugged her shoulders.

"I guess we could bring it up to Thyme."

"Sure," said Sage. "Do Toble and Tanner know about it yet?"

"No, but let me be the one to tell them about it."

"Of course," said Sage. "I'm just honored you spoke with me first."

Autumn blushed.

"Do you want something to drink or eat?" asked Sage, changing the subject.

"No," she replied feeling self-conscious. "I think I will go."

"Don't go," said Sage quickly.

Autumn wondered if he was bored.

"At least let's take a walk together."

Autumn smiled.

"I'll wait for you in the hall."

"What?" asked Sage.

He followed Autumn's eyes up and patted his hair.

"Oh, I'll be just a second."

Autumn walked out into the hall at the same time Tanner walked up to his room. He looked a bit tired but very happy.

"Good morning," he called.

"Good morning." Autumn blushed. "I was just visiting with Sage real quick. I thought you and Toble were busy downstairs."

"We were, but Toble went to the library to look up something he thought he calculated wrong. I'm just grabbing my knife to do a little whittling while I wait for him. So, what are you up to with all of those books?"

"I had a language question for Sage, and I needed examples."

"Well, if you are done with them, I would like to borrow that book on whittling you happen to have, and I think Toble might find the one on flight interesting to browse through as well."

Autumn walked over and handed him the books he referred to. He seemed puzzled for a moment and then shook his head.

Sage walked out of his room in a new set of clothes and looking dashing. Tanner got a sparkle in his eye.

"Hi, Tanner!" called Sage. "Autumn, are you ready to go?"

Autumn looked at Tanner. He grinned.

"You kids have fun," he said as he went into his own room.

Tanner seemed extra happy suddenly to Autumn. She wondered if he had some scheme in his head, but she couldn't imagine what about.

Sage and Autumn instinctively walked arm in arm even though she didn't need the support anymore. They walked quietly for a little while searching for a topic to talk about.

"Could you tell me more about the Huldra kingdom?" asked Autumn.

"Well, it's called Samodivas, and it's a beautiful well-wooded kingdom. The trees are smaller than the lands north of the River Yarrow, but it is filled with hills, streams, and lakes. My family had a large estate in the northeast corner of the kingdom, near the city of Kalinda. We used to visit in the summers. I was born there, and Toble grew up in that city. I haven't been there since Maldamien took over. I just expected Turmeric to take over the estate since the extended family disowned me for not supporting Maldamien like the rest of my countrymen. I think Toble is more troubled by my not inheriting the estate than I am. For me, Vervain was my home. That was where my friends were and my best memories. The rest of our family were arrogant, jealous, and greedy. They used to make comments about how soft I would be growing up in the palace and that it was strange that I had no Huldra friends. I was ready to leave the issue of the estate alone if Turmeric hadn't hunted me down in the Ifrit desert. Apparently, the spells on those old estates won't give access to parts of the home to someone who isn't the true heir. Turmeric felt like I deserved to die anyway. How about you? Do you miss back home?"

"No, not really," sighed Autumn. "I was not very popular, and I don't have any close family."

"That seems strange. You make friends easily here. Everyone you have met, other than Maldamien's allies, likes you."

"It's hard to make friends when everyone knows what you have done your whole life, and no one wants to treat you like an adult. I have always been odd and misunderstood. Does that make sense?" Autumn stopped and looked at him. "I don't know that my whining even makes sense after looking at life and death so closely."

"Everyone needs friends," said Sage, tucking Autumn's arm back into his arm. "It is what..."

Sage stopped and turned around pulling Autumn with him and walking quickly in the opposite direction.

"Sage!" came a familiar female voice.

"Drat!" mumbled Sage in a low voice. "I could smell her perfume, but I was hoping we could get away."

He turned around and bowed.

"Queen Shasta."

Autumn curtsied too.

"Oh Autumn, you are looking well. How kind of Sage to escort you around. I am sorry to interrupt, but Sage, I need an escort to the wedding ball since I will be part of the ceremony."

"Well...uh..." Sage looked a little pale as he tried to think of something to say. Finally, he bowed. "I would be honored."

"Wonderful!" Queen Shasta floated a little higher with giddiness. "Oh, and you will be measured for your suit of clothes this afternoon. I will see you after lunch!" She turned around and glided away.

Sage turned to Autumn. "Why don't you ask Toble or Tanner to escort you to the wedding ball?"

"Don't worry about me," said Autumn as they continued walking. "I'm a big girl."

Sage sighed.

"I need to get away from this place. This wedding stuff is driving me crazy."

They continued to talk the rest of the morning, arm in arm. Autumn realized that Sage was not in love with Queen Shasta at all. In fact, he mentioned how much he hated being involved in planning this wedding two more times. He also seemed to have an insatiable curiosity about Autumn's past and interests. They were in deep conversation until they reached the atrium for lunch. Both Toble and Tanner were already sitting and having an animated debate. At seeing Sage and Autumn, they stopped to watch the newcomers.

"What are you old fools scheming?" asked Sage as they were seated.

"We weren't scheming anything," said Toble indignantly, but his eyes sparkled in contradiction.

"Sage, you need to see the flying machine," said Tanner, changing the subject. "It looks fantastic, and it's almost done."

"If it's almost done, it'll need a name," said Sage.

"How about the Flying Hope?" asked Autumn.

"Perfect," said Toble.

"The good ship Flying Hope," stated Tanner. "I like it."

"Sounds like she has a name," said Sage as their food was served. It was fish again.

"So, what's the schedule?" asked Autumn.

"The wedding ball is at dusk, so I was thinking we could leave early the next morning," said Sage. "That is if the ship is done by then?"

"Oh, it will be done," said Toble. "I was also thinking that for Queen Shasta's safety, she should be left behind. Perhaps we can ask King Fredrick and Queen Oceania to give her an escort home. She might need some troops to take her throne back. I would suggest leaving Autumn as well for her safety, but she is part of the reason we are going."

"Do we know what we are going to ask when we get there?" inquired Tanner.

"I have a list," said Autumn.

"Good," said Tanner. "What about the supplies?"

"That is taken care of," said Sage. "I would like to check on it sometime this afternoon if Shasta would leave me alone."

"You guys have been like that since you were kids," said Toble, shaking his head.

Autumn noticed Sage's frown.

"Yes, we have known each other for a long time. You would think she would understand how much I hate frilly palace party stuff. I have never liked color coordinating decorations and sorting out guest lists and planning seating arrangements. I really couldn't care less if an admiral is at the same table as a magistrate."

Autumn's heart fluttered a little. She mentally reprimanded herself for being such a child. Just because he wasn't in love with Shasta didn't mean that he would then be in love with her. She might be just a little sister to him, a way to escape the wedding stuff and nothing more.

A way of escape and little sister who were walking arm in arm.

"So Sage, are you going to be able to help with the ship at all?" asked Tanner.

"I should have been here this morning, sorry guys," said Sage pushing away his empty plate. "This afternoon Queen Shasta has me scheduled for a measuring."

"That shouldn't take long," said Toble. "Mine just took a little while."

Sage shrugged. "If I can get away, I will be here."

"I would like to see the improvements on the Flying Hope," said Autumn as she finished her own plate.

"Sounds good." Tanner shoved the last bite of his lunch in his mouth and got up.

They all walked to the other side of the atrium from where they had been eating to see the ship. The Viking-styled ship had grown a mast since Autumn had seen it last. A seat and pedals were attached to the back of the boat. A huge pile of cloth sat next to the ship beside the stack of paper Autumn had cut.

"This cloth here will be filled with helium gas and air," said Toble as he started the tour.

"Where are you going to get helium?" asked Autumn.

"Everyone has a helium extractor device to work the kitchen heating coils," explained Tanner.

"Oh." Autumn wondered about the science and safety behind that.

"Then the ship will have water bags that we can empty when we want to get higher. The propulsion forward will be a series of Sprite-like wings on the rotating rudder on the back of the boat. Someone will have to pedal the device. Sage, I thought that would be you."

"This is for not helping to build it," teased Sage.

Toble continued. "Steering will be done with these large oars for the sides. We will also use the wind with the mast for propulsion and large steering."

"It looks great!" said Autumn. "How are we going to get it out of here and outside?"

Toble frowned and rubbed his chin.

Tanner spoke up. "All we need to do is take down the mast and lay it inside. They brought the ship through some cargo doors. We will wait to blow up the cloth bubble and add the finishing touches to the mast when we have it outside."

"Well done, Toble," said Sage, giving him a pat on the back. "Got to go before Shasta starts foaming at the mouth."

After Sage left, Autumn asked, "Where did you find the balloon... I mean cloth bubble?"

"The Merpeople have some large buoys made of some whale organ for their ocean territories. We had the crew of tailors who were already working on the wedding just sew them together real quick," said Toble.

"Well, can I help with anything?" asked Autumn.

"You could attach the paper to those oars, if you would like," said Toble. He showed her how to put the glue on them and left her to work until dinner. Tanner and Toble climbed all over the ship doing various other tasks, shouting at each other and making jokes. When Autumn finished, she stood to stretch.

"Look," said Tanner as he walked up to her. He pointed to the front of the ship. Autumn walked to where he pointed. There, engraved ornately on the ship, was "The Flying Hope" in English.

"That's beautiful!" cried Autumn. "Where did you learn to carve like that?"

"My grandfather was a master craftsman, and he taught me. He wanted me to follow in his footsteps unlike my father, but I chose to study husbandry. That book you had helped, too."

"Can I tell you about something?" asked Autumn nervously. "Did Puck ever tell you about how I understood the Sprite language at Ezekiel's place?"

"Sure, he mentioned it once. Does this have something to do with that book?" asked Tanner.

"Yes," said Autumn. "I found out this morning that I could read the Sprite, Gnome, Brownie, and Undine languages."

Tanner turned and shouted, "Toble, did you hear this?"

227

Autumn looked around to see if anyone else was listening.

"What?" Toble said, bumping his head into a fin-like sail he was erecting.

Tanner beckoned him over. "Did you hear what Autumn was talking about?"

"No, of course not!"

"I can read the Sprite, Gnome, Brownie, and Undine languages," repeated Autumn.

"I think it might be a good time to head to dinner," said Toble.

As they walked, Toble and Tanner asked her all the same questions Sage had earlier. They sat down at the table that they usually ate at and continued speculating on how Autumn might have known those languages. After a lengthy discussion, they didn't reach any new conclusions.

"I wonder where Sage is?" asked Autumn.

"I had hoped he would have been only a few minutes," said Toble. "We should start eating. He may not make it tonight." Toble motioned for a servant and told them that they were ready for dinner.

Autumn couldn't help looking disappointed.

"Don't worry about him and Shasta," said Toble knowingly. "He was over her decades ago. She isn't his type. The more she clings to him the more he wants nothing to do with her."

"So, they were a couple at one time?" asked Autumn.

"Yes, they saw each other for a while before she married the Sprite king, but it was over pretty quickly, for Sage at least. King Coriander was good for her, and they loved each other, but Shasta has always been afraid of being lonely," explained Toble.

"She is gorgeous," said Autumn.

"That is true, but do you think Sage is shallow enough to like a girl only for her looks? There is more to a good relationship that is hard to describe. Sage is not looking for a girl who is just," Toble searched for a word and seemed to settle on, "silly." He took a bite of his fish. "He tends to appreciate women who have a strength of character and a few brains. I have noticed you two getting along well."

"You noticed nothing," replied Tanner, "until I mentioned it this morning."

"So that is what you two were talking about," accused Autumn.

Toble and Tanner looked down at their food, busily shoving bites in their mouths. Autumn smirked. "It doesn't matter. You both know better than I that Sage is four times my age and probably thinks of me as a little sister. I don't know what you are planning, but I don't think it would be a good idea."

Toble looked up and pointed a fork at her. "Age doesn't make a difference. He looks thirty, he thinks thirty, and he acts thirty. The little sister thing is just because he is a man, and he is dense. I know. I happen to be one."

"Besides," added Tanner, "it isn't like we can make him feel something he doesn't already. We just want to bring the unconscious to the conscious level."

Autumn began to feel nervous. "Whatever you're planning, don't do it. I can't handle the embarrassment if it just turns out..."

Sage ran up to them out of breath. "There's been a coup, and the palace is under attack!"

CHAPTER 23: ATTACK

Toble, Tanner, and Autumn just sat and stared at Sage, with his disheveled appearance and drawn sword.

"A coup here?" said Toble.

"Yes, so come on! We need to evacuate everyone to the large dining hall."

"Who's attacking?" asked Tanner. "And where are they? Oh, and who is organizing the evacuation?"

"We don't have time for this!" said Sage. "Queen Oceania's general was a spy for Maldamien and is leading the coup. King Fredrick is organizing the Undine and Mermaid armies. They put me over the evacuation. I have Katrina rounding-up the maids, Aurora rounding up the Merpeople, and other staff getting the guests. So, come on!"

Sage ran off to round up those in the atrium as Toble assisted Autumn. Autumn had felt faint at the news and sat in shock. She saw images of being recaptured by Maldamien and carried off by the Ogres. She was frozen in place with fear when Sage returned with a gathering group of people.

"Why are you all still sitting here?" said Sage.

"I can't get her to move," said Toble.

Sage knelt down to her eye level.

"Sage, I can't go back! I just can't!" Autumn started crying. She was shaking and pale.

"Autumn!" Sage snapped, "that's enough. Snap out of it and come on. I'm not going to carry you. So either fight the fear or stay behind!"

Autumn's eyes grew large in surprise. Then her expression changed to anger. She got up and walked furiously past him in the direction everyone else was going. She felt hot with anger. "How dare he talk to me like that," she grumbled under her breath. "How dare he talk to me like that. How dare this stupid situation ruin this time for me to heal! Don't I get a break?"

Toble and Tanner were able to catch up with her since she was still moving somewhat slowly through the crowd. They followed the bustling crowd of panicked people. Autumn's anger subsided as she watched women and men alike crying or wandering along silently, in terror. The large dining hall was not very far away. The tables had already been moved to the side wall and laid on their sides so that more people could file in. The room was the size of a large banquet room at an expensive hotel. People were sitting all over the place. Toble, Tanner, and Autumn tried to lean against a wall near the door.

"It's going to be a tight fit if all one thousand servants, plus guests, are going to be in here," said Autumn.

"Anyone who can fight will probably join the soldiers, and the royal party will probably be in another part of the palace," said Toble. "I expect we will only have about five hundred people in here."

Sage came into the room following a group of people that included Katrina. He closed the door behind him. Autumn saw some soldiers outside guarding the room before the door closed. Sage sheathed his long shiny new sword and stood up on a nearby chair.

"Everyone check to see if those you know are here. Please report anyone who is missing to the person who led your group here." Sage waited as a general bustle began and people moved around the room.

"Sage," said Autumn as she walked up to him, "where is Queen Shasta?"

Sage knelt down. "She is with King Fredrick and Queen Oceania, but thanks for thinking of her."

People started to come up to Sage. "No one is missing," they each told him.

Sage sighed in relief. "I can't believe it. Good job all of you!"

Autumn was amazed. She looked around at the group of people who were in here. Sage had led the evacuation perfectly. She returned to Tanner and Toble.

Sage stood up again. "As you all know, the palace is experiencing an attack. The Undines and Merpeople are united into one army and should have this under control in a little while. King Fredrick will send a group of soldiers here to protect us if necessary. It is not an attack from Maldamien's main forces, just a group of dissenters from within the palace trying to stop the wedding and overthrow the unified government. Remain calm, and I am sure this will be cleared up soon."

"There has never been an attack here until that Mermaid queen came!" cried a hysterical Undine woman in the corner.

Autumn felt embarrassed for her. Just a few moments ago she had been just as hysterical.

"The queen didn't cause this, Maldamien's lies did. We can't fight among ourselves, or we won't be able to trust anyone. We need each other to survive in this world. Now, relax, and I will keep you informed." Sage jumped down from the chair and walked up to Tanner.

"Do you have any weapons with you?"

"I have my hunting knife," said Tanner, patting his leg.

"Get it out. Do you know where the royal chambers are?" Tanner nodded. "I need you to report to the king in his study and find out what he wants us to do next. All the royal party should be there with him as well, so it will be well guarded, but there might be fighting there too. The general attacked from the north dock and came straight through the front hall. Most of the fight was on the main floor and the throne room, but they were trying to make their way to the royal chambers."

Tanner nodded again. "I'll go through the atrium, past the library."

Sage walked Tanner to the door. Tanner pulled out his knife as he reached the door and left. Sage looked down the hall before closing the door. He drew his sword, sat down cross-legged in front of the entrance, and laid the sword across his lap.

"Why doesn't he join us?" whispered Autumn to Toble.

"Do you remember how you panicked because of fearing recapture earlier?" asked Toble.

Autumn blushed. "Yeah."

"Sage is dealing with his memories of the coup at Vervain. He has had many more years to deal with it than you have, but he never stops thinking about it. He will protect the people in this room with his life, and he is mentally preparing for the worst even though he knows it isn't the same."

"Why was he so mean to me earlier then?"

"You snapped out of it, didn't you?" said Toble. "He had an old Nomad do the same thing to him once not long after Vervain when we were on the run. I think Sage knew you would respond the same way he did. Weaker folks would have crumbled and cried hysterically, like some of the people in this room." Autumn looked around at some of the weeping huddling people. They never expected this. Toble continued,

232

"You are a fighter at heart. Your spirit wasn't broken at the fortress, just damaged some."

Everyone settled down eventually, and all waited quietly. The low whispers and mumbling of those in the room were just as a background hum of noise. As time crept by, Autumn turned to Toble.

"Come on. We should sit with him."

They got up and sat on either side of Sage by the door. "What?" asked Sage startled from his thoughts.

"You need company," said Autumn.

Sage look back down at his sword like he had been doing before she had spoken to him. "Sorry about earlier," said Sage. "I was tempted just to pick you up and carry you, but I think you would have worsened instead of shaking out of it."

"Don't worry about it." Autumn tried not to blush at remembering it.

"I hope no one destroys the ship," said Toble.

"We will see," said Sage. "The general didn't know of our plans to go see Thyme. I don't know if he was concerned about that."

"Do you think the wedding will continue after this is finished?" asked Autumn. "We really can't wait around much longer than we are already."

"I imagine they will push to keep the wedding on schedule. It is too important to delay longer than necessary. They wanted to marry quickly. Nothing could prevent that. This would make them more desperate."

Just then a knock came from the door behind them. They jumped up along with a quarter of the room. Sage opened the door with his sword ready. Autumn pulled out her dagger and noticed that Toble had had his hatchet sitting on his bag right before he too got it ready.

"It's me," said Tanner to the crack in the door. Sage let him in.

"It took me awhile to get in," said Tanner. "There are layers of guards protecting the king. It helped my story that I am obviously a Gnome. It turns out that the general's band is not giving up without a nasty fight. King Fredrick wants us to plan on staying here for the night. In the morning, he will send someone to let us know what to do next."

Sage jumped onto the chair that had been vacated by an Undine woman. Before he could talk, another knock came from the door.

Sage again answered it with his sword ready. James stood there in battle armor and a sword.

"The king said to let everyone go back to their rooms. The rebels have all been slain. We got the report right after Tanner left. None of the traitors would surrender, but at least the palace is safe for now."

"Thank you," said Sage, patting James on the shoulder. Sage sheathed his sword, and James came in, leaving the door open.

Sage jumped onto the chair. "The situation has been resolved. Everyone is to go to their rooms. Avoid the main hall and throne room area. It might be best if you can make your way through the atrium."

Sage jumped down. The people surrounded him, thanking him as they slowly filed out of the room.

"We must leave the day after the wedding," said Sage to Autumn. "Whatever the condition of the ship, we will just have to repair it as we travel."

Toble and Tanner looked at each other. "It will be done," said Tanner, "even if we have to build a whole new one and get no sleep. We will have it done."

"Let's go check on it now," said Toble. "There is no way I can rest until I can see what has happened to it." Tanner followed Toble as he filed into the slow progression out the door.

"I'm going to bed," said Autumn tiredly. The tiredness was overwhelming, as it was with a lot of the folks in the room. "See you in the morning," she said to Sage as she followed close after Tanner.

"Good night," Sage said as she left the room. He continued to shake hands absently and give answers to various questions to those walking by. It seemed to take twice as long to get people out than it did to get them in. Groups of people stood around the room talking happily like they had just come from a dinner party. The change of emotions irritated Sage. Sage passed on the task of directing people to James and left to find King Fredrick.

Sage took the route he had told everyone to avoid so he could see where the main fighting happened. The hall and stairway only sustained minor damage with stains of blood distinctly seen in multiple areas. The door of the throne room stood open. In there, Sage could see multiple dead bodies. Soldiers walked by carrying wounded and corpses through the hall. Sage continued to the king's apartment. The way was littered with blood, but the bodies of wounded or dead were already gone. The king was standing at the door to his study giving various orders and talking to high ranking soldiers. Queen Oceania was next to him, also giving orders and listening to reports. Only Queen Shasta seemed frantic as she sat on a chair in the study being comforted by Queen Oceania's handmaiden.

"Sage!" said King Fredrick. "Excellent job on the evacuation. I couldn't have done better myself. You are a born leader just like your father! Good job." The king turned to talk to a soldier who walked up.

"Sage, darling!" called Queen Shasta as soon as she saw him. She came over and nearly hugged him until he bowed low first. "You truly saved those people!" She sobbed a little into her handkerchief and then composed herself. Her eyes were red from crying, and her voice was shaky. "I can't believe this has happened, but Queen Oceania is determined to keep the wedding day. I am going to need you to help me. There is so much to do and what if all the decorations have been damaged? I can't imagine the wedding guests not being frightened away. Oh, and what about the dining hall being trampled over?" Queen Shasta started crying again.

Sage sighed.

"Is there anything else you need me for tonight?" Sage asked the king.

"What?" he replied. "Oh. No, no. The soldiers are doing everything fine right now. I'll send someone to your room if I need you." The king turned to the new soldier who came up.

"Your Majesty," Sage said to Queen Shasta, seeing how she was frustrating Queen Oceania who was trying deal with some soldiers as well. "Your Majesty, you look tired. Why don't I escort you to your apartment, so you can rest? The wedding things can wait until tomorrow. We will get it all repaired and sorted in the morning."

"That sounds like a good plan," added Queen Oceania as she pushed Shasta towards Sage. "There is nothing else that can be done about that tonight. I am going to retire soon myself in a few minutes, so I will visit with you later."

Queen Shasta took Sage's arm, somewhat confused, and walked with him to her rooms. Shasta continued talking about the issues around the wedding as they walked, but Sage mentally began to process the night's events.

He had gone to be measured, and Shasta found him to ask him to do more errands. In the midst of that, Sage had heard the fighting in the front hall and alerted the king, his bodyguards, the soldiers, and everyone he could. It was inevitable that the palace would eventually get some sort of attack before the wedding if Maldamien had wanted a war between the water people. The Undine had felt like their hidden palace had protected them this long from Maldamien. What they didn't understand was that Maldamien had no reason before now to attack them. King Fredrick made sure to pay all the taxes and to obey every command in public. The Undines lived in fear and were no threat to Maldamien's power. When Maldamien took control a hundred years ago, he didn't bother to overthrow local governments who obeyed him. His destroying the governments of the Brownies and the Hiru was enough to cause fear everywhere without having to expend any more effort. The Undines were not safe in their little bubble, but they didn't see that. Maldamien was out to destroy all the governments not completely loyal to him now. He had something big planned that he wanted no resistance over, if only he could figure it all out.

Sage left an exhausted Shasta at her door and headed straight to his room, crashing into bed fully clothed. He didn't budge until the next morning.

When he woke up, he groaned at remembering his promise to help Shasta. It wasn't that he was lazy, he just didn't like wedding stuff. So much of it was unnecessary and annoying, Shasta's exuberance and hints were even worse. Yesterday, she had assigned Sage the task of handing out the orders to the various servants about decorations and wedding schedules. Of course, that required multiple trips because some of the things she wanted were not possible with the resources available. Sage asked why a servant or footman couldn't do this, and was told she felt that she couldn't trust them to relay the messages properly and that she trusted him to make decisions if they had questions. He did make decisions. Lots of them for various things that didn't matter in the least. It was just that a decision had to be made. Did she want linen tablecloths or cotton? Did she want the pearl china or the stone? Did the name cards for the table need to be in black ink or a color? He just made a decision and told her later. Then he had to go back to half of those places and change the decision he made because it wasn't the right one. She would ask him his opinion about the menu, and when he said it was too extravagant with the food shortage, she started crying! She had so much for him to do that he ended up eating his dinner in the kitchen quickly between errands. The way she was talking last night, he wouldn't get a break all day, and he still needed to check on the supplies for the journey. He was relieved to think that they would be leaving, eventually.

"Tap, tap, tap." The sound was awful to Sage's ears. He had the dim hope that it was Autumn again. If it was Shasta, he would love to tell her to go away, but decided to just deal with it. She was a queen, an old friend, and someone who had gone through a lot lately. He smoothed down his clothes and ran his hand through his hair before opening the door.

Queen Shasta radiated beauty. Her light blond hair and elegant blue gown made her sparkle. With her translucent wings keeping her barely touching the floor, she seemed unreal.

"Good morning," she almost sang. "I was hoping you would join me for breakfast in the drawing room."

Sage softened. "Good morning, Your Majesty. I'll be ready in a minute."

"I'll meet you there," she said, then turned and left.

Sage closed the door and sighed. Why didn't he say no? It was because he couldn't to a face like that, not when he really had nothing better to do. He cleaned up some, shaved, brushed his hair, brushed his tail, and left. He went to Toble's door and knocked. Toble appeared, dressed, shaved, and ready for the day.

"Toble, I am probably going to be helping Shasta all day. Would you let the others know?"

"I think Autumn will be disappointed," replied Toble.

Sage sighed. "Yeah, well, I have no reason not to help Queen Shasta. How is the boat? Do you need my help there?"

"The boat was untouched. Can't honestly say we have to have your help. We will probably finish it today even without you," said Toble.

"Well, other than that, I can't really tell her that I'm busy. You know Shasta."

"Yes, I do know her. Be careful with her. She is trying to make you an emotional replacement for her husband. She hasn't grieved yet, I think, which means she doesn't really know her own feelings. Also, you may not be aware of Autumn's feelings as well. You have a complicated situation developing."

Sage sighed again. "I think the last time I had this much girl trouble I was eleven. Besides, Autumn is just a friend, a little girl, right?" Years

237

of experience with Toble made Sage take his warning seriously. Somehow, he just saw things in people that Sage never did.

"Toble, where did you learn so much about women?" Sage teased.

"I wasn't always a confirmed old bachelor, Sage," said Toble seriously. "When you are truly in love in such a way that you would sacrifice anything for their happiness or well-being, you learn to pay attention some."

Sage smirked and shook his head. "You surprise me sometimes. Well, I'll see you later."

Sage walked down the stairs musing over Toble's words. So little Autumn had a crush on him. It was flattering. He still kind of saw her as the little girl he first met. It seemed like every time he saw her though he was struck by how grown-up she had become. Then again, she still came out with such innocent child-like questions and behavior.

Sage pushed the thoughts from his mind as he walked into the drawing room. Breakfast was laid out, and Shasta was waiting.

"Good morning Sage," Shasta greeted properly.

"Your Majesty," said Sage as he bowed. He did it on purpose. She would let him be less formal, but the formality created a safe distance between them.

Queen Shasta seemed to read his thoughts. "You don't have to be so formal with me. After all, we are such old friends."

Sage's eyes turned yellow, but Queen Shasta didn't notice as she poured him a cup of tea. Toble was right in his assessment of Shasta.

"We have so much to do today," said Shasta as Sage sat down and began to eat. "Queen Oceania is going to be busy today with her dress fitting and other tasks. I am going to need you to help re-arrange the seating chart. We also haven't created a music list."

Sage listened patiently and wondered why she didn't let the ladies of the court help her or even the housekeeper take care of the menial tasks. It seemed to Sage that she was trying to stay busy and keep Sage busy with her. The events of last night were completely forgotten. She talked on about all that they needed to do or get accomplished. Sage allowed himself to lose any remaining hope of having time to see the others in the atrium. When breakfast was almost over, Sage concentrated to hear the last of what Shasta was saying.

"We need to get some music books from the library, and I need to speak with the royal conductor."

"Why don't I get the books for you?" asked Sage relieved for a task away from the more frilly obligations she had listed during the meal.

"Why Sage, that would be perfect. And on your way, you can talk to the master gardener about what flowers will be available for the wedding. The gardener might be in the atrium. Now when you get the music books, remember to get Undine love songs. I am not interested in a multicultural mix and especially nothing too loud," explained Queen Shasta.

"You mean no Huldranian folk songs," said Sage with a teasing smirk.

"You know what I think of that kind of music," replied Shasta. "We weren't raised around that."

Sage shrugged. She had only lived at Vervain for three years, and the goal of the palace was to be multicultural, but Sage didn't want to argue.

"Could you bring the books to the south study? Thank you," she said but left without waiting for an answer.

Sage made his way toward the atrium. He would check on his friends first. Autumn came to his mind as he walked. He really enjoyed the time he had spent with her this week. He had felt comfortable and relaxed. She was interesting, even though she claimed to be very normal. In Sage's experience of a hundred years of wandering, no one was 'normal.'

He shook his head sadly. Even though his appearance looked like he was in his early thirties and a good match for her, he was old enough to be her great-grandfather. She was really still a child.

Then again, he didn't feel like an old man, and he didn't act like one either. Were they really so unsuitable? Could he ever remember being around someone who brought out the parts of himself that felt real? She was comfortable to be around and fun to spend time with.

Sage walked into the atrium. He saw Toble and Tanner working on the Flying Hope.

"Hey, where's Autumn?" asked Sage.

Toble looked up at him and then pointed upward. Sage looked up at the sails that had been erected. There was Autumn on a ladder stringing ropes on a sail.

"What are you doing up there? Aren't you supposed to be resting or taking it easy or something?" he exclaimed.

Autumn looked down and smiled enthusiastically. She started to climb down, and Sage went over to help her. He grabbed her by the waist and helped her down. She turned to him. He was struck by the glow of joy on her face. She was stunning.

Sage noticed in the corner of his eye that Tanner elbowed Toble. Those silly old men were trying to match them up. Sage stepped back from Autumn a little.

"Hey, I didn't think we would get to see you today," said Autumn.

"Shasta sent me over to talk to the master gardener about flowers," he replied.

"I guess she didn't know we were working in here," said Autumn.

Sage was surprised. He hadn't thought about that. Would Shasta try to keep him away from his friends, away from Autumn?

"Do you have time to see what we have accomplished so far?" asked Tanner.

"No, I probably need to run my errands," said Sage. "If I take too long she might send a messenger after me."

"It was nice to see you anyway," said Autumn as she headed back up the ladder. Sage watched her a moment.

He slowly left and found the gardener. As they spoke, Sage could see the Flying Hope from where he stood. The gardener told Sage what he needed to know, which was that there were very few flowers available, and it might be better to use decorative leaves. When the gardener was finished talking, he followed the direction of Sage's constant glancing. He tilted his head.

"She's a beauty," said the gardener.

Sage looked at him. "Who?"

The gardener frowned. "Queen Shasta, of course. Everyone in the palace has been talking about how much time you two have been spending together. There seems to be speculation that you might stay here and marry her and let your friends go on without you."

"What?" Sage felt his eyes turn red. "I would more likely marry Autumn than Queen Shasta! Who started these rumors?"

The gardener nearly dropped his tools. "I'm sorry. It is just general palace gossip. I didn't know."

Sage sighed and left for the library.

In the library, he found the music books Shasta wanted. He also found a small book of Huldra music. Shasta hated this stuff, but

Autumn had seemed to take to it, or at least to the main instrument for it. He wondered if Autumn could read it and if she would be interested in playing any of the songs on the bolerita. It was just one of many things he felt refreshing about Autumn. He put the book into his pocket.

Before leaving, he looked out the window into the atrium. He just watched Autumn for a few minutes and left. He had not really noticed her before somehow. Not as an equal in maturity. When they thought she was going to die, he had been desperate to help her, but that wasn't anything more than normal compassion. Something was different now, though, and it may have started then. Autumn was a partner in this adventure. Sage may have rescued her, but she had rescued a couple of nations already. He didn't have to protect her like most women, she had seen the worst, and it hadn't crushed her. Even so, he never wanted to let that happen to her again. Still, it wouldn't be like protecting a child or most women. He respected Autumn.

Sage walked into the south study. Shasta wasn't there yet, so he sat in a chair in the corner. Was Autumn right about Shasta? The implication was that she was trying to keep him away from his friends. He may need to finally say something.

Queen Shasta walked in with a bunch of papers in her hands. "Well, I have the list of tasks here that we need to go through and some paper for writing out the list of songs and the order for the ceremony. Queen Oceania said that she didn't care what songs we chose. The ceremony needed to follow their royal customs, so she is going to send a servant with a book from her collection. What did the gardener say about flowers?"

"No flowers, but we can have decorative leaves."

"What a shame! I guess everything is going to have a watery theme anyway. Maybe we can use candles shaped like flowers."

At that point, Sage stopped hearing what Shasta was rattling on about. She sat behind the large desk in the center of the room. She was still talking as she got out a piece of paper to write more errands for Sage to do. After a half hour, a knock came at the door.

"Enter," said Queen Shasta.

A servant entered, bowed, and announced, "Queen Oceania has requested to see Lord Sage whenever he is available."

Queen Shasta looked up in surprise. "She probably wants help with King Fredrick's part of the wedding. He keeps saying he doesn't care what we plan. Here is a list of errands, if you don't mind. I will be using this room all day, so you know where to find me." She smiled in a way that said 'I know you love me and can't wait to get back to see me.'

Sage stood up, took the sheet of paper from Shasta, and bowed. He followed the servant out of the study. He frowned deeply at the mess he was finding himself in. This was why he never belonged in a palace.

As Sage and the servant walked, he glanced over the list. It was more of the same: talk to the cook about..., talk to the candle maker about..., talk to the calligrapher..., and so on.

They arrived at Queen Oceania's apartments. The servant entered the room to announce him, then opened the door wider for him to enter.

Sage had been to the queen's sitting room before, but it was always so exotic. The room was a wall-to-wall shallow pool only a few feet deep. The floor was tiled in a colorful mosaic. The shell-shaped furniture was anchored to the floor with decorative weights. The room was illuminated by glowing stones in the floor which reflected the water patterns all over the walls. The ambiance of the room was of being underwater. Sage had to continually remind himself to breathe while there. He stepped forward into the floating chair by the door and grabbed the stick attached to the chair for the purpose of punting over to where the queen sat in a similar shell. Her long fishtail dipped in the water while she talked to the mermaids around her.

When Sage arrived at the group, the talking and giggling stopped. The queen spoke. "Sage, I am so glad you came. You have been such a great help in planning this wedding and for warning us of the coup. I am eternally grateful. I have made the arrangements for your supplies. They will be carried to the surface with you and your ship the morning after the wedding. I also have some guides who arrived not too long ago. They would be of much use to you, but their identities need to be protected at this time."

"Thank you." Sage attempted to bow but almost knocked over his chair.

The mermaids suppressed a giggle.

The queen continued. "Sage, I must admit that my main reason for asking to see you was to request another favor. I have reminded and explained to Queen Shasta that I do not want to drain too many resources on this wedding. I want things royal for the political statement it makes to our people, but I still want it simple. She has not understood me clearly. I get reports from the housekeeper that she is requesting too much from the servants and staff. I do not want to embarrass her or insult her. She was married during the golden age of our world, she is mourning the loss of her husband, and she is doing a great service for me to help this wedding happen as quickly as we would like. I want our countries to be friends, and I intend on helping her get her throne back. I understand that you know her well."

Sage frowned just a little. He hoped she didn't believe the palace rumors, too.

Queen Oceania noticed Sage's frown but continued. "Queen Shasta has often talked about how you both grew up at Vervain. I believe that you understand the world conditions as they are now. Would you please influence her? If necessary, I give you permission to make tactful changes in my name or in the name of King Fredrick. His main concern now is the security of the palace and our two countries. He is not going to be involved in any more wedding planning. He has told me that if your taste in swords is as good as he observed, then he would probably like anything else you like as well. I really don't know what else to do in this matter." Queen Oceania touched her forehead as though she had a headache.

"Don't worry," said Sage. "I understand what you mean, and I will take care of it. I think I can make some tactful changes that she will never know about and influence her towards the direction you wish."

"Thank you, Sage, that is a huge worry that you have eased. I cannot wait for this wedding to be over with!"

Sage tried to bow again, just a little, and punted the floating chair to its dock by the door.

Sage immediately headed for the kitchen. He knew exactly what Queen Oceania was referring to. There was a reason that the luxurious meals at the palace were always fish. As he walked in, he heard the cooks talking.

"Nine courses! Nine courses! For over five thousand guests! Where are we going to get that kind of food?" The cooks hushed and then looked pale as they saw Sage. Sage smiled.

"I agree. Do you have the menu?" he asked. The head cook handed him the paper in her hand. "Do you have something to write with?"

An assistant cook pulled a pen from a small desk in the corner. Sage put the paper on the work table in the middle of the room and marked out five of the courses. He also marked out a few items in each course. This was going to be something Queen Shasta would notice at the wedding, and he would take credit for it. He wouldn't let the blame be put on Queen Oceania for something he didn't mind fighting with Shasta about.

"This is the new menu, but don't tell Queen Shasta. If she finds out and asks, say that a Lord walked in here and told you that she said to change it. If that doesn't appease her, then just tell her that it was Lord Sage, and she will find me, I'm sure."

All the cooks looked at each other and smiled. "What about the cake?" said one of them.

"What about the cake?" asked Sage.

The head cook spoke up. "She wants a cake the size of a man. This is the design she approved." The cook handed Sage a drawing of a cake with sixteen tiers. Sage shook his head. Queen Shasta was living in a dream. She was trying to forget the trauma of Maldamien's prison by living in the luxury of a royal wedding. She had not been treated too badly as far as Sage could gather, but she would have seen many things and had feared for her life. She did not have the strong fighting spirit Autumn had, but was easily scared by what she went through. Still, she was one of the good guys, and Sage didn't need to lose his temper over her mild insanity. Hopefully, it was just temporary.

The cooks watched Sage closely. "How many layers would it take to feed a thousand guests?"

The head cook looked at the drawing and answered, "Eight should do it."

"Then make eight and used boxes or wood for the rest. Just cover it in frosting."

"What about the other guests?"

"Don't worry about that. Oh, and plan the menu for only a thousand guests as well."

The head cook and Sage shook hands as though they had just agreed on a conspiracy, and Sage left. He stopped at the calligrapher and ordered a reduction of name cards, wedding programs, and whatever else he was working on. He discovered that Queen Oceania had already beat him to that. She had, at the beginning of the week, reduced the invitations to 1,500 without telling anyone and so Sage's guess for who would arrive was probably going to be accurate.

Sage stopped at all the places on his list to do what Queen Shasta requested and also corrected the amounts. Finally, at noon, he returned to the south study already tired of errands.

"Hi! So what did Queen Oceania want?" asked Shasta as soon as Sage walked in the door.

"Our supplies for our trip to find Thyme," said Sage.

"Oh, that's great," said Shasta looking back down at her work. "So, when are we all going?"

Sage paled a little. "Well, Queen Oceania was going to help you get your throne back, so we thought we would take off the day after the wedding."

Queen Shasta looked up confused. "My throne?"

"Did you not know that Maldamien made Lord Jacob king after you left?"

"Oh, that gutless rat, he will step down as soon as I show up."

"Yes, but not Maldamien's soldiers and Nomads."

"I see." Queen Shasta sat back blinking. It seemed to Sage that Shasta had not thought about life beyond the wedding yet.

Queen Shasta shook her head. "I'll worry about that later. Look at this mess! I am now going to have to change a lot of things because the only responses we got from the invitations were from Undines and Merpeople. I don't know what happened to all the other countries. I have been waiting for replies, thinking that since they were farther away, the dragonfly messengers must need more rest breaks or something."

Sage sat down. "A lot is going on out there. It was last minute. They may just think the journey is too risky or too publicly against Maldamien's wishes. It would bring a lot of danger to their kingdoms."

"It's always a dangerous time to travel, and why not unify against Maldamien? It's just a wedding, for goodness' sake!" Shasta began to tear up.

Sage felt trapped. Now, what did he do?

Shasta continued. "I'm doing the best I can, and I feel like everyone is against me!"

Sage moved his chair next to her. "Perhaps you are doing too much."

Shasta started to cry harder. "But I want to do this!" she wailed.

"Shasta," Sage said gently, "are you doing this so you don't have to think about all that happened to you, or are you just doing this to help Queen Oceania?" Sage offered her a handkerchief from his pocket.

Shasta dried her tears. "I miss Coriander so much!" she wailed again. "How am I going to live without him?"

Sage sighed. "You live one day at a time. Some days will be tougher, and some days will be a little easier. It won't completely go away, but you will be able to live again."

Shasta stopped crying and looked at Sage. "How old were you when your parents died?"

Sage shifted uncomfortably. "Twelve," he said flatly.

Shasta nodded. "It was the year after we had moved back to Caoineag. Dad's term as Ambassador had ended and he took a position in the court instead. Do you think about them a lot?"

Sage stood up and studied the woodwork on the fake books. "Very often." Then he turned. "I'll go to the kitchen and tell them about the guest list. Is there anything you would like me to do after that?"

Shasta flipped through her papers and pulled out a sheet. "If you could do these tasks, I would appreciate it. I need to eat lunch with the wedding party and then we will have a rehearsal to finalize the order of events. I'll send someone to you if I need you." She sniffed, whipped her eyes, and handed the handkerchief back to Sage. He absently put it back into his pocket as he glanced over the list.

"Then I will see you tomorrow." Sage bowed and left.

Sage went to the kitchen first and was greeted by the pleased staff. He informed them that the guest list had been officially shortened by order of Queen Shasta. They cheered and fed him a hearty lunch. He continued to do his errands and began to look forward to the possibility of eating dinner with his friends. He passed by Katrina in the hall as she was carrying an armful of clothes.

"Katrina," he said to stop her, "I would like to have my dinner in the atrium with the others. Who do I need to inform of that?"

"Don't worry. I'll take care of it."

"Thanks!" He started to look forward to talking with Autumn and showing her the book in his pocket. Suddenly, he thought about Toble's words to him that morning. Perhaps he needed to be more careful of his own emotions.

He rushed through his list of tasks and still got done later than he had hoped. He hurried into the atrium.

246

Toble and Tanner were seated eating, but Autumn was gone.

"Where is Autumn?" asked Sage.

"We had to start without you because Autumn was scheduled for some beauty treatment or hair or skin oil or something," said Toble.

Tanner added, "Katrina postponed it so that Autumn could eat with us."

Sage sat down and sighed. He couldn't help but be disappointed.

An Undine servant came and delivered Sage's meal. Sage pulled out the music book from his pocket.

Before Sage could take a bite, another Undine servant walked up. "Queen Shasta sent me to let you know that your fitting has been scheduled for tonight. Your presence at the royal brunch will be needed in the morning, attired in your wedding garments."

Sage replied to the servant, "Let Queen Shasta know that I will be there."

When the servant left, and Sage was able to taste his cold fish, Tanner remarked, "Kind of demanding, isn't she?"

"Yeah," grumbled Sage. He picked up the music book and handed it to Toble. "I got this from the library for Autumn. Could you give it to her to look at?"

"Sure, but what is she going to do with a music book?"

"She can play the bolerita. She says it's like an instrument from the human world. I don't know if she can read the Huldranian music notation, but she may have fun looking at the words or something."

Sage took another bite of the fish in front of him dejectedly.

"I'm sure she will enjoy that since we finished the ship today," said Tanner.

"Really?" said Sage with a pang of guilt. "Sorry that I didn't help."

"You have been busy," said Toble. "You would have been in the way anyway."

Sage smirked. They spent the rest of the dinner talking about the ship and the trip. Sage left for his fitting after a longer than average dinner. Tomorrow was the wedding ball, and then they would be off. He couldn't wait.

CHAPTER 24: THE WEDDING BALL

Sage woke with a start and looked at the wooden clock on the wall. "I'm running late!"

He jumped up and began to get ready. He dealt with his floppy hair, tried not to cut himself shaving, and gave his tail a good brushing. Then he dressed in this new suit of clothing: a black and silver embroidered tunic, black trousers, and shiny new leather boots. He fastened his new sword and sheath on the black leather belt around his waist. He looked at himself in the mirror. Not bad, but he didn't look like himself. He messed up his hair a little and nodded. That was better.

Sage hurried to the door and saw a note on the floor that had been slid under the door. *Sorry I missed you at dinner. Thanks for the book. - Autumn.*

It was written in a rough Huldranian script. Sage smiled, folded it up, and put it in his pocket. It would be nice to hear her play the bolerita again before they left, but they would probably not have the time. He wondered if she asked Toble or Tanner to escort her. He would see tonight either way, but he felt a pang of jealousy towards those two silly old men. He was starting to think of her as his girl and didn't want her with anyone else but him. He sighed.

Sage walked down to Shasta's door and knocked. Shasta opened the door. She radiated beauty and perfection in her sparkly pink ball gown. Her blond hair was up in curls on her head and was accented with diamonds everywhere. Sage bowed and then offered his hand.

"You look beautiful," he said as she took his hand and gracefully floated out of her room.

"Thank you. You look very nice yourself."

The brunch was in the same dining room that had held the dinner they'd attended just a few days before. The table was shorter and pushed against the wall holding various finger foods so that the wedding party and guests could mingle. Unlike the dinner, the conversations were dull as Queen Shasta dragged Sage with her from one group of people to another. Ambassadors who were in residence at the palace from various kingdoms were there, including representatives from Fenodryee and Dwende. The ambassador from Caoineag had been recalled with the shift of government when Queen Shasta was arrested, so Queen Shasta was the only Sprite there. Sage was also the only one of his kind there since most Huldra would have been supporters of Maldamien and not welcomed there.

"How have you liked it here?" asked one of the Mermaid ladies-in-waiting.

"Very well. It will be a shame to go," Sage said politely.

He took a sip of the sour yellow fruit juice in his glass goblet Shasta had just handed to him.

"You don't have to leave," teased the Mermaid looking at Shasta knowingly.

"No, I do," Sage said flatly.

The Mermaid's expression diminished some, and she moved to join another nearby conversation.

Sage then heard Autumn's name from a conversation behind him.

"I heard that she was the last student of Puck and when Maldamien interrogated her, she spit in his face!" said an Undine man to two Mermaid ladies-in-waiting.

Sage turned around amused. One of the ladies noticed him listening.

"Is that true?" she asked him.

Sage smiled. He didn't know if it was true, but somehow he could imagine it.

"It very well may be true." Then he added mischievously, "but I do know that she did slap his face."

The group gasped.

Before Sage could continue, Shasta leaned over and whispered to Sage, "I think people see us as a couple."

She giggled.

Sage frowned.

"Shasta, you know that we are only friends, don't you? I mean you just lost King Coriander, and it was over between us a long time ago, right?" Sage whispered gently.

Shasta paled a little.

"Oh yes, of course," she said with forced flippancy.

Sage did not feel convinced, but he could not be any blunter without being mean.

He turned back to finish his conversation with the Undine man and two Mermaids, but they had moved on.

The brunch lasted an eternal four hours. After the socializing and ever important small-talk, the wedding party moved to the front hall to greet guests.

The evidence of the attempted coup was completely erased, and people greeted each other with elegance and splendor. Since most of the Merpeople were limited to the raised pool in the center, Sage assigned himself to greet them while Queen Shasta greeted those who walked in. When the majority of the guests had finally signed the guest book, collected a program, and entered the ball, Sage and Queen Shasta made their way to the door they needed to use for their entrance. They had to wait in the back of a group to be announced in a manner that was appropriate for Shasta's rank.

Sage looked at Queen Shasta again. She was beautiful in an untouchable way, like a star in the night sky. Autumn was so different from her. Sage always returned to the image of a wild red rose still on the vine, thorns and all. When he was young, he was drawn to Shasta's kind of beauty, but Autumn's internal strength, child-like innocence, and earthy beauty was more appealing. With Shasta, he felt trapped and restless. She was a good person and would become a great queen and leader. That was where she belonged. Sage had nothing in common with Shasta from the time they were kids. It was so different with Autumn. He felt like he was really himself, more so than even with Toble. In every topic they talked about they had a common interest. He found that despite all he had thought before, he was definitely falling in love with Autumn.

"What are you thinking?" asked Queen Shasta.

"How nice you look this evening," said Sage.

They moved forward into the ballroom on top of a grand staircase. Sage looked across the ballroom. A balcony surrounded the room a little above the staircase, and it poured a gentle shower of water down the walls of the room into a pool surrounding a central dance floor. Floating tables near the floor area were surrounded by Merpeople, leaving a large swimming area between them and the wall. The pool wrapped around to either side of a raised throne area and under a small footbridge leading to the dance floor, creating a smooth circular river. The two pearl thrones sat behind a small shallow table on their shell shaped platform. The circular dance floor was also edged with circular tables matching the floating ones. These were also filled with guests. The floors and walls were mosaics of the historical events and fables of the Undine people. The ceiling was a rich painting of the night sky with a chandelier hanging down from the middle of it. This was not the main source of light because light glowed from everywhere, creating a misty, magical feeling.

The announcement came, "Queen Shasta Aurora Coriander, ruler of Caoineag, and Lord Sage Petro Goliad, son of General Fennel Petro Goliad, Captain of the guard for Queen Anemone of Vervain."

Sage escorted Queen Shasta down the steps and toward the thrones. The nearest table to the thrones on the right sat Toble and Tanner. They stood and bowed to Queen Shasta. When she was seated, they all followed suit.

"Where is Autumn?" asked Sage.

"We thought she was coming with you," said Tanner.

"No, she is an Undine and Merpeople national hero," said Queen Shasta. "She is going to be announced last, right after us if she is not late."

Sage was still in a state of surprise when he heard, "Lady Autumn Diane Lewis of the Human Realm, the hero of the Unified Water People."

Sage gasped. The lone figure of Autumn in a dark aqua gown and long dripping translucent sleeves gracefully descended the stairs. The hue of her gown made her eyes a rich grayish blue. Her hair twisted around her shoulders in large curls. Sage had not noticed her perfect hourglass shape before, but it was now accentuated by her heart-shaped neckline and very low back. Everything she wore sparkled tastefully.

"Why did the poor girl come in alone?" whispered Queen Shasta.

Sage immediately got up and walked to the foot of the staircase. He bowed and then offered Autumn his hand. She lightly placed her hand in is.

"You look... You are... a."

Blast, he thought. He sounded like an adolescent boy. He coughed. "I am sorry you had to come alone," he finally said.

"I chose to," said Autumn.

"Well, you are very beautiful tonight."

"You look dashing yourself."

Sage walked with Autumn towards the table as the music started to play. He looked at Queen Shasta, Toble, and Tanner sitting there and was overcome with the desire to keep Autumn to himself a little longer.

"Would you like to dance?" he asked as he turned to her.

Autumn's eyes sparkled.

"I would love to."

Sage took her into a hold and whisked her away from their destination. The soft music was accompanied by an Undine crooner singing in their traditional language. A moment passed as Sage looked down into Autumn's face. Her cheek was glittering with a tear.

"What's wrong?" he asked urgently, wondering whether any of her injuries were hurting her.

"Puck was the one who taught me to dance," she said. "I miss him so much."

"He taught you well in such a short time," said Sage truly impressed, "but of course, Puck was always an excellent teacher."

"Did you know him well?" Autumn asked as she looked up at him.

Her eyes were so irresistible that Sage kissed her forehead. He looked away as she blushed. He wanted to just put her in his pocket for some reason.

"I knew Puck as well as the massive group of his acquaintants. I believe that in the short time you spent with him, you probably got to know him better than me. Tanner probably knew him better than anyone else."

Autumn still seemed sad. Sage spun her around, and her face lit up with surprise.

"Autumn, how are you so... something? You capture people's hearts almost the moment they meet you. You belong here, Autumn. You belong in Gryphendale."

Autumn lowered her eyes. "Sage, what will happen to all of us?"

"We keep fighting until everyone is safe to live their own lives," said Sage more confidently than he felt.

"Are you ever afraid?" she asked.

"Yes," said Sage, "but the only thing that matters is what you do with that fear. You're not afraid now, are you?"

"No," she said. "How can I when you seem to have everything under control," she teased.

"Of course." Sage turned as he was tapped on the shoulder. Toble stood there.

"You've danced two songs. It's my turn. Plus, Queen Shasta is biting the bit to dance with you."

Sage frowned and released Autumn to Toble. He reasoned with himself that it was only right to dance with Shasta since he'd agreed to escort her. Sage walked to the table where Queen Shasta sat and bowed to her. He offered Queen Shasta his hand and asked, "Would you like to dance?"

Queen Shasta was thrilled, and they were off dancing. She was a far superior dancer than Autumn, but she talked endlessly about the preparation it took Queen Oceania to do this and congratulating herself on how well it was all going. She even quizzed Sage on what he was to do for the ceremony even though it was minor.

Suddenly, horns sounded.

"King Fredrick Alexander Colon, ruler of Berehynia and the great rivers of two worlds."

The king proceed down the steps with his royal court following. They were all dressed in suits of silver and navy blue. The king's suit was decorated with metals and a darker unique material that had more of a sheen than the rest.

All the dancers parted for him and his party. The room bowed as he walked to the thrones. The Undine men following him lined the edge of the floor near the water on both sides of the little footbridge.

Another set of horns sounded.

"Queen Oceania Aquatica Triton, ruler of Derketo and the great oceans of the world."

From an opened underwater door came Queen Oceania and her Mermaids up to the surface of the water near the left side of the throne. They swam around the room as Merpeople parted for her and her court. Everyone again bowed as they came to the left side of the thrones. King Fredrick greeted her by offering his hand. As she took it, one of the Mermaids put a golden belt around Queen Oceania's waist. A silvery glow covered her and dripped down her shoulders and torso in waves. As she walked up a set of stairs to the shell-shaped platform, the silvery light became solidified into a layered silvery-white fitting gown in the style aptly called a mermaid style. The whole gown was covered in shimmery shell-patterned lace. Queen Oceania's dark hair lay in tumbled curls with shimmering pearls throughout. King Fredrick and Queen Oceania stood in front of their thrones, looking at each other with so much love in their eyes that it made Queen Shasta sniff back a sob.

The Undine men lining the pool reached down and offered their hands to a Mermaid each. Each Mermaid fastened a silver belt around their waist and stepped out of the pool as light dressed them in navy mermaid-styled gowns.

Sage escorted Queen Shasta to the center of the room, then toward the king and queen at their thrones. Sage then bowed and moved to the side out of the way, and Queen Shasta took a step closer.

In a loud voice, she said, "Please, now exchange your pledges."

King Fredrick picked up a crown from his seat and said, "The ancient crown of Undine queens will now be yours for now and ever more as a promise of my love, loyalty, and devotion. Let our kingdoms be united as we are now united."

Queen Oceania knelt as King Fredrick placed the crown on her head.

Queen Oceania stood and picked up a crown from her seat and repeated similar vows, "The ancient crowns of the Mer-kings will now be yours for now and ever more as a promise of my love, loyalty, and devotion. Let our kingdoms be united as we are now united."

Queen Shasta turned toward the people.

"I, Queen Shasta of Caoineag, am witness to the union of these two people and these two kingdoms. Let no one and nothing force apart what has been joined together this day."

King Fredrick and Queen Oceania kissed, and the whole room cheered. Sage walked up and escorted Queen Shasta back to her seat as the music began to play. Undine men and Mermaids danced. When they were finished and seated at the tables to the left of the throne, the servants arrived in procession with the dinner.

The first course was a fish broth and herbs. Sage, Toble, Tanner, and Autumn bowed their heads and lifted their bowls as they had been doing for every meal.

Queen Shasta leaned over to Autumn and patted her hand.

"You don't have to feel compelled to do that."

"Oh, but I do," replied Autumn.

Queen Shasta was annoyed, but Sage was pleased.

"This soup is excellent," said Toble. "Did you help prepare the menu for tonight?" he asked Queen Shasta.

"Yes, I did," she happily responded. "I was included in a great deal of planning."

"Is there a particular format for weddings here, or does everyone invent their own vows?" asked Autumn.

"I haven't been to a wedding in a long time," replied Tanner, "but in the Gnome tradition, we have vows that everyone follows very closely."

"All the kingdoms have their own traditions," said Toble.

"Yes, but this, like my own wedding, could not follow the traditions," explained Queen Shasta. "This wedding was a mix of Undine and Merpeople traditions. My own was unique because Coriander's father had died and couldn't marry us in the traditional Sprite way."

The second course of salad made with underwater herbs was served.

"Ugh," grunted Tanner. "Seaweed."

"Oh eat," said Toble. "It won't hurt you."

Tanner placed a leaf in his mouth and made faces while chewing it. Autumn giggled like a little girl as Toble coaxed, "Now swallow!"

Tanner gulped and pushed the bowl away.

"No more!"

The king and queen stepped down from their thrones and dinners, hand in hand, to greet all their guests, table by table.

"Thank you for staying for the wedding and for helping our people over and over again," said Queen Oceania to Autumn and Sage's table.

"I understand you are all leaving tomorrow," said King Fredrick.

"Oh!" Queen Shasta exclaimed, turning to Sage. "I forgot to let you know that I will be journeying home next week with an escort from here."

"That is an excellent plan. I hope you have safe travels," said Sage. Queen Oceania must have convinced Queen Shasta the importance of it and helped arrange it as a return favor for Sage. He appreciated it and gave Queen Oceania a quick glance to convey the appreciation.

"I hate to part with everyone so soon, but we hope for the best in all of your endeavors. Let us know if there is anything else we can do to help," said King Fredrick as they moved on to the next table.

The next course of baked fish was served.

"Wow," said Tanner. "Fish again."

Queen Shasta made a sour face at him.

"It tastes excellent," said Autumn to appease the situation. "I hope, though, that this is the last course before dessert. I think I'm getting full."

"Oh no," exclaimed Queen Shasta, "there is the shrimp, then crab, then the lobster, and cheese before the dessert."

Autumn's eyes got big. "Where did they get all that food?"

Sage's eyes turned blue. Autumn's response amused him.

"Oh, but this is a historic occasion," said Queen Shasta.

Sure enough, dessert was served next, and Queen Shasta was indignant.

"Those cooks shortened my menu!" cried Queen Shasta.

"Maybe they lost it," suggested Sage.

Tanner stood up once he was done eating and asked Autumn to dance. They were an awkward pair, and they both had difficulty because of the major height difference, but they laughed and finished the song anyway. Sage thought they managed pretty well considering.

Toble quickly stood up and asked Queen Shasta to dance. When she accepted, Toble covertly kicked Sage and looked at Autumn. Sage took the hint. He met Tanner and Autumn before they reached the table.

"May I steal your partner?" asked Sage.

"Yes, of course," said Tanner. "That is all the dancing I will do tonight."

Autumn and Sage waltzed away as Tanner returned to the table.

"Are you enjoying yourself?" asked Sage.

"Oh yes!" said Autumn. "I have never been to a ball. Do you know how you feel the day after a terrible fever? You know the calm light feeling?"

"Yes," answered Sage, admiring her eyes.

"Well, that is how this week has felt with tonight being a dream," said Autumn.

The song ended. Sage began to lead Autumn back to the table. Suddenly, Sage heard a strum on the bolerita. He looked at Autumn. She shrugged, not understanding his look. Sage then looked at Toble and Shasta who were at the table again. Queen Shasta looked pale and shocked.

Toble mouthed, "Dance!"

The bolerita again.

Sage turned to Autumn suddenly and whispered, "Try to follow me."

The bolerita strummed a third time, and Sage struck a dramatic pose. Autumn copied a little later. As the music began to play in an intense rhythmic fashion, Sage aggressively danced around Autumn, then stopped. Something seemed to trigger in Autumn, and she mimicked the movements around Sage. Sage arched an eyebrow as his eyes turn a deep dark navy blue, then green, then back again. He took Autumn into a firm hold and began to dance to the building speed and intensity of the music. Sage intensely focused on Autumn's movements.

The floor cleared for them since no one else knew how to dance to Huldranian folk music. Autumn and Sage marched, spun, posed, and snapped from side to side. They aggressively danced close to each other and then away again. Autumn's eyes burned into him in response to the building passion of the music. Finally, Sage spun her, pulled her close, and snapped her down into a dip. The song ended equally suddenly into a roaring silence.

Everything, even time, seemed to freeze.

Sage looked into Autumn's eyes and then kissed her deeply.

Autumn pulled herself closer to Sage kissing him back. Then Sage pulled Autumn back up, so she could stand.

"You followed well," he said quietly.

She smiled, blushing a little, "You led well."

The room erupted in clapping. The next song continued as Sage and Autumn walked back to their seats. King Fredrick and Queen Oceania walked up to them.

"You danced that well!" exclaimed King Fredrick.

"I hadn't danced Huldranian folk music in a very long time," said Sage, "but it was a pleasure."

"I loved it. You must teach it to me one day!" said the king.

"Oh, you two were so beautiful together!" exclaimed Queen Oceania. "It has been ages since I saw a faerie ring!"

Some people began to gather around.

"That was amazing! Did you practice that? How did you learn that spell?" they asked Sage and Autumn.

King Fredrick and Queen Oceania moved back to their seats. People surrounded them and continued to ask various questions.

"Move it, people! The show's over," cried Tanner as he pushed through the crowd and helped Sage and Autumn back to the table.

"You old goons!" said Sage when he sat down. "Did you guys ask the musicians to play that?"

Toble sat back.

"I only gave the conductor one of your favorite songs before giving the book to Autumn. It was King Fredrick's choice to allow it to be played, and you performed the faerie ring. I had nothing to do with that."

"What is a faerie ring?" asked Autumn.

Queen Shasta dabbed her red eyes with her handkerchief as she spoke.

"A faerie ring is a magical glow and rings of color that appear around two or more dancers." She then started to cry. "Coriander and I used to do it when we danced, too!"

Tanner continued where Queen Shasta left off.

"Some people think it is an indication of love or passion, but really it is very old magic for a very pure unity of emotion such as joy, love, passion, or even anger. When the faerie ring is created in dance, and it has the power of one emotion fully expressed, it can cause a variety of things to happen."

Toble added, "It is something that used to happen more often than it does now, but since the weakness in magic in the world, it hasn't been seen in a long time."

Sage thought about what had been said. He had seen a faerie ring once as a child, but he had never created one before. He was never good at magic to begin with. He looked at Autumn. What was it about her that caused unusual things to happen?

The dancing continued, but the friends at Sage's table just sat and watched. The king and queen announced their gratitude to the guests and left. The guests began to leave soon afterward. Toble, Tanner, and Autumn left together. Sage escorted Queen Shasta back to her room.

"Sage," said Shasta, "I am sorry I have caused you so much trouble this week."

"What made you think that?" said Sage. He now felt terrible for all his complaining.

Queen Shasta looked at the handkerchief in her delicate hands.

"I had not noticed how much you cared for Autumn. I was obsessed with trying to focus your attention on me. I know now that you can't replace Coriander for me. I have never seen you in love like that." She looked up at Sage. "Try to hold onto her. She is good for you. Everyone knows that Maldamien won't let her go. If he personally interrogated her, then he will personally try to find her again. I am afraid for you both."

Sage stood dumbfounded. She was right, but he never expected to hear such insight from her.

"I won't see you all off tomorrow. I hope you understand. I hope you have a good journey. I expect to see you in less than two months to lead your army."

"I still don't know why I said that to those prisoners," said Sage.

"Yes, I think deep down you do. You are ready to make a last stand. If everything you have told me about Apollo's predictions is true, in less than two months the world is going to end. It might as well end with a fight."

Sage bent down and kissed Queen Shasta's hand. "You will make a great queen," said Sage, and he meant it.

Queen Shasta smiled, said good night, and went into her apartments. Sage turned and absently walked to his room. The euphoria of this evening was melting away and the reality that they were going to face tomorrow was hitting hard.

Sage stopped at the door of his room but then continued on downstairs to the smaller atrium by the dining room that he and Autumn had visited before.

Sage walked in and went to the waterfall. He wanted to think about Shasta's words. Autumn was in very real danger. Sage had been able to hide in the desert for years, but she could never do that. He wanted to protect her. The outside world looked different to him suddenly. He didn't want to just fight for those other people out there. He wanted to fight for himself and Autumn, and the life he wished with all his heart could be a possibility.

"It's very relaxing here."

Sage turned around and saw Autumn still in her evening gown sitting on the ledge to the planter around the large center tree.

"Aren't you supposed to be sleeping?" he teased.

"What about you?"

"I just needed to think some."

"So did I." Autumn sighed. "I am wishing we could just hide and not have to do all of this."

"Yes, I know what you mean. Neither of us has a choice in the matter. You must run from Maldamien, and I from Turmeric."

"All because of a house?" asked Autumn.

"Turmeric is my cousin," said Sage. "He personally killed my mother. He has hated me from the time we were children. His father was always in trouble with the law and a general criminal. My father was a hero and well respected. His father was the oldest and would have inherited the estate, but he was disowned. Turmeric despised my privileged upbringing. Even though he is ten years older than me, he wanted my life, our property, and my father's reputation. He has our property, and he was celebrated as a hero when Maldamien took over, but as long as I live, he will hunt me."

"Your cousin? He killed his own aunt? How can you be related to such a monster?" said Autumn.

Sage shook his head and shrugged.

"Why does anything happen? I really don't know."

"I wish I understood why I went through everything I did," said Autumn. "I meditate on the Gryphon, and he seems to teach me so much about the world, but he stays quiet on that point."

"You never told me what happened to you at Odemience."

Autumn looked down and moved the gravel around with her foot. "I went through a lot there. He did various things so he could read my mind. When I blocked him with thoughts of the Gryphon, he had me beaten and brought back to him. He did that over and over again."

Sage watched her in awe. He remembered what it was like for the short time when the Red Ladies tried to take control of his mind. It turned his stomach.

Autumn continued.

"It was dreadful, and I never want to go through that again. The one good thing... the only good thing is that I was able to see some of his thoughts and learn some things about him. The more he pushed on me, the more his own mind had to open up. It was horrible to see and just full of poison."

"What kind of things did you find out?" asked Sage as he came

260

closer to her.

"Well, do you remember the story Puck told us when we were hiding at Ezekiel's house?"

"The one about the beginning of time and the kings who wanted to be gods?" asked Sage sitting down next to her.

He was beginning to see where this was going.

"Yes. Maldamien is obsessed with a different version of that story. He knows a version of the story where the Gryphon was a creature just like one of us. In his story, the Gryphon kills the kings and becomes a god instead of them. For Maldamien, death is the key that made the Gryphon a god. Somehow, he wants to mimic it, but I can't imagine how. I don't even know how he learned this version of the story. I couldn't see his past or his plans, just his emotions and his surface thoughts. I don't even know completely what information he got from me. I do know he is afraid of the possible return of Queen Anemone. She is the only one he thinks might possibly be able to stop him."

Autumn was shaking as she talked. Sage slid next to her and put his arm around her.

"If I have anything to say about it," said Sage, "you will never go through anything like that again."

She turned and buried herself in his arms. He felt an overwhelming desire to protect her and keep her safe at all cost, even if it cost him his life

CHAPTER 25: TRAVELING

The problem with building a ship inside of a building is getting it back out. Toble had worked on this issue with Tanner, and they had made many parts of the ship removable. Each of these pieces was carried separately by a parade of Undine servants. Most of the palace inhabitants came out to watch this curious parade to the nearest dock. There the ship was loaded with the pieces, supplies, equipment, and various luggage the queen of the water people felt would be helpful to them.

Finally, James introduced their guides. One was a well-covered Nomad man named Hao, and the other was an easy-going Dryad woman named Hazel. The husband and wife team only had a small bag each that was also loaded. At around noon, the six people boarded the heavily loaded boat and began to row down the passage. The crowd of observers cheered for them until they were out of sight, which was only a dozen yards past the dock at their first turn in the passage. They rowed by the light of the glowing stones and up the series of lochs. They passed through the watery curtain where the sunlight was blinding. It took a moment for their eyes to adjust as they tried to steer the boat into the main river.

"We need to get this mast back up," said Toble. "I need the pedaling seat here, and the bubble unit over there."

Autumn and Hazel were left steering the ship with the paddles while the men re-attached the ship pieces that didn't fit when they were still in the underground passage.

"What is this stuff?" asked Tanner looking at all the luggage. Sage, Tanner, and Hao began to go through the luggage as Toble tweaked the devices on the ship.

Autumn noticed how amused Hazel looked.

"What's so funny?" asked Autumn.

"Oh, just how men of any race act like little boys when it comes to luggage." She then turned to look more at Autumn as she periodically rowed to keep the boat on track. Autumn could more clearly see her features. She was a slightly tan, athletic woman in her prime with the characteristic floppy ears of a Dryad folding out from her long curly brown hair.

"I have heard much about you," said Hazel. "I am glad to finally get to know you. Please accept my condolences concerning Puck. He was a great man. I met him about ten years ago, and he was very wise and kind. I am sure you miss him."

"Thank you. Yes, I do miss him," said Autumn. "He was the one who told me to go see Thyme. How do you know Thyme?"

"I lived in the monastery for a while in my younger days. After Hao and I married, we were not accepted as much among his race. You see, Hao is a Hiru."

Everyone looked at the Nomad man as he pulled off the scarf that hid most of his face and lowered the hood of his cloak. Autumn recognized the jet-black hair, light skin, Asian eyes, and pointed ears that she had tried to mimic in her disguise when she had traveled with Puck. Hao returned the hood of the cloak back up but packed the scarf in his bag.

"Things are not much better now than they used to be. In fact, two of our children live in Cuelebre with their spouses, one lives in Shenlong, and one is in the Ifrit desert. We lost a son to a skirmish with the Ogres some years ago. He helped with the underground quite a lot. None of them were accepted among the Hiru."

"Was that Cordy?" asked Sage.

"Yes, did you know him?" asked Hazel.

"A little," said Sage. "He was a good and brave man. He would give the shirt off his back to anyone in need and often did."

"That would be him," said Hao. He coughed a little.

"Hey!" said Tanner from the other end of the ship. "We have enough food here to feed all of us for a month and a couple sets of travel clothes for each of us."

"Are we going to have to lighten the ship to fly?" Hao asked Toble.

"No, no, it should be strong enough," said Toble.

Autumn looked back at Hazel. "Thank you so much for helping us and being our guides. You have taken a great risk since Maldamien is after us."

"We are very honored to help," said Hazel. "Hao and I want to help you as long as you can use us."

"Really?" said Sage looking up from the bag he was digging through. "After what everyone did to your people? I thought Hiru had a noninterference attitude these days," Sage said to Hao.

"My people did go through a lot, but it was Maldamien's doing more than all the other nations. No one who fought Maldamien at Vervain came home alive. The Hiru's anger was spread in myths and rumors to all their children, but I have since heard different stories from those who had been there from a variety of nations. All the other armies did run when faced with Maldamien. They were scared, and they saw that it was a losing battle. Very few who retreated felt proud of it afterward. They had forgotten about those in the palace, and they had not realized what they were leaving them to experience. The Hiru that fought that day are honored in the memories of everyone who I meet. Their actions were very brave, but their stance did not save anyone. Instead of being the better good as it should have been, it rained down Maldamien's anger on our nation while the other nations cowered in fear. Our cities and homes were destroyed. The only men who live today were children then, saved by mothers who hid them in the woods or sent them away from the battle. Some women fled with massive groups of children from their villages. It is easy to understand the anger and feeling of abandonment by the world, but we must move on if we are going to survive as a people. We must defeat Maldamien if we are going to never let that happen again."

"How many of you are left?" asked Sage mesmerized by Hao's speech.

"After all three of Maldamien's expeditions, there are only a hundred and fifty families left of our race," said Hao. "The Hiru live in complete poverty with primitive society so that our magic can be used to have children. It takes a lot of magic for a child, and there is so little of it left."

"How many are in a family?" asked Autumn trying to get a picture of what Hao was talking about.

"There are rarely more than four generations in a family, and we have developed a tradition that when a young couple gets married, everyone who has had four or more kids will bless the couple with as much magic as they can so they might have children. This prevents families from having much more than four, but quite a few young couples only have one or two these days."

Autumn tried to do rough math in her head.

"Somewhere around seven thousand people," whispered Hazel. "It is not much of a population. They all live in the city of Merrow because it's walls are still intact."

"Wow." Autumn tried to imagine a city of seven thousand, but the smallest city she had ever lived in was ten times that size.

"With so few to guard Thyme, why was his monastery still in Cuelebre?" asked Tanner.

"The land is large and wild. The island is not easily found there. Also, it guards the fire portal that borders the land and the oceans," explained Hao.

"So, we are going all the way to the ocean?" asked Autumn, wide-eyed.

"Almost," said Hao. "We may want to fly the last bit though."

"So, it will take us a full two weeks to get there," said Tanner. "We hadn't really discussed that when we left."

"I told the queen that I didn't want to make the details of where we were going known for security reasons. That is partially why she provided so much. She didn't know how much we might need."

They ate dinner just as the sun was setting. Toble had not created a rudder because he thought they would be flying more, but the with the nice cool wind blowing, the ship was moving much faster in the water than it would in the air.

"I'll make a rudder tomorrow when we stop, and I will remove the pedaling seat until we are ready to take off," said Toble as an announcement to everyone after Hazel was the second person to point out the missing rudder. Sage had done so earlier.

Everyone went to sleep in the front of the boat except Toble and Hazel. The two Dryads would have to wait until they stopped in the morning to rest. They steered the ship with the oars and talked all night about their people and their dreams for their people's freedom from slavery.

In the morning, they steered the ship to the shore. Everyone got out to do various chores. Sage made the rudder for Toble while he and Hazel rested as nearby trees. Autumn gathered some herbs she recognized for future use, and Hao and Tanner disappeared to scout the area. When they returned, everyone piled back in the boat and took off.

"We couldn't find anyone," said Tanner. "I am worried that we have gone so long without knowing what Maldamien is up to."

"I saw signs of Ogres having been by recently," said Hao. "I think we should stop at night since they travel during the day when they have a Nomad with them."

"We will be safer from them on the water if we could go as long as possible," said Sage.

"Don't worry about me," said Hazel. "I can go a couple of days at a time without resting."

The day passed calmly. The new rudder worked well, and the wind blew steadily. They were making good time.

The next few days each of the group found an activity to keep them occupied in between boating chores. Autumn taught Sage some meditation principles, but Sage struggled with it. Tanner taught Hao some wood carving basics. Hao taught Toble some more about the principles of flying. Toble taught Hazel some of the tricks for spacing out her need to rest. Hazel taught Autumn some ways to store herbs while traveling that would keep them fresh for as long as possible. Sage taught Tanner some combat strategies.

Autumn noticed Sage and Tanner both periodically staring at the thickly wooded shoreline as though something was wrong with it. Tanner, Sage, and Hao regularly went out scouting for signs of danger each evening as well. After the fifth day, Sage seemed worried.

"We have not seen any Ogres, Huldra, Red Ladies, or any of Maldamien's people. Where are they? I have never gone so long without running into someone."

"Perhaps we are just lucky this time," said Hao, only half believing it himself.

Sage frowned and shook his head. "I don't think so."

"There is nothing we can do about it right now anyway," said Autumn. "We just need to focus on what we are going to do."

"Do you think it might mean trouble later on?" asked Hazel.

"I don't know what it could mean," said Sage. "Our last guess is that he somehow successfully opened the earth portal while we were in Tangie waiting for the wedding."

"The unusual rain and influx of fruit seem to point to that," said Autumn.

"The next portal would be the fire portal then," said Tanner, "which makes me nervous about all this quiet."

"If Maldamien was going our way, you would think we would see signs of him," said Hao.

"Look," said Tanner as the city of Vervain came into view through the trees. Everyone silently watched as the city passed. Somehow, they all felt like something terrible would happen just being near it. Autumn struggled with the memories of Puck and their time there. She felt her waist for the sash she always wore that held the ring, the picture, and the keys. Finally, she might get some answers.

"Autumn," said Sage, "what happened to that ring? Did Maldamien get it?"

"No, I still have it."

"How did you do that?" cried Tanner.

"She hid it," said Toble proudly.

"Did we ever find out what they wanted with it?" asked Tanner.

"No, but Turmeric seemed pretty desperate to find it," said Autumn. "I wouldn't be surprised if there were still Ogres there searching for it."

"What ring?" asked Hao.

"The royal seal of Vervain," said Toble.

"That ring cost us a lot," mused Sage. "I wonder if it was worth it."

"The Ogres were after us either way," said Tanner. "It doesn't matter now anyway. Hopefully, it will slow down Maldamien's plan until we figure it out."

Autumn concentrated on what she had seen of Maldamien's thoughts to see if she could recall anything about the ring, but she couldn't find a thing.

It took another week of sailing before the ocean came into view. By this time everyone was sick of sailing, sick of the boat, and sick of everything. The ocean was a relief from the constant shoreline of trees, hills, and more trees. The wide blue horizon felt too open and made Autumn a little nervous. She had never asked Puck if one could fall off the edge of this world.

"All right Toble," said Hao. "Let's take off."

Toble replaced the rudder with the pedal chair, and everyone took a place by an oar. Toble started a little motor. The motor rotated some gears, and a giant balloon expanded over the boat and its mast. As the balloon filled up, the boat began to lift out of the water and into the air.

Sage sat on the pedal chair and began to work the rotating propeller on the back of the ship. Everyone else worked the oars to row in the manner Toble instructed. The ship moved forward at a decent speed. Autumn looked around in awe as she rowed.

"It works!" exclaimed Tanner.

"Of course it works," said Toble indignantly.

Hao looked over the edge as he rowed. "It's kind of slow. Would you want me to get out and push?"

"If you think it's necessary," grumbled Toble.

"I think it's wonderful!" exclaimed Autumn.

They floated upward and arched over the trees on the southern bank. They soared higher and higher towards the clouds, but before they entered them, they leveled off. The balloon was just hidden in the clouds so that it looked like the boat was flying without help. The giant white fins and oars gave the ship an exotic fish-like look.

When the sail was lowered and adjusted, they picked up speed immediately. The pleasant sailing weather began to change as evening approached. The darker sky also brought with it more wind. Hao helped Toble adjust the sails and gave him directions in which way they should go.

Sage continued pedaling as the ship rocked violently in the night sky. He suddenly heard something like thunder. He looked up at the sky and didn't see any storm clouds even though everything was dark now. When he heard it again, he looked down.

An army of a variety of nationalities was marching underneath them in the direction they were flying. Maldamien and Turmeric were in front, magically paving a wide treeless road with a wave of their hands. The thunder-like noise happened again, and a chunk of forest flew to the right.

"Maldamien is on the march!" Sage announced to the busy crew. Everyone looked over the sides of the boat.

The army was huge, made-up of Ogres, Nomads, Huldra, and various other races marching in columns. Wooden structures were also being transported. Giant insects were pulling huge boats on wagons. Dryad slaves were driving the wagons and carrying various loads.

"Are they after the floating island?" asked Hazel, wide-eyed.

"No, I think they are after the next portal with those boats," said Tanner.

268

"That doesn't mean he won't exterminate whoever he finds," said Hao.

The Flying Hope shuddered as a gust of wind blew. Everyone got back to work. Sage paddled as hard as he could, and everyone tried to work on the rocking boat. The wind ripped through one of the sails.

Hao shouted, "Get some rope and drop it over. I'll pull us!"

Hazel found a rope and tied it to the stern of the boat. She threw the end to Tanner. He tied a huge loop into it.

Hao turned to Sage. "Keep pedaling Sage. We need to hurry before Maldamien's army reaches Merrow." Then Hao jumped out of the boat.

Autumn muffled a scream. A huge red oriental dragon flew up with the rope around his serpentine neck. He was as big as the ship itself.

Autumn looked over the side as she bought in her useless oar and saw that they were speeding through the air. Sage was pedaling, but also gripping the handles in front of him to keep from flying off his seat.

Less than an hour later a herd of dragons swooped down from the sky. The fierceness of the group made Autumn really glad that they did not take this journey alone. The herd was made up of six different colored Asian dragons about the same size as Hao. It seemed as though the group had intended to attack but then changed its mind. Two of the dragons came alongside the ship and practically carried the boat the rest of the way.

When the floating island came into view in the midst of the clouds, Autumn gawked at the scene. The island looked like an upside-down mountain. The top was green and flat while the underside was rough and sloped to a point. The island was also very small with only one large medieval structure on it that filled the surface of the top to the edges. The square-ish monastery sat directly in the center of the island with gardens around it dripping off the edge, a garden in the center courtyard, and a small lawn in the front. Dragons flew around it as though guarding it. The dragons carrying their ship set the boat down on the front lawn. Toble deflated the withered balloon, and Sage hobbled off of his seat. Each of the dragons changed into Samurai Hiru warriors.

"We must see Thyme!" exclaimed Hao as soon as he changed back into his normal self. "Maldamien is heading this way!"

"Luke, Lee, Willow, go check it out," said the slightly graying warrior Hao spoke to. Three younger warriors ran off the edge of the island, changing back into dragons as they went.

"I will speak to Thyme on your behalf," said the graying warrior.

As he marched off, he looked at two of his soldiers as though to tell them to guard the guests closely. The two warriors escorted the group to the covered arcade. All the soldiers, except the commander, looked like they couldn't be much older than Autumn. The two warriors who guarded them both had dark bluish-black hair tied in a samurai style. They stood still and professionally, but their facial expressions were nervous and inexperienced.

As they waited, Autumn leaned against one of the columns and looked around at the building. It appeared to be mostly one story with a second floor in a small more ornate chapel-like section to the left and a long narrow dormitory area to the right. The gardens around the building had plants Autumn had never seen, and they were all greener than anywhere she had seen in Gryphendale.

The commanding warrior returned. "Thyme has been expecting you, but you are a little early."

CHAPTER 26: THYME

"Early?" asked Autumn. "How could Thyme know we were coming?"

The commanding Hiru warrior snarled. He turned, leaving them standing in the arcade as he shouted orders to his soldier in his native language. Dragons flew to the island from every part of the night sky.

"What is happening?" Tanner asked Hao.

"They are evacuating the city. I think Thyme verified our story. They apparently were attacked three weeks ago as well and lost a lot of people. Had I not been with you, they would have killed you on sight. The anger is strong with Riven. I think I am under suspicion as well," said Hao quietly.

His face showed the lines of worry and sorrow as he watched the influx of dragons and their children.

The Hiru guards watched the foreigner with no pretense of hospitality. The more folks arrived, the fiercer the guards looked. The families transformed back into their faerie state and gathered their children and supplies. Everyone seemed to know where to go. They immediately entered the complex through the main set of doors to the right of the foreigners.

The guard on the left of Autumn finally spoke up. "I don't know why Thyme wouldn't let us kill all of you. It seems convenient that you came at the head of the army."

"Like scouts or spies," added the second guard on the right of them.

"Right, so we can warn you of Maldamien's arrival because he is so much more interested in your primitive city and supplies than exterminating our race through a surprise attack!" said Hao sarcastically. "Do you think a Hiru would even be able to be seen by Maldamien without being killed on sight, let alone be a spy for him? Use your head, Calvin. Being a warrior is not just about using a sword. Think a little, Steven!"

The guards both frowned even more, and Hao sighed, folding his arms as he concentrated on the evacuation that was going on.

"We didn't need your warning," said the guard on the left who Autumn thought might be Calvin. "We beat Maldamien off the last time, and we will again."

Hao glared at him. "At what cost? Even if every man, woman, and child picked up a sword this time, Maldamien has an army of tens of thousands of well-trained soldiers with him. This time he is after the portal and will destroy anything and anyone in his way. He is ready to wipe out the Hiru completely if necessary."

The two guards paled slightly but tried to maintain their expressions. Autumn wondered if they were just teenagers trying to prove their worth.

They watched as the progression continued. There weren't as many children as Autumn had expected. Each child had a circle of adults hovering around them to attend to their needs or carry them. It was obvious that children were a priority in this society. The very basic rough wool clothes, hand-woven baskets, and rough leather luggage also verified Hao's description of the economic state of his people. They were just subsistence farmers, all of them. The men and women all looked as though they had to work the ground hard to get what they could out of it. Leathery hands, lean bodies, and worried faces showed the signs of the rough life they led. They looked like their existence was even more dangerous than that of the Brownies. Once the last family had entered the building, Riven returned.

"The dorms are full. You will have to sleep in the chapel after your audience with Thyme."

Suddenly the ground began to shake.

"What's happening?" cried Autumn as everyone braced themselves with a pillar.

"The island is moving," said Hao. "That explains all the wind we experienced earlier. Thyme was gathering magic."

"Come this way," said Riven without emotion.

The group followed him quietly into the monastery's side door and traveled down a long narrow hall with very few doors. The bare stone walls echoed their steps as they walked. Most of the way down the hall, the commander stopped at a plain green door on their left. He knocked briefly and then opened the door.

"Your visitors, sir," announced the commander.

"What?" came a small old voice from behind stacks of books on a large desk in the small office. The group gathered into the room, struggling to fit in and not step on any of the stacks of books on the floor. The messy office had no windows. Bookshelves lined every wall, floor to ceiling. Papers and books were piled on every surface. The room was lit only by a small lamp on the desk.

"Your visitors, sir," repeated the Hiru, louder.

"Yes, yes!" said the voice. "I hope you were nice to them. They are our friends, you know."

The Hiru warrior grunted and left the room, slamming the door behind him.

"Tut, tut, tut," said the short old Sprite as he came into view from around the desk. He looked around for a place to sit and saw that everything was covered in books. He pushed a stack of books off the front desk of his desk and sat down on the cleared spot. Autumn had not noticed until now how Sprite wings moved through objects like they were just made of light. With such a small office, Thyme would have been in trouble otherwise.

"Don't worry about General Riven. He won't harm you. He is just a stubborn one. So now, who are you?"

The group looked at each other confused. "I thought you knew who we were," said Autumn.

"How can I until we are introduced?" said Thyme.

"What about what you told General Riven?" said Tanner.

"Oh! Magic senses like magic," Thyme said, waving the question away. "Introduction now."

"I am Hao, and this is my wife, Hazel. Surely you haven't forgotten us," said Hao.

"Oh, the exiled prince! Of course not. Shame the people won't give you your throne. Stubborn folk, these Hiru. As pigheaded as any I've met. No, no, I haven't forgotten. Now, who are you, my dear? I see you have studied with Puck. How is my old friend?"

"My name is Autumn. I came from the human world and did study with Puck. Puck died to save our lives from Maldamien."

"Oh dear! Oh dear!" Thyme jumped up from sitting on the desk. "This sudden increase in violence is disturbing. To lose such a scholar, too! Tut, tut!" Thyme began to sort through some papers, mumbling to himself for a minute, then realized he had an audience.

"Oh, yes, the rest of you. Names please!" Then he continued looking at his papers.

"I am Sage Goliad, son of the Captain of the Guard for Queen Anemone, this is Toble, who was the ambassador at Vervain at that time, and Tanner, who was the groundskeeper for Vervain."

"Ah yes, from Vervain all of you? Yes, that seems appropriate." He turned around and got a book from his shelf and began to read it.

The group fidgeted a little as they waited.

After a couple of minutes, Autumn couldn't stand it. "We came to see if you could help us," she said.

"Oh?" said Thyme, not looking up.

"Well, we have some questions we were hoping you might help us find answers to. I wrote them down on a list so we wouldn't waste your time." Autumn pulled out her list from her trouser pocket.

"A list? Hmm. I think we should get more comfortable." Thyme then left the room from a door on his left.

Hao sighed. "Thyme will be a great help if he can focus, but it might take some time."

About a half hour later Thyme peeked in the door the group had entered earlier. "Are you coming?"

The group filed out of the room following the old Sprite down the narrow hall to another plain green door. They went down a narrow winding staircase. It took a while to reach the bottom to another door that Thyme open and entered. The whole group found themselves in a huge library three stories tall and about twice that long and wide, with aisles of books everywhere. Thyme walked through the narrow aisles to an open area in a niche in the wall. To the left of a door, there were chairs and tables enough for everyone to sit.

As they got comfortable, Thyme sat back in his over-stuffed chair and talked. "These years of study and collecting by all the Asiri has produced this bank of knowledge, yet I am the only one left who can enjoy it. It isn't unavailable to anyone who really wants to use it. Perhaps the Hiru scare off quite a few, but I find that most people who seek this library are trying to find some secret treasure or some great power. They just don't understand that this is about knowledge and preservation!" He sighed.

Autumn felt uncomfortable with the idea of changing the subject, but the importance of it was on her mind. She plunged in. "Sir, would I be able to ask you my questions now?"

"Yes, yes, ask your questions." He leaned back and closed his eyes.

Autumn opened her list. "How did Maldamien become so powerful?"

Thyme lifted his head, opened his eyes. He looked at Autumn with a clarity of focus that she had not yet seen. His eyes sparkled, but were sad. "It was one hundred years last Thursday when Maldamien took over. The prophecies are all about to be fulfilled. Wars, battles, and murders have taken place, yet no one has come to me and asked that question. I spent years researching this issue, and when I found the answer, I had no one to tell. By that point, most of the world just existed and tried to just survive under the current government. Knowledge and wisdom deteriorated just like the art and culture of the world." Thyme got up and began to walk through the library as he continued to talk, and the group got up to follow.

"The fighters just fight and don't think. The thinkers, like me, can only think and not fight. The world's knowledge lays here and here," he said as he pointed around him at all the books. "There we have all the answers. The Creator gave us the key from the very beginning, but we turned our back on him. Even the Hiru, who I love like my own children, are so close, but so far. Only now, when they can't fight anymore, do they come to me for help. They have protected this island's secrecy, but never saw it as a place of help. Now, they don't ask for knowledge, advice, or wisdom. No. They just want a place to hide so they can fight another day. Will the world not learn before it is too late? The stars, the wind, the prophecy, everything in the world is shouting that it is almost time, yet who will lead this charge?" Thyme sighed as he continued to walk. He reached the back wall of the library and then looked around. "My dear, what was your question again?"

Autumn repeated, "How did Maldamien get so powerful?"

"Oh yes!" said Thyme. "Now I remember where I was going." He turned left and continued to walk. "That is quite an easy question to answer, though it took me a while to find it. You see, it was mother's fault."

"Queen Audrey?" asked Toble.

"She didn't know that, of course. She thought she was doing the best thing for the world in creating the spell of immortality. Well, in my research I found out that she didn't create it, and it isn't a spell of immortality at all. According to her journal, the idea was given to her by Maldamien, and he helped her through the entire process of researching it, creating it, and then he tried to hide the evidence of his involvement in it by dumping her body in a field of rosemary." Thyme stopped at a glass cabinet in the far corner of the library, opened the door, and pulled out a small leather-bound book. He turned and handed it to Autumn.

"This is her journal. You will need it to understand the details of what I am going to summarize. The spell that they created was really a spell that re-channeled the four rivers of magic into Maldamien. The world, not receiving any of its own magic, is frozen, at least in appearance. These rivers are slow, so it took a couple of centuries to really feel the effects. The world is really in decay. Maldamien is stealing the magic of our world to become stronger. Our immortality is just a symptom of the impossibility for there to be any aging. The wisdom of age, maturity, and all that comes with that take a great deal of magic. That was the first to go, children being born was next. I don't know whether it has happened yet, but the physical bodies of those in between will be the next to go." Thyme started to walk back the way they came.

"You mean we will turn into ghosts?" asked Tanner following after Thyme.

"I guess that may be the right idea," said Thyme. "Closing the portals has limited this spell to our world. I don't know if that was what Queen Anemone was trying to do, but it was a beneficial effect. Maldamien could only get so strong that way. Half of this planet's magic is in the human world. The main problem is that when this world runs out of magic, it will collapse. The destruction of this world will destroy the human realm as well." Thyme returned to his seat and sat down. The others followed suit.

"So, is it a bad thing or a good thing that the portals are being opened?" asked Tanner.

"Oh, definitely a good thing, if it wasn't Maldamien."

"That's what Apollo told us," said Autumn.

"He would know," said Thyme.

"Could we just break or reverse the spell?" asked Hazel. "Wouldn't that fix it?"

"If one could put together the elements of the spell and then figure out how to reverse an element of it, one might be able to do it. The problem is that this spell ended with a death. I believe that Maldamien murdered mother to make this spell practically impossible to reverse. You can read the journal yourselves and see if you can discover something I missed. I am certainly not infallible. So, does that answer your first question? Though, I have forgotten what it was. Perhaps I was already on a different one."

Autumn looked over her list. He had answered a couple of questions, but created new ones. If the rest were that simple, they should be off by tomorrow and be working on this spell thing.

"Well, I guess the next question is how do we defeat Maldamien? I mean, if we break this spell, will it solve everything?" asked Autumn.

"Everything as in what?" asked Thyme.

"I think what Autumn is trying to say is if we break this spell, will it break the shield over his fortress, make it so we could kill him, free the slaves, free the people at the mines, weaken all his agents, and anything else that depends on his power?" said Sage.

"And is this how to save the world from being destroyed in a month and a half?" said Tanner.

"Hmm," mused Thyme. "This is a good question. It would require one to think about the cause and effect line of magical events." Thyme closed his eyes and leaned forward with his hand under his chin in a thinking position. All was quiet for a while.

Finally, after some time, Tanner whispered to Toble, "Do you think he is asleep?"

"Ah!" said Thyme suddenly. "It may. You see when the spell of immortality, or whatever you want to call it, is broken, all the magic Maldamien has been storing up will be reversed and flow out of him with him being the source. Since no one but the Creator can be the source, this should kill him instantly. Once he is destroyed, all spells he created with this magic should lose their power too and break. This should help return the balance of magic in the world and stop the deterioration and impending doom."

"I thought Maldamien's goal was to be a god and the source of magic in the world," said Autumn.

"Is it?" said Thyme. "That may cause a problem. He may know of something I do not. His use of dark magic is beyond what I am willing

277

to delve into extensively, but I may need to research this. That makes sense, but that changes things. Come with me." He stood up and went to the door they had entered by. They followed Thyme up the winding staircase to the long narrow hall. Thyme then turned right, leading them to the end. There stood a lone set of huge blue doors. Thyme walked straight to them and pushed them open like they were as light as feathers. The group walked into a well-lit chapel that was two stories tall. Every wall was covered in stained glass windows about the blue Gryphon, with the largest windows being at the end of the rectangular room right in front of them. Instead of pews or seats, the chapel was full of desks; instead of altars or a pulpit, stood a small cabinet of books. Other than those spaced out furnishings, the room was very simple, yet beautiful.

"This is where the books about the Gryphon are housed," said Thyme, leading them up between the desks to the cabinet. "There are so many variations of these stories in circulation, causing many problems. I am certain that whatever plans, spells, or goals that Maldamien has towards becoming a god must be a distortion of one of these stories. He would have to base his spell off of what he thought made the Gryphon god. Who knows what variation he is working with, but we must start with the truth first and then figure out the fallacy."

"If he is not working with a true story or a true spell, won't it fail?" said Hazel.

"Oh yes," said Thyme, "but who knows what it might destroy in the process. Read these stories, and the journal, and I will do my own research."

"We won't have much time," said Sage. "How long do you think this research will take?"

"I do not know," said Thyme.

"How long do we have?" asked Autumn.

"We have only a month until the portal has to be opened according to Apollo, but we need to travel to the Sprite kingdom to meet up with the army, do whatever it takes to set up the breaking of the spell, and then have time to get to Yarrow to stop Maldamien," said Sage.

"A week to Caoineag, a week to Yarrow," said Tanner.

"So, if we leave here in a week, we may still have time to do something," said Sage.

The group looked at Thyme. He shrugged. "I only have

information. I can't create miracles. I will research what I can, but that is all I can offer. It's late. Perhaps you should rest. There is food in the kitchen if you're hungry. If you have the energy to read, please do."

"Wait!" said Autumn as Thyme turned to leave. "I haven't asked the questions about how I ended up in the middle of all of this."

"Tomorrow, my dear. I am tired. Have Hao or Hazel bring you to my office in the morning." With that Thyme left.

"Well," said Hazel, "I guess we are left to fend for ourselves."

Autumn walked up to the cabinet of books. "There are only twenty or so books in here," said Autumn. "Why so few and so damaged?'

"Those are the few books that were saved from the various burnings Maldamien had. These books were rare even before that, from what I understand," said Hao.

"Even twenty volumes will take a little while to work through," said Sage. "Let's unpack the ship and get settled in here for the night. Hao and Hazel, do you know where a few more blankets are? We certainly won't be able to have a fire in here, and I am sure they won't want us camped in the gardens. This is going to be an uncomfortable week."

"In more ways than one," mumbled Autumn, thinking of the poor reception from the Hiru.

CHAPTER 27: THE TRUTH

That evening was full of activity, and the travelers did not get to lay down until late that night. Right after Thyme had left them in the chapel, Hao gave them all a quick tour of the complex. It seemed pretty simple on the outside, but Autumn gave up trying to remember all the halls and paths.

The complex was made up of a parlor in which all the Hiru refugees had entered. The dining room and kitchen to the right of the parlor were locked to them. The long two-story building beyond that was the dormitories. To the left of the parlor was the short arcade where they had been when they first arrived, and it was open to the yard in front of the monastery and to the cloister vegetable gardens in the center of the complex. The square courtyard style cloister was surrounded by blind arcades or arched porches. The building directly across the garden from the parlor was offices and apartments that had been used by all the Asiri. It was badly damaged and never used anymore. To the left of the whole complex was the chapel that they were staying in and the building which housed Thyme's apartments, study, observatory, and any other room that he used. The giant library they had visited was underground. The halls and passages throughout the complex were all so dark and narrow that Autumn only had a mental map of things Hao pointed out to them from the outside. Luckily, there was a door from the chapel that led to the arcade which everyone used to unload the ship.

They moved all the desks in the chapel against the walls and were able to make a reasonable camp, excluding the fire. They sorted their personal belongs in various corners, stacked the rations by the door, and passed out any extra clothes or tools to those who could use them to keep with their stuff. They ate their rations for dinner since it was obvious General Riven had intended the kitchen for just the Hiru. They talked some about what Thyme had told them and tried to read some of the books by the light of the glowing rocks that Queen Oceania had thought to pack them. It wasn't long though before everyone was dozing off. Hazel and Toble left to see if they could squeeze into the gardens somewhere, and the rest tried to settle down onto the cold hard stone floor.

No one slept well. By the time there was light in the sky, most of the group was done trying.

"Well, Autumn," said Sage as he handed out more rations, "you will get your meeting with Thyme this morning."

"Yeah," said Autumn.

"Why so sad? I thought you would be excited," said Sage.

"I thought I would too, but I feel nervous. What if I find out something I don't want to know?"

"Like what?" Sage sat down next to her and put his arm around her shoulders.

"I don't know."

"We will be here looking through these books when you get back," said Hazel.

"I can lead you to Thyme's office whenever you are ready," said Hao.

Autumn took a few bites of the make-shift sandwich she had made from the dried fish, cheese, and stale roll that were her rations for breakfast. She handed the last half of it to Sage.

"I think I'm ready when you are," she told Hao.

Hao nodded, and they both left quietly. The walk to the office was quick. Before Autumn could get properly composed, she was walking into Thyme's study.

"The Gryphon be with you," whispered Hao as he closed the door behind her.

"Good morning," chimed Thyme, unseen from behind the books on his desk.

"Good morning," Autumn replied.

"Move the books and sit down," said Thyme as he walked around his desk and sat on the spot he had cleared yesterday. The books were still on the floor where they had landed.

"Go ahead and ask your question," he said when she had settled.

Autumn took a deep breath and pulled out the list, the picture of the queen, the keys, and the ring.

"Well, the simple version of the question is how did I get here and why? I guess, though, I should tell you my story to help you understand the question."

"Yes, that would be best," said Thyme. He seemed genuinely interested, which made Autumn more nervous, but happy to be able to finally tell someone her story who might have answers.

Autumn began to relay all that had happened to her from the very beginning. Thyme's attention wandered, and soon he was up pulling a book from the shelf and reading through various volumes. All the while he interjected, "Yes, I see," or "continue, that is fascinating." Autumn wondered if he was researching what she was telling him or just bored. When she finished, he looked up and asked, "Is that it?"

"Well, yes," said Autumn.

"I am surprised you haven't figured it out yet. Then again, I suppose you have been working with a memory disadvantage," said Thyme, closing his book.

"You are missing much more of your memory than you realize."

"Am I?" said Autumn.

"Oh, yes," said Thyme as he dug through a drawer in his desk. "First of all, you know how you got here. The Gryphon brought you. You practically told me that yourself. So, it might not be through a portal that was supposed to be open, but stranger things have happened." Thyme paused. "Where is that... if I could just find..." He continued to dig into other drawers of his desk. After a minute he looked up at a shelf next to him. "Oh, here it is!"

He picked up a small paddle-shaped object from the shelf and walked over to Autumn. He gave her a plain hand mirror. Autumn looked at Thyme questioningly.

"Look at the picture of my niece. Do you not see the resemblance?"

Autumn was still confused.

"There! The picture you have of Queen Anemone, my niece. Do the features not resemble your own?"

Autumn looked at the picture and then herself. They were definitely not the same person. She couldn't be the queen. She had too many human memories. Autumn was trying to understand what Thyme was getting at. Then she saw it. Her face shape was the same. They both had the same smile. It was just a similar feature here or there. She had always looked a great deal like her father.

"Are you saying she is my mother?" asked Autumn.

Thyme smiled.

"Did you really suspect nothing? The languages you know, the items you have, the ring's response to you. These were all clues to the blood that flows in your veins. I had thought the magic imprint I saw on you was just Puck's influence because he taught Queen Anemone as well, but I can see it clearly now. You are most certainly her child."

Autumn looked at the picture again. Did her father know who her mother really was? The Faerie queen of all the folktales he studied and taught about was his wife and her mother? Something inside of her knew what Thyme said was true. It made sense. She had never met her mother's family. She had never heard stories about her mother before her parents had met. Her mother never had a past and no profession during her parent's short marriage. She just existed and was gone. Autumn knew she died. She had been to her grave numerous times with her father.

"But she died!" exclaimed Autumn. "Everyone is waiting for her to return, but she can't and won't."

"So the Gryphon brought you," said Thyme.

"What? To be some sort of long lost princess and save the world?" Autumn felt dizzy. What did it all mean?

Thyme sighed. He moved books off a nearby chair and moved the chair in front of Autumn. He sat tiredly into it. "You are not necessarily expected to rule or even save the world. All rulers here have a choice whether or not to take the throne, and then they are voted in by representatives of each country. It usually does pass on to relatives, but that isn't the issue at the moment. As to saving the world, you were trying to do that before you discovered who you were. Does this change that? This puts you in a good position to try and break the immortality spell, but it shouldn't affect you fulfilling what you have always felt like your created purpose was. You made that choice a long time ago."

Autumn looked down at the things in her hands. Yes, she was already trying to save the world, but somehow she felt tricked into it.

"Well, that leaves us with two more matters. The first is seeing what memories your mother chose to leave you, and the second is finishing our research on Maldamien."

"You didn't mention the actual process of defeating Maldamien. You make it sound like it is just an academic exercise. Are you not going to help us fight?" asked Autumn.

283

"With what? This island? My fists? No, my dear, I can only research. It is all I am good for. Now let us return to the subject of your memories before we have to assemble."

"Assemble?"

"Oh yes, we must assemble with the Hiru to discuss what Maldamien has done, but we will worry about that later."

Thyme moved his chair closer.

"All right, let me see your hand."

Autumn gave him her right hand.

"No, this one won't work. You already have runes on this hand. Give me the other." Autumn did what he asked. "No, this one has runes too. Of course, you told me. You have touched a contract and a unicorn's horn. Same runes, of course. They just say, 'Bound by magic unbreakable.' Much older than that silly master-slave thing that folks use it for. It is really for a unity of created purposes, a magic bonding and strengthening, to become a team. Your mother must have left something for us to access. Oh, your head, of course. Queen Audrey did that too. Very unusual to have three bonds."

Thyme stood up.

"Now, please bow your head." He placed his hands on her head and said, "Hidden bond and concealed memories long gone, here you belong through the power of the Gryphon's song."

When he finished speaking, Autumn could see the light from her forehead shining on Thyme's robes. When Thyme sat back down, she looked into the hand mirror. As she suspected, runes appeared across her forehead in the same tattoo style as her wrist, creating a tiara-like effect.

"You will now remember everything," said Thyme tiredly. He pointed to the door that was on the left side of his desk. "You can use my sitting room. You will need time alone as your memories return. The room opens to the hall whenever you want to rejoin your friends. I'll let them know what has happened if they come looking for you."

Autumn nodded dumbly and walked to the door he pointed to while still carrying her items and the mirror. She entered a sparsely furnished room. It had a couch and a small table and lamp. There was nothing else and no windows. As Autumn went to sit, the world suddenly turned upside-down as she collapsed.

Memories came rushing back like a tidal wave. She remembered her father's funeral and the despair at losing him. She had gone to her father's house immediately afterward. In her anger at losing him, she grabbed a box and began to pack up his things. She started in his bedroom. She pulled out clothes from the closet, personal mementos from his past, and pictures of relatives. She didn't look at much as she cried. How could he have left her alone in the world?

She was suddenly struck with the unusual look of a particular photo album in one of the boxes. She opened it and saw pictures of her father as a young man right out of college, at a house deep in the woods. On the next page was a woman who was sitting in a chair with a blanket over her as though she wasn't feeling well. The next page had her well and with some of her father's friends. The book proceeded to a wedding, and then the woman was pregnant. Autumn began to recognize that this woman was her mother. The last page had a pale woman with a baby girl, her.

Autumn decided to go through her father's house and see what else her father had about her mother. She couldn't find anything. She finally resolved to find this house in the woods to learn more about her mother.

The next few months were filled with trips to the library and interviewing her father's friends. They couldn't even agree what her mother's name was. Some said "Annie" or "Ann" or "Amy." She finally found the address of the house, which was an abandoned rental property.

She quit her job and got rid of her apartment to go on an extended trip to this house hundreds of miles away. The house was a disappointment. She had brought a tent and camping gear in case the house was not inhabitable. It was a good thing she did, because the whole thing was about to collapse with rot. She spent a couple of days looking around and found nothing. She drove to the nearby town and asked people about her mother while showing them a picture from the photo album. She could only find one crazy old lady who recognized her mother. The old woman told her of the doorway in the woods and that her parents were obsessed with it. She thought it might be a family house or historical site. Autumn then searched the woods for this door for a few days before finding it.

Autumn felt like she was getting to the end of the memory when another one hit.

She could hear her mother's voice. "Her name will be Autumn. She was born in the Autumn, and that has always been my favorite name."

Then another memory hit.

"I'm dying," Autumn's mother whispered to her father.

"I can't lose you!" he cried.

"The portal is closed, and I need that world's magic to live. I am over a hundred years old, and my body is in disunity with this world. I cannot pass my memories to you, but I can give them to our daughter."

"Will she be able to handle them? What will it do to her?"

"I will lock them away for when she needs them. She will be a queen now if she ever goes to my world. She will have the memories of my life to help her, but I can't give her my grandmother's. You must tell her of that. We Sprite can only pass on one generation of memories. You must tell her everything when she grows up."

Autumn's mind rushed with memories from her mother's eyes, from growing up in luxurious palaces, to knowing Queen Audrey to Queen Audrey's death, and her own ascension to the throne. She saw the years as queen ruling in Gryphendale's golden age, but the decline in the way of the Gryphon. She could see the signs of plotting and scandals from Maldamien and his constant attention to her. Autumn shared her mother's repulsion at Maldamien's attempts to woo her and even his proposals. Finally, Autumn experienced the events of her mother's final days in Gryphendale trying to capture Maldamien and his escape. She learned of Maldamien's plan to use the power of the portals to become a god from an informer. She didn't specifically know how he would do that, but temporarily closing the portals would slow him down and prevent his escaping into the human realm. Autumn saw Sage's father die trying to save Queen Anemone and her consequently being trapped in the human world, injured and alone. Using her magic, she hid her wings and faerie traits. The effort caused her to pass out. A group of young men hunting in the woods found her and took her to the hospital. One of the young men, Autumn's father, was the love of her life. Autumn saw the courting and marriage, but that was where the memories ended. Her mother died before giving her the last few years of her life.

All these memories began to settle down in Autumn's mind as though they had always been there. She wondered at never being curious who her mother was until after her father had died. Somehow, she had been protected from that curiosity.

Autumn opened her eyes with a little bit of disorientation and sat up. She was still in the sitting room. Nothing had really changed, but for Autumn everything had changed. She wasn't completely human; her mother was Queen Anemone. That made her half Sprite. Autumn looked back towards Thyme's office. Anemone was Thyme's niece. That made Thyme her only family.

All this information was overwhelming. Why had her father not told her? Maybe he never had the chance, but he should have found the time. Was he waiting until she remembered things? Did he think that she would need that information? Who would have guessed she would be here?

After a while of contemplating all that had just happened, Autumn reached up to touch where her new marks were. Her skin was smooth just like her wrists, but she knew everyone would be able to see the marks.

She put all the items, except the mirror, back into her pockets. She then cleared her mind.

Gryphon, thank you for the memories of my mother. I know that I am now marked as being dedicated to you, and in return, you have made me whole. I didn't even know that part of me was still missing. I understand why I so fiercely didn't want to leave this world. You were bringing me home. Thank you.

Suddenly, Autumn felt an urge to go tell Sage and her friends what had happened. When she opened the door to the hall, she was shocked to see the hall full of people walking and pushing in various directions. Mothers with children and couples trying to find parents. How long had she been laying in the sitting room?

Autumn pushed through the crowded hall following the way she had come. She found Toble. He had his back turned to her, looking at Hazel farther down the hall.

"Where is Thyme?" called Hazel to Toble over the noisy crowd.

"Yes, we are running out of time!" he nodded in response.

"Where?" called Hazel.

"What?" called Toble.

Autumn made her way to Toble and shouted to Hazel, "He is in the study."

Hazel moved through the crowd towards them. "Well, we need him to move the island again. We are under attack," she shouted over the noise.

Autumn turned around and worked her way back to Thyme's study. When she got there, she was out of breath.

"They need you to move the island. We are under attack," Autumn relayed as she tumbled into Thyme's peaceful study.

Toble looked over his books. "They move it. I just unlock it."

"Could you unlock it now? They seem to be ready."

Toble shook his head as he disappeared behind his books. "You do it. I can only work on one problem at a time."

Autumn gasped. "I don't know how to do it!"

"You're a child of the Way now. You have your mother's knowledge, and you need the practice."

Autumn sighed and left. The hall was beginning to clear some as people were filtering into the library. Autumn guessed they were using it as a bomb shelter.

Autumn made it back to Toble and Hazel in only slightly less time than before.

"Well?" asked Hazel.

"He wants me to do it," said Autumn.

"What? Do you know what to do?" asked Hazel.

"Maybe," said Autumn honestly.

"Well, let's go." Hazel grabbed Autumn's hand. She led Autumn through the crowd and Toble followed behind. They made their way to the arcade where Sage, Tanner, Hao, Riven, and seven of his warriors stood debating. There was snow covering the whole island.

"Thyme told Autumn to do it," said Hazel interrupting them.

"What?" said General Riven. Autumn could see the stress from the situation all over his face even though he was calm and acted in control. "Well, go ahead then!"

Autumn felt lost. She didn't even know what was going on. She stepped away from the group trying to focus on the Gryphon with her eyes closed. It would only be through his power that this could be done.

Okay then, she thought, *what do you want me to do?*

She waited. She had learned to listen and to concentrate on what he wanted in each situation. After a moment, Autumn opened her eyes.

"By the Creator's will, let this mountain be moved."

The whole island shook. Hao, General Riven, and his warriors ran out into the snow and transformed into dragons. The whole island moved up and to the southeast. They moved for about an hour until the island suddenly jerked to a stop.

"Why did it stop?" Autumn asked Hazel.

"It just does and then it is locked there until Thyme unlocks it. He says it's the Gryphon who does it."

"Don't you believe in the Gryphon?" Autumn asked.

"Sure, I guess." She shrugged as she walked off to greet her tired husband as he landed in the snow.

Sage walked up to Autumn and hugged her shoulders in a quick squeeze. "You did well."

"Thanks," she replied. "What happened?"

Sage explained. "When it began to snow, General Riven sent out some scouts to see where Maldamien was. Apparently, he had completely destroyed their city, opened the Fire portal, and was on the march towards the island. Most of what you saw was just panic."

A small Hiru boy pulled on Sage's cloak. "Thyme would like you both to meet him at the observatory. I also need to find all your friends and General Riven. Have you seen them?"

"They are all over there," Sage pointed to the arcade. The boy nodded and ran over to them and repeated his message. Sage and Autumn followed and joined the group so they could follow someone to the observatory.

"Do you have anything to eat?" Autumn asked Sage as they followed General Riven into the building.

Sage handed her some dried meat. "That's all I've got."

General Riven led them up a stairwell in the building with Thyme's study. They ended up in a dome that Autumn had not noticed from the outside. The entire dome was filled with contraptions and charts with a huge telescope in the center of the room.

"Good, good! I'm glad you are all here now," said Thyme. Toble wondered off like a child in a toy store, but Thyme continued. "The snow has shown me how precarious our situation is so..."

"I thought you had caused the snow to protect us," said General Riven.

"Long ago I could have done that, but not this time," said Thyme. "This was caused by a combination of a surge of magic from the human world through the Fire Portal and the cooling of our world as it dies."

"Dying!" exclaimed General Riven.

"Yes, as the leader of the Hiru, I thought you should know this information. There is only one portal left, and that is the Water Portal at Yarrow."

"We need to stop him!" said General Riven.

"Yes, yes, yes. That is what we are all here for," said Thyme.

"And you trust these?" said General Riven.

"Of course," said Thyme. "The daughter of Queen Anemone, the son of General Goliad, the faithful servant of the late Queen, and the Ambassador are all beyond question. Also, you should have never questioned the loyalty of Prince Hao and his lovely wife."

The General eyed the group still uncertain.

"Daughter of Queen Anemone?" said Tanner looking at Autumn in surprise. "And those marks are new too!"

"It's a long story," said Thyme. "Let her explain it to you later. Now if you please, let us focus on the chart here." Thyme pointed to a diagram of the two worlds with arrows pointing the path of some currents. "I had done some research since we last met. I hope you all did the same."

"Yes, we did," Sage said who gave Autumn another quick squeeze around the shoulders.

"Good, good. Well, I believe, according to my recording of Maldamien at the Fire Portal, that Autumn is correct. He does want to be a god. To do this, he is going to try to reproduce the spell he created with Mother at the same time he opens the last portal. Now, he can't do the same exact spell because he doesn't have a powerful Queen to sacrifice. Instead, he is going to have to create a similar effect and use the opening of the portal for a power boost. It is a fascinating idea, but very dangerous."

"Wait, I don't get it. Why does he need to do all of this? He has all the magic of our world already right?" said Sage.

"Of this world only," replied Thyme. "He would want all the magic, even from the human realm, to be god-like. Of course, ultimately destroying both worlds. Our world is almost dead, so he will most likely march his army into the human world to conquer it and rule until it's magic has drained as well. Then if he was a 'god,' which he actually won't be, he would expect to create a new world after this one is destroyed."

"So, all of that is going to happen at this one portal?" asked Tanner.

"Yes, some of it is just speculation, but I think that considering the evidence I am confident that is what his plan is."

"And why does he need to go through all of this to make the new immortality spell? Why doesn't he just use the magic he has and do the spell?" said Autumn.

"It would be too dangerous for him to do that," said Thyme. "He is not creating magic by using the natural abilities of things the way they were intended. He is grabbing the magic and forcing it to his will. If he uses the magic inside himself and something goes wrong, he could destroy himself. He, like all users of the Dark arts, prefer to put the risk outside of themselves."

"How did he learn all of this?" asked Hazel. "I mean this isn't common knowledge. Even when we were reading through the stories about the Gryphon we didn't discover this."

"Oh no, of course not," said Thyme. "This is very dark magic. It has a similar feel to the magic used by the Red Ladies. Many of these spells have never been written down. He is inventing spells using many magical things and forcing it to do his will. He is only trying to get the end result that he believes the Gryphon was able to achieve."

"So the stories of the Gryphon being the source of all magic and the various things that the Gryphon does is what he is trying to accomplish?" said Hazel.

"Yes," said Thyme.

"What should we do?" asked Autumn.

"I was about to get to that," said Thyme, turning to his chart. "As you see in this diagram, the currents of the worlds should pour into each other. If we were to open the portal right now, the vacuum in our world would cause a great deal of magic to rush through the portal. This could cause massive destruction in both worlds, but it would save our planet in time at the cost of many lives in both worlds. I think Maldamien knows this and is fine with these consequences. It would be best, though, if we could prevent such a disaster. So, we need to open the portal before him, but with Maldamien's original spell being broken or reversed. This way, the magic he is holding onto would pour out at the same time and keep the balance in the two worlds."

"Could we just kill him? Would that do it?" asked General Riven.

"Well, yes. Sort of. If you could kill him as he is, but I don't think you would be able to do that. With how much magic he has, he would probably be able to heal himself. I think that breaking the original spell before the portal is opened would cause the magic to pour out of him and destroy him. He won't be the source of all magic at that point, so there is no chance of him being god-like, if that were even possible. Now if you are able to break his spell, you must remember to open the portal afterward, because that is the only way to restore the natural order of things and reverse the dying trend of our world. The planet's magic needs a bit of mixing with fresh life in it. Maldamien has held onto the magic so long that his stale magic may only prolong the dying trend instead of curing it. We are so far gone from where we should be that only a complete restoration will fix all these issues." Thyme looked at the strange expressions on everyone's faces. "That's it," he said.

"So it comes down to breaking the immortality spell that Queen Audrey created," said Sage. "How do we do that?"

"I gave Autumn Queen Audrey's journal. She is going to have to figure that out. I am afraid I have told you everything I can."

"What happens after that?" asked Hazel.

"After Maldamien dies?" said Thyme. He waved his hand dismissively. "I never liked politics. That is your business. All the countries have rulers or leaders, and they will fight or rule or do whatever they like. At least the world is saved, and the natural order of things will be restored."

"What if Maldamien goes to open the portal right now? How much time are we going to have?" said Tanner.

"Oh don't worry," said Thyme. "Maldamien will wait until the last moment to open the portal to get the greatest effect. He may have been able to do it now had he obtained the royal seal Autumn has so graciously hidden from him. The magic held in that one artifact could have thrown off the balance of this whole event in Maldamien's favor. I imagine you will have all the way until the day of remembrance before Maldamien can accomplish his ritual."

"That's only a month away!" said General Riven.

"Yes, yes, that is true. Does anyone want to go to dinner?" said Thyme as he walked over to the door of the observatory.

The group dumbly followed Thyme into the dining hall. The large rectangular open room was easily able to accommodate the whole of the Hiru population. Autumn noticed the beautiful solid wood rafters and beams that held the roof in a style similar to a Viking longhouse. Hiru were already sitting on long wooden benches at long wooden tables eating from simple wooden bowls. The group waited in a line at the far end of the hall where three Hiru men were ladling some stew from giant iron caldrons. The first Hiru man stopped pouring when he saw Autumn.

"Serve them," said General Riven.

"Are you sure?" asked the cook.

"These folks are going to save us all. Serve them," said the general. The cook poured the stew and handed the bowl to Autumn.

When the whole group had their stew, they went and sat together at the table back by the door. Thyme lifted the bowl to his forehead in thanks to the Gryphon. Sage, Toble, Tanner, and Autumn did the same. Hao and Hazel embarrassingly followed suit. Only General Riven seemed to ignore the gesture entirely.

"I think we are still going to need the army," said Sage. "We need to get to the portal when the spell is broken, deal with Turmeric who will try to take Maldamien's place as ruler, and establish some sort of order when this current government falls apart. We don't need the Huldra, Ogre, or Nomad countries trying to conquer everyone else. That also is assuming we don't need to get access to Maldamien to break the spell to begin with."

Sage ate some of his steaming hot stew as most of the table nodded in agreement. Autumn couldn't even taste her food it was so hot, so she just sat and stirred it until it cooled.

"And you will lead this army? Who is going to be fighting? A bunch of farmers? Are you going to make yourself the next dictator?" said General Riven.

"I will lead because no one else will. The army will be of volunteers from the freed prisoners of Odemience, those supplied by the Sprite kingdom, and those who come to us from the water people. If your people wanted to join us, that would be fine too. As to the ruler, that will be voted upon, but I think that if Autumn is the rightful heir, she will have a lot of support," said Sage as he looked up from his stew. His eyes were orange, bordering on turning red.

"Our people will not be in this battle. We have already done enough," said General Riven.

"Done enough!" exclaimed Hao. "So all you will do is sit here and hide!"

"It only seems fair," said General Riven looking at Hao challengingly.

"How many of our people are slaves? None! How many of our people have been tortured? None! How often have we been raided or attacked in the last eighty years? Only the two times this month! We may be a small people who suffered great violence at the beginning of all this, but we have lived many years of relative peace, being ignored and left alone, while the rest of the world has suffered much more than their fair share. What have you been through? Have you been touched at all by the wrongs done to your father? How many people from all the nations have lost fathers, brothers, children, and friends? No, we are equal in suffering with the world, yet you want to sit here and reap the benefits of the blood of others without even pretending to stand with them. That is worse than what was ever done to us! Our fathers would be horrified and ashamed!"

Hao was standing and shouting by the time he ended, and the whole room was looking at him.

"Enough! I will not sacrifice the few lives we have for your pride and delusions," said General Riven. "You all had better leave tomorrow morning, or you will regret ever setting foot here!" He took his bowl of food and left.

Thyme shook his head and sighed as he finished his food. "Same argument. Well, may the Gryphon guide you on your way tomorrow."

He patted Hao's shoulder as he stood and left. Hao sat back down.

"Hazel and I want to go with you," said Hao.

"That's great," said Sage. "Toble, do you think we can repair the ship tonight?"

"It doesn't need too much. It should be ready to go tomorrow," said Toble.

"So, I guess we are going to Shellycoat in Caoineag where Queen Shasta's palace is?" asked Tanner.

"That is where I told all the prisoners who wanted to fight to go," said Sage. "We will see if we have a couple of hundred men. I also hope to ask Shasta for some troops as well."

"Against an army of thousands?" said Hao.

"Are you changing your mind?" asked Sage.

"No. I am very aware of the dangers. Couldn't we rally a few

294

more?"

"I hope we have enough time. It will take us a week to get to the palace and a week to get to Yarrow, so we only have a little over a week to rally, train, plan, and equip an army," said Sage. "I wish my dad was here. I have never done anything like this. It seems almost impossible."

"You may not see it, but you have been training your whole life for this moment. You are probably more equipped for this particular battle than your father ever was," said Toble.

Autumn squeezed Sage's hand.

"We each have our purposes and our tasks. I am certain the Gryphon has prepared you for this time. I am going to the library to start reading the journal. I hope that I can find the steps we need to do to break this spell."

"The Gryphon be with you," said Sage.

His eyes were watery blue and sincere. Autumn smiled. She had learned that meant, "I love you."

CHAPTER 28: FLYING AGAIN

Autumn curled up in one of the overstuffed chairs of the library with Queen Audrey's leather journal. She opened to the first page but was not reading it. She needed to be alone with her thoughts. Everything was overwhelming her. She was now part of this world. She knew what this world was supposed to be like. She had a mother who loved her dearly. She would be reading about her own great-grandmother. Sorting through these new memories and emotions made reading difficult.

Autumn forced her attention to the beautiful Sprite script on the parchment pages.

The fifth day of Spring:
My dearest husband was buried a week ago. I have begun this journal to help sort my thoughts and emotions. My life has been left empty. The throne and grave responsibility of this world is now mine alone. My granddaughter and all my advisers have been a source of comfort and support, but yet I feel alone. A great man, a scholar, artist, and heroic leader, has left a void in the world in which I cannot see any who would be able to fill. He died too young, too quick, and all because of a tragic illness. With all of our technology, science, and advancements we still are the slaves of mortality.

Autumn could relate to some of the sentiments the queen had written. The loss of Autumn's mentor, Puck, and her father were devastating. The introduction of all the memories also created the feeling of loss for her mother and the weight of an awesome responsibility on her shoulders. Autumn could never hope to hide in some wilderness now. This mess was her family's fault. Her mother and great-grandmother didn't stop Maldamien when they could have. Autumn felt like it was up to her.

Autumn looked up as Sage pulled a chair up to her.

"I wanted to check up on you. I was worried. How are you doing?" said Sage.

"You mean now that I found out that I am someone completely different than who I always thought I was? I'm doing great."

Sage reached out and took Autumn's hand.

"You aren't really that different. You have a past and a heritage, the future is still yours."

"Sort of," said Autumn as she shifted to sit properly in the chair. "I now have all the memories of my mother. It turns out I had them the whole time, but they were hidden away. That is how I knew these languages. With all that I now know, I feel a lot of responsibility to fix all of this. My family caused this problem. I remember my mother fighting Maldamien and all that he did. Having all this knowledge isn't a bad thing though. There are a lot of things that are clearer now and make more sense. My strong desire to stay in this world makes sense now. You were right, I do belong here, but my life looks different. I am different."

Sage looked down at Autumn's hand that he was holding.

"I know you are right. You could be the next queen. You remember farther back than I do now. I don't know what that does to a person. I know this isn't the best time, but I think you know... Well, I am 113 years old and have never really fallen for someone. I have not had the time, patience, or inclination to. Very few women could lead the life I do or have had much in common with me. I am an outcast. You are so different than anyone I have ever met. We are similar... or were similar. Either way, I have fallen in love with you. I think you have known that, but I just want you to know that this doesn't change that if you don't want it to."

Sage's eyes were a deep blue.

Tears fell onto Autumn's cheek.

"I have wanted your love and have fallen for you as well, but this does change things. I feel responsible for breaking this spell, no matter what that costs. I don't feel like I am my own person anymore. My life has been taken from me. My happiness is not my biggest priority. I just don't know anymore."

Autumn gave Sage a quick kiss.

"If I am truly honest, I have loved you from the moment I saw you.

Maybe it was a schoolgirl crush at first, but I know that it is much more than that now. I would spend the rest of my life with you if it was my life to spend. What if we both die? Or what if we are successful and both live? I haven't decided if I am equipped to be a queen, or if these people would have me as queen. If they did want me, would you be happy in a palace obeying your wife's orders? I can't turn my back on the knowledge I now have to help these people. Honestly, I don't know what expectations even tomorrow is going to bring."

Sage kissed Autumn's hand.

"I love you. When all of this is over and whether or not you become queen, I will still be here for you. In this life, we are not promised much to hope for, but I think that if you love me, and I love you enough, we can make a way for it to work. I care about this world too. I have spent my life fighting for it. We can do that together. I want to help you, so don't shut me out. If we die, then we die, but I need to know that I am fighting for us now, and not just for everybody else out there."

"Fight for us then," said Autumn, bringing Sage's hand to her check. "I need to dream and know what I am hoping for. I still don't know if we will have our dreams or if the world will end or what, but I feel better equipped to deal with it knowing you are there fighting with me, too."

Sage knelt down in front of Autumn and kissed her. Then he looked into her eyes.

"I know you need to read, and I need to prepare for us to go, but find me if you need anything. We will have this happily ever after. I am sure of it. Then we will get married, have about a half a dozen fat babies, and take care of our people together."

Autumn nodded with tears in her eyes and a crooked smile on her face.

"That sounds wonderful."

Sage kissed her again and left.

For the rest of the evening, Autumn happily read about Queen Audrey's introduction to the idea of trying to prevent the death of so many great people in Gryphendale It was interesting to note how often a young adviser named Maldamien began to be mentioned in the entries.

When Autumn was too tired to read more, she left the library. She wandered the empty halls trying to process all the events of the day. The monastery was plain and barren. No rugs. No curtains. It was built like a university, but with less focus on comfort and more focus on practicality and economy. Everything was either made of gray stone or wood. Even in its plainness, it vibrated with energy and seemed to make things easier. There were no distractions. The problem was, she was too tired to think.

She returned to the chapel where everyone was already asleep and curled up in her blankets to another uncomfortable night of sleep.

The morning was full of activity, but none of the Hiru came to help the group. They were boarding the loaded ship with everything they had brought when Thyme walked out into the snow towards them.

Autumn jumped out of the boat to meet him. He took her hands.

"Take care of yourself, my dear," said Thyme. "This will not be easy for you. May the Gryphon lead you and help you."

"Goodbye," said Autumn.

She squeezed his hand and joined Sage on the ship. Thyme waved to them as they quietly took off and rose into the clouds.

Everyone agreed to let Autumn skip the ship duties so she could read through the journal. She felt like it was a little unfair that she could just wrap a blanket around herself and comfortably read while everyone worked hard, but she also knew that everything depended on this journal and they were running out of time.

As Autumn read farther into the journal, she was absorbed with the notes the queen made of her research. The journey to learn this spell was a strange puzzle with disturbing pieces. It was amazing how subtly Maldamien fed her information or pushed her in specific directions. It was also interesting to Autumn how the Gryphon never came up in the queen's thoughts or research. This was an academic and scientific issue to her. It had nothing to do with religion in her mind. It took two days of reading before Autumn began to get into the spell itself. Autumn felt the hair rise on the back of her neck as she read:

I was able to get the consent of Puck and Anemone to be bound to me. They are both such powerful wizards. It should help me to be strong enough to do this spell. I also called Apollo with the royal seal this afternoon. When he bowed to me, I touched his horn and was bound to him as well. He was not very happy with me and told me that I was seeking too much power. He warned me that it would end badly. I wanted so badly to tell him the wonderful plan that I am working on, but I must agree with Maldamien that very few people would support me in this. Everyone is too content with the way things are. I couldn't tell Apollo that with the bond I have with him now I would be powerful enough to do any spell I needed.

Autumn looked up. Queen Audrey had the same three bonds she did with the same three people. The coincidence was too remarkable to be an accident. There had to be a divine hand in this matter.

Autumn continued reading and came upon another interesting passage.

In my research, I realized that the container I used to combine the elements of the spell is just as important as the elements themselves. I researched the properties of gold, diamonds, and various rare and exotic materials. I think though that the most powerful container is a living being. I suppose I could try anyone or any creature, but what would be more powerful than a faerie and a queen, with three bonds at that. I have decided to use myself as the container to combine the elements. After all, I am working on trying to change the very fabric of life. To use myself as the container for this spell would make the spell in contact with life at its completion.

Autumn started to shake as she processed this information. The ship shuddered, and Autumn was relieved that everyone was too busy rowing, passing out rations, or repairing things to notice her huddled in the stern of the ship. She felt sick at how gullible her great-grandmother had been. She was a little old lady being conned into sacrificing herself for the benefit of a horrible villain. She gave no one the slightest chance or clue to save her. Perhaps Puck and Anemone should have guessed something was strange, but what could they have even imagined that would have been close to what Queen Audrey had planned? Now Autumn was going to have to walk in the exact same footsteps as her great-grandmother. No one else had the marks. No else had the blood of the queen in their veins. No one else was going to be able to do this.

Nervously, Autumn continued reading as Hazel handed her a bit of food.

"Are you all right?" asked Hazel.

"I think the reading is giving me a little motion sickness," Autumn

300

lied.

"Oh, here," Hazel went into her bag and dug out a dried herb. "This will help."

"Thanks." Autumn chewed the nasty weed.

"Have you found anything yet?" asked Hazel.

"I am beginning to get into the spell itself now," said Autumn.

"That's great!" said Hazel. "We have four more days until we get to Shellycoat. Do you think you will know everything by then?"

"Well, I think I will know how the spell was created, but that doesn't mean that I will know how to break it."

"Good luck then, and we all will help if we can."

"Thanks," said Autumn with more of a smile than she felt. As Hazel walked off, Autumn continued reading.

That night, Autumn didn't sleep. She felt the anxiety rising in her as she read about the way the queen went about researching in books that Maldamien brought to her. The queen started to see the elements that she needed for her spell in these books. She needed something of death, something of life, something to block the cycle of them, and something to channel them. Autumn wondered why the queen never asked where this was going to be channeled. She was so obsessed with the result that she never looked to see what the spell was really doing.

The queen finally decided to use the water from the pool of the dead for the element of death, a phoenix feather for the element of life, rosemary for blocking this cycle, but she struggled with the final element. The entries became separated by more days as she started suspecting people of interfering with her research.

Autumn was annoyed when, instead of telling about how she went about acquiring the water from the pool of the dead, she just quickly wrote that she had drunk some that day. No mention of where this pool was, if there was any trouble getting to it, or if it was an easy task. Autumn made a mental note to ask everyone if they knew of this pool.

Autumn looked around at the dark ship. She was reading by the light of a glowing stone. Toble and Hazel were the only ones awake, talking to each other at the other end of the ship. It would be best to ask in the morning.

Autumn shifted and went back to reading. The queen talked some of the political issues in her kingdom, Anemone's birthday party, and various projects. Again, the queen quickly mentioned that she had eaten a phoenix feather with no mention of how she got it or what kind of trouble it caused.

Autumn sighed. Maybe this would be easier than she feared. Autumn hoped that perhaps the pool of the dead and the phoenix feather were common things, easy to find. Something told her that if that was true, than this spell would have been done before now. Autumn went back to reading.

I am so excited! Today I will complete the spell. I will be traveling to the rosemary field with Maldamien. He said he discovered the last element for me, and it was a very simple thing that we can do today. Today will be remembered throughout history as the day that death was defeated!

Autumn felt her skin crawl. She flipped the page. It was blank. The rest of the journal was blank. Autumn flipped back through the last pages. There was nothing else. The last element was either Maldamien's secret or Queen Audrey's death. How would Autumn be able to find out what it was? Autumn just stared at the blank pages. Sure, she could copy everything the queen had done so far, but it seemed important that this last element be the one reversed to break the spell. Now there was a dead end. What was the last element? If it was death, then how would one reverse it?

"Drat!!!"

Autumn felt tiredness sweeping over her. She put away the glowing stone and the journal and laid down to think. She reviewed the steps of the spell that the queen did: drink from the pool of the dead, eat a phoenix feather, and do something with rosemary. What was it that she did with the rosemary?

Autumn was so tired that she fell asleep.

In her sleep, Autumn had unsettling dreams. She kept trying to remember things the queen wrote. The chaos of her thoughts seemed to settle down on: *I also called Apollo with the royal seal this afternoon... the royal seal...*

Autumn woke with a start. The royal seal! She dug into her pocket and got out the ring. The ring was large enough to fit a man's thumb, but when she put it on her ring finger, it shrank down to fit perfectly. The ring glowed slightly in the early morning light. Autumn remembered back into her mother's memories. This ring was not just an ordinary signet ring. It had magical properties to help the monarch to rule all of Gryphendale, to call magical creatures, and to protect the wearer. Autumn was going to need it now. She needed to find the pool of the dead as her first step, and maybe the ring could help with that.

Sage came over and sat by Autumn. "Good morning. It is the first time in days that I haven't seen you with your nose in the book. Did you finish it?"

"Yes, sort of," said Autumn.

"Sort of? That sounds like it wasn't very helpful," said Sage.

"Oh! No, it was helpful. It just doesn't end. It just stops before I had everything I need to know. I have an idea of how the spell was done, but I don't really know how it ended."

Sage frowned. "What can we do to find out about the rest?"

"Well, I just think we should do what we do know and then..."

"Sage!" shouted Hao.

"Wait a minute," Sage told Hao.

"No! Look, there is an army down there heading towards us!" said Hao.

"What?" cried Sage, scrambling to his feet and looking where Hao was pointing. It was a small detachment of the previous army made up of Ogres and Nomads being led by Turmeric. Unlike before, the Flying Hope was spotted.

"All hands rowing!" cried Sage as he ran to the back of the boat to sit and pedal.

A fireball was shot towards them. Tanner pulled out his hunting knife and sliced a couple of ropes quickly, forcing the ship to lurch left to miss being hit. Toble turned the helium on to raise them up into the clouds. Autumn and Hazel put out a small fire caused by another near miss. Sage jumped off his seat as a fireball hit it. Hao jumped overboard and turned into a dragon, so he could push the boat while shooting flames at the army. A fireball came straight for the balloon.

Sage pulled out his long, curved sword.

"Duck and hold on!" he shouted as he whirled around slicing all ropes.

Hao tried to slow the fall of the ship as the balloon burst into flames just a little bit above them. Toble and Hazel immediately grew a canopy of leaves to try and act as parachutes, but the ship still crashed hard behind a hill out of sight of the little army.

"Everyone all right?" asked Hao as he turned into his faerie form.

"Yeah, just sore," said Autumn as she looked around.

"We need to hide!" said Hazel.

"No, we have to run. They will find us," said Toble.

"Wait, look!" cried Autumn pointing to a small path leading down into the hill.

"We have no other choice," said Sage. "Everyone grab as much as you can carry." Sage picked up two bags, his own and one with rations. He headed quickly down the path into the hill. The path narrowed until everyone had to walk single file. Then they had to bend down in half to dodge hanging tree limbs and rocky overhangs. Even Tanner, the Gnome, was bending over to walk on.

"What if we get trapped down here? asked Hao.

"Can we get anymore trapped than we already were?" said Sage.

"At least we have a chance in hiding," said Autumn.

"If no creature lives here," said Tanner.

Sage stopped suddenly, and everyone ran into the person in front of them.

"Hey! What happened up there?" cried Tanner who was almost crushed by Toble.

"There is a singing tree in front of a cave that has ancient writing on it," said Sage.

The statement was repeated back, and Autumn heard a mummer in return of, "Gungil Caverns."

"We need to turn around," said Hazel.

"No, we need to go forward," said Hao.

"What is Gungil Caverns?" she asked Sage who was in front of her. It seemed familiar, but she couldn't place it.

"A place filled with ghosts," said Sage.

"We have no choice," said Autumn. "We must go on."

The group was silent as they continued forward. They entered a large area in which they could gather around the cave and stand upright. It felt like the bottom of a giant well. In front of the group was a giant silver weeping willow that sounded like its leaves were tiny wind chimes. Slightly behind and next to the tree was a large entrance surrounded by ancient writing no one in the group could read. As they walked closer to the door, they could see the entrance was covered by a large black door with a large seal on it. Sage and Tanner pushed the door, but it was locked closed.

Voices came from the path behind them.

"We're gettin' closer," growled the Ogre's voice.

"We're trapped!" said Tanner.

"No," said Autumn. "This is the royal seal on the door. I wonder if one of my keys can open it."

Autumn pulled out her keys. She felt like she just knew which key it was. She put the key into the hole in the center of the seal. The door opened on its own. Everyone stood stunned momentarily, before suddenly running into the cavern. As Autumn pulled the key back out, the massive door slammed shut behind them.

The cavern was large and spacious with bowls of shining white liquid lining the walls. The light revealed the wall's multi-toned golden color with jewel-toned streaks. The ceiling looked like it would drip solid rock onto them. It would have made a good secret place for a palace like the Undines had built. A sad tune reverberated through the void. Autumn's skin crawled, and her heart felt like it would turn her inside out with sorrow. Tanner pointed at a handsome legless faerie playing a harp to a small handful of very pitiful souls. None of the ghosts could be easily identified as to what nationality they were from. The tearful melody paused a moment as the door slammed and continued as the musician began to speak.

"What has brought the living dead to us, the dead living?'

The group was speechless as they ventured closer to him.

"Well, since you cannot bring yourselves to answer my question, I will introduce myself." He continued to play without much thought. His skill was extraordinary. "I am Paul."

Some of the group gasped.

"The royal minstrel?" asked Tanner. "You died two hundred years ago!"

"We are the forgotten ones who pay the price for immortality. We are slowly absorbed into the magic Maldamien has been using from the beginning, but we have never died. Do not look horrified. None of us have been here longer than a couple of hundred years," he said bitterly.

"Is that what happened to your legs?" asked Autumn.

"Yes, Your Majesty." he smiled at her. "You are the first of the royal house who has been here since the curse."

"Why?" asked Autumn. "If you all have been here for only two hundred years, why would anyone come before then?"

Paul laughed bitterly.

"No, my living queen. It is the reverse. People do not come now that we are here. This is the place of magical treasures, a place where one could get healed, or do miracles. This was a place flowing with living power, but now it is where magic is held captive, used up, and destroyed. The doors were once used for the protection of precious treasure, but now it is a prison. Once this place was shared with all who were worthy, now it is forgotten and feared. Pass through and weep with us, my queen! Weep long and hard at what the inside of the world has become!"

Autumn continued on as Paul had indicated, deeper into the cavern with her friends close behind.

CHAPTER 29: GUNGIL CAVERN

The group ventured on, fearful and quiet. The cavern was littered with groups of ghosts everywhere. The farther they went, the more there were. Soldiers from battles, mothers with children, and even a few animals sat around talking quietly. The cavern then led to an area where it split off into multiple directions.

"Where do we go?" Tanner asked Autumn.

"Do we know that any of these lead out somewhere?" asked Hao.

"Let me ask someone," said Autumn. She walked up to a ghost of a young woman.

"May I ask you where these passages lead and which one is the way out?"

"They all lead out, but not all can be traveled safely," she replied and turned back to her conversation.

"So, which is the safest way to go?" asked Autumn, frustrated at the first response.

"It depends on where you are headed," replied the woman.

"I'm trying to get to the Sprite kingdom," sighed Autumn.

"Maybe. You must search inside to know for sure."

Autumn was not satisfied with that answer but went back to the group anyway. "I didn't get anything out of her!" Autumn complained.

"Well, look!" Sage pointed to the tops of each entrance. There were symbols of different things on each one. A golden harp decorated the top of a small entrance to the right. A pot of gold decorated the next one to the left of that which also had a lot of heat coming from it. A sword decorated the next one which looked straight and smooth. A scroll was the adornment on the top of a roughly carved passage. So the symbols and passages continued on. There were almost twenty different passages one could choose from.

"How can one pick with so many?" asked Hazel.

"Can no one tell us anything?" said Tanner.

Sage pointed to the one on the left that had a symbol of a blue gryphon. "Why don't we stick with what we trust?"

Everyone agreed and went to that entrance. The tunnel progressively got smaller, and it continued a long distance without any souls in sight.

"I wonder if Turmeric's troops are gone," said Hao. "Perhaps it would be better to turn around than to get lost."

"We have been walking too long to do that," said Tanner.

"Maybe we should stop for some food," said Sage.

"It might be good to get a little sleep too," said Autumn.

Toble shook his head. "We cannot eat or sleep here. We may not ever be able to leave if we do."

The passage went on for miles. The friends became fearful as the way became narrower and narrower.

The group continued on for hours. By this time, most of them were dragging their feet in exhaustion. There was no way to tell how long they had been walking or how far they had gone. Hazel and Toble were beginning to sprout branches as tiredness was consuming them. Tanner and Sage were focused on keeping Autumn from passing out. Just when they were about to give up, they turned a corner and there sat the Gryphon in front of a fire with a fully cooked meal. The fire produced light and heat, but there was no smoke and no fuel for the fire. It just floated inches from the ground.

"Well done. Eat and rest. You will be safe."

The Gryphon said this with a voice that was carried in a wind. He then just faded away.

The group was so hungry and tired that no one questioned the command.

"If we die, at least we die with our stomachs full!" said Hao with his mouth full of bread.

The group practically passed out around the fire with Toble and Hazel as bent over trees, one on each side of the hall with the rest of the group between them.

The hazy transition between sleep and awareness overtook Autumn. She found herself dreamily sitting in a gondola on a large canal lined with nondescript houses and buildings close together in a very plain version of Venice. Everything was monotone in color so that it was unidentifiable. In the gondola, Autumn recognized the entire group, each absorbed in their own thoughts. The gondola was being punted by a plain human man who was staring straight ahead and not looking at any of them. The gondola passed under a bridge and then stopped by a little pier. Sage stepped out and walked into one of the buildings. The gondola then continued on, stopping as each one of the group entered a different building. Finally, Autumn alone sat in the gondola.

The gondola stopped again, but Autumn did not feel like stepping out. Moments later, a small satyr stepped into the boat.

"Puck!" cried Autumn. As tears poured from her eyes, she leaned over and hugged him. "I missed you so much!"

He felt so real to her.

"My dear, dear girl!" replied Puck emotionally. "I have missed you, too."

The gondola continued moving on into the canal.

"Am I dead?" asked Autumn.

"No," replied Puck, "you are still in Gungil Caverns."

"Oh, how I have missed you and your wisdom!" cried Autumn again.

Puck laughed. "You are much wiser than you realize or allow yourself to be. Had I any children I could not have been prouder of them than I am of you."

Autumn looked at Puck's sincere expression. "Did you know who I was? That I was the daughter of Queen Anemone?"

"No, not really. That was a surprise to me."

"But then how did you know to be bonded with me and to lead me to all the places you did?" asked Autumn.

"I had a dream a couple of days before I had met you. I had mentioned it before. In that dream, I saw a giant blue gryphon. He flew down and handed me a slave bracelet. A voice on the wind spoke and said, 'Now is the time. Go to the Wind Portal and bind yourself to the human child. Death will surround you and overcome you, but I have overcome death. The curse will be no more, and the great evil will be no more. Do this in love. For that purpose, all was created that was created.' Then I woke and did what I was told."

Autumn pondered this for a while. "The Banshee queen was washing some grave clothes when I first met her. Were those yours?"

"I had no grave clothes, remember?" said Puck.

"Are they mine?" asked Autumn.

"We all die. Haven't you seen that this illusion of immortality is completely fake?"

Autumn frowned. "You didn't answer my question."

"I must show you some things," said Puck as the gondola pulled up to a little pier. "Follow me."

Autumn got out behind Puck. She turned to look at the boat.

"Don't ever look back. Regrets will haunt you," said Puck.

Autumn turned back towards him and walked with him into one of the plain buildings. Inside looked like a hospital room. The angelic woman lying in the bed was her mother, Queen Anemone. Autumn's father was weeping heavily with his face toward the wall. Autumn's mother opened her eyes weakly.

"Lewis, please let me see my daughter."

Her father wiped his eyes on his sleeve, went to the bassinet next to his wife, lifted out the tiny baby, and laid her on his wife's lap. Anemone looked at the baby, and a tear fell onto her cheek. She placed her right hand on the baby.

"My only child, Autumn, I give you the gift and curse of being my heir. Take now my memories, my hopes, and my responsibilities." She looked up. "Creator of all things, be with my husband. Comfort him until we can be together again. Be also with my child. At the right time, open the portals for her. Make her way clear. Let her deliver the world of my birth as I would. May they honor her as queen. Help her to grow strong, wise, and good. Prepare her and keep her safe. Let her forgive me and all those who came before her for the burden she will have to bear." Anemone looked down at the child and reached for her husband.

"My last gift... forget..." Then she died.

The room grew dark. Puck led the tearful Autumn forward into the blackness until they found themselves in a rosemary field. Coming from the opposite direction came a little old lady Sprite with a basket in her arms full of rosemary, and the same Maldamien Autumn had met.

"This is a good spot," said Maldamien.

"I am so excited," said the old woman. "To think that death will be erased. No one will ever have to go through the heartache of losing a loved one, the arts and sciences will expand with no interruptions or redundant work, and families will know the multitude of their descendants. The world from this day on will be such a happier place!"

"Yes, my queen," said Maldamien. "Now to finish this spell, you must fill your pockets with the rosemary."

The eager queen put down her basket and filled the pockets of her traveling cloak and gown with rosemary. Maldamien had his back to her as she did this.

"I am finished," she announced when every pocket was full.

Maldamien turned around suddenly with a silver dagger and rushed towards her as he screamed, "Die, hag!"

Autumn turned her face away from the scene. When she looked back, all was black again. From the darkness came Queen Anemone walking towards her.

"Mother?" said Autumn.

"Oh my child!" said the queen as they embraced for a while.

When they let go, Queen Anemone spoke. "Listen now to me, my daughter. You are queen of this world now in my stead until the council votes you in or out. All the things that listened to my voice in my lifetime will listen to your voice now. That ring called Gungil Caverns to you. It can call others to you as well. You are my daughter, and if you call on the Gryphon, you will have the power to break this spell. You have already done the first steps, and you have discovered what the rest of the steps are. You must find the pool of the dead in these caverns and drink of it. You must find a phoenix and eat the feather that he will give you. You must find the last rosemary field and fill your pockets with rosemary. Finally, you must trick Maldamien into killing you with the silver dagger that the water people have given you. The rosemary has now become poisonous because of the spell. When you need strength to continue on, drink this potion a little at a time. It will help you fight the pain. Be brave, my dear, and forgive me for leaving this to you to do."

Autumn took a small metal canteen from her mother's hands.

"But this is all exactly the way Queen Audrey did it. What step do I reverse?" asked Autumn.

"Not all spells are as easy as that to break. Do what I have told you and leave the rest to the Gryphon. I am so sorry, my child. My failures have been felt by the whole world, and you must forgive me!" said Queen Anemone with tears in her eyes.

Autumn looked at the canteen. Her mother was telling her that she must die. "Is this the only way?" asked Autumn.

Queen Anemone nodded. She began to fade away.

Autumn cried out, "I love you, Mother! I DO forgive you."

"Thank you, my sweet girl. Thank you!"

When all was dark again, Puck took Autumn's arm gently. "Let us go as well."

Autumn walked quietly as Puck led her. All she could think of was Sage. Her hope for the future, her love and dreams would all have to be sacrificed. She didn't have a choice. If she didn't break the spell they would all die, and if she did break the spell, she would die. She felt the despair and fear sweep over her. She began to shake thinking about the torture she went through under Maldamien's hand. She was going to have to face her greatest fears.

Puck led her to the small pier as the gondola with all her traveling companions in it glided up.

Puck turned to Autumn. "You know now that those burial clothes were for you. You will die. How you die is your choice."

"Do I have a choice?" asked Autumn.

"You know that you do, and you already know what you will choose. Your compassion makes it seem that you are faced with no choice, but it is because your heart will not let you choose any other way. We all die. Some young and some old, but it is what we do with what we are given that matters. No one is guaranteed a certain amount of years. Life isn't fair. You will deal with many emotions, but make your choice and stick with it."

Puck hugged Autumn. "Goodbye, my dear, and may the Gryphon be with you and guide you."

Autumn couldn't say anything in response, so she stepped into the gondola. She then began to turn to look at Puck as the gondola pushed off.

"Don't look back," said Puck.

Autumn looked down into her lap at the metal canteen. The gentle rocking of the gondola gave way to the harsh shaking of someone trying to wake her.

"Autumn! Autumn!" Sage was shouting in her face.

"What?" cried Autumn.

Sage sat back and breathed hard. The whole group was around her.

"We thought we lost you," Sage explained. "We all woke up, but you did not. I was afraid that since you were Queen Anemone's daughter..."

"That the cave would keep me," finished Autumn, sitting up. "No,

I'm here. I just had the strangest dream." She lifted her hand, and in her hand was the metal canteen that her mother had given her.

"We all had strange dreams," said Hao holding up his golden dagger. Everyone in the group had a unique gift. Toble had a magical three-dimensional map of anywhere, and it could be rolled up as though it was flat. Tanner had a hunter's horn that could call any creature. Hazel had an enchanted harp.

Autumn turned to Sage, "What about you?"

Sage turned a little red as he held up a golden helmet from a suit of armor that had a crown around the top. "It was the helmet of Arthur Pendragon the deliverer, third king of the unified kingdom of Gryphendale." He looked at it and swallowed.

"Each of our gifts are quite legendary," explained Toble. "They seem to pop out of the pages of history and mythology. Show us what you have."

Autumn held up her canteen hoping that it didn't reveal too much about all she was told.

"What is it?" asked Hazel.

"It's a potion to use when I can't continue on," said Autumn. She was trying to be vague.

"It might be the same potion the Gryphon gave away in the legend of the early wars to King Wallace so he could keep fighting and win the battle," said Hao.

Autumn nodded. It didn't matter if it was legendary, she knew what she needed to use it for.

Autumn got up, and the group picked up their things to continue traveling. Autumn had noticed how Sage wrapped the helmet up and put it in the bottom of his bag. Almost everyone else held onto their gifts as they traveled.

Hazel talked about the legends surrounding her harp. Mermaids had created it. Some evil Sprite stole it and used it to lure sailors to their death on the rocks of a dangerous shore. Then they would steal the sailor's cargo and treasures. It was also used in another legend to put a monster to sleep to save a village.

Hao talked of the legends of the golden dagger and how it was said that it could pierce any armor or any substance, even diamonds.

Tanner just looked over his horn as he walked.

Toble opened his map and was continually surprised at what he would see. He finally put it away when he almost tripped over Tanner.

Only Sage and Autumn didn't look at their gifts. They walked hand in hand at the front of the group, quietly meditating on their own thoughts.

Sage was thinking about his conversations with all the heroes of the past, including his father. He never saw himself as a hero, but they were encouraging him not just to wait for people to follow him during this important time, but to lead and take the initiative to win this fight.

Autumn, though, was wondering if or how she would tell Sage of her impending death. She wasn't sure she could follow through with what she needed to do if he knew, but she worried about his always resenting her never telling him. She needed someone to encourage and help her, but she could not stand to see the pain in his eyes as she worked towards that end.

The group traveled on like this until they again lost all sense of time. Their stomachs were growling again as well.

"I wish we were close to the end," said Tanner. "I have no way of finding out with so much magic here."

"Without seeing the sun, it is hard to know anything. We could be making a circle for all we can tell," said Hazel.

They all stopped as they came into a large cavern filled from edge to edge with a pool of water glowing in a bluish color. They could see the faint outlines of the ghosts of Merpeople and aquatic animals swimming around in it.

"Now what do we do?" asked Hazel.

Autumn knelt down and called one of the Mermaids. "Sorry miss, but could you tell me how we should get across?"

The ghostly Mermaid looked at her strangely. "Let me see your hand."

Autumn showed her hand.

"No, the one with the royal seal," said the Mermaid.

Autumn hesitated, but then held out her hand with the ring. The Mermaid grabbed her hand and pulled her into the pool. The group all shouted, but before Sage could throw off his bags to jump in, a crystal walkway to the other side rose out of the water with Autumn lying on it. Sage rushed to her. She coughed and stood up with Sage's help.

"Are you all right?" asked Sage.

"Would you call this the pool of the dead?" asked Autumn.

"Yes," said Toble as the group gathered around her. "There is only one in the world. Why?"

"I just had heard about it before," said Autumn.

"You must have drunk gallons of that water. Can it hurt her?" asked Hazel.

"I don't know," said Toble.

"I'll be fine," said Autumn.

Sage held onto her anyway. The group continued walking cautiously on the walkway until they reached the other side. Once the group reached solid ground, the walkway sank back down into the pool.

It wasn't far before they reached a door like the one they had entered by with the royal seal in the center of it. Autumn took her key and opened it. The group walked outside into a circular area identical to the area they had entered by.

"Look, the singing tree and the alcove. We must have made a circle," said Hao.

"How long have we been traveling?" asked Autumn, shivering some in the snow. Sage pulled off her wet cloak and put his dry one on her.

"Look, the sky is different," said Toble, looking up the tall shaft. "We have exited in a different part of Gryphendale."

"Let's go," said Sage. "We need to build a fire, get our bearings, eat, and rest."

"I hope we didn't lose too much time," said Tanner. "When we stop, I'll scout the area."

When they had walked through the snow into the low passage, and then out from the hillside, Autumn immediately recognized the distinctive size of the trees.

"These trees are huge," said Autumn. "We must be in the Sprite forest."

The group stopped to look around. Tanner placed his hand on a nearby tree. He closed his eyes. A low glow came from his hand. "Yes, Autumn is right! We are in the center of that region."

"How far are we from the palace?" asked Sage.

"We are in the right area, but I can't tell you exactly where it is because it isn't on the ground. It's difficult to get readings of things up in the trees," said Tanner.

"Look!" said Hazel. "The hill is gone!"

315

Everyone turned to where she pointed.

"Just like the stories," said Toble in awe.

"That's magic for you," said Sage with a shrug. "Well, let's go and see if we can find a place to camp so we can eat soon."

The group fell into line behind Sage as they trudged through the snow. Hours went by with very little change of scenery.

"Tanner, are we going in the right direction?" asked Hao.

Sage growled slightly under his breath.

"I think so," said Tanner looking up at the sky.

"Hello there!" called a familiar voice.

The group all stopped. Coming towards them from their left was Martha with a bag of groceries.

"Sage! Toble! Autumn! I am so glad to see all of you. We have heard the sad news about Puck. Oh my goodness, girl, you must be freezing! Oh, and you have company."

"Yes," said Sage. "These are friends. I trust them with my life."

"Good! We have a new place. It is much smaller but come and rest yourselves. It will be tight, but you will get a good meal and a warm room."

Martha led them as she waved her arms about in an awkward way. Autumn turned around and saw that a light wind was covering their trail. They traveled only fifty yards to a small boulder. Martha knocked a different rhythm than what was used before, and the door opened.

"Friends!" cried Ezekiel.

The large man greeted them with his arms wide open and hugged nearly the whole group at once.

"Sit down and tell me about your adventure. I have heard tales, and tales of tales. I want to know the truth straight from the source. Martha, we have hungry guests. Oh, Autumn, you are soaked and freezing! Martha, do we have anything she could wear?"

Autumn had the spare clothes that the Mermaid queen had given her in her waterproof pack, but Ezekiel and Martha didn't give her a moment to say anything. Martha had her in the room the girls would be sharing and had opened a trunk to look for something that wouldn't be too huge, and all the while she talked on without a break.

"I have clothes," said Autumn. "I'll be fine. I will join everyone once I change."

"Are you sure, my dear?" Then Martha heard a whistling noise.

"Oh, the tea! I will see you in a little bit. Sorry!" Martha bustled out, and Autumn closed the door behind her.

The little bit of quiet was a relief. Autumn was freezing and changed clothes as fast as she could. Her dry clothes were also still cold. Autumn rubbed her toes and limbs until she felt warmth in all her extremities the way Puck had taught her long ago. Autumn didn't linger too long though. She didn't want to think too much about want she was going to need to do. She just wanted to enjoy some dinner and the feeling of being at home among friends once more. Autumn returned to the sitting room where everyone was sitting around the fireplace enjoying some hot tea. There was no more tonic and no more inn. It was a normal family home. She suddenly missed those days not so long ago.

"Autumn! I can't believe you went through so much!" exclaimed Martha when she saw her enter the room. "I can't believe you are Queen Anemone's daughter! Oh, my! A queen in my house! You are the rightful heir to the throne! Oh dear!" Martha was all flustered. She got up and led Autumn to the most comfortable seat by the fire, pushing her husband out of the way.

"I am the same Autumn. Don't treat me any differently!" said Autumn.

"Your friends have been telling us of your adventures," said Ezekiel as he settled down into a different seat by the hall Autumn came in from. "I had thought folks were exaggerating, but really everyone was telling only half-truths. Martha, is that soup done?"

"Oh, yes, come into the dining room, and I will bring it out."

Everyone filed into the dining room. Amazingly the table was big enough for all of them.

"We couldn't afford another inn, as you see, so we have the meetings at other places, but we had to have room for guests, or we would never have any information!" said Martha as she came in with a small tray of soup. She placed the first bowl in front of Autumn and the other three for those next to her. Martha then bustled back into the kitchen for a second load.

"So, what is the plan now?" asked Ezekiel. "Eight thousand troops are hiding all over this area waiting for your command."

"Eight thousand troops!" exclaimed Sage. "How did that happen?"

"I found out what you had told the freed prisoners," said Ezekiel as he took a sip of the soup Martha put in front of him. "They told all the

317

undergrounds, their family members, and their friends. They all just came. We even have a few Ogre and Huldra defectors, which caused a bit of a stir. I helped create a little order to the mess, but those folks came in droves. Everyone wants to fight in Lord Sage's army. Sorry Autumn. I am afraid no one knows your true identity yet. We have been waiting for close to a week for your arrival. I am sure Maldamien must know about it by now, and he has a huge force on the march. It has folks nervous. Do you know if he is heading here?"

"I don't know if he will stop here. I expect we will have to go and meet him at Yarrow," said Sage. He paused a moment to lift up his bowl in homage to the Gryphon, and then continued. "Maldamien has a time limit for his plans. It would be good to continue to scout out where he is going, though, just to make sure."

"With that many soldiers, we can really make a difference," said Hao excitedly. "Why now? What has everyone so excited about fighting?"

"It has to do with all of the things all of you have been doing," said Ezekiel. "The adventures and deeds you have accomplished, from rescuing the prisoners at Odemience to stopping the war of the water peoples, to Autumn facing Maldamien alone and living to tell about it. These are the stories of legends. Everyone can feel that this is a historic turning point. They will either fight now or never."

"We are still dealing with a lot of farmers with pitchforks," said Sage. "We need to get some trained troops from Queen Shasta if we can. No matter how much she gives us, we will still be outnumbered close to ten to one. Even with trained soldiers that is not good numbers."

"It's certainly better than the few hundred you had told me a week ago," said Hao.

"Yes. True. With good planning this can be won," said Sage, "but we need to be smart about it and not just charge in. The way we have done these fights before would result in a sure massacre even now."

"Well, Queen Shasta is having a banquet tomorrow," said Martha as she sat down with her own soup. "It is to celebrate her return. We can probably get some tickets."

"A banquet?" said Autumn. "How can she throw a banquet at this time?"

"In my opinion, it is probably Lord Jacob and the nobles who are throwing the party to get in the queen's favor. Queen Shasta returned to the city in secret with some soldiers from the water people to see if she could secure her throne and protect herself from being recaptured. We were able to help some, but there wasn't much need. Most of the Ogre and Nomad troops in town have been recalled. From what I've gathered, Maldamien strategically over-turned all the governments that give him problems and then has abandoned them. Even his loss of prisoners doesn't seem to concern him much. If you are right about his plans to become a god, it explains a lot. He has created the biggest army he can and is unconcerned with what will happen to this world after he is done," said Ezekiel.

"That verifies what Thyme said about Maldamien conquering the human world," said Tanner. "I don't think anyone had any doubt about him being insane, but this is just nuts!"

"We are just going to have to work fast to stop him," said Sage. "We should go to the banquet and speak with Queen Shasta."

"That sounds like a plan," said Ezekiel. "It's late, and I am sure everyone needs to rest. The men have the nearest room on the right of the hall. Autumn can show Hazel their room on the left."

Martha began to clear the empty bowls even though she had only finished half of hers. Everyone filtered out of the room. Autumn went to the room and thought about talking to Sage alone. Hazel walked in before Autumn could act.

"I'll leave my things here, and I'll see you in the morning," said Hazel. "Even with the snow, I will just rest better as a tree outside."

"Okay, take care," said Autumn.

Autumn tried to follow Hazel out, but the hall was congested with the men trying to carry their stuff in. Autumn turned back to her room and closed the door. She began to unpack her bag completely. There were very few things that she had remaining that had been hers from the human world. Her human clothes and shoes were lost at Vervain. She only had the few items that she moved back and forth from her secret pouch to her pockets. She still had the picture of her mother, she was wearing the seal, and she had the keys to Gungil Caverns. The rest of the stuff had been given to her. The silver knife from the king and queen of the water people, the two sets of clothes, the food, and random supplies. She picked up Queen Audrey's journal that Thyme had given to her.

A knock came at the door.

"It's Sage. Can I come in?"

"Sure."

Sage walked in and closed the door behind him. "Are you all right? You haven't said much all evening. Did you get sick from being wet in the cold?"

"No. Oh, here is your cloak," she said as she handed him the garment. "I just have had a lot on my mind, and I am very tired." Autumn put down the journal and turned to face him. "Sage, I think I haven't said it enough, but I love you so much. I just needed to let you know that. No matter what happens, I will always love you."

Sage pulled Autumn close to him.

"I know this battle, and everything is frightening. War is full of uncertainties, but with the Gryphon on our side, I have learned to hope. It's just one spell and one battle. We may live through this yet, and when we do, we should get married, have a home, invite friends over all the time, and have lots of fat babies. We should live out all the things that we have ever dreamed and hoped for. I will never let you get hurt again or be unhappy or even let a frown touch your face. We will be the happiest, most loving family you have ever seen. You'll see. Even if you become queen or whatever, I'll still build the house myself. Just name the spot, tell me how many rooms you want, and I will make your dream home. I just feel like we can do this."

Autumn buried her face in Sage's chest and let the tears fall.

"I would like that," she whispered. "I would like that very much."

"Autumn, I have never felt so alive as I do when I am with you. I have spent my whole life fighting for other people. Life was just unfair to me. I never had a family, a home, or the comforts everyone else had. I had tried to get rid of any hope that I would have those things. It hurt too much. I fought so that other people could have those things, but I knew it would never be me. Then I met you and all that changed. I can so clearly see the life we could have together. I can almost touch it. I have never wanted anything more in my life. I love you more than I can even describe."

They stood there in an embrace for a while. Autumn let the tears flow. Finally, Sage let her go and kissed her.

"I'll let you get some rest. You look worn out. Don't worry about the battle, just think about the banquet tomorrow and our future."

Autumn nodded, wiping away the tears.

"Good night."

"Good night!" said Sage, kissing her again before he left. His eyes were bright blue, and he was giddy as he left.

Autumn closed the door gently behind him. She then returned to her bag and began to repack her things. She let the tears continue to fall freely. She took some of Hazel's rations and put on some of her extra clothes over her own. Autumn left her wet clothes hanging to dry in exchange.

She would have to leave. She wouldn't have the strength to do this with Sage so happily dreaming at her side. She couldn't tell him. She had to do this alone and let him find out later. The news of her death would hit him at one time when the battle was over. He would learn to deal with it instead of brooding over it for weeks before the battle was even fought. She couldn't do that to him or to the people who followed him. They needed him strong and hopeful.

She sat down to write Sage a letter. Once everyone was asleep, she slipped out into the cold winter night, determined not to let them all down.

CHAPTER 30: THE SPRITE BANQUET

Sage woke up with the golden helmet staring at him. Obviously, Toble had unpacked it and set it on the nightstand next to him, but it annoyed him. It ruined the good dreams he'd had last night. Autumn's declaration of love was not unexpected. She had pretty much told him that before, but something in the bluntness of her declaration made him feel free to dream and plan. They would marry, and he would have a family again. That thought made even the helmet less irksome. He felt alive and ready to do battle.

The other guys were already up and out. There were two beds in the small room, and Martha was able to bring in a camp bed that appealed to Tanner. With Toble and Hazel sleeping outside, everyone had a good night in a warm bed. Sage was the last one getting up, and he didn't feel like rushing much. If they were going to battle soon, he was probably not going to have more sleep like this in a long time.

He walked out into the sitting room, shaved and ready for the banquet that afternoon. He looked around. He wondered if Martha would help Autumn find a dress for the banquet. He looked forward to what she would wear. She had looked so beautiful at the wedding ball.

He sat down and saw Ezekiel and Tanner both reading, Toble was tinkering with some new gadget, and Hao was sharpening his knife. Martha came in with a tray of drinks. Some things hadn't changed even though the inn was gone.

"Do you want some tea?" asked Martha.

"Sure. Have you seen Autumn this morning?" asked Sage.

"No," said Martha. "Hazel just went back into the room a moment ago. Oh, wait, here she is." Martha's words faded at seeing Hazel's pale face.

"Autumn's gone," announced Hazel, holding a note.

"What!" said Sage, standing up and spilling tea on himself.

"This note is for you," said Hazel handing the letter to Sage as

Martha tried to clean up the spilled tea with the dishcloth that was on her tray.

Sage sat down as the color washed out of his face. His eyes grew almost clear green as he read. He then handed the letter to Toble who had walked up to Sage as he was reading. Toble read the letter out loud.

"Dear Sage,

I am sorry that I left without telling you or anyone. It was hard to leave without saying goodbye, but I was afraid you would try to stop me. I am Queen Anemone's daughter and Queen Audrey's great-granddaughter. I am the only one who can break the spell of immortality. We can't all go and break this spell together because we don't have time. I must travel fast to get the things I need in time. I know how to break the spell, and I can do it. I need you to lead the army as you planned. I know you would have wanted to go with me, but they need you. Only you can make the most out of this battle. I will need to be able to get close to Maldamien to break this spell. I need you to help me do that. I need you to fight like the whole world depends on it, because it does. Tell everyone how sorry I am to have not told them. I love you, my dearest Sage, with all of my heart.

Autumn

P.S. I don't know if this will help, but as the only daughter of Queen Anemone and heir to the throne of Gryphendale, I declare war on Maldamien, his forces, and his allies. I also declare Sage Goliad as the commander and chief of the Gryphendale army. His commands are to be followed as though they were my own.

"She sealed it with the royal seal," said Toble.

Sage was sitting with his head in his hands as Toble read. Suddenly he stood up and headed for the door.

"I must stop her!" he said.

Hao and Ezekiel grabbed hold of Sage to stop him.

"No, you can't," said Ezekiel. "She is right. There needs to be two teams. You have no time to help her break the spell."

"But it's dangerous out there!" said Sage. "I nearly lost her in Gungil Caverns. Who knows what else she is going to come across."

"Let me go, Sage," said Tanner. "You need to lead this army. I am no soldier, but I can track her better than anyone else here, and I can help her. I promised Puck that I would help her, so let me go after her."

Sage relaxed some and the two men holding him let go. Sage knelt in front of Tanner. "Go after her, help her, and protect her. She is my very life."

Tanner nodded. He went into the room, packed his things, and left only a few minutes later.

Sage sat with his head in his hands and his fingers in his hair until Tanner left. When the door closed, Sage sighed and looked up. "Ezekiel, where is the list of our recruits? Toble, could you bring your map to the dining room? Does anyone have some extra paper? Oh, and Toble, keep Autumn's letter for me to show Queen Shasta at the ball tonight. The royal seal will make a big difference in proving Autumn's identity, since no one but the ruler or heir to the throne can use the seal like that."

Sage worked furiously in the dining room figuring out how many troops he thought Maldamien might have total, analyzing the lay of the land around Yarrow, thinking through the different races and their strengths in battle. When Martha had asked him if he wanted lunch, he declined it. He needed to work on this some more before going to the banquet, he had told her, but in his mind, he needed to work out his anxiety over Autumn. He didn't want to let her down, but he also kept having to tell himself, "Tanner will find her and help her, and the Gryphon will be with her and help her. The sooner this battle is over the sooner I can see her safe again."

About a half hour before they needed to leave, Toble came into the dining room. "Are you ready to go?" he asked.

"As much as I plan to be," said Sage without looking up.

"Sage, look at me," said Toble sternly.

Sage looked up, confused. "What?" he asked as everyone started walking in.

"We have been talking," said Hao.

"We are about to face Queen Shasta and the messy politics that remains at her court," said Ezekiel. "We can't go in there asking to join her army or agreeing to leave this in any of the hands of her noblemen."

"Eight thousand people came here to fight in your army because they believe you can lead them to victory," said Toble. "They don't want to be under the command of someone else. They believe in what you are fighting for."

"What we are saying," said Ezekiel, "is that we want to ask Queen Shasta to join us and ask her troops to fight under your command. I know that is what all the volunteers want, that is what we want, and that is what Autumn wants. You are in supreme command of the war against Maldamien, so don't back down to anyone, don't give up your command, don't make compromises with the noblemen. Above all, you need to have your head in this. You are rightfully upset by Autumn leaving us, but you are going to have to get a hold of yourself and be the leader that you are capable of being. You will be facing a bunch of fools who will want to command the army to get glory, power, or fame. They will lead us to ruin if you aren't up to challenging them and demanding your right to lead."

Sage looked over the group. Toble, Hao, Ezekiel, Hazel, and Martha all had been in this fight as long as he had. "I am honored," said Sage sincerely. "I was told in Gungil Caverns that this would happen, but I wasn't certain what they were talking about. I will do the best I can. I know that for this army to work, whoever commands it must not question themselves too much, so I won't. I will let the Gryphon and Tanner watch over Autumn, and I will be here to command, both physically and mentally. I do expect advice and input from all of you with the understanding that I have to make decisions that everyone may not like. Once the dialog has ended, my decisions must be obeyed completely. This has to be different than anything we have ever done before."

"We know," said Ezekiel, "and you are the right one to lead this."

Sage nodded. "Have you decided who will be coming with me to the banquet, or do I need to make an executive decision?" teased Sage.

"Just me and Toble," said Ezekiel. "Martha doesn't feel like she has a dress that she could wear to a banquet. Hao and Hazel don't want to let it be known that a Hiru is involved in this."

"I guess we need to be going then," said Sage, getting up. "Who would have thought it would be a group of men going to this kind of banquet? I remember most banquets at Vervain being dominated by women."

"It isn't like we are going so we can dance," said Ezekiel as they walked through the sitting room and out the front doors.

325

The three men did not have to walk far in the snow before they came to the lift. As they boarded the tulip-shaped device, Sage thought of the irony of this war being dependent on the delicate rapiers of the materialistic Sprites. They had never been known to be decent warriors, but any trained soldiers would be an asset at this point.

The lift passed two floors of ordinary city to reach the top of the forest canopy. Sage had never been to the Sprite court by the front doors, and the sight of the wedding-cake styled palace was breathtaking in the bright colors of the setting sun. It had multiple tiered towers that were all gleaming white. Each of the towers was topped with onion-shaped domes. The lattice windows were lined with carved woodwork leading to pointed tops. The walls were covered with some sort of vine pattern that gave the impression that the towers were wearing wedding dresses. The palace just dripped with adornment and detailed work to the point that it was overwhelmingly sweet, like eating too much candy.

They walked out of the lift and headed towards the tiered complex. The palace seemed to be floating lightly on the leaves. The men walked along the silver leaf walkway through the lacy gate that had been left open for the guests. In the courtyard were hanging gardens and layered paths going up and down with no clear pattern. At the door to the center tower stood a Sprite guard who watched as guests entered. He only gave a quick nod when Ezekiel showed him their invitations.

Once inside, beautifully ornate staircases branched upward like a tree. Two branches curved to the right and left for each of the six floors. There were several doors on each side as the branches formed balconies to get to every door. The pattern of the latticework on the balconies and the decorative touches of everything else were done with small white branches twisting around each other in an organic symmetry almost too perfect for nature. Vines and leaves were engraved on the doors and white porcelain steps. The main trunk of the staircase led straight to the large double doors on the seventh floor. Sage, Toble, and Ezekiel climbed the stairs as Sprites flew past them.

"Why don't they build a lift to the dining hall? Do they think that every faerie in the world can fly?" grumbled Ezekiel.

Sage smirked. Ezekiel had wings. He just didn't like heights or flying.

When they reached the top of the stairs, the doors were opened for them by some Sprites who had landed in front of them. The large dining hall presented itself before them. A long curved rectangular table surrounded a central area in a U shape. An elaborate white throne sat directly in front of them at the height of the curved U so that all the guests could see the royalty when sitting. Glass windows surrounded the room with carved white vines in between each panel. The colorful sky could be seen from every direction. All the white vines from in between the windows met on the ceiling in an elaborate and active design, pausing only to hang down over the tables as softly lit chandeliers. The light in the room was golden in color. The tables also matched the atmosphere, with the legs of the white tables sprouting from the ground. The plates, cups, and dishes were all glass with hints of gold trim, either from the lights or from gold itself. The palace was the way every fairytale palace should be.

The sounds of people laughing and talking filled the air as servants hustled and bustled about in a great hurry. The servants looked like the only ones who were not happy, in fact, they seemed miserable. They served the guests appetizers on golden trays with respect, but anger was deep in their eyes. The neatly starched uniforms were almost able to hide their underfed forms. Sage, Toble, and Ezekiel followed a footman to their seats, observing everything as they went.

A side door that the servants were coming and going through crashed open as a very thin woman fainted through it. A young man hastily picked her up and whispered to another young man that she had not eaten in three days. They then disappeared behind the door. No one seemed to even notice the episode. Sage's eyes met Ezekiel's. He had noticed and was reflecting the same frown Sage had. The crowd of people moved around like butterflies, oblivious to the world around them.

"Sage! Nice to see you my boy!" cried a nobleman that Sage did not recognize. Sage stood, bowed, and made the appropriate small talk before the nobleman moved on to another conversation, with his wings fluttering as he went. A footman came a moment later.

"Queen Shasta has requested you to come to her sitting room."

Sage stood up and followed the footman through a short hall to the room he had named. It was a large room decorated with the same patterns as the dining hall, but with drapes and a bit more upholstery.

"Sage!" exclaimed Queen Shasta when he walked in. "I was so glad to hear that you were here. I have been waiting for your arrival!"

Queen Shasta looked wonderful, not just beautiful in her elaborate embroidered gown, but in her steady composure and confident bearing. He bowed low.

"Thank you for seeing me. I am glad you have returned safely," he said.

"The journey was uneventful, thankfully, but I have found things in very bad shape around here. The people are starving, and this ball is a ridiculous maneuver of Lord Jacob to save face."

Sage smiled a little. She had changed some, in a good way.

"I did not come with good news," said Sage.

"I did not expect it. I know you are looking for help and equipment for your army. I have heard about the troops flowing into this area. I will bring the issue to the people during the banquet. We will come to a decision tonight. I have only been in the palace for two days, and I am sorry that I haven't brought it up until now. You will need to present your proposal when I introduce you, but I am afraid it will not be easy to get support as I would like. Be prepared. I will see you in a little while."

Sage bowed and backed out. He felt encouraged that she would support them. He had hoped that she would come to her senses after the wedding ball and he wasn't disappointed. Now he would have to convince a court of selfish aristocrats to lend their troops and resources. Shasta was only a constitutional monarch. Without the vote of the nobles, she would be able to do very little.

Sage walked through the short hall to return to the banquet. As soon as he walked into the dining hall, he saw Philip talking to Lord Jacob. Philip had always been a loyal attendee of the underground meetings at Ezekiel's inn. Suddenly Sage was suspicious of Philip's loyalties. Was he the one who had betrayed them to the Ogres that night the inn was burned down?

Sage walked around the edge of the room and returned to his seat between Ezekiel and Toble. Before he could tell them what he had seen, horns announced Queen Shasta's arrival.

"Queen Shasta Aurora Coriander, ruler of Caoineag," announced a short male Sprite with a grand baritone voice.

Queen Shasta entered the dining hall from a side door. The whole room stood and clapped warmly, bowing as she passed by. She stood in front of the throne at the head of the tables.

"Thank you for your warmth and love in welcoming me upon my return home. Much has happened while I was gone, but I am honored that you have chosen to continue to call me your queen. I will continue in the footsteps of my late husband and will honor our traditions as I always have. Thank you."

The room erupted in applause. Lord Jacob bowed and then addressed the queen. "Your Majesty, we are all very glad to have you home again safe, well, and happy. Maldamien's heart must have been moved by your grace and wisdom to return you to us at a time when we need you most. May your reign be long and peaceful."

Queen Shasta's eyes widened with anger as her face took on a reddish tint. "Maldamien! Maldamien did NOT send me home! I have returned in spite of Maldamien! Even now I am still confronted by the trouble he is causing us all. Cursed be the day of his birth!"

The color completely drained from Lord Jacob's face. "Forgive me, my queen. I made a mistake. Please accept my humblest apologies and my wishes for your reign to be a long and peaceful one." Lord Jacob bowed deeply, then directed for the meal to be served. He looked around as though he was verifying his support.

Sage looked around too. There were no Ogres or Nomads. It would be a good thing for him, but it was very unusual. All of Maldamien's supporters were with him now, but he left behind the spineless, useless spies such as Lord Jacob.

Queen Shasta was still visibly irritated, but she sat down so the rest of the room could do the same.

Three Sprite musicians entered to play their stringed instruments while everyone ate their first course of dried fruits in an herbal salad. The next course was a broth of root berries. The third course was a light sauce over some purple spotted truffles. By the fourth course Sage, Ezekiel, and Toble had completely lost their appetite at the lavish waste. Sage noticed that even Queen Shasta was playing with her food and not eating. Finally, the queen stood to speak.

"Before we continue with this meal, I must bring before you an issue of great concern that has come to my attention. Lord Sage will explain the details of this matter."

She indicated that Sage was to come. Sage stood, bowed, and then walked around the room to the center open area. Murmuring filled the room as he walked. Once he was sure he could see everyone and everyone could see him, he began to speak.

"We are all aware of the strange behavior Maldamien has been exhibiting these days. Even the few of you who support him must see that he has interfered more than usual in the local governments, then recalled his troops, and now has been on the march. What you may not have been aware of is what Maldamien's ultimate goal is and how quickly he thinks he will attain it.

"Maldamien is opening all the portals, and is even now planning on opening the last portal in Yarrow. You may say this is a good thing. Some of you may even be excited about this, but this isn't a good thing. Maldamien has been absorbing all the magic of this world and is trying to recreate the immortality spell for the human world so that he can absorb all of their magic, too. His ultimate goal is to become a god, but what he will accomplish instead is the destruction of our planet. Queen Anemone will not be able to help us. She died long ago and has sent her only daughter, Autumn, in her place. I have a letter," Sage held up the paper for all to see, "from Autumn with the royal seal declaring war on Maldamien. As you know, only the heir to the throne can use the royal seal to declare war. Autumn is currently working to break the spell that Maldamien has created to absorb Gryphendale's magic. She has asked for the underground forces to fight and stop Maldamien so she can complete her mission. I have come here to ask you to help us. We are going to stop Maldamien from destroying us and the world."

A lot of murmuring followed and even some heated conversations.

"What?" cried Lord Jacob, standing suddenly from his seat at the table. "You want us all to be massacred! Do you not remember all the battles that people have tried to fight against him and how he crushed everyone? Now he is even stronger than ever before! Who is this Autumn? How did she get here from the human realm? I say we let Maldamien do as he wants and leave us alone. Do we want the violence that came to the Hiru and the Brownies on us as well? Why should we draw the wrath of Maldamien down upon ourselves? We have done just fine as we are. I for one don't believe your warmongering. We should focus on preserving ourselves the way we are, and leave the humans to deal with whatever Maldamien has planned."

"Autumn is working on breaking the spell that gives him that power even as we speak. Her story is too long to tell right now. Just look at this seal. It doesn't lie, and it verifies who she is. I have come here for help, but we already have recruits from other countries. This is not going to be a little skirmish. This is an all or nothing fight. The world is in the balance now. If you fight, you might die. If you don't fight, you will die. The more who fight, the better chance we have of winning this. You have tried to stay out of Maldamien's way, and he still came and killed King Coriander. Do you think that you will be able to escape what is to come? Even your description of the state of things now is skewed. You say you are fine, but that is a lie. The common people are starving. You can't have children. Your kingdom is rotting from the inside out," said Sage.

"You are not asking for a simple thing. This will cost lives. We need to think about this and plan. Come back next week," said Lord Jacob. Some of the noblemen nodded in agreement.

"We don't have a week!" said Sage. "Maldamien has to do the spell before the Day of Remembrance. We must march next week. Whose side are you on?"

"That's impossible!" said Philip, leaning back in his chair and folding his arms.

Sage narrowed his yellow eyes.

"How much more time do you need than a hundred years!" said Ezekiel.

"I agree!" said a young nobleman sitting with his wife at the end of the table farthest from the queen. "You shouldn't be trying to use delay tactics, Lord Jacob. We should all be pledging our swords as King Coriander would have done. Queen Anemone has sent her daughter. How can we refuse to follow her?"

"You forget that we are immortal, Jordan," said another nobleman next to Lord Jacob. "Delay tactics or not, we have no reason to rush into this."

"Did you not hear Lord Sage?" said Jordan. "Maldamien is going to destroy everything in three weeks."

"That seems a bit unlikely," said Philip. "I know Lord Sage, and he tends towards drama and exaggeration. I even wonder at the legitimacy of this so-called daughter."

"Ah!" said Sage. "I see where your loyalties lie. You tried to have us killed a couple of months ago! Would you have said the same thing if Queen Anemone was standing here?"

"See what I mean?" said Philip to the room.

331

"I can vouch for what Lord Sage is saying," said Queen Shasta. "I saw what Maldamien was trying to do to the water peoples. I saw what he did to Autumn. I have met this Autumn. She is a selfless and honest woman who was willing to give her life for what is right. I know about the portals. Apollo himself predicted the date of this battle, the character of whom none of us can doubt. That seal cannot be forged. I can see it's magical glow from here. These events are real. This war will happen with or without us. We have an opportunity to equip and train these volunteers and to be of more service to the world than we have been in a long time. I am in favor of this action, but as you know, I cannot declare war or help in a war without the majority of parliament in support of it."

"Who is going to lead us into battle? This little girl who we haven't seen? Who is going to pay for it? How can we just blindly vote for this when we know nothing about it?" said an older nobleman sitting next to Toble.

"I am commanding the army," said Sage. "The cost of the battle will be whatever you choose to give. We have some support from the water people as well. The troops will need to be fed for a month, but no one volunteering for this is asking for pay. Everyone is doing it because they want life, freedom, and a chance to make a better world for themselves and their families. You know everything that there is to know. People have already left their homes to fight this battle, not because it is a suicide mission, but because they believe we can win it. With the Gryphon's help, we will win it!"

"You are going to lead this army!" said Lord Jacob. "Shouldn't we vote for a more qualified and capable leader? I mean when have you done anything other than petty crimes and spying?"

"Sage is a great leader and has led many successful rescue missions, of which Queen Shasta has benefited," said Toble. "What other person has been more actively at battle with Maldamien's forces than Sage?"

"Does he know how to lead an army?" said the nobleman next to Lord Jacob. "Does he know tactics and strategy? Has he studied any past military campaigns or successful generals? An army is different than a little skirmish here or there."

"Again, I ask who is more qualified than Sage?" said Toble. "I know of no one who fits your description. Sage has experience in a variety of situations. He learned what he could of the past when he could, but experience counts very heavily when it comes to a high-stress situation like war."

"Lord Jacob has spent his whole life studying war," said Philip. "I think he would do much better in such an important conflict as this."

"Does this mean you are now in support of this conflict?" asked Sage.

"Only if the right person is leading it," said Philip. Sage hardly recognized this person in his fine clothes and sly ways. Somehow Philip was able to be just a poor peasant like all the other poor souls at Ezekiel's inn for all those years. This man sitting before him was the complete opposite in every way.

"Enough of this foolishness!" said Queen Shasta. "If we enter this conflict, it will be under Lord Sage, or we don't enter it at all. I am tired of this useless arguing!"

"But Your Majesty," said Lord Jacob, "we still don't know what the plan will be once Maldamien is stopped. Will this scoundrel make himself king? Will we be trading one dictator for another?"

"When Maldamien has been stopped, then a council will be created like the days of old, and a ruler will be voted upon," said Sage. "I for one will be voting for Autumn, the only daughter of Queen Anemone and heir to the throne."

Some murmuring followed with a few nodding heads.

"Are there any more questions?" said Queen Shasta. Lord Jacob blustered like he wanted to say something but couldn't think of anything. "I am now bringing this to a vote. It will be a public vote. All in favor of us going to war, please stand."

For a moment no one moved, and everyone looked around. Ezekiel and Toble stood even though their votes didn't matter. They were hoping to encourage some action. Noblemen around the room began to stand nervously one at a time. Soon the majority of the room had joined the first few. When all the movement stopped, only six noblemen were still sitting. Lord Jacob and Philip were two of them.

"The decision has been made," announced Queen Shasta sternly. "We go to war." She took a deep breath. "In light of that decision, we will end this banquet early. If you want to take something with you as you travel to your cities, ask the kitchen. I am calling for an immediate standing army, and I am channeling all resources into this endeavor.

Each of you must report to me how many soldiers you will be sending from your cities and what equipment. If it does not meet expectations, I will put a hold on your portion of public funds. You are all free to go."

Murmuring filled the room again. Sage heard Lord Jacob complaining about the wasted meal.

Sage walked around the room to get back to where Toble and Ezekiel were seated. He noticed how many noblemen looked excited.

"How is it that Queen Anemone's daughter has come into this world without the portals being opened?" one nobleman asked Sage.

"It's a long story," said Sage, "but it could be described as a miracle."

"Does she look like the late queen?" asked a Sprite noblewoman.

"No, she looks more like her human father," said Sage.

The questions kept coming from various people until Toble and Ezekiel met Sage halfway to his seat.

"You did well," said Ezekiel.

"We were lucky," said Sage.

"No, we were blessed," said Toble.

The group made their way to Queen Shasta. She was leaning to the side of her chair talking to a servant.

"Serve the poorest first. It may be the only meal they have had in days. No one should take food with them. We won't have enough for that. Any of the guests who ask for food for their travels get one meal packed and no more. If anyone has a problem with this, send them to me."

The servant bowed and left.

"Your Majesty is very compassionate," said Sage.

"I saw some of the villages when I was traveling home in secret. The poverty I saw shocked me. I feel so ashamed of the way I behaved at Tangie. I just could not see outside of my own little world. This battle is so important on so many levels. I will give your army everything I can, but you must succeed!"

Sage's face became completely serious, and his eyes turned dark green, almost black, as he thought of Autumn.

"We will."

CHAPTER 31: AUTUMN

The snow had turned the whole world gray and colorless. Autumn trudged on alone with the weight of her memories and thoughts for company. She had been pushing herself hard to get some distance from her friends... and Sage. It was more of an emotional drive to push the heartache down. She had chosen to do this. That statement became her mantra as she thought of everything she should have done or the things that could have been. She wondered if this was the way a person with a terminal disease felt, the main difference being that she had made the choice to do this.

She continued her pace all night and the next day. She didn't stop to eat until late the next night when she found a very shallow cave on the side of a hill. She made a small fire and ate the rations she had brought with her. Some of the rations were dried pieces of the goat Sage had killed a month ago. She wondered if it was still good. It didn't matter. It was food, and in this weather, she would be lucky to find anything else that was edible.

As she ate her rations, Autumn studied the night sky. Puck had taught her how to know which direction she was going by the stars. They were fake stars, he had said. Just light reflecting on crystals inside the earth's crust, but to Autumn they looked like real stars in a vast night sky. She had been using them to head northeast. She wasn't quite sure why she had picked that way. She needed to find a phoenix and then a rosemary field. The journal didn't say anything about where to look first. She should have gotten information from her friends before she left, but that would not have been possible without telling them everything she knew.

She looked at the ring on her right hand. Her mother said it could call things like Gungil Caverns. She wondered if she could call on someone for help and information? She thought about the Gryphon. It had been close to a week since she meditated on him. It wasn't like she was sitting around playing cards during that time.

"Creator, I need help. I am trying to do what I think is best. I know this is what you want me to do, but I don't know where to go next. I can't return to my friends and accomplish this, but I can't do this alone either. I need help."

Autumn was overwhelmed with tiredness. She hadn't slept last night and had been depending on adrenaline today. The tiredness was catching up with her. She lay down and fell quickly to sleep.

The night went by quickly and the morning light was an unwelcome reminder that she needed to wake up and make some plans. The first thing she saw when she awoke was Tanner sitting by the fire she had made. He had added some more wood and was just staring at it, facing her. She then noticed the tall, elegant form of Apollo standing next to Tanner and talking with him. She rubbed her eyes to make sure she wasn't dreaming. The Unicorn and the Gnome were an odd pair, but she couldn't have picked two more welcome faces.

"Hi!" said Autumn enthusiastically as she sat up. "How did you find me here?"

Tanner looked up and then pointed to the trail that looked like a miniature snowplow had come through.

"It wasn't too hard. How are you doing?"

Autumn blushed a little. She still had a lot of survival skills to learn.

"Fine. What brought you two after me? You aren't going to try and take me back are you?"

"No," said Tanner. "Sage read your letter to us all. He was very upset, but we all decided that I would come to help you and Sage would lead the army as you suggested. Apollo says that you called him for help as well."

"I guess that's true. I wasn't sure who would come, though," said Autumn as she combed her hair with her hands. "I know what I need to break the spell, but I don't know where to find them."

"Tell us," said Tanner. "We have already promised to help. There is no reason to keep any secrets from us."

Autumn pulled out Queen Audrey's journal even though she didn't need to look in it.

"The spell of immortality was invented by Queen Audrey and Maldamien both. Queen Audrey was bound by the same three people I was so that she could use their power to strengthen the spell. I have

336

done that, but not intentionally. The next thing she did was drink from the pool of the dead."

"Which you happened to do in Gungil Caverns," said Tanner, nodding as he poked the fire with a stick.

"Right, and that represents death. She then ate a phoenix feather to represent life."

"The last of the phoenix lives in the rosemary field between Dwende and Fenodryee," said Apollo.

"That's convenient," said Autumn. "I then need to fill all my pockets with rosemary, which the queen used to stop the flow of magic."

Tanner looked up when Autumn went quiet. "Is that it?"

"No. The last step is to get Maldamien to kill me with this dagger." Autumn pulled the dagger that the king of the water people had given her out of its sheath on her hip. Tanner looked at it and then back at her.

"That is why you left us, isn't it," said Tanner. "It wasn't that we needed to split up for more time, but that you couldn't let us stop you from dying."

Autumn nodded as she put the dagger back in its sheath.

"Was I wrong in leaving?"

"I can't say," said Tanner. "It is hard to predict how people would act with such news. I don't like it myself. You should be queen, happily married, and starting a family. You are much too young to have this weight on your shoulders, but the young die here every day at the hand of Maldamien, and we still claim to be immortal. I wish I could doubt the accuracy of your information or question your sources..."

"What she says is true," said Apollo. "I can see the pieces of history fitting together with the information she has given."

Tanner nodded.

"Then I will help you until the very end."

Autumn smiled. "I'm glad you are with me."

"I could do no less," he said as he stood. "We should be going then."

Autumn packed up her bag as Tanner buried the fire.

"Get on my back," said Apollo. "We do not have time to waste, and it will still take me three days to get there even if I travel at full-speed."

Apollo knelt down so that Autumn and Tanner could climb onto his back. When they were settled and holding on, Apollo took off. The speed he traveled was exhilarating. Having the wind blowing through her hair lifted Autumn's spirits. Tanner, who was sitting in front of her, remained grimly quiet.

The snow covered everything in every direction. The lack of leaves in the trees revealed the various Sprite villages as Apollo passed under them. By the end of the day, they were at the edge of the Sprite forest and overlooking the broad plain of Dwende. Autumn could see some of the groupings of large trees that created each of the Gnome villages. They made camp for the night in a makeshift shelter half buried in the snow. They had to dig to create enough dry ground for a fire and a dry place to sleep.

"When we get to the rosemary field, I will not be able to follow you into it," said Apollo after they finished their dinner of dried meat.

"Why not?" asked Autumn.

"Since the day Queen Audrey was found dead in the rosemary field, the plants burn when they are touched. It gets worse with every passing year," said Tanner.

"I will leave you both there and return when you need me," said Apollo. "I must take care of a couple of things."

That night Autumn spent a long time thinking about Sage. He would make a good king if the people voted for him. She imagined him leading the army and being the high king of Gryphendale. It was a happy thought, even if it made her heart ache.

The next two days were very similar. With breath-taking speed, they traveled the width of Dwende, passing clumps of gigantic trees and a few bundles of traveling Gnomes looking bewildered or in awe when they passed. Tanner remained grim and talked very little. Apollo maintained his aura of distant otherness. In many ways, Autumn still felt very alone.

At noon during their third day of travel, the field of white was interrupted in the distance with a puddle of purple. The puddle grew as they moved closer to it. By the time Apollo stopped at its edge, the purple field of rosemary seemed like an ocean.

"I will leave you here and return tomorrow," said Apollo.

Autumn and Tanner dismounted when Apollo knelt down for them. He then turned and left them without another word.

Autumn and Tanner turned to the dangerous field of purple.

"How will I find the phoenix in all of this?" asked Autumn.

"You could try calling him the way you did Apollo," said Tanner.

Autumn looked down at her ring and concentrated on calling the phoenix, then they sat down on their bags and waited. After about an hour, Tanner stood up.

"I am going to try my horn that I received in GungilCcaverns."

Tanner lifted the horn and blew. The crisp, clear call echoed in the distance. Tanner and Autumn looked around in expectation.

"That's too bad," came a voice from the field.

"Hello?" said Autumn. "Who are you? Where are you?"

"Don't talk to me like that, missy," said the voice. "Where did you learn your manners?"

Autumn looked around at the field of rosemary. She was certain the voice was coming from there. She stepped near the field and felt the heat rising from it.

"I'm sorry. I just don't have any way of knowing how to act when I don't know who you are or where you are."

She tried to part some rosemary to see what was hiding in it but screamed when it burned her hands.

"Ha! That's what you get," said the voice. "You should treat everyone with the same respect no matter who they are."

Tanner handed Autumn some cloth to wrap around her hands.

"I hope that I do act in that way," said Autumn.

She had kept her eye on the spot where she thought the voice was coming from last. She lunged towards it, parting the plants with her newly wrapped hands.

"No!" cried what looked like a plucked turkey. "Leave me in my misery!"

Autumn allowed the branches to fall back to the way they were.

"We are both miserable creatures," Autumn sighed. "Please tell me who you are and where I might be able to find the phoenix."

"I was once the very beautiful and elegant phoenix. When I became old, I would die in a marvelous flame and from the ashes be born anew," he said.

"What happened?" asked Autumn.

"With this dreadful spell of immortality, one cannot die from old age. If I cannot die, then I just molt and deteriorate."

"Then I am very sorry for the one question I must ask you. Do you have one feather that I could have?"

339

"What?" cried the bird.

"I need it to break Maldamien's spell of immortality," Autumn explained.

"I cannot help you," answered the bird.

Autumn sighed.

"Then the world is lost."

"Humph!"

The bird flapped around until the rosemary around it was trampled enough for him to see her.

"If you put it that way, then I might help you, but you must do me a favor first."

"Oh! Thank you," said Autumn.

"We will see if you are thankful afterward," said the bird. "There, to the south about a mile, is a herd of wild horses that some Ogres penned up years ago. I want you to free them, so they run wild again."

"That sounds easy enough," said Autumn. "I will be back soon."

"We will see," said the bird.

Tanner and Autumn walked in the direction the phoenix had indicated. Just as he had said, there in the middle of the snow was a herd of ten gaunt white horses. The large stallion had a silver medallion with a red jewel around his neck. The herd was surrounded by a simple wooden fence creating a corral of about a half acre. There were no other structures anywhere nearby to be seen.

"This should be easy," said Autumn.

"I wonder if it will be," said Tanner, "but there is no way to find out until we get started."

Autumn grabbed the first plank as the horses ran around in the pen. The wood just softly fell apart in her hands. Tanner found that the wooden plank he grabbed was rotten as well. They both had half of the fence down before they stopped and looked at the horses in confusion.

"They should be running free now. Why do they act like the fence is still there?" asked Autumn.

"I have seen this sort of thing before," said Tanner. "When an animal, or any living thing for that matter, is trained a certain way it is very tough to get that original training out of them. They must have been shut up in that pen so long that they stopped seeing or caring about the world outside it."

"What can we do?" asked Autumn.

340

"Let's see if we can startle them out of it," said Tanner.

Tanner and Autumn spent a few minutes trying to chase the horses out, but they pretty much ignored them and stayed out of reach.

"I'll try my horn. Maybe I can call them out."

Tanner held up his horn and blew a clear call. The horses stopped, looked up at him, and then returned to their circular path around the edge of their prison.

"I don't think the ring will work in this case," said Autumn, "but we could try food."

Tanner and Autumn set out some of the dried herbs from their rations just outside the corral, but the horses ignored it.

"It is getting late," said Tanner. "Apollo won't return until tomorrow, so we have a little time to think about this."

Autumn and Tanner dug into the snow and created a little camp. Tanner was able to use the rotted fence pieces for the fire. They ate some cold rations as Tanner made a hot tea in a little metal pot that he had in his sack.

"I suspected it couldn't have been too easy," said Tanner. "That sly bird was trying to get out of giving you a feather. He had at least one left. It isn't like it keeps him warm or helps him fly."

"I still made a bargain, and I can't go back on it now," said Autumn.

"Those horses remind me of the people of Gryphendale," said Tanner. "I wonder if they would know what to do once they are freed from Maldamien's tyranny."

Tanner poured the hot tea from the pot into two little metal cups he also had in his sack and then handed Autumn a cup.

"There is no way of knowing until it happens," said Autumn. "It is interesting to me how in this land where magic and the Creator's work can be seen so clearly, the people still don't understand that they were meant for more. The people act like slaves when they were created to be scientists, artisans, musicians, and inventors."

Autumn grabbed a stick and poked the fire.

"You have grown a lot in your comfort and confidence with the way of the Gryphon," said Tanner. "You don't question him the way most people do."

"I find that most people don't question him enough," said Autumn. "I question him a lot, but I ask him instead of asking everyone else. Most of the time he gives me the answers, sometimes he doesn't. You

341

would think that the torture at Odemience would have made me doubt him, but it did the reverse. I trust him more than I could ever trust anyone. He was there for me. He didn't keep me from the pain, but he never let me go through it alone. He protected me in a way that was most important to me. I don't know how to explain it well. I found that I could depend on him in ways that aren't completely logical. I think most people want everything to be perfect all the time, or they should be able to ask for something, and the Gryphon just appear and do it for them. It isn't like that. I find that I can't even see everything he sees. I don't know how everything works. I don't know why Puck had to die, and I don't know how that event affected other events. It is a complicated web of lives interwoven together. He created us each to play a part and will guide us through the best life that we can live on this planet with the time that is given to us. It's a messed up world. He lets us mess it up so that we can have a choice to follow him, but he is also always working to make the world better through us. The complicated nature of things, the dialogue that we can have with him, the strange freedom one has in knowing what you were created for and fulfilling it, all of that is why I can seem so confident in my trusting him."

"You sound like Puck did long ago," said Tanner, sipping his tea.

"What do you mean?" asked Autumn.

"Puck didn't teach you about the Gryphon early on because he had lost trust in him," explained Tanner. "When times got hard though, I think Puck realized that you both needed the Gryphon more than you needed to continue doubting him."

"What made him lose confidence?" asked Autumn.

"All the evil he saw Maldamien do when he took over."

Autumn looked at the fire.

"He wanted to know why the Gryphon had allowed it. I remember Sage saying the same thing. It is a hard and complicated issue, and it would be nice to have the luxury to question the Gryphon about it until he answers. I am not saying that we shouldn't ask that question, but what I am saying is that I need the Gryphon more than I need to know the answer to that right now."

Tanner nodded.

"That is at least the most honest answer I have ever heard."

Autumn looked over at the horses who were still running even though it was dark. She knew how they felt. She was once like that in her old life. Afraid. Afraid of what was out there, afraid of the pain they might feel.

"I'm going to go to sleep," said Autumn as she lay down with her head on her bag and her cloak wrapped up tight around her.

Autumn's sleep seemed to merge with her meditating on the Gryphon. She was revisiting her own words, but somehow the horses began to get mixed in with what she was saying. Autumn woke up with a jump that startled Tanner.

"I have it!" said Autumn and she got up and walked towards the corral.

Tanner followed.

Autumn stood in front of the corral where the horses were. She closed her eyes and thought about the Gryphon's purpose for them and the potential inside them. Autumn poured her own potential and abilities into them the way Puck had done for her.

Autumn began to subtly glow silver-ish.

The horses stopped and watched her while neighing nervously.

"Wild horses of the Fenodryee valley, listen to me! You have been held here for a very long time. You have been hungry, dependent, and limited, but that is not who you are. You were created to be wild and free. You were born to roam and travel to distant lands. You are not a mere beast of burden groveling for the next morsel of food. You are the greatest of horses, ridden by kings and queens of old. Remember who you are! Now, run free!"

The horses began to snort and paw at the ground. They reared up. Only the stallion was still. He stared at Autumn intensely as though waking from a deep sleep. Suddenly, he took off in a sprint past Autumn and all the horses followed. The horses ran hard and fast in a wide circle, fast enough to be almost running on the surface of the snow. The stallion led the herd back to Autumn and bowed.

"Thank you, Autumn, daughter of Queen Anemone, heir to the throne of Gryphendale and chosen one of the Gryphon. You have done a marvelous thing, and we thank you. You have opened your magic to us, and now we can see what your purpose is as much as we can see our own. Take the medallion from around my neck. I know that the phoenix must have sent you, so I will return the favor to you both. You must cut all the rosemary that you need from the field and set it aside. When you are done, throw this medallion into the field. It is the only thing which will cause the rosemary to burn, so make sure you stay a safe distance away when you throw it. May the Gryphon guide you and make your way smooth."

Autumn took the medallion off the neck of the great horse.

"Thank you," said Autumn.

The stallion tossed his head and took off at full gallop, passing Autumn and followed by his herd of white horses.

Tanner walked up next to Autumn from where he'd been observing everything. "Should we get some sleep before going to the rosemary field?" Tanner asked.

"Sure, you rest. I'll take the last watch," Autumn said.

Tanner nodded. He looked tired, and Autumn was too excited to sleep. She was both happy that the spell was going to be able to be broken, and nervous about how they were going to have Maldamien kill her in the right way. She sat up all night thinking about how she wanted it to be quick and without all the pain she had endured at Maldamien's hands before. It was a strange thing to be planning her own death, and it filled her with unpleasant morbid emotions. By the time Tanner woke up, Autumn was relieved that she could focus on the task at hand.

It was a short walk back to the rosemary field. Autumn wrapped her hands in cloth and Tanner pulled on his heavy working gloves. Then they set to work cutting a large stack of rosemary. The heat from the plants caused them both to sweat as they worked. Within a couple of hours, they had plenty of the herb.

"Should we warn the phoenix that I am going to burn the field?" asked Autumn as they walked a safe distance away from the field with all of their stuff.

"Why do you think the phoenix picked this task for you to do?" said Tanner.

Autumn shrugged.

"So that I might get the medallion and burn the field. It is probably the only way he would be able to die and be able to rise again. That makes sense," said Autumn. "Well, here we go."

Autumn dropped her bag and threw the medallion into the field. The field burst into flame. The fire spread furiously to the edge of the purple ocean of flowers. Tanner and Autumn had to cover their noses and mouths from the smell. Even from their distance, the heat was too much, and they had to move back farther. The snow around them melted as quickly as they walked. A loud squeal came from the field like a bottle rocket taking off. Autumn and Tanner turned to see what it was as they shielded their faces from the heat. A ball of fire shot up out of the field, and golden wings unfolded from it. The flames took the form of a bright golden bird, larger than an eagle, with long elegant plumage dripping from him.

"Thank you, Queen Autumn, daughter of Anemone, tool of the Creator and friend of the world!" shouted the Phoenix as he flew above them.

He dropped a large feather as he flew away.

"Oh, catch it!" said Tanner as they tried to see where it would land.

Autumn grabbed it from the air.

"Eat it before it bursts into flame!" said Tanner.

Autumn had never tried to eat a feather before, and it was a horrible task to try to accomplish. It had the texture of straw and fur which made Autumn gag. Tanner handed her the canteen of water which helped a little. Eventually, Autumn was able to force it down and ate a few pieces of dried meat to help it digest.

After she had finished eating, Autumn began to fill her pockets with the rosemary they had cut. For some reason, more pockets appeared on her clothing. They had thought they had cut more than enough, but Autumn was only barely able to fill every pocket that appeared. The pockets then merged back with her clothes and turned everything she wore purple. The heat and light burning sensation all over her were so intense that it made her dizzy.

Then Autumn opened her eyes, Tanner was looking down at her with concern.

"What happened?" asked Autumn. "I was standing a moment ago."

"You passed out," said Tanner. "This isn't a good sign for the rest of the journey."

"No, but the silver canteen in my bag is specifically to help me endure. Could you get it for me?"

Tanner opened Autumn's bag and found the canteen. He brought it to her and helped her drink some of it. Autumn sat up all the way as the swimming sensation in her head cleared.

"I feel hot!" said Autumn.

"You are emanating the properties of rosemary," said Tanner. "I don't think I will be able to touch you without my gloves."

345

"I'm not going to be able to drink much more of this," said Autumn. "It is going to have to last a week."

"It will take all that time and more to walk to Yarrow. You won't be able to sit on Apollo's back, and if you are as ill as you look, you won't be traveling very fast."

Autumn tried to force herself to her feet and then sat back down. "We have to get there in time. The whole world is depending on us."

"Apollo should be here soon, keep your faith." Tanner turned and looked at the horizon with a worried expression. They had to make it in time. There was no other choice.

CHAPTER 32: A PLAN

Sage stood at the door of his tent and looked out at the volunteers camped before him. The sprawl of tents filled the forest floor as far as he could see and more people were coming every day. The encampment before him seemed to leap from the scenes of legends and tales that he had heard as a child. He had never been a part of an army this big. He'd rarely even slept in a tent before, but Queen Shasta had sent this one for him to use as headquarters and a place befitting a commander.

The tents of all the troops of the rebel army (as Toble and Ezekiel had started to call themselves) showed the distinct differences of each of the races gathered there. The Sprites camped together in their bright colored tents of silky material. The Gnomes were grouped in their leather tents. The Brownies were in their tiny canvas tents. The Undines and few Merpeople were in some tarp-type tents. Scattered about were the Dryad shelters. Few Huldra, Ogre, and Nomad tents were visible, but even the fact that there were a few was encouraging.

It was also encouraging how well the races were getting along with each other. Sage was having to settle a few squabbles, but not as many as he'd thought he would. The entire ordeal was like nothing Sage ever thought he would be a part of and most definitely had never expected to lead. For the past few days, as he had been gathering the volunteers to this point from their various hiding places. Sage felt like he was moving through a dream or going back and living his father's life rather than his own.

"We are ready," called the general for the Brownies.

Sage walked back into the tent. All his generals had settled down into chairs around a large square table. The group was still a little crowded, but they had left a chair for Sage at the head of the table. Sage felt like standing though. He needed to move to think. As he looked around at the group, he saw a representative from every kingdom sitting there. He was struck by the fact that this was not his doing. The

Gryphon was pushing events along, and people could feel the importance of this battle on the wind. It sent electricity into the emotions of all who knew of these things.

"I have called this meeting for the purpose of getting us all on the same page. Since we haven't had an official meeting with us all present at the same time, let us go around and introduce ourselves. I will begin, even though you all know me already. I am Sage Goliad, son of General Goliad who was Queen Anemone's Captain of the Guard."

The Brownie sitting to his right spoke up, "You don't need to tell us who your father was. You are a legend in your own right. You should say you are Sage Goliad, freedom fighter and leader of the rebel army." A few people grumbled their approval.

"Thanks, I'll remember that. Why don't you go next and then we will go around the table," said Sage.

"I am Timothy Browntongue, leader of the Brownie underground and survivor of Odemience."

The gray-haired Gnome next to him spoke up. "I am Calsusa, the leader of the Gnome underground, brother of Tanner and an exile of the Gnome court on behalf of the queen."

Hao spoke up next. "I am Hao, leader of the Hiru resistance and heir to the Hiru throne and also an exile."

The athletic Undine in leather armor next to him spoke, "I am Sola, sister to the king's steward, and brigadier general in the Undine army. I have been placed over those who have volunteered to fight from both the army and civilian services."

The brawny man next to her was wearing a broad gold belt and distinctive black armor. "I am Petras, the lieutenant commander of the Merpeople. Only a small portion of us are equipped to fight with you, but we brought weapons and armor to distribute."

"Thank you, Petras," said Sage.

The next person around the table was a young man with horns down his spine. "I am Trey, one of the few Nomads. I was also told to tell you that there are fifty Huldra who look to you as their representative. I'll introduce them to you after the meeting."

"Fantastic! I wasn't expecting any of my people, but I did notice a couple of their tents a moment ago. I will look forward to seeing who has joined us."

Sage then nodded at the uncomfortable Ogre sitting next to Trey. At almost seven feet, he was kind of small for an Ogre, but he seemed cramped in his chair. "I am Milkweed, the leader of the twelve Ogres who have joined the army. We left Maldamien's army shortly after I was responsible for Queen Autumn during her journey to Odemience."

"What convinced all of you to defect?" asked Sage.

Milkweed shifted uncomfortably. "Well, it started with her treatin' me with respect. She didn't look at me like I was some kinda animal or monster. After da jailbreak, a group of us started talkin' about how low we'd gotten. We'd used ta be craftsmen once. Da finest metal an' jewels came from us. Some of us were legendary fer the kinda metalwork an' swords we used to make. Now we're just thugs. Our people are trained an' treated like animals an' we tell ourselves that we have da easy life. Maybe we do get food from Maldamien an' eat better than most, but we've lost anything that we were. We wanna be free an' have a culture an' self-respect again. We wanna serve a good ruler who'd treat us right, not like animals. I'd like ta someday stop bein' a soldier an' learn da ancient craft of metal work. I'd like to make somethin' that I'm proud of an' leave a business an' a legacy ta my children's children."

"Those are good reasons, my friend," said Hao.

"We all need that kind of motivation to be in this fight," said Sage. "This won't be easy."

Sage looked at Ezekiel who was next. "I am Ezekiel Cornwing, leader of the Sprite underground and the new general of the Sprite army."

Sage smiled and lifted an eyebrow. Ezekiel frown but then chuckled. "Don't be deceived by my great gut. I was once a great warrior, and Queen Shasta is cleaning house by getting rid of those she doesn't trust in high positions. She replaced Lord whats-his-face with me."

"Congratulations," said Sage.

Toble who sat between Ezekiel and Sage spoke up. "The Dryads asked me to represent them this morning, so I'm Toble the former Ambassador at Vervain."

"And adoptive father to Sage," said Sage as he patted Toble on the shoulder. "Well, we all know each other, and we all are well qualified to be sitting here. We have a representative from every kingdom and region sitting at this table. Look around you. This is what Vervain was about. This is what the old government was about. Each one of our different peoples have strengths and weakness that differ from each other. We may not agree on a lot of things, but we do agree that we need to be free. To win this we must work together, but not as the Sprite army and the Gnome army and the Brownie army. Instead, each of you will be commanding a mixed unit that will have some of every race in it."

The group began to grumble a little. Sage was not pleased with some of the expression he saw on the faces of his leaders.

Sage continued. "We are greatly outnumbered, and we can't win this fight the way everyone has always fought. I sent out teams of Brownies and Sprites to do some scouting, and we received the reports back this morning. The Brownies calculated that Maldamien's army has eighty-five thousand troops. That is made up of forty thousand Ogres, twenty thousand Huldra, ten thousand Nomads, ten thousand Dryad slaves, and five thousand troops of various races. As you know, half of the Huldra and the Nomads will be magic users."

"How are we going to fight such a force!" said Timothy. "From my observation, we only have about ten thousand five hundred thirty troops."

"You are correct," said Sage. He was always amazed at the analytical minds of these small Brownies. That was why he used them as scouts. The Sprites were just their transportation for this particular task.

"But you have a plan?" said Trey.

"Yes," said Sage. "Toble, if you don't mind spreading out your map."

Toble pulled out the rolled-up canvas that he had received in Gungil Caverns out of his bag. He then rolled the map out onto the table. The map took the three-dimensional landscape of the area surrounding Yarrow. Everyone gasped and leaned in towards the map.

"As you know, Maldamien is camped at Yarrow. His tent is in the midst of the ruins and right next to the portal. The leaders of his army surround him, and the army fills this whole valley. The seven hills that surround the ruins have guards stationed at the peak of each one. Only this hill to the southeast has ruins of a tower to protect the lookouts. The landscape of this valley is going to be our friend in this battle. The trees that surround the valley will be our cover, and if we can take the hills, we will have an advantage over those in that exposed valley."

"If we can take the hills?" said Calsusa. The Gnome scratched his head under his pointed brown hat.

"Yes," said Sage. "The first part of my plan is to split up into seven units with a mixture of all the races, like what I talked about earlier. Each unit will travel separately to Yarrow and specifically to their assigned hill."

"Why a mixture?" asked Ezekiel.

"I had mentioned that every race has strengths and weaknesses. Our only chance in this fight is to make the most of the strengths we have and work together to minimize our weaknesses. When each of you plans out how you will specifically take your hill, keep this in mind.

"The Sprites can fly and can use the magic of the wind. They are great for transporting the Brownies, dropping items on foes, and surprising an enemy who is not looking up. Sprites tend to be good with the rapier but ask your troops for any specialists in other weapons. Also, you can use the Sprites to blow away the noise of a surprise attack or the tracks you have left behind. Their weakness is in hand to hand combat. They are just not very strong fighters. The good swordsmen can attack and retreat well, but don't use them as your first option for that.

"The Gnomes make a fantastic cavalry. Their skill on their ponies makes them fast and good for taking out an enemy as they ride by. They also can unsettle enemy horses well or even steal them without being seen. Their skill at tracking and quiet movement is without comparison. Don't use your Gnome troops for foot soldiers. They are slow and small. This will put them in a dangerous situation.

"The Brownies are amazing scouts. They can remain completely hidden and get the most accurate information in an instant. Remember that they are farmers though and are very small. They can hamstring their enemies, but the kill is hard for them. They work well in teams with the Sprites for both combat and scouting. Brownies make great front line surprise attackers on large opponents like the Ogres because they go unseen and can lame them for a killing blow by those who follow them.

"Dryads are great in hand to hand combat in the woods, especially the magic users. They can get the trees involved in the battle. Also, even with their leather armor, they tend to be hard to kill because they can turn various parts of themselves into wood. They are not good against the fireballs of the Huldra or Nomads, and they, like most races, can't handle the crushing blows of an Ogre with a mace. Still, let the Dryad use the forest to their advantage. Also, use your Dryad archers with your Gnome archers. Gnomes go for power, while Dryad go for distance.

"The Merpeople are fierce warriors and are strong in hand to hand combat since they don't have the resistance of water, but they do get easily hot and worn out. Send them in for bursts of activity. Their strength is the water, so I will probably put more of them in the units taking the hills by the river. If we have a few magic users, we can cause some flooding in the south here." Sage pointed on the map. "A muddy battlefield is very difficult on the Ogres."

"The Undines can help with some of the water magic as well. They tend to do well in surprise attacks rather than a straight hand to hand combat situation. When you take out your hills, you may want to send tiny groups of quiet killers to take out the Ogres by surprise. The Undines would do well in these teams. On the battlefield, intermix them with some of the stronger fighters. The Undines are quick and can protect the others from a surprise hit, but they may need help if faced with an Ogre alone."

"Hiru can be fierce when doing hand to hand combat with a katana, but most often they like to fight in their dragon form. Their magic is fire, and all the dragon forms tend to breathe fire. They are great fliers who can swoop in and kill quite a few foes at a time. I wish we had more of them. They are vulnerable to magic attacks due to their soft bellies. It would be good to have some sort of armor for them if we can quickly invent something, but that may slow them down too. Also, since they are attacking in broad strokes, save them for the battlefield. They do get worn out with a long battle as well. We need to send them out in waves.

"Our Ogre friends will be the strongest foot soldiers that we have, but don't use them in the surprise attacks, they are not known for stealth. Instead, bring them in when you have a full hand to hand conflict. Their height and reach, and even their thick scaly skin is perfect for battle. Also, use the Ogres for information on how to attack their people. I wish we could turn more of them to our side, but we are going to need their advice if we are going to win this.

"Huldra are natural hunters. Use them in your teams with the Undines to surprise attack the guards on the hills. Huldra can climb trees well and set traps. They tend to be trained on a few weapons from childhood so use them on the battlefield too. If we have any magic users, they would be able to shoot fireballs, create magic shields, and lure an enemy away from a group. Don't use Huldra alone though. They are often more worried about attacking than protecting themselves or defending their back.

"Nomads will vary the most. You have a variety of race mixes and even a few races that are not well known. Make the most of what you have. Their skills can surprise you. Some Nomads are magic users. Some are specialists in weapons that others have never seen. They can also advise you on how to fight other Nomads. If we are lucky, we may have a few who are good at this device that looks like a wheel with chains on it. When they spin it around above their heads, they can protect a group of people from a shower of arrows.

"These hills will be assigned clockwise, starting with the northernmost hill here. This one will go to Timothy, then Ezekiel, Cassius, Sola and Petras will work together, Milkweed and Trey will work together, Hao, then Toble and me. Sola and Petras will have the hill with the tower, which I suspect will be the hardest one to take, but it is the one closest to the river. We will all leave separately and take different routes to Yarrow. Try not to let any scouts see your army and try to take your hill as quietly as possible. Remain hidden. Be creative. Use the Brownies to lure the guards into the woods so the Dryads can capture them. Or use Undine and Huldra together to kill them silently. Use your Sprite to disperse the sounds. Whatever you do, make it quick and quiet. We will all take our hills a week from today at exactly dusk. If we hear something or one of us is discovered, the rest of us will still be there. At midnight, report to me at the foot of the tower hill at the nearest point to the river. At that meeting, we will talk about the plan for attacking Yarrow, which will happen at sunrise."

"What is Autumn doing during all of this?" asked Trey.

"Autumn is working with Tanner on breaking the spell that makes Maldamien so powerful. She will need to get close to Maldamien or the portal, so that is our top priority," said Sage. "If we can accomplish that, than the world will be saved even if we are all killed. When the spell is broken, Maldamien will die, and we can try to take back our world."

"What if Autumn is late or can't break the spell?" asked Petras.

"Don't worry," said Milkweed. "We will all be lucky if we live

353

through it to begin with."

"You are both right," said Sage. "If Autumn fails, then we will be annihilated, but I believe in Autumn."

"The way you're talking, it sounds like you don't want us to use everyone for the battle?" asked Sola.

"No, what I mean is that we need to be strategic in how we fight. Toble has an invention that he will give you the plans for. It will throw boulders down into the valley. What I am envisioning is sending the Sprites with a small boulder to drop and letting the archers start the attack first. That will not do much damage. Knowing Maldamien, there will be a shield around his army. But to send all his army to fight us, he will have to lower the shield," explained Sage.

"So, we are throwing sticks and stones until we can awaken the hornet's nest?" said Ezekiel.

"Yes, we want them to come into the woods for the hand-to-hand combat. That is where we are strongest. Once the battle is in full force, we will send everyone in, but in waves."

"It sounds good," said Petras. The Merman leaned back in his chair. "Especially if you are trying to draw the soldiers away from Maldamien. That will give them less magical protection."

"Right," said Sage. "Autumn will take care of Maldamien, but I will be searching for Turmeric. This battle will not end if Turmeric survives it."

Sage looked around the room. Everyone studied the map and were deep in thought. "Here are the lists of those who will be in your units," said Sage as he began to pass out the papers on his camp bed. "Any questions?"

"It looks like you have thought of everything," said Timothy. "We may survive this."

"Maybe even win it," said Ezekiel.

"Let me know if you see a problem, but that is my goal. I am not in this fight to commit suicide or to become legends. I am in this because I think we can finish this once and for all."

"Right!"

"Here here!"

Everyone banged the table with their fists in agreement.

"You may leave with your unit whenever you like. I will see you in a week after you have conquered your hill." Sage sat down finally as

Toble stood to roll up his map. The generals were talking with each other and leaving with their lists. A few of them patted Sage on the back as they left.

"You did well," said Toble.

"Thanks," replied Sage as Toble left. Only Milkweed remained.

"All of us know da cost of dis battle. If we all die, it don't matter. We have somethin' ta fight for that's worth it," said Milkweed. "You're a good commander. If anyone could'a led us ta win, you will."

Milkweed walked out of the tent as Sage sighed and leaned forward against the table.

Milkweed might be right, but this wasn't a battle he wanted to die in. For the first time in his life, he had so much to live for. He slammed his fist down. Dadgummit! He wanted to win this thing, once and for all!

CHAPTER 33: THE WAR

Autumn watched Tanner put some more of the twigs and grass on the fire as she shivered involuntarily. There was nothing they could do about it. She needed to save the rest of the liquid she had gotten from Gungil Caverns for when she was dealing with Maldamien. She would just have to push through it.

"How do you feel?" asked Tanner.

"I feel comfortable. I just can't stop shaking."

Autumn was trying to put Tanner at ease. Tanner instead looked at her with concern.

"When Apollo gets here, perhaps we can stop at a Brownie village and buy a pony and cart. It would be very small, but you could sit in the back and rest as we travel."

Autumn wondered if Tanner had enough money for a cart and pony. That was a luxury very few seemed to have.

The afternoon was very long. She wished she could get some bark from a willow tree to help with the cold burning, but the field was flat and empty. Autumn meditated on the Gryphon as Tanner grimaced at the fire.

After a few hours of meditating, Autumn became distracted by the gray sky. The world was not well. She could feel it. She turned her mind away from those thoughts and tried to distract herself with watching Tanner. She felt a little better after meditating.

Tanner sat with his knife carving a long stick. When he saw Autumn watching him, he stopped what he was doing and handed her the stick.

"Here is a walking stick for you. I found it when I was looking for fuel for the fire. There must have been some saplings in the rosemary field when it burned. It will help you travel."

He stood to make some dinner with the rations. Autumn watched him work. In the distance, past him, she saw a figure approaching on the horizon in the dusty glow of evening.

"Do you think that's Apollo?" asked Autumn.

Tanner turned from the fire to look where she pointed. "I hope so because we have nowhere we can hide."

They watched as the figure headed straight for them.

"That's too slow to be Apollo," said Tanner as he pulled out his knife and moved closer to Autumn.

"I think it is a cart and horse," said Autumn.

Tanner nodded. He was preparing for a fight.

"Wait! I think that is Apollo. He is pulling the cart," said Autumn.

"Impossible!" said Tanner. "It might be a white horse, but Apollo is no beast of burden. He was very kind to subjugate himself to carrying us the two times he did, but he would never be tied to a lowly cart!"

"Who would have known we needed a cart?" asked Autumn.

"I am worried that it is some Nomads who have come to carry us away," said Tanner. "You never know when Maldamien finds out these things."

Tanner stood ready for a fight even after it was obvious that it was Apollo alone pulling the cart. Autumn stood up unsteadily from behind Tanner and walked around him to greet Apollo. Tanner seemed frozen in shock.

"Hello Apollo!" said Autumn with a little bow. "How is it that you are pulling a cart?"

"Good day, Your Majesty," greeted Apollo. "You were going to need a cart to finish your task."

"But you are pulling it!" exclaimed Tanner. "Why didn't you get a common beast to do it?"

Autumn did agree that Apollo looked odd. It was kind of like a prince in his royal garb hooked up to a plow.

"Should I not humble myself and do this thing when an innocent young woman must humble herself to redeem our errors? This is the way of the Gryphon. One does not seek their own glory. This is my task to do. I am glad to be worthy of it," Apollo said, as though he wore a badge of honor.

After a moment of hesitation, Tanner helped Autumn into the back of the tiny cart with his gloved hands and placed the bags around her so she could be comfortable. Tanner climbed into the driver's seat but left the reins where they were tied. Apollo took off at a quick even pace.

It was slower than they would have traveled had they been on his back, but much faster than they could have ever managed on foot.

"How did you get the cart?" asked Tanner as they traveled.

"I have many friends," said Apollo.

"I apologize for my rudeness. I was not expecting you like this," said Tanner, sitting forward in his seat in the way he would have been had he been driving. He fidgeted with his empty hands.

"I am still needed," said Apollo. "You are very much needed too. You must be aware that just because I bring the girl to Maldamien, he will not kill her the way she needs him to."

"That is true," said Tanner as he rubbed his chin. He looked back at Autumn who was half listening and half meditating while laying feverishly in the cart.

"This is where your role is vital," said Apollo. "You are not here by accident."

Autumn fell asleep and was not able to hear all that Tanner and Apollo talked about. Their plans were going to involve her, but she did not have the power to give input. She had never been so grateful for help in her life.

When she woke up, Tanner was trying to wake her enough to get her to lay down by the fire for a nice breakfast and to give Apollo a break. They had traveled all night.

Tanner woke her again to feed her.

"It is a good thing that she sleeps so much," said Apollo. "She will save her strength and won't be able to mourn over her life."

Tanner nodded but remained quiet.

"You too must not mourn over her. Not yet," said Apollo.

"I wonder why the Gryphon is allowing this or even pushing for it," said Tanner.

"You may be able to understand it once it is all finished," said Apollo, "but even if you don't, is it not his right as master of all things created to do as he wants?"

"That is not the way he is described in the books at Thyme's monastery," said Tanner. "He is supposed to be a good and caring being willing to sacrifice his own life for the sake of all those he has created. How does letting all of this happen fit into that?"

"I see," said Apollo. "I had to ask that question long ago. It isn't a simple answer. Could we see the hearts of all who are remotely involved and observe the tapestry of history, we may begin to have answers for specific events. Unfortunately, the complex inter-working of one's life in time does not soften the blow of losing a good person or one so young. How many times has the question been raised 'why do bad things happen to good people?' Why was nature created to be an indiscriminate source of good and evil in the world? The question is as old as time and yet is new for each person who asks it. Everyone thinks they are the first to go through events that raised the question in their hearts. In many ways, they are both right and wrong."

Autumn fell asleep even though she really wanted to hear the rest. It was frustrating to feel so ill and so tired at such an important time. Now that they were finally talking, she couldn't be involved. Over the next days, Autumn did hear bits of conversations, but most of the travel was done in silence. The bits of conversation Autumn did hear had to do with their plans for interacting with Maldamien. The pieces of the plan just floated around in her mind, though, and would not connect into a sensible course of action.

They detoured from the path east to the river's edge. There Tanner harvested a large amount of willow bark and made a concentrated brew. It was only a half an hour after drinking this that Autumn's shaking nearly disappeared and she was able to function normally. Every couple of hours, though, she needed a swig of the concoction that was probably destroying her liver.

****

Sage looked over the tired group of generals sitting around the table in his tent. Each one sat proudly as they had each taken their hill quietly just a few hours ago. Sage also felt an emotional boost from the accomplishment. They would all need it for the battle that was coming next.

"We only have a few hours before we will start the battle," said Sage. "I am very proud of each one of you. We have already heard about some of our victories as we waited for the others to arrive. Each one of you have proven your worth and thought on your feet. You made the most of what you had. Timothy, you were the last to arrive. What happened?"

Timothy stood from his seat. "They were changing guards when we attacked so we ended up fighting twice as many as I had planned. We lost two men, but the Ogres on that hill were killed before making much noise. I assigned one of our Ogres to pace the hill like the lookouts were doing to keep the illusion going. We hope that the returning patrol would not be missed. It didn't seem like they were expecting an attack though."

"Good!" said Sage. "A few of us did lose men, but did anyone have significant trouble that you want to report?"

Everyone looked around and shook their heads no. Sage's smile broadened.

"I sent out more scouts," said Sage as Toble rolled out his map again. The three-dimensional form of the valley popped up. "The scouts indicate everything is the same as before, but apparently some young women are being held in a cage next to the golden altar in front of the portal. Our goal is to lead the troops away from there. I will be going in after Turmeric and the women prisoners. Everyone needs to keep watch for Autumn. She may not be with those women. She must be able to get to Maldamien if she needs to. Above all, we can't let Maldamien hurt those young women or open the portal or do anything major."

"Sounds easier than it will be," said Milkweed.

"I know," said Sage as he pulled out some papers from a pouch on his belt, "but here is the plan for the battle. Hopefully, we can keep them guessing for a while."

****

In the darkness, two dark figures crept between the Ogres' tents nearest the woods. The figures moved slowly and quietly, working their way from shadow to shadow avoiding the maze of activity. An Ogre walked out of the first tent they had hidden behind since starting, and he sniffed the air.

"Somethin' stinks," he muttered.

The two Ogres around the fire nearest him turned to look around and sniff the air.

"Yeah, it's just da rosemary Lord Maldamien has piled on dat there altar thin'. Da wind's picken it up sometimes."

The first Ogre wrinkled his nose. "That stuff smells awful. I wish he'd have gotten somethin' else." He continued to move towards the fire to warm his hands.

The figures in the darkness gave a silent sigh of relief as they continued their task. They moved on carefully from one tent to another.

Periodically an Ogre would sniff the air, but the same sort of conversation would ensue. The rosemary covering Autumn was hiding their presence well. Autumn took a long swig of the potion that she'd received at Gungil Caverns and felt better immediately. She and Tanner were able to creep into the ruins of Yarrow. They carefully hid as Turmeric walked by, then decided to follow him at a safe distance. He led them into the chamber that held the Water Portal, the golden gem-studded altar, and Maldamien's massive tent. Nearby stood a cage of young Sprite women who all had three sets of runes on them. Maldamien walked out of his tent as Turmeric approached and bowed.

"My Lord, did you feel the magical disturbance?" asked Turmeric.

"Have you sent any magic users throughout the camp to check it? The shield over the army should not be flickering until the change in guard is due," asked Maldamien.

"Yes, my Lord."

Autumn smirked. Apparently, the magical shield didn't like rosemary too much. Even so, the shield was weaker away from Odemience, and Apollo would have been able to open a hole large enough for them to get in.

Maldamien walked over to the cage of women. He pulled out a handkerchief to put over his nose as he got nearer to the rosemary laden altar. Turmeric followed Maldamien and produced his own handkerchief to deal with the smell.

"Do you think those women will work for the spell?" asked Turmeric.

"One will not, but the blood of all of them should do it," said Maldamien. "If we had that royal seal, it would have made things a lot simpler."

"I am so sick of hearing those weepy women," said Turmeric. "Tomorrow will be a glorious day."

"Yes, it will be a day that will change history."

Maldamien slowly turned and looked at the shadows where Tanner and Autumn hid. "I think a better plan has arrived right on schedule."

Tanner and Autumn instantly turned to run. Autumn chided herself for not being more careful. They had gotten in too easily, yet how could he see them?

Maldamien moved his hand and both Tanner and Autumn were frozen with their weapons in their hands and in mid-run. Maldamien levitated them over to himself. His smug look of triumph irritated her. At the same time, it also caused fear to shudder through her bones.

"Hello my dear, did you miss me?" said Maldamien. "My, you have grown into such a lovely young woman, just like your mother was. You look surprised. Did you think I could not taste your royal blood when you were here? I have been following your progress. I was concerned you may not get here in time to help me."

Turmeric seemed almost as surprised as Tanner and Autumn were.

"Her mother?" asked Turmeric.

"Oh yes," said Maldamien. "She is the daughter of Queen Anemone. I had thought to make her tell me where her mother was, but my spies tell me that you said she died in the human world. Such a nice neat package you have given me."

Maldamien moved Autumn's hair with his free hand.

"See she went to all the trouble to set up my old spell. She has all three runes. I will have to taste her blood in a moment, but I suspect that she went and drank from the pool of the dead and ate a phoenix feather. The smell of rosemary is on her as well. You even remembered to wear the royal seal. How nice."

Maldamien took the knife from Autumn's hand.

"You brought back my old knife. I had lost this years and years ago. I couldn't have hoped for more. Turmeric, as soon as the sun rises, we will begin the ceremony. Bind them and put them in my tent until then."

"What about these other young women?" asked Turmeric.

"We will sacrifice them too," said Maldamien. "You can't have too much blood with a spell like this."

With the magic that kept them frozen, there was not much struggling Autumn and Tanner could do. Turmeric called an Ogre for some chains and had them bound. Once they were in the tent, the spell was loosened. Unfortunately, they were in the presence of Maldamien or Turmeric at all times and were not free to re-plan their strategy. Only a few hours remained until morning. Autumn needed to think quick. She may have just handed Maldamien the key to destroying the world.

As the morning light peeked over the tree-covered hills, Tanner and Autumn were dragged out to the altar area. Nomad magic users surrounded the inside of the ruined hall. Autumn could see the sea of tents for the army and noticed observers to the south sloping down towards them. The valley created a natural amphitheater for the drama unfolding. Turmeric and Maldamien had everything set up perfectly. Turmeric had the key to the portal in his hand ready for action. Maldamien had the sharpened knife and some other tools on a tray near the altar. The young Sprite women were lined up, chained together and sobbing. Autumn counted six of them. All of them looked identical. Long blond hair, flawless features, and all with three sets of runes like she had.

"You are all witnesses to this momentous occasion," announced Maldamien. "You will soon see your master and king go from glory to glory. The last heir to Anemone's line has graced us with her presence to help me do this spell. Thank you."

Maldamien made a mock bow towards her. A rumbling of whispers and surprise ran through the crowd of spectators. Confusion crossed the faces of the many Ogres.

"These women will increase the power in this altar for the ultimate sacrifice. Please bring the first young woman," said Maldamien.

The Sprite woman screeched as two pairs of Nomad hands grabbed her, unlocked her chains, and dragged her frozen form to the altar. Autumn wildly looked around for something she could do. Tanner just stared ahead as if in a trance.

The Nomads lifted the Sprite woman up and placed her on the altar. Her screams seemed to cheer Maldamien, and so she just gave herself over to sobbing uncontrollably. As Maldamien took the knife from the tray and lifted it over the Sprite, the room shook.

"BOOM!"

Boulders were flying down in all directions followed by smaller stones. Maldamien had to maintain his balance by holding onto the altar. Shouts and screams could be heard coming from the camp.

"Go check that out! Find out what happened to my magical shield!" shouted Maldamien to Turmeric. Turmeric ran out of the hall, handing the keys to the portal to a nearby Nomad. Another Nomad ran into the hall past Turmeric.

"My Lord," said the entering Nomad, "we are under attack by an army of rebels!"

"I want a second shield around us!" shouted Maldamien to the Nomads in the hall.

They created the invisible shield Maldamien requested around the ruined chamber. Maldamien turned to Autumn, who was smiling and thinking of Sage.

"This is your doing!" said Maldamien. "Well, they won't succeed."

He shouted at the Nomad who came in.

"Destroy them! Kill every last one of them just as we have done hundreds of times before."

The Nomad bowed and ran out of the hall. The invisible shield flickered as the Nomads creating the shield allowed him through.

Maldamien turned back to Autumn while still holding the dagger. The smirk on Autumn's face irritated him.

"Don't think your petty farmers with pitchforks will make any difference," said Maldamien.

Autumn looked up at the hills. As red and orange rays of a sunrise filled the sky, soldiers also began to pour out of the woods in every direction. Autumn could see the battle erupting on every side. Maldamien followed Autumn's gaze. His eyes narrowed. Those who had not gotten up early to watch the sacrifices, half-dressed Ogres and groggy Nomads, were running out of their tents in every direction. They grabbed weapons and were looking around trying to get oriented. Fires broke out in the camp as a rain of flaming arrows poured down on the chaotic scene.

"I think we are doing pretty good actually," said Tanner. "As long as their queen still lives, there is hope for a better world. They will fight until the very end."

"Their queen!" said Maldamien. "She will be dead in a few minutes."

He turned from the altar and looked back at the chaos of the camp. He reached out his hand and put out the fires. Then thousands of little flames reappeared as fireballs being shot by Maldamien's magic users.

"No, I think we have only begun."

He turned back to the woman who lay on the altar, stabbed her, and then magically blew her off the altar.

Autumn gasped.

"Bring the queen here. We will open the portal now. You with the key, get ready by the portal."

The Nomads grabbed Autumn. She screamed and fought against them, but they magically froze her so she couldn't move. They laid her on the altar. Autumn searched with her eyes for Sage in the fight. This was not going right!

The front line of rebel troops took to the air, their Sprite wings seemed to be almost invisible with speed. Hand to hand combat was being engaged in all over the place. Waves of rebels attacked and then disappeared into the woods like phantoms. Autumn thought she saw the shining golden helmet that belonged to Sage, but then it was gone. Trees started to reach down and grab Ogres and throw them across the field.

"Burn the woods!" shouted Maldamien when he followed what she was looking at.

"Get control of your units!"

His eyes flared with anger. He lifted his hand towards the battle, the shield flickered, and fire flew from his hands as he shot at random areas of rebels.

"I am their queen!" said Autumn. "You can't win this! I will overcome your army, and I will overcome you. Your reign has ended. You will never be a god! I will rule Gryphendale. They are loyal to me! You are just a worm, and you will die this day!"

Autumn didn't know why she said that, but she was angry. She wanted Maldamien to stop hurting her people.

Maldamien turned to Autumn in a fury.

"No, my dear, you will die."

He lifted the dagger with both hands.

"Open the portal now!" he commanded as he quickly lowered the dagger.

A flash of white flew into the hall. The speed of Apollo's majestic gallop was hard to see clearly as his mane flew, leaving streaks of light in the air. Apollo speared the Nomad holding the keys at the portal door.

Maldamien, unable to stop his momentum, thrust the dagger into Autumn's chest.

CHAPTER 34: SPRING

Sage stabbed his sword into the belly of the Ogre he was fighting and turned towards his goal, the gem-studded altar. He had seen that Autumn had been captured, and he was working his way to her as fast as he could. This time when he looked, he witnessed Maldamien's murder of Autumn.

"NO!!!" he shouted from inside his helmet.

He ran like a madman towards the scene until Turmeric stepped into his path.

"Let me by!" said Sage as he swung his sword blindly, enraged.

"You pathetic fool!"

Turmeric's icy voice washed over Sage, and his eyes fixed on his opponent. Sage slowed his breathing and pushed down his emotions as best he could. He needed to concentrate.

Sage regained his composure just in time to dodge a fireball by crouching low in an animal-like posture. Sage twirled his sword in the Nomadic fashion as both a shield and to create momentum for an attack. Sage often switched from his more straightforward combat lessons of childhood to the exotic techniques of the Nomads. It kept his opponent off balance and guessing.

Turmeric stood tall and smirked with his decorative sword sheathed at his side and his hands in front of him, ready to fire another spell at any moment.

Sage pushed down his rising anger. He focused on Turmeric. The battle around him seemed to slow, and his mind began to clear.

Sage leaped forward to attack Turmeric forcing him off balance. Turmeric fired a couple more fireballs of various colors. They were old pros. They both maneuvered quickly in a series of attack and blocks. Sage was slightly faster, exposing Turmeric to some slight cuts. But Turmeric wasn't slow. He still singed some of Sage's clothes.

Turmeric's haughty bearing was unshakable.

"She's dead!" said Turmeric. "You can't win. Everything is almost over now."

Sage attacked, but then cursed himself as Turmeric nearly sliced his arm open with another fireball.

"Look around! Your pathetic band is being slaughtered. Did you lead them? Whoever you are, you are a traitor to the Huldra people!"

Sage was surprised that Turmeric didn't recognize him, but then he remembered the helmet.

Fires erupted all over the woods as Maldamien's troops set fire to the trees that the Dryads were using. The rebels poured out of their hiding places. From the center of the camp boomed a voice.

"For the queen and a free Gryphendale! For the queen and a free Gryphendale!" chanted the voice.

Maldamien shouted, "What are you all doing? Get them! Kill them all!"

Sage finally identified the chanting as coming from Milkweed. He was bleeding profusely and sitting on top of Apollo as they stormed into the battle. Apollo had a ring of keys hanging from his bloodied horn. The rebel army rallied behind them and charged. They cut right into the heart of the largest group of Maldamien's troops. Some of the Ogres in the camp began to switch sides and fight their neighbors, picking up the chant.

"For the queen and a free Gryphendale! For the queen and a free Gryphendale!"

A couple of Ogres fought between Sage and Turmeric. Sage moved around them to find Turmeric.

Before Sage could completely see what was happening, Turmeric was pointing his hands for another fireball, but then nothing happened.

Sage took this opportunity to attack him. Turmeric only just missed being pierced in the gut. Instead, he suffered a wound on his side when he turned to dodge the attack. He was clearly unbalanced and disturbed as he drew his sword.

"Well, Turmeric," said Sage. "It isn't over until it's over. With my very last breath I will see you and Maldamien dead!"

Turmeric narrowed his eyes with recognition of Sage's voice. He attacked with a ferocity that surprised Sage.

"Sage! You will never defeat me. You will see the afterlife long before I do!"

The movement of swords sped up, and the attacks were more intense. Sage could no longer think about anything, even his next move. Everything was instinct and reflex. Every thrust, block, or dodge was pure muscle memory. With Turmeric's magic not working, skill alone would decide their fate.

Somewhere in the distance over the roar of battle Sage heard Toble cry out in pain. Sage turned his head only a fraction. It was enough. Turmeric lunged at him. Sage fell on his back to dodge the blow. Turmeric was at him in a second, ripping his helmet off and shoving his sword under his chin.

"This is the way I always wanted to kill you."

Turmeric sneered.

Suddenly, the world turned dark. Turmeric hesitated and looked up briefly. That was what Sage needed. Sage grabbed his sword and drove it into Turmeric's chest. Turmeric died with a look of shock frozen on his face.

Sage looked up to see what had saved him. Directly above him was an upside-down mountain with fire-breathing dragons flying through the air and swooping down on the battlefield. Sage pulled his sword out of Turmeric's lifeless body and dodged the nearby fighting Ogres.

One of the dragons passed into Sage's line of vision. That dragon had a little old man riding on it, shooting lightning bolts at Nomads and Ogres. Sage smirked. Thyme had come.

Sage scanned the field of battle. It was very evenly matched now. Fires and fighting stretched as far as Sage could see in every direction. It was a horrific spectacle.

Sage focused on his goal.

Maldamien.

Sage made his way to the horrific scene. Maldamien had dragged Autumn's body off the altar to the side where Tanner was mourning over her. Maldamien was having one of the Sprite women being dragged to the altar.

"I will fix this!" growled Maldamien under his breath.

His hair was a mess, and he was rapidly aging. Sage had never seen Maldamien in such a state. Sage hoped that Autumn was able to break the spell before she died because he was about to join her if she didn't.

"Die you horrible snake!" shouted Sage as he attacked Maldamien.

Maldamien spun around, pulling his sword from its sheath and meeting Sage with unnatural speed. He easily blocked Sage's attack.

"You are very annoying, boy!" said Maldamien. "How many times have you escaped my people? Well, not today."

Sage was surprised at Maldamien's speed and agility. He was barely able to defend himself at all. They parted suddenly as Maldamien caught his breath. Maldamien looked even older than he had a moment ago.

"You fools have ruined my magic!" Maldamien growled.

He lunged at Sage, but the attack was much slower, and Sage blocked the attack more easily.

"It doesn't matter," said Maldamien. "You will all die now. You have ruined everything, and the world will die soon after me."

Maldamien looked like a gnarled old man now. He started to laugh. "So you think you have saved yourself and your people? No. My fate is the same as yours. Your queen is dead. Your world is dead. Soon you will be dead!"

Maldamien was now a bent over, shriveled old man. He looked past Sage with wide eyes. Sage turned slightly with his sword still pointed at Maldamien. Sitting next to Autumn's body and Tanner was the giant blue Gryphon.

"Look!" said the Gryphon as he turned his head toward the battlefield.

Sage and Maldamien turned to see that the battle was over. Maldamien's troops had thrown down their weapons. Everyone was moving toward the center of the field in front of the fortress ruins.

Maldamien's wrinkled old face darkened. Then he smirked. "At least I will have the satisfaction of seeing you destroyed," said Maldamien to the Gryphon.

The Gryphon shook his head no.

"Everything will be as it should be."

He then blew Maldamien's altar to the four winds so that no part of it remained.

Maldamien's face looked frozen in a state of shock. He started to choke. He reached for the sky as he gasped for air. Then his withered form collapsed and died. His body turned to ash and also blew away.

Sage let the point of his sword fall to the ground.

The battle was over.

Sage moved like he was in a trance over to Autumn's body. Tanner walked out of Sage's way as he knelt down by Autumn.

The warmth was already gone from her pale skin. The wound in her chest had stopped bleeding, and her clothes were covered in the drying maroon blood. He brushed the hair from her face. Her face was tranquil like she was asleep.

Sage's breathing was heavy as a knot formed in the depth of his stomach. The emotions rose to lodge in his throat. He studied her face in the faint hope that she would just wake up.

"After all of this... after all we have finally accomplished. You're gone."

He stared at her porcelain expression. She was the one person in all of Gryphendale who was innocent of this whole affair. She was the one person who should have had a long peaceful life for saving the world. She was the one person in the world who could have made him happy. His one reason for fighting. His one reason for living now that the fight was over.

She was gone.

The moments passed in a timeless, speechless vacuum. The emotions were overwhelming. A sob escaped his lips as he stroked her hair. She was so beautiful. He loved her so much it hurt every part of him. How was he going to live without her? He had nothing left.

Sage's sorrow began to burn. They had given up everything to do this, for what? The heat of Sage's rising anger spread through his body as he became aware of the Gryphon's presence. Sage looked up at him with fiery red eyes.

"You could have saved her! You could have prevented this! We chose to follow you! We were faithful to you even when we didn't understand! We did everything you asked! We depended on you, and you betrayed us! It is just like you betrayed Puck and my parents and the queen! You are petty and heartless!"

Sage grit his teeth, felt for his sword, and pointed it at the Gryphon.

The Gryphon didn't move. He met Sage's stare but said nothing. His expression was completely unreadable.

"Answer me!" Sage shouted, crouching down ready to attack and shaking with rage.

The Gryphon still said nothing.

Sage let out a roar of anger as he leaped towards the Gryphon with deadly aim. The Gryphon was prepared for Sage's attack in a moment.

He knocked Sage's sword away with his claw.

Sage continued forward into the opening the Gryphon made to grab hold of the Gryphon's feathery neck with his arms. As Sage began to wrestle the Gryphon down, the Gryphon pushed Sage off balance to loosen his grip. Sage instead shoved against the Gryphon's body while still having his arm around the Gryphon's neck, requiring the Gryphon to move his claws back to the ground to maintain balance.

"What are you doing?" shouted Toble as he ran up next to Tanner. Toble's right arm was severely injured, but Toble's only focus was on Sage.

"Sage, are you crazy?"

Tanner touched Toble's left arm.

"Leave them be. Sage needs to do this."

"Do what? Get himself killed?" said Toble. "This is the Gryphon! He can't kill him. Is he trying to wrestle him to the ground? This is just stupid!"

"No," said Apollo, moving next to Toble. "He is wrestling with his own faith and grief. The Gryphon is just accommodating him."

Sage swung himself onto the Gryphon's back and again put his arms around the Gryphon's neck. Sage's eyes were insanely red with anger.

The Gryphon then reached back with one of his claws and grabbed Sage's waist, trying to pull him off of his back.

Those who watched this could hardly believe the strength and full might of the conflict. The entire battlefield closed in to watch an ordeal that most had only heard about in legends. Not every day did a man or faerie wrestle with a god.

The Gryphon roared as he finally pried Sage off of him. Sage quickly maneuvered out of the Gryphon's grip and rolled underneath the creature to grab onto one of his great wings. The Gryphon swung his wings, lifting Sage into the air. The Gryphon was able to shake Sage off and caught him. Instead of the Gryphon being able to thrust Sage to the ground, Sage was able to get his footing. The Gryphon sat up on his hind lion legs, and the pair were locked in a hand to hand wrestling match.

"The Gryphon doesn't look like he is accommodating him," said Toble. "It looks like they are in a life or death struggle."

"In many ways, they are," said Apollo. "The Gryphon is not pretending to struggle, but Sage could never win. This is about men

371

working out a conflict that words cannot express."

The tension in the bodies of both the opponents were at full strength as sweat dripped down Sage's brow. The intensity of their focus was severe, and none who watched could doubt that they were both putting full effort into this battle. Finally, Sage's strength failed and his knees buckled. The Gryphon let go as the crowd could hear the pop of Sage's hip joint. Sage fell to his knees in front of the Gryphon. The Gryphon tiredly sat down as well so that they were face to face.

Sage gasped for breath while looking down toward the ground. Tears fell down his cheek.

"You could have saved her."

"Yes," answered the Gryphon.

"You betrayed us."

"Do you really believe that?"

Sage's head jerked up as he looked into the Gryphon's face. He still could not read his expression. The Gryphon turned and looked toward the battlefield. Sage followed his gaze. Thousands of people from every nation stood there watching Sage and the Gryphon. Many had thought that the Gryphon was only a myth, and gawked like children. The wounded and dead littered the valley. Toppled tents and burned woods were just the beginning of the destruction caused by the battle.

Sage looked back at the regal king of heaven. The Gryphon continued to look at the people as a tear fell down his feathery cheek.

"It had to be this way. The world would not listen, though I gave them every chance to turn from their ways. Because of my love for them and the stubbornness of their hearts, the whole world suffers."

"Was there no other way?" asked Sage.

"No."

Sage bowed down before the Gryphon with his face into the dirt.

"I have nothing left. Nothing to give, nothing left to fight with, and nothing to live for."

"Will you trust me?" asked the Gryphon.

Sage closed his eyes and covered his head with his arms. He felt beaten and crushed. There was no fight left in him, but there was also no life and no hope. He had nothing left to lose except his life, and even that was worthless to him. Who else could he turn to? He just felt empty resignation.

The pause between the Gryphon's question and Sage's answer was only for a minute, but the Gryphon's question seemed to echo through a lifetime.

The tension in Sage's body finally relaxed. He sat up and looked into the Gryphon's eyes. Sage could finally see compassion in them. He sighed.

"I have no choice," said Sage.

"You always have a choice," said the Gryphon.

Sage closed his eyes as another tear fell.

"Yes, I will trust you."

Again, the knot returned to Sage's throat.

"Then bring the girl," said the Gryphon.

Sage got up and turned to where Autumn was. A group of greenish banshees surrounded her. They had come when Sage had been fighting the Gryphon, but no one had noticed them until now. They lifted their heads in unison and gave a mournful wail that echoed throughout the valley.

Sage looked around as they wailed their distinctive unearthly cry again and again. Out of the edges of the valley came more people, animals, and creatures. Queen Oceania and King Fredrick walked through the crowd up to Sage.

The king and queen bowed to the Gryphon and then turned to Sage.

"We heard the banshee's wail," said King Fredrick. "More will come. The wind will carry the message to every corner of Gryphendale. Might we see the one who is to receive the ancient and most honorable funeral?"

The group of Banshees parted. Autumn's body had been cleaned and dressed in a white burial gown. The king and queen gasped. Sage picked Autumn up. Toble and Tanner joined Sage as he carried her while hobbling on his injured hip to the Gryphon and laid her before him.

"Friends of Gryphendale, prepare a funeral mound worthy of a sovereign," said the Gryphon to the crowd of onlookers in the valley.

Hazel, Hao, Milkweed, and many others, including Riven, stepped forward to begin building the mound in the place that Maldamien's golden altar had been. It didn't take long to build because so many people were piling wood nearby for them to use. At the same time, people, animals, and magical beings continued to filter into the valley from all over.

Once the mound was built, Sage picked up Autumn's body, hobbled over to the mound, and laid her gently on it. He smoothed out her hair and kissed her forehead as tears wet his checks. He stepped back next to the Gryphon.

The Gryphon nodded.

The funeral pyre burst into flames. Tanner and Apollo ran to the portal. Tanner pulled the key off of Apollo's horn and unlocked the door as Apollo mumbled some words.

Sage looked around confused.

The mass of onlookers shouted in protest.

The portal flew open as the flames leaped up.

The Gryphon flew up into the air as light poured out of the portal in every direction.

"Amen and amen!" shouted the Gryphon.

He then vanished in the light of the portal.

As the light from the portal began to fade, everyone looked intensely at the scene to see what would happen next. Around the edges of the portal floor and in the cracks around the floor stones of the hall the snow melted, and thick green grass rapidly grew. The snow melted farther and farther out from the portal, radiating into the valley and beyond. The grass followed with flowers and growth in the trees.

The fire on the funeral pyre had gone out, and the wood was sprouting leaves. Autumn's porcelain body still lay on top of the pyre, untouched by the flames. The green growth moved out beyond the valley and the woods surrounding it was sprouting leaves. The sky took on a bluish tint and turned bluer and bluer. The entire world transformed from bleak winter into spring in moments.

Thyme stepped up in front of the portal and addressed the crowd. "We had thought we had lost everything only days ago. We had thought we lost our world, our queen, our lives, everything today. What these brave people, what Autumn did, was break the spells that held our world captive. Maldamien destroyed himself in killing Autumn. He drained all of his own magic by breaking the spell that let him steal it in the first place, and then the portal was opened to restore the balance of power in the world. This day will be remembered throughout the ages! Let the portal never be locked again. Let the stories of these dead always be remembered. Tell this to your children. Sing this in song. Don't let it be forgotten that..."

Out of the clear blue sky, it suddenly began to rain heavily.

Sage rushed forward past Thyme to where Autumn lay. He thought he saw...

Well, he was sure it wasn't just the wind blowing. He looked into Autumn's face. She began to glow and rise off the funeral pyre. Little fireflies of light flew around her faster and faster until she was in a cocoon of soft golden light. The cocoon lowered onto the mound and then faded away.

Sage hesitated a moment, but then walked up close to the funeral pyre again.

Autumn's pale features had transformed into a more angular fairie complexion. Her ears were pointed, her eyes slightly more almond. She also had pale moth wings.

"Autumn?" whispered Sage hoarsely.

Autumn's eyes opened, and she smiled.

"Sage!"

Sage lifted Autumn off the woodpile in an embrace.

"You're alive!" cried Sage.

"Of course I am!" said Autumn. "Death created the spell; only life could break it."

"Oh Autumn! I thought I had lost you. Why didn't anyone tell me?" said Sage, still holding onto her but looking intensely at her face.

"I don't think anyone knew. Even I didn't realize it until after I had died. It is so clear now. My death only stopped Maldamien, but the spell could not be reversed until I was alive. Even with the phoenix feather, I couldn't have done the spell without the Gryphon setting the right flame."

Tanner shouted over the roar and cheers of the crowd at Sage, "Stop talking to the girl and kiss her, man!"

Sage smiled, grabbed the back of Autumn's head, and created a faerie ring that folks said did not wear away for two weeks at least.

Thank you for reading Gryphendale.

If you liked this book, please post a review at:

amazon.com/author/laralee

If you loved this book, explore the world of Gryphendale in:

The Shadow of the Gryphon

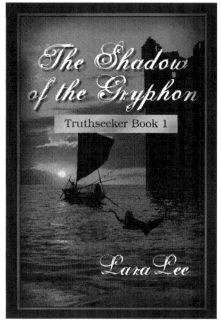

About the Author

Lara Lee is the author of young adult fantasy fiction novels. Sometimes, she is also a graphic designer, wife, mother, and Sunday school teacher. After growing up in Florida with her head stuck in various books, she ran away to Oral Roberts University to obtain a Bachelor of Science degree in Graphic Design and a husband. Then, she worked professionally with the children's curriculum publisher, Mentoring Minds in Texas before following her husband on a crazy adventure in Scotland for four years. She has lived in three states and four countries and has visited even more destinations with an insatiable curiosity that shows up in her writing. Currently, she lives in Texas with her husband and two sons who all regularly participate in her misadventures and random schemes.

laraswanderings.wordpress.com

facebook.com/Gryphendale/

twitter.com/Gryphendale

goodreads.com/author/show/13773505.Lara_Lee

GRYPHENDALE

THE SHADOW OF THE GRYPHON
TRUTHSEEKER BOOK 1

(Sample Chapter)

GRYPHENDALE

CHAPTER 1: A BROWNIE

All journeys begin and end at a crossroad. The Plough and Thistle Inn was built at the main crossroad of Grassmarket and was the only lodging in the entire country of Aberdour that could accommodate all the races of Gryphendale, no matter the size. In fact, it was the only inn in Aberdour, which explains why old Arthur chose it for his musings and his temporary home. The small, wooden two-story building sat on the edge of the tiny market town near the few major dirt roads in that predominantly rural country of Brownie farmers. Being the only inn for miles was the only way it had enough business even to stay open.

Unlike his fellow home-loving Brownies, Arthur had traveled a great deal in his lifetime. He felt comfort at seeing the various strange faerie people coming and going. The inn was one of his favorite places in the world. Unfortunately, his reclusive Brownie nature was winning tonight, and he felt glad to see the evening rush of guests go home or to their rooms.

Hickory, the tall, old Dryad with large, floppy, pointed ears and white, messy hair had built the place. One could find him sleeping in front of the building in the form of a large hickory tree at night. This widely known Dryad behavior was viewed by the Brownies of the area with suspicion, and it meant that poor Hickory was accepted in the community about as much as Arthur was, which wasn't much. His food and drink were consumed mostly by Brownies who wanted to satisfy a mild daring or rebellious urge by dining on something exotic, such as stew with parsley added to it. Those traveling across Aberdour to visit relations on the other side had no choice but to stay at the strange inn.

Arthur was Hickory's most regular guest, and they maintained a quiet friendship and understanding between them. On this solemn stormy night, they left each other with their own thoughts. Hickory collected dishes and cups from the small, emptying tables to wash behind the bar, and Arthur smoked his polished wooden pipe by the imposing fireplace.

The few travelers in the inn hardly noticed Arthur, a two-foot-tall, rat-like figure, in his little wooden chair. His flopped-over pointed ears and his oversized nose was typical of the gnarled and hairy Brownies. His brown and gray speckled hair and unshaven face, leathery, wrinkled skin, and brown clothes blended in with the wood of the spacious open dining area crowded with tables, benches, and chairs.

Arthur enjoyed his customary spot by the large hearth and smoked while staring into the warm flames. The orange and red crackling fire drew him back to the events of just a month ago. He should hate the fire for destroying his life, but instead, he felt like he was watching an old friend playing a familiar game.

Fire had devoured his little yellow farmhouse, which is why he had come to live at the inn a month ago. It was a dreadful accident. All his friends and relations rushed to his farm to help put out the raging kitchen fire. Even with the great community effort, all he had built over the last thirty years with his late wife was gone. Her grave lay by the ruins of their lives together. He only had a single small portrait of her left that he kept with him in his pocket. Their two sons were grown-up, married with broods of children of their own. They each offered him a room in their homes, but he chose the inn so he could have his own independent life rather than depend on his kids.

He told everyone that living at the inn was temporary. He had originally planned to rebuild, but after a few weeks, he realized he felt too tired and too old to build over again. He hated the idea of starting yet another farm. It was his wife's passion to farm. His sons were just like her in that way. Arthur wasn't good at it. He had just kept farming after she passed away five years ago because he had nothing better to do. He mused over the idea of just staying here at the inn. He had enough savings that he could live like this for the rest of his days, staring at the familiar fire.

The door to the inn swung open as two tall young men with large backpacks walked in from the pouring rain. Their brown traveling cloaks dripped water all over the wooden floor.

"Innkeeper, do you have lodging and food for two weary souls?" asked the lighter-haired young man as he pulled the hood of his cloak down from over his head.

"Yep," said Hickory. He started to prepare something behind the bar. "Take a seat and supper will be right out."

Arthur watched the two men take off their brown cloaks and drop their canvas bags at a small square table near him and the warm fire. They plopped down in the simple wooden chairs looking tired and worried.

They were both the same human-sized height and in their early twenties, no more than twenty-five years old. Arthur noticed the resemblance to their father immediately. He had fought with their father in the Great War before he was made the High King of Gryphendale.

The few remaining Brownie guests in the inn didn't seem to recognize them, though. The men wore common travel clothes and had not shaved for a few days. They carried nothing that would indicate that they were extremely rich or royal. At the same time, they weren't in disguise or being secretive.

Arthur knew the princes were fraternal twins. Nathaniel and Timothy were the youngest sons of King Sage and Queen Autumn. Prince Chevil, the heir to the throne, was their older brother and well respected. He was also easily recognizable by his red hair. There was always talk of the royal family. It was a worldwide hobby to gossip about them.

The blond-haired man, Timothy, wore wire-rimmed glasses, a distinctly human device. He was training to be an Asri to take the place of his mother's great-uncle, Thyme, the legendary scholar. Timothy took after his Sprite mother with his light hair, light eyes, and a pair of dragonfly wings that were folded down near his body. His mannerisms, face shape, and facial expressions were all his father's though. He was tall, lean, and athletic.

The tan, dark-haired man, Nathaniel, carried a curved Nomad saber. He was a well known warrior and was expected to lead the army in the footsteps of the King. He looked similar to his older brother, Chevil, and almost identical to his Huldra father. He had the fox tail of the Huldra, and his eyes changed colors from dark brown to green as he glanced over the room. Out of all the royal children, Nathaniel reminded everyone of a young King Sage the most, but there was a poetic gentleness to his expression that was a marked difference. Nathaniel just didn't have the hardness in his jaw or the fire in his eyes that King Sage did.

Both men were the same height and same build and carried

383

themselves confidently. They both had pointed ears, and, other than coloring and race, their facial features were the very same proportions.

Arthur looked back at the fire wondering what brought the two princes alone into this boring, flat land of farmers. Plenty of trouble brewed in the other countries even though they had voted for the High King and Queen of Gryphendale. Constant squabbles between the countries and threats to leave the union were common, especially among the southern lands. Aberdour, though, liked the stability of the High King and Queen.

"This rain will delay us," said Timothy to his brother, "but we really need the rest. We shouldn't kill ourselves before we even get there."

Nathaniel sighed. "It may stop soon. We might be able to leave before sunrise."

"No, this is a true storm. It'll rain all night," countered Timothy as he took off his glasses and cleaned them with the edge of his tan shirt. "Besides, you need sleep. You're pushing too hard. We have traveled what usually takes a week in three days. I'm tired."

Nathaniel sighed again and leaned his head in his hands as though that would help him think better. "I hate waiting. I hate how slow we are traveling. I hate this whole mess. Give me a battle and I can fight it. Give me a task and I can do it, but this just grates on me!"

"Sorry," said Timothy. "I know you are worried about her, but this is the fastest we can go. We aren't going to solve anything overnight. She'll be all right."

Hickory brought out some hot drinks in each hand for the young men. "This will warm you up," he said, placing the mugs on the table before them. "What are your names, and what brings you to this part of the world?"

Arthur snorted. If Hickory thought for half a minute he would know who these boys were. Perhaps it was in the best interest of an innkeeper to be ignorant at times. Then again, maybe he didn't know. Arthur was always surprised at how little people noticed things.

"We're just passing through," said Timothy. "This is the road towards Rokurokubi, correct?"

Arthur tilted his head. Rokurokubi was the mountainous Ogre homeland. That was a rugged and dangerous place to go.

"Well, yes," said Hickory slowly. He scratched his scruffy chin. "It isn't a straight road there, though. Most people around here don't travel in that direction much. Poor farmland and too many rocks, you see. You can get there from here, but I might need to draw you a map. If you go as the crow flies, you'll march right through some crops. You don't need angry farmers in your path. Also, as you get closer to the border, you'll be facing more bandits and trouble."

"I don't mind that so much," said Nathaniel. He took a sip from his mug.

Arthur smirked. If Nathaniel's reputation was accurate, he tended to search out bandits on purpose. Arthur was not the nosy type, but since the princes sat so close to him and didn't seem to mind being overheard, he spoke up.

"Sorry, but I might be able to help, depending on what you are looking for in Rokurokubi."

The young men jumped. Apparently, they hadn't noticed Arthur.

Nobody uses the eyes on their heads anymore, thought Arthur.

Timothy spoke first. "We are going to the Odemience Mountains in the Ogre homeland. Do you know the best way to get there?"

Arthur turned in his little chair to look at them better. "The main pass into the heart of the mountains is near the caves where bandits tend to live. Are you trying to find them?"

Timothy shook his head, "No, we are trying to find a particular cavern. Here, look at my map."

Timothy opened his canvas bag next to the table and pulled out an old, rolled up parchment. Nathaniel moved his cup as Timothy rolled out the parchment on the table. Then, Timothy used his and Nathaniel's cups to hold it open. It was a map that had the whole world of Gryphendale on it with each of the nine countries marked and the main highways drawn.

Gryphendale was a small floating island in the center of the earth. Humans had all sorts of other names for Gryphendale in their legends, such as the Faerie world or the Seelie kingdom. The west side of Gryphendale was a large sea that the Merpeople ruled, while seven small countries divided the land. A great lake and a river that cut through the continent were ruled by the Undine. The south and southeast were abandoned deserts filled with Nomads of various races. Timothy pointed to the northeast side of the map where Aberdour bordered Rokurokubi. He moved his finger east to an isolated mountain in the middle of the Odemience Mountains, solidly in the dangerous

Ogre lands.

Timothy stood as he explained, "Only the main roads are drawn on this map. They stop here at the inn, turning either north or south. I have no roads on this map going east to the mountain range." He tapped his finger on the mountain on the map. "We need to get to Tabletop Mountain. I was expecting to see the Odemience Mountains by now, but I guess rain or fog is obscuring them. We can just go in that general direction, but we don't need to pick fights with angry farmers, like you said. It would also be nice to avoid Ogres or bandits when we cross the border."

Hickory whistled.

"Can't help you there, but you are talking to the right Brownie."

"What do you mean?" asked Timothy, looking up at Hickory and then Arthur.

"This is Arthur's kind of half-baked adventure," said Hickory.

"Oh, go bake a cake," growled Arthur. "I haven't been on an adventure in fifty years."

"Thirty years, but who's counting." Hickory crossed his arms enjoying his jab at Arthur.

Arthur pointed his pipe at Hickory.

"No adventures!"

"Maybe it's about time you do something with your old carcass," said Hickory as he turned around and walked away with a smirk. He went back to his bar, pleased with himself, and began to cook a stew on his little black iron stove.

Timothy and Nathaniel watched the exchange curiously.

"I thought Brownies were allergic to adventures," said Nathaniel. His eyes turned from brown to green.

"Do you want help or not?" growled Arthur. He was regretting speaking up at this point.

Timothy sat back down.

"We know what we are looking for, but we could use a little guidance."

Arthur stood up and walked over to the table where the young men were sitting. He looked at the map where Timothy had pointed.

"The best way is the market roads between the farms. They aren't drawn here. You have to go through Stone Face Pass to get to Tabletop Mountain unless you want to go all the way south near the Undine

River. The Ogres live in the mountains here and here." He pointed to the very eastern edge of Gryphendale. "You shouldn't have trouble with them in the middle of summer. It's too bright and hot for them."

Timothy and Nathaniel watched where Arthur pointed on the map.

"Are these market roads pretty easy to find?" asked Timothy. "I am not familiar with that pass, either. Are the roads a grid where we can head east at any point?"

Arthur puffed on his smooth English pipe some more and then held the pipe in both hands. "No, it's more like a pile of yarn. You're going to have to take the right roads or it will turn you back this way."

Timothy looked up from the map to Arthur.

"I think a guide to Rokurokubi would be welcome." He turned to Nathaniel who shrugged in response. "We can pay you. It should only take a couple of days."

Arthur chewed his lip, looking at the map. A little adventure and fresh air wouldn't hurt. Then again, he knew how these things worked. One step led to another. Arthur moved his chair up to the table with the princes. His gut told him this was going to be more than a stroll through some farmland.

"Why you are wanting to go there? I do not want to be responsible for the death of two young princes who are just bored and trying to find a random thrill. You boys ought to be wise enough not to just go looking for trouble." Arthur was trying to provoke them on purpose. What kind of men were these? What kind of trouble were they after? He wouldn't get sucked into something he didn't agree with.

Nathaniel narrowed his eyes angrily and the color of his eyes turned from green to a reddish brown color. Timothy, on the other hand, smirked and raised an eyebrow.

"We don't need his help," said Nathaniel to his brother. "We aren't children to be coddled. We have enough information to find our own way."

"No. I think that he is precisely the sort of person we need," said Timothy. "He has some perception. We never said we were princes, and he knows we are wanting to do something dangerous. He does not know the kind of people we are. We both have friends who would foolishly risk their lives for a thrill. I perceive that he isn't just an ordinary Brownie." Timothy leaned forward, looking at Arthur in the eyes. "What adventures have you seen, old man? What secrets do you hide?"

Hickory just then brought over plates of food for the princes. Timothy quickly rolled up his map and put it in his bag. Arthur was relieved. He hadn't expected Timothy to see through him. He watched them eat for a couple of seconds thinking about the two men's responses. It told him a lot about them. There was no boasting, no bravado, and no interest in proving themselves. One brother wanted to just leave him and the other saw through him. There was confidence in both responses. They were certainly hungry enough to drop the conversation for some mouthfuls of hot stew.

The doors to the inn opened again. For a stormy night, Arthur thought, there seemed to be a lot of travelers. A tall Nomad with gray, bumpy skin swaggered into the inn and went directly to the bar. He wore the Nomad keffiyeh over his head, covering part of his face. His loose, dark gray tunic and trousers were tied with a cloth belt. His clothes were worn out and soaked.

The Nomad spoke quietly to Hickory at the bar. Hickory looked extremely upset at seeing the Nomad, but he served the stranger a drink. The Nomad untied his keffiyeh and laughed loudly. He carried the drink to a table in a dark corner. He sat with his back towards the wall so that he could keep an eye on the princes and the few Brownies in the room.

Timothy looked up from his food.

"If we do tell you everything, would you be our guide? It would only be for a few days. You don't have to come with us to the other side. It would be faster to have a guide than to wander around with old maps from the archives."

"The other side?" said Arthur.

His eyes shot back to Timothy. There were multiple things Timothy could mean, but Arthur felt the hair on the back of his neck stand up. He narrowed his eyes as he studied the young men. Could they mean what he thought they meant? It would be impossible.

Timothy and Nathaniel looked at each other. They had not expected Arthur to catch that. Their expressions caused Arthur's insides to shake. He puffed on his pipe again.

"What are you boys trying to do?" he asked.

It was impossible. He hoped that they weren't trying to attempt what he suspected.

Nathaniel leaned forward over his food, looking at Arthur intensely.

"You are a highly unusual Brownie. You seem to know what we are saying before we even say it."

The grayish Nomad on the other side of the room drank his glass and shouted out, "Barkeeper! I need another one! Just leave the bottle!"

Hickory and Arthur met eyes for an instant. It was enough for Arthur to know that Hickory was worried. Arthur sighed. This evening was completely ruined.

Timothy whispered, "Let us not jump to conclusions. We are not traveling for amusement but on a rescue mission. The Huldra ambassador from Samodivas has a daughter."

"My fiancée, Lady Peony," said Nathaniel.

"She was turned to stone by some people who claim to be from the other side. We have a letter they left demanding some sort of jewel be returned to their fortress." Timothy watched Arthur carefully as he said this. He was gauging Arthur's response. It was as though he was gathering as much information as he was giving.

"So the royal family, army, and politicians sent you two alone with no other help," said Arthur.

Timothy laughed, but Nathaniel growled.

"Do you think we are unqualified?" said Nathaniel.

"No," replied Arthur as he sat back chewing on his pipe.

They left on their own, he thought. It wasn't unlike something he had done at their age.

Timothy put his hand on his brother's shoulder, which seemed to calm him some.

"I like you, Arthur. You understand what is going on quickly. The palace was greatly upset by the event and has made poor decisions. Other events, such as the flooding in the coastal towns, were distracting them from taking action."

"I see," said Arthur. "Who knows you are here?"

"Ambassador Toble," said Timothy.

Old Toble, the ancient Dryad inventor and ambassador for the newly established Greenbow country! They might as well have not told anyone. He was over two hundred years old. He had had a hard time staying in reality thirty years ago when Arthur had last seen him.

Arthur shook his head. So these princes were taking it on their own shoulders to save the girl. Their parents wouldn't be too happy, but these men certainly inherited their parents' adventurous spirit. Arthur wasn't

389

sure if they were foolish or brave. It was best to wait and see.

"So, you are talking about the other side of the world," said Arthur, "the shadow side of our floating island. You do know that people have only gone there in myths and legends. Even then, they only went with magic. There are no paths to the other side through Rokurokubi."

Timothy smirked, leaned back, and crossed his arms.

"Leave that to me. We will get there from Rokurokubi. You just need to take us to where we need to go."

Arthur puffed his pipe, looking at Timothy and Nathaniel. Could these boys do it? Could they really make it to the other side? It was a death wish.

The Nomad on the other side of the room drained another glass and burped loudly.

"That man is here to cause your friend trouble," whispered Nathaniel, watching the Nomad as he took another bite of his supper. His eyes glistened black. "I have seen him before. He is wanted in Dwende. He goes around threatening innkeepers and store clerks, then offers to not follow through with his threat for a fee."

Arthur shrugged.

He didn't have to say anything. Hickory had the money. He had been through this before. It wasn't a new trick. Sometimes it was worth spending the money so the riff-raff would just move on to another town. Arthur would have liked to help his friend, but Hickory didn't want to damage his inn. Something in Arthur wanted to see what the young men would do, though.

Timothy glanced back at the stranger. The last Brownie guests walked out of the inn into the rain. It was now just the five of them. The Nomad walked up to the bar where Hickory stood and slammed the empty glass down.

"I want double the payment!" He slurred his words drunkenly. His keffiyeh fell from his head down to his shoulders. He was a half-Ogre who stood taller than Hickory. His snout-like nose and pointed ears stood out from his bald, gray head.

Nathaniel stood up from his chair and walked to the bar. His brown fox-tail swished casually. He wasn't quite as tall as the nomad, but close enough to look him in the eye.

"I think you are supposed to pay the bar for that drink. Not the other way around," said Nathaniel. He leaned against the bar in a nonaggressive way, but Arthur could see the tension in his arms. He was ready for action if needed.

"Who are you?" said the gray-skinned Nomad, still slurring his words together. "This has nothing to do with you."

"Pay the barkeeper and go home." Nathaniel straightened up with authority and placed his hand lightly on the hilt of his sword.

The Nomad had an incredulous expression.

"What?"

He half grunted as he turned towards the bar slightly as though to ignore Nathaniel. Suddenly, he pulled out an old, rusty dagger and swung back to stab Nathaniel in the gut.

Nathaniel was ready. He deflected the Nomad's stabbing attack with his forearm. With his other hand, he grabbed the Nomad's arm that held the dagger. Nathaniel twisted the arm around, and, in the same movement, stabbed the Nomad in the leg with his own dagger. The whole thing lasted less than a second and was over.

The Nomad screamed out in pain and fell to the floor. He rolled around on the ground as blood surged from his leg with the dagger still in it.

Nathaniel looked at Hickory.

"He will need a doctor, and the royal guard will be interested in his activities."

"Right!" Hickory handed Nathaniel his bar rag and ran out into the rain to fetch both.

Nathaniel knelt down to help the Nomad. The dagger had sliced into the Nomad's thigh muscle. With how much he was bleeding, it probably had hit an artery. There was no way he could walk on that leg for months, even if the bleeding was stopped quickly.

"Get away from me!" he shouted at Nathaniel.

The Nomad tried to get up and fell back down while crawling towards the door. He shouted out in pain as he gasped for breath, holding his leg.

Nathaniel sighed. He threw the rag at the injured man and went back to his seat in front of his supper.

By the time the Nomad crawled to the door, Hickory was already back with a group of people who carried the screaming man to another room.

"What a pain," said Nathaniel, taking a bite from his stew.

Arthur stood up with his pipe. He felt confident that the young men could at least take care of themselves.

"He got what he asked for. I will see you both in the morning. I'll be your guide, not just to Rokurokubi, but to the other side and back." Arthur felt startled by his own words. When had he decided to do that?

Timothy and Nathaniel looked up at Arthur in surprise.

"You don't have to do that. We know full well that we are risking our lives on this adventure. It won't be easy," said Timothy.

"Why would you even want to do that?" asked Nathaniel.

"Because you will need me," said Arthur ending the conversation. There was a lot more that they could talk about, but he was emotionally tired of the evening.

Arthur walked up the stairs at the back of the inn to his room. He turned into the first door on the right, closing it behind him. He sat on the simple wooden bed in his room and puffed on his pipe.

He had just volunteered for his first major adventure in thirty years. The princes were both well qualified to deal with the average bully and bandit. They had more experience than he did on his first adventure. They weren't baby-faced farm boys.

Then why was he going on this adventure? What made his heart race at the idea? He had ended his adventures a lifetime ago. Why do this now?

Arthur looked at himself in the mirror that sat on the dresser. He frowned at the old, hairy man he saw looking back at him in his reflection. His short, brown and gray hair had more gray than brown. His wrinkled, leathery skin, large nose, and large pointed ears that stuck out from his head was a stark contrast to the chiseled, good-looking young men who sat downstairs.

"You aren't seventeen anymore, you know. You are an old fool weighing down two well-trained young princes. You need to mind your own business and spend more time with your kids and grandkids. If they get themselves killed, it isn't your business."

Arthur frowned deeper.

"Not going to happen," Arthur told himself, pointing at the mirror with his pipe. "I don't want to just sit in front of the fire and rot. I don't want to build a farm. I don't want to get old without a fight. Clara was a good wife. Basil and Hansel are good sons, but they know I wasn't made for this. I need this adventure. Yes, I am an old fool, but that's what happens when young fools don't die young."

Arthur looked at the thick scar that ran from the middle of his forehead into his hairline and around toward his ear. There was a second scar going from his neck around to his back.

"Those boys don't know what is waiting for them on the other side, but you do. They need you. Old fool or not, they will need you. The great Gryphon led those boys to the only person in this entire world who could help them. For some reason, all three of us were chosen. This isn't an accident. One month ago I would have never gone with them. Yet here I am."

Arthur grunted and nodded to himself.

He spent the rest of the evening packing and writing letters to his sons.

Made in the USA
Columbia, SC
21 November 2022

71311003R00215